Christian's over-the-top laughter struck me again. So did Adrienne's downright panicked expression when she heard it.

Was she supposed to bbe. That was the only ex went still, like a frightene her boss approached.

Christian didn't seem p there. "Ms. Dowling!" he barked. "Shouldn't you be in your magical workshop, coming up with some tasty treats for later?"

"Um," Adrienne began. Her gaze darted to me. "Uh—"

Christian's abrupt clap made her jump. "Yes! Get on it!"

"I'm sorry," she mumbled. "I'll leave right now."

As Christian turned to his retreat guests—presumably making sure they'd witnessed his masterful employer-employee relations—Adrienne caught my arm again. Her intent expression riveted me.

"*Take this*." She whispered the words harshly, shoving a thick rectangular item at my midsection. "Please, Hayden. Take it! I can't let Christian have it. Just . . . keep it safe for me, okay?" Her fearful gaze zipped to her boss. "I'll get it later."

Criminal Confections

COLETTE LONDON

KENSINGTON PUBLISHING CORP.
http://www.kensingtonbooks.com

KENSINGTON BOOKS are published by

Kensington Publishing Corp.
119 West 40th Street
New York, NY 10018

All Kensington Titles, Imprints, and Distributed Lines are available at special quantity discounts for bulk purchases for sales promotions, premiums, fund-raising, and educational or institutional use. Special book excerpts or customized printings can also be created to fit specific needs. For details, write or phone the office of the Kensington special sales manager: Kensington Publishing Corp., 119 West 40th Street, New York, NY 10018, attn: Special Sales Department, Phone: 1-800-221-2647.

Kensington and the K logo Reg. U.S. Pat & TM Off.

ISBN-13: 978-1-61773-345-1
ISBN-10: 1-61773-345-8
First Kensington Mass Market Edition: February 2015

eISBN-13: 978-1-61773-346-8
eISBN-10: 1-61773-346-6
First Kensington Electronic Edition: February 2015

10 9 8 7 6 5 4 3 2 1

Printed in the United States of America

To John Plumley, with all my love.

Chapter 1

You probably already know not to eat French fries with your fingers in Chile, not to shake hands across a threshold in Russia, and to sit in the backseat of a taxi (never up front with the driver) if you're a woman traveling solo in Costa Rica. But you might not know that ordinary chocolate contains over five hundred unique flavor components—more than twice that of vanilla or strawberry. You might not know that you should let your next bite of chocolate melt on your tongue (don't chew it!) for the ultimate flavor experience. And you might not know that the *most* chocolaty chocolate mousse is made with high-quality chocolate and *water* (not cream). Not many people do—not even the restaurateurs, TV chefs, and chocolate-company executives who hire *me* to troubleshoot their *Theobroma cacao* cookies, cakes, and confections.

But I'm getting ahead of myself. You didn't ask for a compendium of travel- and chocolate-based tips, and the fact that my on-the-job adventures have included bushwhacking through the jungles of Africa, rubbing elbows with Academy Awards-catering chefs, and being blindfolded (*not* to do something kinky, I promise!)

for a chocolate tasting doesn't mean *I* never come up stumped. I do. Sometimes. But I never quit, and I never tell clients I'm mystified by their gloopy ganache or freaky frappés, either. I always keep trying until I find a solution.

In my book, perseverance counts.

My clients appreciate the effort, and I appreciate their loyalty. I'm a freelancer. That means I can't goof around (much). My work demands expertise, attention to detail, and a thick skin when it comes to criticism . . . but it *doesn't* usually demand hobnobbing with chocolate-industry bigwigs and members of the media at a fancy-schmancy San Francisco resort spa with a five-star rating and a "room service" option featuring Frette linens, sterling silver, Bernardaud china, *and* a personal butler. That's what I was facing at the moment, though.

The prospect had me shaking in my single pair of "dressy" flats, which spent most of their time being ignored while crammed into a corner of my (always packed) suitcase. I don't usually need to wear anything swankier than a pair of Converse or some kitchen clogs. But today I was making a grand entrance into the world of the San Francisco chocolate-industry elite. I was doing it on the spur of the moment. And I wasn't entirely comfortable with it.

See, most of my work is done (necessarily) under-cover. The companies that hire me don't want it known that they need *me,* Hayden Mundy Moore, to improve their prized confections. I've gotten pretty good at troubleshooting on the QT, building my high-profile client list through discreet referrals. I work one hush-hush job at a time and let the next assignment take care of itself. My globe-trotting background means I'm fairly adept at blending in when necessary, too. But knowing how to navigate a Milanese street without a map or negoti-ate a good price at a Lebanese market doesn't necessarily equip a girl to face the elite of her industry with perfect composure.

Not even if that "girl" just turned thirty, like me.

Look, I can backpack with the best. I can make instant friends with the back-of-house staff at a restaurant or the line workers at a chocolate factory. I can tell a wicked Dutch dirty joke that will make a sailor blush, and I can confront a squat toilet in Bangalore with equanimity and (enviable) balance. But put me in a ballroom with canapés, champagne flutes, and polite chitchat, and I suddenly come off like a monkey on NoDoz. It's not pretty. But it's me. That's just the way it is.

Truth be told, as I crossed the Golden Gate Bridge from the city toward the Marin Headlands, arrived at Maison Lemaître, and saw the cadre of well-dressed, wineglass-holding, chitchatting executives, suppliers, and restaurateurs gathered on the resort spa's manicured grassy grounds among a bunch of gauzy tents—smaller versions of the ones caterers like to use at chichi outdoor weddings—I seriously considered telling my taxi driver to turn around. Then I went ahead and did it.

"Turn around, Jimmy. I changed my mind."

He looked at me in the rearview mirror. He shrugged. "It's your thirty-eight bucks, Hayden. Where to, instead?"

Aha. That was the crux of the problem, wasn't it?

"Noe Valley?" I suggested with a grin, naming one of my favorite San Francisco neighborhoods. "I know a fantastic little bakery there. The strawberry-rhubarb macaroons are on me."

They were so delicious, they almost made me want to settle down in the City by the Bay. Which was saying a lot. For me.

"Sounds good. I like macaroons." Jimmy glanced at me in the rearview again. "I didn't peg you for the chickening-out type."

He was right. I wasn't the chickening-out type. Never had been. "This is what I get for bonding with you on the drive from Russian Hill to here." I sighed. "Rain check on the macaroons? I already said I'd put in an appearance at this industry retreat."

Jimmy nodded and kept driving toward the hotel. I bit my lip and stared out the window, knowing I didn't have any place else to go at the moment. I couldn't spend all day at a bakery, no matter how tasty their lattes and pastries were. And I wasn't technically finished with my last consulting job, so I couldn't leave town altogether. I still owed a comprehensive report to Christian Lemaître, who'd hired me for my last job and whose family owned both Lemaître Chocolates and Maison Lemaître.

Christian was the one who'd invited me here to his annual high-powered industry get-together. (I had the impression he saw me as kind of a trophy to be bragged about: "Step right up and see the real, live chocolate whisperer!") He'd agreed to let me slide on our agreed-upon due date for my report, if I'd attend. Put that way, the decision had been a no-brainer. I was going.

Any inveterate procrastinator would have done the same.

Plus, I'd already invited my friend Danny Jamieson to fly in from L.A. and be my plus-one for the retreat. He was supposed to meet me here, at the chocolate-themed resort where I now sat parked, deliberating over whether I wanted to go through with this, in full view of the quizzical valets. One of them ambled out from behind his stand and headed for the taxi's door, ready to give me the full white-glove treatment.

Decision made. I opened the door first and stepped into the breezy coolness of a northern California springtime afternoon, lugging my duffel bag and single wheeled suitcase with me.

"Welcome to Maison Lemaître! May I take your bags?"

"No, thanks!" Breezily, I maneuvered them both. Hoisting fifty-pound sacks of cacao beans and equally heavy bags of sugar on a regular basis is *great* for the biceps. I'm only average size for a woman—about five-foot-six, barefoot—but I'm strong. And stubborn. "I can handle them. I do it all the time."

The valet tried to insist. I held my ground. It may be quirky, but I don't like handing over my stuff. Not even under such innocuous circumstances. Pretty much, my two bags contain everything I own in the world. Just call me the urban nomad.

The valet seemed confused by the way I was body-hugging my duffel. I smiled to let him know my protectiveness with my stuff wasn't his fault and then looked around the place, checking out the hotel division of the venerable Lemaître Chocolates corporation. What I saw was par for the course for a modern luxury-resort spa—a sprawling hotel complex with a sparkling whitewashed finish, a hushed atmosphere of indulgence, and a nod to "locality" in the form of co-sponsorship of tonight's welcome reception with a local winery. Several ultra-attentive uniformed staff members milled around. Surrounding the hotel and its long, curved drive, the aforementioned grounds, low outbuildings, and precise landscaping lent the whole place an air of serenity.

Maison Lemaître smelled like . . . money.

And chocolate. Lots and *lots* of chocolate.

Mmm. I guess I should have been jaded (or immune) to the way cocoa butter permeated the breeze at Maison Lemaître, since chocolate is my job. But I *love* chocolate. I love the way it smells, the way it tastes, and even the way it snaps—faintly but distinctly—when it's expertly made. I love the way it melts just below body temperature, creating the decadent sensation that it's *melding* with my tongue.

Hands down, eating chocolate has got to be one of the most sensual experiences on earth.

Being eyeballed by a befuddled valet is not.

"Thanks, but I've got this. Seriously." I tipped the valet, then shooed him away. With that accomplished, I peeled off a few more bills. I leaned into the taxi's open passenger-side window to hand over my fare plus a tip. "Thanks for the ride, Jimmy. Good luck with that screenplay you're writing. Have fun at your niece's birthday party tomorrow at the Exploratorium, too!"

Jimmy saluted me with a grin, then drove off. I waved, feeling sorry he was abandoning me so soon. You might have guessed by now that I have a flair for making friends easily—just maybe not with grabby valets or bigwigs. My friend-making knack goes hand in hand with my always-packed luggage and my well-traveled upbringing—and the assortment of chocolate bars, truffles, and cocoa mixes I typically keep on hand to give out to people I meet. Usually, they're postconsultancy samples from grateful chocolate companies. I can't possibly eat them all.

I know, tough life, right? *Too much* chocolate is a real first-world problem. But it's what I deal with every day.

Unfortunately, considering what passed for my usual daily travails only reminded me of the *unusual* event awaiting me today: the Lemaître industry retreat. Just glancing toward the suit-and-tie business types on the lawn made a wave of pure monkey jumpiness wash over me. The effect was like knocking back four espressos and then trying to name all the U.S. state capitals—doomed from the start due to lack of focusing ability.

I glanced at the hovering valets. "Big event today?"

"Huge!" one confirmed, nodding toward the lawn. "All the TV networks are here covering it. They've got satellite vans."

I looked. I saw the vans, the local media . . . the potential disaster that awaited if I tried to "network" with my peers, freestyle, on an empty stomach. Those rhubarb-strawberry macaroons at the bakery in Noe Valley had never sounded better.

Maybe I'd better check in to my room first. I could stow my stuff, freshen up, and have a snack. Maybe I could track down Danny, too. His flight from southern California should have already arrived at SFO. We could lighten the mood with a little harmless teasing, solidify our plans to check out the resort's famous all-chocolate brunch buffet, and catch up on old times.

Then I'd network.

It was an excellent plan. Feeling less monkeylike already, I seized my luggage and headed for the Maison Lemaître lobby.

In my third-floor room, silence enveloped me. *Ah.*

I like the buzz of cities—and I'd adored being immersed in the energy, grit, and fickle weather surrounding my downtown San Francisco hotel—but there was a lot to be said for luxury, too. Just as long as I wouldn't be expected to perform cogently while immersed in it, that is. What I needed was an adjustment period.

Maison Lemaître was ready to give it to me. The resort was chic, comfy, and welcoming. The décor struck the perfect balance between starkly minimal (but modern) and lavishly cushy (but outmoded). My room featured a pillow-piled king-size bed, a sitting area with windows overlooking the Golden Gate Bridge, and an enormous spalike bathroom stocked with Maison Lemaître's house brand of cocoa-themed personal-care products. I uncapped the shampoo and sniffed. Notes of cacao and vanilla struck me first, followed by something with a lingering floral note.

Orange blossom water, I discerned. Interesting choice.

Its citrus notes blended well with the chocolate essence, but it seemed a little too sweet to me. More like candy than shampoo. Little girls would love it, but I wasn't sure if grown women and men would get on board with the idea of lathering up with Orange Crush and Tootsie Rolls. The blend could use some refinement.

Making a note to pitch Christian Lemaître about tweaking the company's nonfood products next (because there was nothing wrong with diversifying, right?), I padded around the room, automatically going through my post-check-in ritual.

I didn't fully unpack, of course. That was a waste of time. But my trusty pashmina went on the foot of the bed, where I could grab it if I got cold. My favorite fig-scented candle went on the bureau, where I could light it to feel at home. My framed photos went on the nightstand, where I could see the smiling faces of my family and friends . . . and wonder where the heck Danny was, anyway? The front desk had said he hadn't checked in yet.

Yes, I was a chronic procrastinator. But Danny was a chronic late arriver. From where I stood, *he* was worse.

Feeling more at home with my things around me, I flipped open my Moleskine notebook and consulted my running to-do lists. Nothing serious leaped out at me—just my reminders about working on my Lemaître report. I usually made those reminders (with all good intentions) around midnight . . . only to abandon them at dawn for a plan of action that featured working on my report *later,* when I would undoubtedly feel übermotivated and energetic.

Yeah. Right. If you believe *that* one . . .

Hastily, I snapped shut my trusty notebook and shoved it back into my crossbody bag for safekeeping. Over the years, friends had nagged me to transfer my myriad to-do lists to my smartphone. But if you traveled to the kind of remote places I did, Wi-Fi coverage was about as reliable as brand-new stilettos were comfortable. It was a crap-shoot, is what I'm saying.

It was better, I'd learned through experience, to go low-fi for the important things. It was better to be safe than sorry.

Heading to the room's windows, I looked out at the proceedings below. Maison Lemaître was built on a promontory that jutted slightly into the bay, which meant the hotel boasted fresh breezes, slightly cooler weather, and a craggy-topped nature trail surrounding it on three sides. From my vantage point, I could see hotel guests tramping along that rocky sliver of pathway, laughing and shading their eyes. Probably the views were spectacular—if you didn't mind roughing it a little.

More retreat attendees had joined the early arrivals I'd noticed earlier. Now they formed an even larger group of fancy-pants CEOs, pastry chefs, PR reps, and other corporate types whose goodwill could only boost my consulting business, if I got to know them. It was probably time to get down there. I'd checked in, gotten settled, and boosted my blood sugar with a complimentary gianduia truffle. I'd made myself presentable with a simple springtime knee-length dress (to go with my flats) and a ponytail to corral my shoulder-length brown hair. I'd reviewed my notes and lists, and I'd even swiped on some lip gloss.

Okay. *Showtime!* But first . . .

I pulled out my cell phone and considered texting Danny, then changed my mind. I wasn't the nagging type. Besides, although our adjoining rooms were being generously comped by Christian Lemaître, I'd covered the airfare for Danny's end of this impromptu trip myself. It hadn't been a big deal. I could afford airfare from L.A. to San Francisco—even at the exorbitant last-minute rates airlines charged. But I didn't want Danny to think I expected anything in return—at least not anything beyond his looking fantastic in a suit. *That* was de rigueur.

For Danny—a private "security expert"—it was easy, too.

What *wasn't* easy was managing the guilt and complicated feelings that came along with flying your best friend upstate on a whim. It was extravagant. He knew it. I knew it. Those feelings hit me hard sometimes. Not that I intended to kvetch to Danny about it. I'd inherited a lot of money when my (admittedly eccentric) uncle had died, and although I had to jump through some hoops to get it, I knew I was lucky.

Reminded of that luck, I looked at my phone again. There was *one* person I could call guilt free. *And* I'd enjoy it. A lot.

Ten seconds later, my call connected with the office of my appointed financial advisor (and trustee of my uncle's will), Travis Turner. Travis's deep, raspy "hello" traveled over the line. He sounded like a supersmart Barry White— like a man who could (and did) make derivatives and stock sales sound hot.

That's why I called Travis so often, of course. It wasn't because I was fascinated with the intricacies of economics. Travis didn't know it, but I liked his voice. I liked its masculine pitch, its timbre, its shiver-inducing huskiness. I'd never met him in person. At this point, Travis could never measure up to his voice, anyway. But for him, I made an exception to my texts-are-efficient rule and actually dialed the phone.

"So, Travis . . . what are you wearing right now?"

"Hayden. Aren't you supposed to be at the Lemaître retreat?" He sounded as though he might be consulting an up-to-the-nanosecond atomic clock. "It starts in five minutes."

Damn his perspicacity. It was really inconvenient.

As much as I yearned for Travis to help me kill time with a little sexy-sounding banter, he clearly wasn't up for it.

"I wanted to talk to you first. You know, to check in."

"Right." In my imagination, he started a timer labeled BILLABLE HOURS, then picked up a pen. "Go ahead. I'm ready."

"Don't you want to tell me what you're wearing?"

"You go first." *There it was*—a hint of playfulness.

I lived for that. It made me feel I was winning every time I coaxed Travis into teasing me. "I'm wearing my fancy shoes."

"And? What else?"

I was tempted to say, *Nothing else. Just shoes.*

But Travis didn't sound in the mood for innuendo. Just for an instant, I wondered if something was troubling him. But then I remembered that was just *him*. Travis was responsible. Settled. Excellent with numbers *and* domesticity. He was also—at twenty-seven—younger than me and simultaneously more authoritative.

That realization nudged me into getting serious for a second.

"What else?" I echoed, musingly glancing down at myself. "A respectable dress. I might not mind being fashionably late to the retreat, but I want to make a good impression. I *have* absorbed one or two cultural mores in my life, you know."

"I know." Travis paused, polite and efficient. "So . . . you've checked in to Maison Lemaître, then? Let's have the details."

Dutifully, I gave him Jimmy's taxicab medallion number and driver ID (in case of lost items or a misplaced receipt), then reported my hotel room number and expected length of stay, along with a rough itinerary. It was our regular routine. As a solo female traveler, I liked knowing someone else knew where I was.

Especially someone reliable, trustworthy, and hyper-intelligent. Someone like Travis. If you had to have a keeper, he was the kind to have. But I'd rather have heard *him* talk than me. I'd rather have heard more of his bed-room voice.

"So," I went on, still gazing out the window at the choco-latiering crowd milling around on the verdant grounds. "About that question I asked before. What are *you* wearing?"

Travis laughed. I liked the sound of that, too.

It was really too bad we'd probably never meet. Travis was (inexplicably to me) phobic about air travel. He couldn't even drop off friends at the airport without get-ting antsy. Whereas I . . . Well, you already know all about my footloose ways.

Sadly, Travis and I are fundamentally incompatible.

"Are you wearing . . . a kilt?" I guessed. "A loincloth? A—"

"I'm wearing a sandwich board," Travis interrupted before I could get too carried away. His seductive voice sounded amused, though. "It reads, STOP PROCRASTINATING, HAYDEN MUNDY MOORE."

"Mmm. Anything else underneath that sandwich board?"

"Just take the hint, Hayden. Get to work, okay?"

"Okay. But be careful. Sandwich boards chafe."

"Not if you wear them correctly."

"Leave it to you to know the correct way to do *every-thing.*"

"That's right. I do." Travis's deep voice made it sound as if he were right in my hotel room with me. "Don't you forget it."

But just at that moment, I could scarcely concentrate on what Travis was saying . . . even as (I swear) his voice gave me goose bumps on my goose bumps. Because just at that moment, I glanced down at Maison Lemaître's lush lawn, saw a familiar-looking fortyish redhead in a skirt suit and Bluetooth headset handing out colorful Lemaître-brand T-shirts to the retreat attendees, and realized I had just been offered a get-out-of-jail-free card.

The woman in the corporate kit and headgear was Nina Wheeler, Christian Lemaître's right-hand gal and the company's PR exec. I recognized her. The T-shirts she'd handed out came in conspicuously matching colors, three shirts per shade, to what appeared to be teams of players. It didn't take a genius to notice that pattern. If the recently unfurled banner snapping in the breeze was any indication of what was to come, I knew what was next, too. Specifically, a 100 PERCENT CHOCOLATE SCAVENGER HUNT.

Because that's what the banner said.

I was quick with details like that.

I was relieved, too. Spouting niceties about current events while making knowledgeable comments about Napa Valley Pinot Noir wasn't my scene. But an icebreaker game was right up my alley. I wouldn't even have to stand still! Scurrying around to find chocolate scavenger hunt items suited my monkey mind perfectly.

Besides, I liked winning *almost* as much as I liked listening to Travis talk. Being humble was not my strong suit. Not when it came to things I did well. Like chocolate.

"I never forget a thing, Travis," I told him truthfully. "*Especially* when it comes to you. Talk to you later!"

Then I signed off on our call, heaved a regretful sigh for Travis's refusal to indulge me with sexy talk, and grabbed my bag. Within moments, I'd eschewed the hotel's molasses-slow elevators and was headed downstairs the old-fashioned way (via the chilly, deserted-but-efficient staircase), ready to show the San Francisco chocolate world a thing or two about Hayden Mundy Moore . . . and what she could accomplish when it came to being the world's first (and only) chocolate whisperer.

I even made house calls. For the right chunk of cacao and a nice referral, of course. A girl had to have standards.

And maybe, today, she had to have the right color of T-shirt, too. When it came to that, time was wasting.

For the sake of scoring a good team, I decided to run.

Chapter 2

By the time I'd practically skidded to a stop downstairs (my fancy flats left me surprisingly spry), things were hopping.

The resort's driveway was packed with cars and taxis and gleaming SUVs. The guests who'd driven (or been driven) in them impatiently awaited bellmen or valet service or both. The valets ran to and fro clutching keys and wearing anxious expressions.

The fragrance of fine chocolate wafted over everything, of course. I couldn't tell if it emanated from Maison Lemaître's Michelin-starred restaurant or its expansive spa or both. I made a note to double-check the spa treatments that were included in the retreat, then gauged my best path across the driveway.

Crossing was like playing a real-time game of Frogger (albeit an upscale version), but it was nothing compared with crossing streets in Paris. I made it alive to the hotel grounds where the gauzy tents and chocolate VIPs were. There, the scent of chocolate was weaker, but the mingled fragrances of Merlot and mown grass were stronger. So was the breeze. Ruffled by its force, men shucked their suit jackets and tugged on T-shirts atop their dress shirts and ties; women shrugged and giggled and wiggled their way into their T-shirts, preserving their modesty by layering them over their dresses or shirts or lightweight, ideal-for-northern-California short-sleeve sweaters.

At least most of them did, I noticed. One woman, standing near a tent featuring Lemaître Chocolates press releases and promotional items, simply turned her back to the crowd, shimmied out of her white-sequin-spangled cashmere T-shirt, and handed it to an older, white-haired man waiting nearby. Then, clad only in her pristine white skirt and jeweled sandals, the woman pulled on an orange Lemaître-logo T-shirt. When she turned to model it, I saw that she was a pretty, olive-skinned woman about my age, with expertly applied makeup, dark hair, and a lot of élan.

Wow. I wanted a woman like *that* on my team. She had audacity. She wasn't afraid to go for broke, either, no matter what it took. While everyone else was gawking at her immodest (and braless) way of changing clothes, I grabbed a yellow T-shirt from a box near Nina Wheeler's elbow. I zeroed in on a woman standing nearby with her back to me, then nudged her.

"Trade you?" I offered, keeping my gaze fixed on my prize—her orange T-shirt—while simultaneously offering her my yellow one in trade. "You don't seem up for a striptease today."

"I'm not! Take it." All but shoving her orange shirt at me, the woman completed the swap quickly—as though she was afraid I might change my mind. In an irked and preoccupied tone, she grumbled, "I should have known Isabel Lemaître would make a scene. She doesn't usually attend the retreat."

"*That's* Isabel Lemaître? Bernard Lemaître's wife?"

A general murmur of assent met my question. Apparently, there was no such thing as a private conversation at a company retreat.

That was understandable, though. The world of chocolate was a small one, really. Everyone knew Bernard Lemaître. More than a hundred years ago, his family had founded one of the most successful chocolate companies in the world. Bernard had brought that company to new heights. He'd turned it into a San Francisco institution as familiar as cable cars, Lombard Street, and Pier 39. He'd partnered with a local television kids' show, making children of all ages love Lemaître Chocolates—and love *him*. He was an icon unto himself. When I'd accepted the consultancy at Lemaître, I'd hoped to meet Bernard. Christian had insisted his uncle Bernard was "too busy" to drop into the office regularly.

It seemed apparent to me that Bernard was "too busy" with his dishy-looking younger wife. Even now, as I held my newly won logo T-shirt, I glimpsed my team's other two members canoodling. Isabel Lemaître gave her husband a kiss, then stroked his orange-T-shirt-covered chest in a very possessive and lusty fashion. For all her ardor, anyone would have sworn that Bernard had six-pack abs and shoulders of steel under that T-shirt. In reality, he had the body you'd expect of a sixty-two-year-old man who'd made a fortune in cocoa butter, sugar, and cream.

They were both sweet, really. Rumor had it that Bernard Lemaître had been forced out of the company (for all intents and purposes, at least) by his nephew, Christian. But from the looks of things today, Bernard seemed pretty content in "retirement."

I guessed that's what happened when a die-hard bachelor like Bernard discovered the joys of wedded bliss *and* qualifying for AARP membership at the same time. Isabel was his first wife.

"Wait a minute," someone blurted beside me. "*Hayden?*"

I was donning my orange T-shirt, getting ready to join what I felt sure would be the winning team, so I didn't

answer at first. I couldn't do much besides yank, hoping to
see who my questioner was. I was blinded by orange. It
was, however, the best quality "gimme" T-shirt I'd ever
encountered. *Mmm. Soft.*

"Hayden?" came the voice again. "Ohmigod. It *is* you!"

I felt a hand grab my arm. I inhaled harshly, then froze.
All my muscles tensed, reacting instinctively to the
contact.

This is not an emergency, I reminded myself. Although
I'd had a few helpful self-defense lessons over the years
from well-meaning Italians and Spaniards and once (memorably) a Frenchman, this situation didn't call for an eye
gouge or a knee crack.

I gave a hard tug, and my questioner's face came into
view. It was Adrienne Dowling, Lemaître's head chocolatier and one of the most talented people I'd ever met
while on a consulting job.

While I'd been undercover troubleshooting for Lemaître
Chocolates, Adrienne and I had gotten to know one another fairly well. We'd shared lunches, after-hours drinks,
and a giddy appreciation for cute 49ers football players.
We'd also shared a similarly scrupulous approach to recipe
development.

I liked Adrienne. I admired her. I knew she was forty-
six, but with her blue eyes, curly blond hair, and petite
frame, she looked more like a fragile teenager—a teenager
dressed in her mother's frumpy business wear, admittedly,
but still a teenager. I wondered if Adrienne knew how
openhearted she always appeared.

I also wondered if she was the only person attending the
retreat without a plus-one. (Well, except for *me,* so far, but
that was temporary.) Everyone else had brought spouses or
dates to the annual event, just as Christian had told me they
would.

I thanked my lucky stars Danny had agreed to join me.

"Adrienne!" I yelled back, laughing at my own goofy self-defense impulses. I hugged her, embarrassed to have been so preoccupied earlier. "I'm sorry. I was so focused on getting a team orange T-shirt that I didn't even recognize you."

"That's all right. It happens, especially to me." With cheerful, self-deprecating charm, Adrienne waved off my apology. "I'd rather have this yellow T-shirt, anyway."

She aimed a meaningful look at Isabel and Bernard, who were now holding hands and trading pet names for one another. It was endearing, like I said. But it was probably awkward for Adrienne to see Lemaître's founder under such intimate circumstances. No wonder she'd been so keen to switch T-shirts with me.

As a decidedly *unmarried* woman (remind me to tell you about my three ex-fiancés sometime), *I* felt more comfortable with Adrienne myself . . . even if I couldn't quite tear away my gaze from Isabel Lemaître. Her laughter was engaging. Her free-spirited attitude toward wardrobe changes reminded me of the European countries I'd lived in, where nudity was featured without fanfare in everything from movies to cereal advertisements.

It was . . . liberating. And natural. And so, it seemed, was Isabel. Which made me curious about her. I turned to Adrienne.

"You said Isabel doesn't usually attend the retreat?"

"*Never,*" Adrienne said emphatically, swerving her gaze away from a good-looking man with black curly hair wearing a yellow T-shirt that matched hers. *Hmm. Maybe there was another reason Adrienne wanted to be on Team Yellow.* "Isabel has always said Lemaître is too 'stodgy' for her trendy tastes. But now that Bernard has been all but ousted from the company, Isabel won't stay away. It's downright perverse." Adrienne frowned. "I'll never understand that woman. I don't want to, either!"

I'd have sworn that mild-mannered Adrienne actually muttered a swearword aimed at her erstwhile boss's wife. But at that instant, Nina Wheeler charged up—with a cell phone in each hand and her Bluetooth headset crackling static—and interrupted us.

"You two! Get with your color-coded groups, please!" Nina said. "We're about to start. We're already three minutes late!"

Her wild-eyed demeanor surprised me. Usually, Nina was the epitome of self-assurance. Evidently, being in charge of the Lemaître retreat was a stressful event. Nina and I had met during my consultancy, too. We hadn't spent much time together, though—and the double take Nina gave me as she looked up from her pair of cell phones showed her surprise at seeing me there.

"Hayden Mundy Moore? What are you doing here?" She frowned. "I thought your consultancy at Lemaître was finished."

"Almost. Just a few loose ends left to tie up." *Like a thorough multipage report,* I remembered guiltily. "Don't worry. I'm not a gate-crasher. Christian invited me." Hoping to calm Nina's obviously frazzled nerves, I smiled and added, "He's probably already included me in the seating plan for the welcome reception and . . . everything else, too. I won't be any trouble."

Nina's eyes narrowed. "We'll see about that." Shoving her dual phones in her suit pockets, she consulted a clipboard hanging from a bungee clip around her neck. Then she spoke into her headset. "Yes, that's Hayden Mundy Moore. Verify, please."

As I listened to Nina spell out my last name—which tended to confuse people, especially in alphabetical-order situations, due to its nonhyphenated nature—to the person on the other end of the line, I traded a concerned glance with Adrienne. My chocolatier friend only shrugged and raised her palms in a "what can you do?" gesture. Evidently, this wasn't unusual for Nina.

The redheaded PR rep got off the phone, scribbled my name on her clipboarded list, then looked up. Tensely. "Well? What are you two waiting for? Get with your groups, will you?"

Then she stalked off, muttering and shaking her head.

"Yikes." I frowned after her. "Poor Nina."

"We'd better do what she says," Adrienne said. "I only have a few minutes to spare, anyway. I'm supposed to be in the hotel kitchen, working on my contribution to the welcome reception."

Before I could ask Adrienne what her contribution would be—undoubtedly, something creamy, dark, chocolaty, and scrumptious that *I* would need to gobble up for "testing purposes"—Mr. Black-Haired Yellow T-shirt strode up. Impatiently, he gestured at Adrienne. "I think that's our cue. Shall we get started?"

"Of course!" Adrienne accepted his hand. "Right away."

The two of them crossed the lawn to join the third member of their team—a nondescript-looking cacao bean supplier—for the scavenger hunt. I hoped Adrienne and Mr. Yellow T-shirt hit it off. Stranger things had happened. After all, Adrienne deserved a fun, confidence-boosting fling. If he was flying solo, too . . . well, maybe they'd connect. Sometimes industry events like this one were hotbeds of intrigue, gossip, and secret alliances.

Under those circumstances, hookups weren't unthinkable.

Except for me. Because I was teamed up with the king and queen of chocolate: Bernard and Isabel Lemaître. Hauling in a deep breath, I plastered on my brightest smile and headed off to start winning my first-ever chocolate scavenger hunt.

* * *

Winning was not *quite* as easy as I'd first anticipated.

For one thing, the items we were meant to scavenger hunt had been placed all over the resort's expansive grounds, so it was a trek to find them in my unwelcome fancy flats. For another, some items were actually tests to be passed rather than objects to be found, which was kind of a letdown for a competitive type like me. For another, the other teams took a quick lead, since they weren't hampered by Bernard and Isabel's habit of ducking behind leafy trees and beside flower beds of geraniums to make out.

Dispirited but not defeated, I rallied my team and kept going. At each station (identified by the gauzy tents I mentioned before), Lemaître employees waited with chocolate samples and on-the-spot quizzes. Ostensibly, the only trick was acing the quizzes and collecting the rewards: embossed gold foil stickers, which were placed on a bingo-style scorecard.

The team with the most stickers won the scavenger hunt. As a PR stunt for Lemaître, it was effective. As an in-person alfresco advertisement for the company, it excelled. As a fun and challenging icebreaker activity . . . it was not the best.

The trouble was, the quizzes were too easy. They didn't have the intricacy to inspire much conversation or strategizing, so all the teams whipped through them with lightning speed.

I'd expected to be doing something like differentiating a Tanzanian single-varietal cacao bean from a premium Grand Cru blend, or picking out the essence of a single-bean 73 percent Côte d'Ivoire cacao from the bite of an arabica coffee bean after it had been brewed into a creamy café mocha. Instead, the "challenges" asked me to identify milk chocolate from dark, explain what white chocolate consisted of, and identify the original recipe for Toll House Chocolate Chip Cookies.

At that station, I peered at the artificially antiqued recipe cards laid out near a tray of cookies. I pointed. "This one. Ruth Wakefield's original recipe for Toll House Chocolate Crunch Cookies called for baking soda dissolved in hot water."

"Yes!" Beaming, the Lemaître employee gave me a sticker.

I pasted it on my scorecard—which now looked like a shiny gold flyer for Lemaître chocolates, because the stickers all bore the company's familiar embossed logo—and hastily moved on. It took a while for me to corral Bernard and Isabel after each station, but by this point, that wasn't a big deal. The other competitors were starting to get bogged down with tasting all the chocolate samples. Team Orange was actually in the lead.

I'd do my chocolate tasting later, I'd decided. Good chocolate deserves to be savored. Being outdoors, blown by the wind and surrounded by competitive chocolate-industry insiders, was not conducive to proper enjoyment. While eating chocolate, I believe in doing just one thing: eating chocolate. That's it.

A girl had to have priorities. That was one of mine.

In the meantime, I tried to win. I yearned for my practical Chuck Taylor sneakers as I navigated the marshy area near the single boat dock, then crossed the hilly zone closest to the wind-scoured Marin Headlands. I completed two more challenges.

I spied Adrienne and waved to her. Before long, Team Orange needed only one more sticker to win. Bernard Lemaître seemed impressed by my performance. His approval was like a shot of adrenaline, driving me toward the waiting finish line. After all, Bernard was a verifiable chocolatiering hero! His approval meant a lot to me—even if he was, at this point, behaving like a kindly but horny grandpa out for a nature hike. Bolstered by the real possibility of winning—and by the idea that *I* could restore a little luster to Bernard's reputation by sealing a victory on his behalf—I took a bold shortcut across the jagged promontory point I'd observed from my hotel room window.

There, I almost took a header into the frigid bay waters.

"Whoops! Watch yourself there, Hayden!" Bernard chuckled and hauled me to safety just in time. He gave me a gruff pat with his bearlike arm. "It's pretty steep around here."

"You're not kidding." With my heart pounding, I gawked at the gray-looking bay waters swirling at the rocky point's edge, fifteen or twenty feet below the designated trail. "Thanks!"

"You're more than welcome." Bernard's warm smile, twinkly blue eyes, and kind, wrinkled face made him look every inch the chocolate company mascot. If he told you chocolate-covered bees were delicious, you'd believe him. He was just that likable.

"Are we done yet?" Sounding bored, Isabel cast her gaze on the gold-stickered scorecard in my hand. "I'm cold, Bernie."

At that, Bernard's eyes twinkled even more. He seemed oddly touched by his wife's use of her nickname for him. It was . . .

Okay, it was *sweet.* You guessed it. I couldn't quit thinking that Bernard and Isabel were sweet together. They were!

Tenderly, Bernard hugged his wife close to him for warmth. "We'll go down to the spa and have a nice hot-cocoa mud bath after this, all right? That will warm you up in a hurry."

Isabel smiled. "You're always so good to me, Bernie."

I was tactfully trying to look away to allow them some privacy, gazing studiously across the resort's grounds to locate the final challenge station. But as luck would have it, I accidentally chose that moment to let my eyes wander back to Bernard. His expression looked hard. And . . . guilty? What the . . . ?

An instant later, I decided I'd imagined it. Because that's when I spied the challenge station I was looking for—*and* Team Blue T-shirt, heading straight toward it for the win.

Ordinarily, I'm not *ultra*competitive. I mean, I might not know how to change a carburetor or grow cucumbers from scratch, but I have my areas of expertise. I'm fine with my skill set just as it is. I don't usually feel the need to grandstand or brag.

Yes. Okay. I can work magic with chocolate. But that's not going to change the world or anything. I have to be realistic.

I have to accept that I'm not going to conquer *everything*.

But for whatever reason, as I squinted across the resort's grounds and saw the blue team—headed by the unmistakably boyish Christian Lemaître, the company's CEO, my host, and the man who clearly was about to win his own scavenger hunt (which basically defined "poor sportsmanship")—something in me snapped.

I had to get down there and win.

"We'd better get going!" I said brightly to the Lemaîtres.

Then I took off at a loping run/walk, mentally reviewing the most arcane bits of chocolate trivia I knew in an effort to prepare for anything. Other competitors waved. I waved back but kept going. Colored T-shirts and green grass and flowered shrubs flew past me. The deluxe resort's windows glinted in the distance. I was almost there, and I *knew* I could win.

I couldn't wait to tell Danny I'd won. Travis too.

Fifty yards from the final station—whose challenge seemed to involve a taste-off between various chocolate liqueurs—I glimpsed Adrienne at the Toll House cookie-themed station. She looked beleaguered. Neither of her teammates were in the vicinity, but she did have a messenger bag slung crossways around her torso, bulging with papers. Maybe, I reasoned, she'd come prepared for this event with research notes and tips?

"I don't *know*!" she was wailing. "I'm having a brain fade!"

Or maybe not. Struck by Adrienne's fraught tone, I stopped.

"I *know* I should know this. I *do* know this," she was telling the Lemaître employee who was manning the cookie station. "But I didn't sleep much last night, and I've been busy working all day, and I wouldn't even be here at all, except—"

That's when I butted in. "Hi, Adrienne. Need some help?"

Startled, the chocolatier glanced from me to the cookie station to a spot behind me—probably the spot where Bernard and Isabel were bringing up the rear. Or maybe giving each other hickeys. Anything was possible. Adrienne waved her scorecard.

"Hayden! I'm such a dummy. My team split up for efficiency. I was supposed to do this station, but I missed it somehow." Adrienne bit her lip. She cast a frantic glance at the grounds, as though looking for Mr. Yellow T-shirt and his cohort. "If I don't do it, we'll lose! But for some reason, I can't remember—"

Her gaze dipped to my scorecard. Comprehension

crossed her face. She glanced over her shoulder at the final station.

"Never mind. You should go!" Adrienne shoved me—pretty hard for such a small woman. "Hurry up! You can still win!"

I could. I cast a wistful glance toward my original goal, then shrugged. "I'll win another time. No biggie." I eyed the cookies, chose a particularly tasty-looking chocolate-studded specimen, then handed it to Adrienne. "Try eating this. Maybe you just need a boost, so you can think straight. If I don't eat, my ability to concentrate goes right out the window."

"Oh, it's not that! I've been sampling test chocolates all day." Nevertheless, Adrienne chomped off a giant bite of cookie. Nervously, she chewed, casting another fretful glance at the retreat attendees. It seemed that she was looking for someone—probably her yellow-shirted potential paramour. "Caffeinated chocolates. You know, for the new Lemaître nutraceutical line?"

Her worried gaze probed mine. All I could do was shift uneasily. Part of my report on Lemaître concerned that line of chocolates. They were supposed to have healthy—even medicinal—benefits. Hence the "nutraceutical" tag—a mashup of "nutrition" and "pharmaceutical." Christian was putting a lot of emphasis on the line, but I knew it had issues.

I didn't want to go into it. My analysis of the caffeinated chocolates line could wait. I knew it might devastate Adrienne, who'd already spent months developing it. Those were the breaks in the chocolate business, but I didn't revel in that fact.

Reassuringly, I patted her shoulder. "You're very talented, Adrienne. Just take another look at the Toll House quiz. Okay?"

To my relief, my diversionary tactic worked. Adrienne

still seemed jumpy and apprehensive, but that might be explained by the fact that she'd apparently been main-lining the equivalent of mini chocolate-covered caffeinated energy drinks for hours now.

Me? After one of those drinks "with wings," I'm a goner.

My vice is chocolate. I definitely don't need extra "energy" revving up my already manic simian tendencies.

I nudged Adrienne. "Go ahead. Which recipe is it?"

With one hand hovering over a Toll House cookie recipe, she hesitated. She exhaled, then gave me a shy smile. "You've always been so nice to me, Hayden. I really appreciate it."

Aw. Unfortunately, I'd chosen that moment to sneak a glance at the final station. Christian had thrust both arms in the air, I saw. He seemed to be performing a victory dance while his Lemaître lackeys and other guests applauded. On him, that ridiculous spectacle actually looked pretty good. Christian was fit, forty, and brilliant enough that even his competitors lauded the way he'd updated his company's quaint confectionary.

Discomfited to have been caught *not* being so nice to Adrienne at a crucial moment, I shook my head. "If only I could do more," I told her guiltily, knowing my report to Christian might well torpedo all the work she'd done so far. "I really wish I could help you"—*not have your work wasted*—"even more."

She gasped with evident delight. "Do you mean it?" She grabbed both my arms. "Oh, Hayden! That would be *great*!"

Ruefully, I wriggled free, not wanting to commit. I'd been hoping to devote some one-on-one attention to Danny during my downtime at the resort. I was mostly booked solid with warm chocolate-fondue body wraps and cacao-nib-and-espresso-bean pedicure scrubs, but on my off-hours, I'd hoped to have fun.

I'd missed Danny. He understood me. He made me laugh.

He was more to me than just a tardy stud in a suit, there to make me look as if I had a modicum of normalcy in my life.

"I'm not sure how much more I can do, Adrienne," I hedged, but before I could say more, Christian Lemaître spotted me.

"Hayden Mundy Moore!" he bellowed jovially. "The chocolate whisperer herself! You made it! That's *excellent*!"

Uh-oh. I recognized that tone. I hadn't worked with Christian long, but for all his brash intelligence, he wasn't exactly complicated. He liked to seem important. The end.

This time, he meant to use *me* as a means to that end.

"Not that *I've* ever needed Hayden's services at Lemaître, of course," he lied in a smooth undertone to his associates. "But I'm happy to introduce all of *you* losers to Hayden!"

His guffaws of laughter grew louder as he came closer.

I looked his way again. Like the Pied Piper of chocolate he aspired to be, Christian strode toward me while surrounded by adoring industry types. His blue crew-neck T-shirt made him look younger than his years; his avaricious expression made him look older. Just then, he reminded me of a middle-aged frat boy.

Bernard frowned as his nephew sailed past. Christian didn't seem to notice. That was Bernard and Isabel's cue to leave.

In their wake, Adrienne's yellow T-shirted pal drifted closer. I tried to send him a mental message to approach Adrienne and ask her out for drinks later. My telepathy failed.

I noticed redheaded Nina, too, bounding along devotedly in her boss's wake in three-inch pumps (on the grass!)

with a grace and alacrity I envied. She seemed to have calmed down a little, with only one phone in hand and her clipboard stowed someplace, now that the scavenger hunt appeared to be a rousing success.

Even *if* the host had won it, I recalled. Lame.

Christian's over-the-top laughter struck me again. So did Adrienne's downright panicked expression when she heard it.

Was she supposed to be working *right now*? She must be. That was the only explanation for the way Adrienne went still, like a frightened rabbit, gazing unblinkingly as her boss approached.

Christian didn't seem pleased to find Adrienne standing there. "Ms. Dowling!" he barked. "Shouldn't you be in your magical workshop, coming up with some tasty treats for later?"

"Um," Adrienne began. Her gaze darted to me. "Uh—"

Christian's abrupt clap made her jump. "Yes! Get on it!"

"I'm sorry," she mumbled. "I'll leave right now."

As Christian turned to his retreat guests—presumably making sure they'd witnessed his masterful employer-employee relations—Adrienne caught my arm again. Her intent expression riveted me.

"Take this." She whispered the words harshly, shoving a thick rectangular item at my midsection. "Please, Hayden. Take it! I can't let Christian have it. Just . . . keep it safe for me, okay?" Her fearful gaze zipped to her boss. "I'll get it later."

Dumbfounded, I accepted it. It was a notebook, I saw after a hasty downward glance, not much different from my favorite Moleskine number. It was the kind of thing pastry chefs (for instance) and chocolatiers typically use to track recipe ideas and formulas. It had to contain years' worth of work, judging by the heft of it. Nodding, I bundled it close.

The whole exchange took maybe fifteen seconds. Ten seconds after that, Adrienne had scurried up the lawn toward the hotel.

Mr. Yellow T-shirt watched her leave. Just like Danny, he was too late. *You missed your chance, buddy,* I told him with a regretful mental shrug. *You just let a great woman slip away.*

Christian's next bellow roared into my consciousness.

"What about *you,* Hayden?" He transferred his gaze from Adrienne's former location, which—if looks could start fires—would have been a blazing inferno. "Isn't there *something* you're supposed to be working on right now, too?"

He had to mean my report about Lemaître's operations, I realized. But he couldn't come out and say so in mixed company—not without letting on that he *had* used my consulting services. Moments ago, he'd sworn he never had.

But he still wanted to needle me about my report?

Christian Lemaître had a lot of nerve. He was a bully.

Determined not to be as easily cowed as poor Adrienne, I held my ground. Calmly, I tucked away Adrienne's notebook into my crossbody bag for safekeeping, just as though it were mine.

Butter wouldn't melt in my mouth when I smiled at him.

"Right now, I'm just enjoying your hospitality," I said.

Christian nodded at me. "Well, enjoy it while you can."

Even nonchalantly said, that statement sounded like a threat. Maybe Christian Lemaître wasn't as laid-back about deadlines as he'd claimed to be, I realized. But I was stuck.

"I'm *dying* to know about that fascinating assignment you were working on. You know the one," Christian persisted while waggling his brows, obviously intending to carry on some sort of double-coded conversation with me while his otherwise clueless guests looked on. Maybe he enjoyed messing with people that way. "Did you ever find out exactly what the problems were?" Eager to appear the expert, Christian turned to a bystander and confided, "Hayden is an absolute whiz at what she does. She's *unstoppable*."

At the fringes of the group, Nina Wheeler narrowed her eyes at him. Evidently, the PR rep wasn't any more fond of her boss's antics than I was. Although Nina didn't intervene—I wouldn't have, either, to be honest—she did cast me a speculative glance.

I nodded at her in shared understanding. *You're right,* my nod said. *You're not crazy—Christian is acting weird.* I'd worked for my share of annoying bosses, and I knew it wasn't fun. Sometimes it was necessary, though. That was apparently the position that stressed-out Nina was in. I felt relieved that someone besides me appeared to recognize what was really going on here.

I'd barely completed that thought before Nina left the group. Probably, she was going to comfort Adrienne, I figured. I was glad someone was. Right now, I was trapped. Christian hadn't paid me for the work I'd (almost) completed. Although I had the money in my trust fund for a fallback, I had a reputation to maintain.

Plus, I didn't want to disappoint Travis—or rile up Danny, who was occasionally frustrated by my "lackadaisical" attitude toward the report-writing part of my consulting business. I understood where he was coming from, but I didn't agree.

I also didn't agree with Christian's intimidation tactics. Adrienne's frightened face still stuck in my mind. For her sake, I straightened my spine and stepped up squarely to Christian.

"Actually, my assignment is going well," I told him. "I'm just surprised *you* weren't already aware of the . . . *troubles* . . . I was looking into. You're usually so on top of things. Aren't you?"

"Yes. I am." Christian tightened his jaw. He managed a blasé-seeming wave. "We can touch base later. That's fine."

"Are you sure?" I widened my eyes as disingenuously as I could. Insincerity didn't come naturally to me. Ordinarily, I'm a take-me-as-I-am kind of gal. But he'd riled me up by being mean to someone as softhearted as Adrienne. "I'd be happy to discuss my findings and all the implications of them now."

I recognized immediately when Christian understood my meaning. *He* could leverage me with my overdue report—but *I* could leverage him with the lie he'd just told about not using my chocolate whisperer consulting services. We were at an impasse.

If anything, Christian somehow tightened his jaw even further. I was surprised his teeth didn't snap. "No. Thank you," he managed. Then, a clap. "Everyone, I think it's teatime!"

He meant Maison Lemaître's well-known British-style all-chocolate afternoon tea service. I'd been looking forward to it.

The crowd meandered toward the hotel. I started to, too—and almost ran smack into Christian on my way. His arm clutched mine. What was it with people grabbing me so hard today, anyway?

"I'm trying to be nice, Hayden," he said with a mean look. "Don't try my patience too far. You'll be sorry you did."

Too late, I remembered he *was* notoriously ruthless.

He'd banished his own uncle from running the family business.

"Don't push me, either," I said. "You need me, remember?"

Scowling, Christian let me go. I waited until he'd stomped away. Then I bolted for my hotel room, suddenly feeling pretty darn übermotivated, energetic, and ready to work on my report.

Chapter 3

I had every intention of working on my report. Honestly, I did. But as I was striding diligently toward my room at Maison Lemaître—scarcely noticing the fragrant begonia beds and tinkling tiled fountains I passed along the way— I caught another intoxicating whiff of chocolate . . . and thought of Adrienne.

Somewhere nearby, poor Adrienne was knocking herself out to create chocolates for her demanding tyrant of a boss, Christian. With the reception only a couple of hours away, Adrienne didn't have a lot of time left, either. She'd mentioned that she hadn't slept much the night before. She was probably exhausted.

Adrienne needed my help, I decided, and veered in the other direction. When I found the kitchen she'd been assigned to—an offshoot located within close proximity of the ballroom and its nearby light-string-bedecked and landscaped patio—I got right down to work. It didn't take much to shuck my crossbody bag, slap a chef's apron atop my orange Lemaître T-shirt, and dig in.

Adrienne was surprised to see me; I was surprised to find her working on her "luxury" line of caffeinated nutraceutical Lemaître chocolates—specifically, gilded "energy" truffles.

Adrienne only grimaced. "This is what Christian wants."

Everyone knew Christian got what he wanted. She didn't need to say it for both of us to know it. Bernard was proof of that.

"With all the changes at Lemaître since Christian took over from Bernard," Adrienne went on, "I *really* can't afford to goof up on this. People lost their jobs! Everyone got reshuffled."

Right. That explained Adrienne's panic at being caught red-handed—by Christian—*not* working during the chocolate scavenger hunt. It also explained her visible agitation now. She talked a mile a minute, seeming almost as frenzied as I sometimes did.

I'd originally planned to return Adrienne's notebook. Looking at her now, though, I decided to wait until morning. In the state she was in at the moment, she might lose it, drop it in a double-boiler of melted chocolate, or accidentally set it on fire. She was just that frantic as she worked on her truffles.

Watching Adrienne scurry to and fro across the kitchen, I felt torn about what to do. The trouble was, I'd thought the caffeinated chocolate line was already an official no-go. I'd voiced my preliminary concerns about it to Christian several days ago, during our agreed-upon "final meeting." I just hadn't detailed them all in writing yet.

At the company's primary San Francisco facility, I'd learned that anhydrous caffeine is extremely difficult to work with. It looks harmless—similar to just-add-water lemonade powder—but it's intense and highly concentrated. It comes with a correspondingly bitter flavor that's difficult to disguise.

Even in the minute amounts used in making chocolate,

that bitterness is evident . . . and unpleasant. It ruins the *terroir* of the chocolate—the unique characteristics given to it by the climate, geology, and geography of the place its cacao beans were grown. It throws off the flavor. No matter how Adrienne and I adjusted the formulas, we weren't able to create a truffle that delivered the necessary nutraceutical "kick" of caffeine while preserving the expected Lemaître Chocolates' quality.

Evidently, Christian had ignored my warnings. According to Adrienne, he'd instructed her to continue developing caffeinated chocolates without me—and to prepare "sneak preview" samples for the welcome reception, too, where the nutraceutical line was to be unveiled. The problems inherent in that had kept eager-to-please Adrienne working feverishly in the days leading up to the retreat. They'd made her a nervous wreck by the time I arrived on the scene, too.

But there wasn't much two diligent chocolatiers couldn't accomplish together. Knowing Adrienne as well as I did, I was able to duck in and out of the proceedings without distracting her. With our energy pumped by the music I switched on for a morale booster, Adrienne and I performed a familiar ballet of chocolate production. We prepared several pounds of dark-chocolate couverture. We measured minuscule amounts of powdered caffeine. We dipped dozens of truffles, then gilded them with edible gold leaf and arranged them on serving trays.

By the time we were finished, I felt more like a mad scientist than a chocolate whisperer. I also felt giddy with relief and buzzed with a glow that felt more like the result of a philanthropic job well done than the effect of the few sugary truffle samples I'd cadged. Giving Adrienne a hug, I smiled.

"You did it!" I told her. "Now, get out of this kitchen, willya? Go take a break. Have a massage! You earned it."

Uncertainly, Adrienne bit her lip. "I don't know, Hayden. There's still more to be done. The formula might not be right."

"It's as perfect as you can make it for now. That'll have to be good enough." If the chocolates didn't deliver the expected "kick," it wouldn't be the end of the world. Firmly, I caught hold of my friend's slight shoulders. I turned her around. "Don't make me march you off to the spa myself. I'll do it, you know! Have something healthy to eat, too. They're bound to have something energizing at the spa café."

"Yes, ma'am." Laughing, Adrienne relented. "I will."

"Maybe you'll run into Mr. Yellow T-shirt on the way," I teased. "It looked as though you two were hitting it off today."

"Oh." Suddenly, Adrienne's pert face clouded. She fidgeted with her apron strings. "Um, it wasn't like that. Not with him."

"Come on." Giving her a nudge, I persisted. "He likes you!"

But Adrienne only shook her head. Then she gave me a long look. "Thanks again, Hayden. You're always coming to my rescue."

Touched by her appreciation, I hugged her. "Anytime."

Then we both undid our aprons, grabbed our things, and went our separate ways—Adrienne to unwind at the spa, and me to track down my errant plus-one and make him model potential welcome-reception attire for me. Danny sure did look good in a suit . . . but I couldn't remember now if I'd told him to bring one.

Hoping I had, I waved to Adrienne and then dashed toward the exit door. Like every hotel kitchen I'd ever been in, it connected with a warren of slightly dingy hallways for staff use, additional stairwells, and—after a little backtracking—the main staircase I needed to get to my room. Grateful for my travel-honed sense of direction (it hadn't failed me yet), I ascended three flights of stairs with my crossbody bag thumping along at the effort, reached the third landing, opened the fire door . . . and found a surprise waiting for me outside my room.

The man standing there frowning at room 332 was tall, tousle-haired, and rakish-looking. He was holding a manila filing envelope. He was handsome and broad-shouldered, and I know what you're thinking: I'm just being coy. He was *Danny*.

Except he wasn't. This man was Mr. Yellow T-shirt himself. I couldn't fathom why he'd be lurking outside *my* hotel room.

Reasoning that he was probably looking for Adrienne (via me, the only one of the two of us who *hadn't* been too shy to look him directly in the eyes), I strode forward.

"Hi!" I said. "You must be looking for Adrienne."

I guess I was more hyped-up on chocolates than I thought, because I spoke pretty loudly. I accidentally startled him. He jerked and almost dropped his manila envelope. When he saw it was me, he recovered quickly, though. He tightened his grip on his envelope and then shook his head. "No, not Adrienne."

He seemed uncomfortable. Up close, I noticed his out-doorsy demeanor *and* his faint hand tremor. His slightly suntanned face sported a sheen of sweat, too. That imperfection didn't mar his good looks, though. It only made him seem more real, less glossy.

"I was looking for *you*," he said . . . and then I understood.

He wanted to hire me. He wanted to do it clandestinely. That's why he was approaching me here, in private, instead of downstairs in the hotel bar or later at the welcome reception.

I wasn't surprised. By the time my clients find me, they tend to be pretty desperate. They're often at the end of their ropes, with no idea how to fix the problems bedeviling them.

Sometimes a new product launch has gone hideously awry and has to be dealt with before the company stock takes a dive. Sometimes a longtime flagship product plummets in popularity and needs to be retooled for twenty-first-century tastes. Sometimes what seemed like a good idea to a CEO can't *quite* be made to work in the real world of fast-casual foodservice. It varies.

"Well, you found me." Smiling, I offered him a handshake. "Hayden Mundy Moore. Chocolate whisperer. Orange team member."

His gaze dipped to my orange T-shirt—specifically to my modest, T-shirt-covered breasts. He leered. For the first time, I felt on edge. I know how to take care of myself, but in this case, my impulse to knee a creeper in the groin warred with my need (constantly hinted at by Danny) to grow my business.

"Rex Rader," he announced in a tone made sloppy by more than one sample (I was guessing) of scavenger hunt chocolate liqueur. I detected it on his breath. "Of *mmm*-Melt."

That's right. He actually said it like that: *mmm*-Melt.

He sounded like a porn star filming an ad for candy bars—candy bars that could make you *much* happier than most did.

I blinked. "*Mmm*-Melt?"

"Melt chocolates," Rex clarified in a less sexed-up tone. "You *must* have heard of us. We're the *modern* chocolatier."

Now that he'd pronounced his company's name normally,

I realized I *had* heard of it. I'd heard of him, too. Rex Rader was, for lack of a better description, the thirtyish Hugh Hefner of the San Francisco chocolate industry. He was smart, charming, and usually accompanied by beautiful women. Now that I knew who he was, I half expected to see a glamazon posse materialize.

It was difficult to take him seriously. But I tried.

"What can I do for you, Mr. Rader?" I asked.

"Call me Rex." He leered at my chest again, then leaned his shoulder against my room's doorjamb with a confident air. He ran his fingertips along the edge of his manila envelope with a suggestive look. "You can invite me inside, for a start."

Ugh. Sure, Rex Rader was *supposed* to be charismatic and fascinating and full of "cool" ideas—the wunderkind of chocolate. But just then, I wasn't in the mood for flirting.

"No, I won't be doing that. But I will tell you my fee for an initial consultation." I did, jacking it up by 20 percent as a deliberate disincentive. His eyes widened with satisfying—and hopefully libido-dulling—surprise. "If you're still interested, we can set up a meeting for later. Downstairs."

Rex breezed right past the public locale I'd suggested.

"But I'm here right now." He pouted, fondled his manila envelope, then looked up. "Come on, Hayden. Let's work together. I *know* you'll enjoy what I have to offer at *mmm*-Melt."

I'll admit it. I almost weakened. There was something about Rex Rader that pulled me in . . . that made me want to know more. Plus, I would need another consulting job after my work for Christian Lemaître was finished, and I liked San Francisco.

Then Rex came out with that ludicrous *mmm*-Melt thing, and all my curiosity about him vanished. Poof! I wanted him gone.

"Look, I have a process. I don't take jobs on a whim."

"It's not a whim! Take my portfolio! You'll see."

"I typically consult with my financial advisor first."

"Go ahead! I'm an open book." Another leer. "Ask anyone."

"Fine." I snatched his portfolio. "I'll consider it."

"*Goood.*" Rex drew out the word in a satisfied purr. His gaze dropped to my legs this time. He leered at them, too. "*Niiice.*"

Wow. Did this technique really work with some women?

"See you at the reception." I squashed his Melt portfolio against my chest, then offered a handshake. "Bye for now."

Rex couldn't have missed my purposely dismissing tone. But he darn well pretended he had. He didn't even quit lounging in my hotel room doorway. But he did raise his gaze from my knees.

"'Bye'? Are you sure?" His liquored-up breath blasted me in the face. He lowered his voice. "We *could* go inside and—"

Thankfully, I never found out what Rex was going to suggest. Because a second later, my longtime friend Danny emerged from the same stairwell I'd used (what can I say—we approach life similarly) and made a beeline straight for us.

His approach had a typically dampening effect on Rex Rader. That happened sometimes, given that Danny Jamieson was more than six feet tall, packed with muscle, and sporadically tattooed. At thirty-two, Danny possessed a swagger that told the world he knew how to handle . . . well, *anything.* It was that quality, I suspected, that tended to make people step out of Danny's way.

Rex was no exception. He actually gawked.

Most likely, I did, too. Danny also had that effect on *me.* It didn't matter that I knew he had two college degrees, more than his share of street smarts, and an endearing, childlike enthusiasm for birthday parties. Every time I saw Danny after a long time apart, all I saw was one thing: beefcake. *My* beefcake.

This time, I also saw my way out of this standoff with Rex. So, drawing on years' worth of time spent trawling SoCal bars with my buddy Danny, I offered him our shared, silent, barely detectable secret signal: a head scratch. Originally, we'd used it while acting as each other's "wingman" to ditch dates that weren't going well. Today I was using it to ditch Rex Rader.

Danny caught my signal without breaking his stride.

Filled with mingled relief, annoyance (he *was* late again, after all), and appreciation, I watched Danny approach. I'd just decided he'd missed my signal when he reached me, pulled me into his arms . . . and planted a big, passionate kiss on my lips.

Uhh . . . that wasn't our usual greeting. I was tingling when Danny released me, deliberately placing his body between me and Rex. He smiled, and I had second thoughts about the cleverness of this rescue. Because while Rex was *supposed* to be charming, Danny actually *was*. He just didn't usually unleash it with me.

"Hey, babe. Sorry I'm late." His voice rivaled Travis's for sheer sexy huskiness. He winked. "I'll make it up to you later."

My heart fluttered. For Rex's sake, I pretended to swoon.

Barely noticing, Danny confronted Rex. "Rex Rader!" He slapped his hand on Rex's shoulder. Hard. "How's it hanging?"

"Uh, fine." Rex cleared his throat. He was too busy keeping a wary eye on Danny to let his gaze wander anywhere near my T-shirt-covered breasts. I was too busy wondering how in the world Danny had identified him so quickly to appreciate the reprieve from being leered at.

"Just trying to convince Ms. Mundy Moore to do some consulting work for me." Rex gave a weak laugh.

"Really?" Danny crossed his arms, appearing interested.

Okay, to be honest, he appeared to be an interested *thug*. No matter what else he did, his rough upbringing never quite got completely sanded off. His short brown hair made people wonder if he was ex-military; his intense eyes could be jovial or hard.

I guessed Rex saw *hard* right now. "Yes, really," he said.

"Well, be sure to give Hayden your card." Danny tossed me a smart-alecky look. "She's awful at remembering faces and names."

You liar! I was about to yell, but then Rex obediently reached for his wallet to retrieve an *mmm*-Melt business card . . . and came up empty, instead. "My wallet!" he yelped. "It's gone!"

Hmm. I stared fixedly at Danny. He gazed innocently at me.

"Have you checked the hotel's lost and found?" he asked.

Swearing, Rex patted his pants pockets. His T-shirt. He turned in a circle, then started pacing. "It's really gone!"

"Seriously. Ask at the front desk," Danny suggested.

Rex nodded. The moment he distractedly entered the distant elevator and I heard the doors *ding* shut, I turned to Danny.

"You idiot!" Frowning, I held out my palm. "Hand it over."

"Hand over what?" he asked with exaggerated guilelessness.

"You know what. Rex Rader's wallet. I know you lifted it."

Danny shrugged, unbothered by my theory. My heart sank at his tacit acknowledgment that I was right. He'd promised me more than once that he would shed his shady past and go wholly legit.

Today's antics only proved he hadn't. I was disappointed, but not entirely surprised. This wasn't the first time Danny's easy-fingered ways had gotten us both out of a sticky situation.

If I knew us, it wouldn't be the last time, either.

As expected, Danny brandished Rex's expensive wallet. He grinned unrepentantly. "We should at least riffle through it once, just to make sure Rader's on the up-and-up," he said by way of a compromise. "Then I'll turn it in to the front desk."

Like the world's most audacious con artist, Danny crossed his hand over his heart. The fact that he used his *stolen-wallet-holding* hand didn't add much authenticity to the gesture.

I gave in. "Fine. Just quit giving me those puppy-dog eyes. I'm trying to be mad at you for being late to the retreat."

"Yeah. It seems like a real classy affair so far, what with you being mauled in the hallway and everything." With a wry look, Danny stuffed Rex's wallet in his jacket. "Why didn't you just drop him cold, like that would-be mugger in Barcelona?"

At the memory of that incident, I cringed. I wasn't proud of fighting back—it had been dumb, frankly—but I'd survived.

"I'm here at Maison Lemaître to network," I reminded him crisply, "not to become the ultimate fighting champion."

"Right. How's that working out for you so far?"

"I'm still optimistic. And *you're* still late."

"The more things change . . ." Danny flashed me a carefree grin. He looked me up and down. "You look great, by the way. Nice T-shirt."

Then he produced a glossy keycard, opened my hotel room with it, and chivalrously stepped back to allow me to enter first. Always a consummate gentleman—that was Danny. I was so happy to see him that it almost didn't occur to me to wonder . . .

How had *Danny* gotten ahold of *my* hotel room keycard?

In the minutes before we were due at the Lemaître welcome reception in the ballroom downstairs, I intended to find out the answer to that question. In the meantime, I decided to hug him.

As you might have predicted by now, I didn't wrangle any answers from Danny—not about my hotel keycard, not about his late arrival, and not about what he'd been up to lately, either.

At my first question (about my keycard), he merely raised his eyebrows in a "who do you think you're dealing with?" way that told me all I really needed to know about my (mostly) former-thief friend . . . although he swore he "only used his powers for good" these days. At my second question, he simply changed the subject. At my third, he began stripping to put on a suit for the gala welcome reception. I was forced to improvise and push his chortling, partly naked self into his own adjoining room.

I'd glimpsed enough bare skin and rippling muscles, though, to know Danny wasn't all talk when it came to his freelance security business in L.A. He was capable of action, too.

Now, ensconced in the midst of the welcome reception, I had more important things to think about than Danny's secrets, his musculature, and that whopper of a kiss. I had to get serious.

The atmosphere should have made that easy. The ballroom

was spectacular, furnished with chocolate brown wallpaper, plenty of mirrored surfaces, lots of gleaming marble, and gold accents galore. A string quartet played, filling the room—and the moonlit patio visible through the opened French doors that lined one wall—with classical music. Waiters passed drinks and canapés and chocolate delicacies; fancily dressed chocolate-industry bigwigs surrounded me, conducting laughing conversations.

I'd dived in an hour ago, having entered the room with Danny, only to split up almost instantly to circulate.

So far, I'd conversed with at least a dozen people, gabbing with the kind of loquaciousness that could only come from my gypsy upbringing in multiple countries. I'd even managed not to fidget too much, which counted as a big victory for me.

But while my initial apprehension faded, I noticed that Adrienne's had never left her. If anything, it had increased.

I glimpsed her running around behind the scenes, wearing a pristine white chef's coat over her party dress, darting into the ballroom with refills of ordinary (non-nutraceutical) Lemaître chocolates. Evidently, Christian had ordered her to wait until the right moment to unveil the caffeinated version.

I hoped the line succeeded. I still had my doubts. But more than that, I was concerned about Adrienne. She seemed unusually tense and pale. Her ordinarily springy blond curls were lank—from the heat of the hotel kitchen, no doubt—and her face was shiny with perspiration. Sweat even darkened the underarms of her whites. When she headed back to the kitchen, she swayed.

Worried, I followed her. But by the time I caught up with Adrienne in the hotel kitchen, she insisted she was fine.

"Look! I've got my patented instant-energy healthy green juice to keep me going!" Manically, she brandished a carafe full of icy green slush. She poured two tall glasses of it, handed one to me, then clinked glasses. "Cheers!"

I took a tentative sip. I made a face. "What is this?"

"Kale, banana, powdered greens, avocado, pineapple, lemon . . ." With a confiding air, Adrienne leaned closer. "*And* a teensy bit of my booster powder, of course." She nodded toward her supply of anhydrous caffeine, waiting where we'd left it earlier, next to the supersensitive culinary scale. "Just enough to keep me going," she added when she saw my dubious expression. "It's like coffee, only better! You were right, Hayden. I *did* need something healthy." Adrienne toasted me. "This is it!"

I stared at its dismal color. "This looks like something a socialite would try to 'detox' with. How about some water?"

"No time now! Gotta run!" Adrienne pointed at my mostly untouched glass. "Drink up, Hayden. It's good for you."

"I don't know about this, Adrienne," I called after her, raising my voice to be heard above the music and the sound of a hundred-odd noisy voices. "I think I'll help you instead."

But by then, my fellow chocolatier was gone, vanished into the ballroom again. When I looked at the array of serving trays Adrienne had lined up—clearly with an elaborate system in mind—I wasn't sure which one to choose. When I glanced at the leftover blocks of chocolate, whisks, and waiting stainless-steel bowls, I couldn't be sure what she'd been working on, either.

With no other alternative, I headed back to the ballroom.

* * *

Isabel was the first to notice my homebrew "energy" drink.

"Hayden! What in the *world* are you drinking?" Tipsily, she peered at my glass. I'd forgotten I was still holding it. Isabel weaved in place, dressed to kill and clearly drunk—but interested. "It looks *disgusting*. Just like my detox drink!"

I saluted Isabel with it, grinned, and kept mingling. I spoke with Nina and Bernard, Christian (briefly) and Rex Rader (ditto). I gave Adrienne an "are you okay?" nod as she passed me. I traded back-of-the-house war stories with a local pastry chef. At the urging of a photographer for a local newspaper, I even posed along with everyone else for a group photo op.

"I'm *sure* I looked horrible!" Adrienne whispered to me as we all regrouped afterward. "I don't take good photos."

"*Nobody* thinks they take good photos," I assured her. "Believe me. Everyone looks better in real life than on film."

"Isabel Lemaître doesn't," Adrienne groused. She examined the assorted drinks that had been temporarily abandoned on a nearby table during the photography session, then chose one. Her (very recognizable) green juice, of course. She handed me mine. "Someone told me Isabel used to be a lingerie model."

I believed it. "That explains why she went braless today," I joked. "I guess she's already worn her lifetime bra quota."

Adrienne guffawed. She almost snorted green juice.

I wanted to hang around and make Adrienne laugh again—if only to make up for the potential devastation I might wreak on her nutraceutical chocolate line after my report to Christian was turned in—but I spied Danny giving me a panicked-looking "head scratch" signal just then and had to run to his rescue.

After I'd extracted him from a clingy blogger from a San Francisco-based culinary site, I pantomimed scratching my head.

"You'd better watch that, pal. Might be dandruff."

"Har, har." He got his revenge by pinching me as I sailed away, but I was okay with that. It was only fair that I helped him as much as he helped me. Danny didn't know it, but that was partly what this impromptu retreat was all about: helping him. Specifically, helping him stay *away* from the lowbrow, bad-influence buddies who tended to congregate around him.

I wasn't sure how much time had passed before I realized I hadn't seen Adrienne for a while. Despite the general sense of urgency, the reception had been running two steps behind all night. The nutraceutical line hadn't even been unveiled yet, and it was getting late. Adrienne must be frantic by now. Thinking I might be able to help, I put down my "energy" drink and went to check on her. Partway there, I spied Rex Rader buttonholing a reporter— a woman who seemed *far* more interested in him than *I'd* been, judging by her enraptured expression—and I decided to make a detour to the ladies' room first.

Some needs, I figured—like Rex's apparent need to be 100 percent smarmy, 100 percent of the time—just couldn't wait.

When I emerged, something was happening. The string quartet's music had stopped. Raised voices rang from the ballroom. Shouts could be heard from the patio. Footsteps too.

A hotel staff member ran past me, looking grave.

Alarmed, I followed him to the ballroom. There, the

retreat attendees streamed toward the open French doors leading to the patio. More guests pushed onto the patio itself, spilling onto the walkway and crowding between the potted topiaries and the tiled fountain that still burbled merrily in the moonlight.

"They said it was one of the chocolatiers," someone blurted near me. "One of the people who works for Lemaître."

"Maybe it's Christian," someone else said with ghoulish zeal, but I couldn't stop to listen. I pushed my way past gawkers and bystanders, ignoring people whom I'd wanted to impress earlier.

All I could think about was Adrienne. I had an uneasy feeling about her. I know it's silly. I do. After the fact, anyone can say they had a premonition of disaster. Anyone can claim to have *known,* in their bones, that something was wrong.

But not just anyone saw what I saw next.

Between the onlookers, I glimpsed Nina. She sat on one of the low stone planters bordering the patio, cradling something. In the dim glow afforded by the now incongruously cheerful white light strings, I saw that she was crying. A man was trying to take something from her. I had the confused impression that Nina was fighting him off. Her agonized wail pierced all of us.

There was anguish in that sound. I'd never heard anything like it. My heart pounded twice as fast. My mouth went dry. I felt dizzy, but I kept moving like an automaton. I had to.

"I'm sorry." Two men wearing uniforms stood. One silently collected his equipment. "There's nothing more we can do."

Belatedly, I realized they were an EMT unit. The police had been called, too, along with the hotel staff. Hazily, I tried to peer around them—tried to see what was wrong with Nina.

Instead, I saw Adrienne. Her limp body was propped in Nina's arms, slumped at a strange angle. Her head lolled. Her chef's coat was stained with blood. Her sleeves were speckled with it, too, as though she'd held up her arms to ward off . . . *something.*

Something, I realized, that had killed her.

Adrienne was . . . dead?

It didn't seem possible. But then suddenly Danny was there.

He was fighting through the crowd, pulling me into his arms, tucking my head against his shoulder. "That's enough now."

Oh, God. That's when I knew it was true.

Danny was pugnacious. Straight talking. Tough as nails. He didn't believe in babying people. He would never have comforted me this way over anything less than a disaster.

I raised my face to his. His gentle eyes looked back at me.

I started trembling uncontrollably. That's when Danny took charge. He nodded. "We're leaving," he said. "Right now."

Then he led me away.

Chapter 4

Danny, being Danny—and my doppelganger when it came to finding an escape hatch—had one destination in mind: the kitchen, with its superfast, behind-the-scenes stairwell.

Unfortunately, getting there proved trickier than hailing a taxi on a Parisian street corner. Other retreat attendees blocked our path, turning what should have been an easy getaway into a five o'clock sharp traffic jam. I stared at the well-dressed industry types surrounding us and felt like screaming.

Or maybe crying. I honestly wasn't sure.

Adrienne was dead. It didn't seem possible.

Confirming that it was, a uniformed SFPD officer was in the process of interviewing people. Her voice pierced the hubbub with authority. "Had she had anything to eat or drink tonight?"

"I know the answer to that!" I stage-whispered to Danny.

Adrienne had been mainlining chocolates and green "energy" juice, I knew. Plus whatever she'd eaten at the spa that day.

I tried to veer in the officer's direction, planning to say

so. My hunky, suit-clad pal dragged me back, shaking his head. Tight-lipped, he carved a pathway for us both through the throng. "Not right now," he said as everyone made way for him.

Too late, I understood. Given Danny's past, his wrong-side-of-the-tracks upbringing, his various run-ins with the law (and his recent pickpocketing escapade with Rex Rader) . . . well, it was no wonder he tensed up around anyone wielding handcuffs, a SIG Sauer sidearm, and a baton. Danny didn't trust the police.

Confirming my theory, he ducked his head. With his face obscured, he swerved deliberately away from the SFPD officer.

Hmm. That wasn't good. If he was up to his old ways . . .

I didn't have time to contemplate Danny's miscreant past, though. Because just then, we passed the area where we'd all posed for that cheesy group photo. I remembered Adrienne's goofy expression when we finished. I remembered her complaining about not being photogenic. I remembered cracking wise about Isabel Lemaître's lifetime bra-wearing quota and making her laugh.

Now Adrienne was dead. A sob escaped me.

If anything, my momentary breakdown put Danny even further into "Hulk Smash" mode. Wearing a scowl, he got us to the kitchen.

There, we almost collided with Christian Lemaître. All of us pulled up short—me with an embarrassingly girly squeal.

Whoops. Ordinarily, I pride myself on not being your stereotypical girly girl. Fluff isn't for me. It never has been. For one thing, "helpless, pink-loving princess" doesn't play well worldwide—not when you're hanging your own mosquito nets. But it had been a tough night. I'm only human. So shoot me.

It was some consolation that Christian squealed, too.

The sight of Danny on a mission tended to do that to people.

Christian leaped out of our way, wide-eyed and flushed. He looked as if he'd been caught doing *something* devious. At that point, I have to admit, I was ready to think the worst of him. More than likely, I figured, he'd been in the kitchen firing someone, just for laughs. Or maybe kicking puppies. The jerk.

Or chowing down on chocolate, I realized, belatedly noticing the telltale brown smudges on his dress shirt. Some of them looked pretty distinct, almost like chocolaty fingerprints.

But by then, Danny had tugged me past Lemaître's personal Napoleon and into the service stairwell, and I was saved.

"I should go back," I said as soon as I realized it.

Isn't that the way of it, though? Superman bravery comes through ten minutes *after* the crisis has passed. Now that I was in the clear, I felt awful about not doing more to help.

"You're not going back." Danny kept moving.

In his wake, I did, too. Not that I could help it. His grip on my arm was like Iron Man's. His attitude forbade argument.

It was that attitude (predictably) that got my dander up.

I yanked back, then stopped cold. Against Danny's momentum, my efforts were pretty laughable. I basically skidded along the floor like a cartoon character. That only made me madder.

I was a good person, wasn't I? If I wanted to go back and help Adrienne, I would. So I dug in my (flats-wearing) heels and held my ground.

"I could have done something," I insisted.

Sure, other people had seen what Adrienne had eaten and drunk that day. I wasn't special. But I wanted to help.

"It's too late for anybody to do anything."

Just then, Danny's usual pragmatism didn't sit well with me. Neither did the dank atmosphere in the deserted stairwell.

I was grateful for its echo-chamber silence, but I could have done without its subzero, frostbite-inducing temperature. I shivered. In fact, I shivered so hard that my teeth chattered.

That's probably what made Danny stop dragging me along like a recalcitrant three-year-old. He stopped and stared at me.

Roughly, he took off his suit jacket. This is probably the part where you're expecting him to gently tuck it around my shoulders for warmth, all Bogey-meets-Hepburn in *Sabrina* style. But that's only because you don't know Danny like I do.

He threw it at me instead. "Take this." He gave my make-do cocktail dress a frown. "Next time, go to the party less naked."

Naked? As if Danny would ever notice. I could gallivant around wearing nothing but gym socks and tasseled pasties, and Danny would treat me (mostly) like a kid sister. As proof? His suit coat, which rocketed at me like a 90 mph fastball. I caught it while it was still warm from his body. That heat was enough to convince me to put it on, despite my exasperation with him.

Ah. Warmth enveloped me in instant bliss. Except for the part where we had just seen one of my friends—*my friends!*—die.

But I didn't want to talk about that. I couldn't.

"It's not my fault Christian is too cheap to heat this place properly." I stamped my feet, wishing I'd worn my motorcycle boots. But they lived at Travis's place, where all my stuff that didn't pack well—but had sentimental value—cooled its heels. Possibly in alphabetical order, knowing my accountant.

"Big news. Christian's an ass, even when it comes to utility payments." Impatiently, Danny gestured. "Ready now?"

I wasn't. "Do you think she's really dead?" I whispered.

Danny wasn't having any part of my incipient meltdown.

"If you're angling for me to carry you—" Dubiously, he eyed my glammed-up ensemble. And me in it. "I'm not going to."

"Real chivalrous." He *did* think Adrienne was dead. Oh no.

"We've still got two flights to go," he argued further.

"You're up for the challenge, He-Man."

But even before he shook his head, I started moving. I knew better than to rely on anybody else for help. Even my old pal.

Another flight up, on the next landing, I stopped again. Danny's *now what?* expression was not enough to budge me.

"I should have stayed with her." My head swam with visions of poor Adrienne, blood splattered and limp. "You know, to—"

"To keep her company on her ride to the morgue?" He shook his head, probably wishing he'd turned down that gratis LAX to SFO plane trip I'd offered. "She won't know any better."

"Danny!"

"Besides," he added in a softer tone, "Nina was there."

That was true. She had been. Adrienne hadn't been alone.

I was glad about that. I was. Not for the first time, though, I wondered about Danny's pragmatic side. It tended to veer toward merciless sometimes. At least it did with outsiders. He hadn't done much more than exchange nods and hellos with Adrienne. He wasn't invested in her. Not the same way I was.

A clatter of footsteps—and accompanying voices— from the landing below sent Danny into motion again. He grabbed me.

Moments later we lurched into my room upstairs, me still shivering and him still stone-faced. He pocketed his room key.

Scratch that. *My* room key. "Where did you get that?"

"Do you really want to talk about that now?"

I didn't. But I wanted to do *something* my way. I had my pride. Like I said, humility isn't exactly my forte.

Besides, being annoyed at him felt better than being freaked out and upset about Adrienne. *Poor Adrienne.*

"Yes, I want to talk about that now." I watched Danny stalk to the window, then look out. He pushed the button that drew the drapes. With silent, luxurious efficiency, they obscured the expansive view. *Bye-bye, sliver of the Golden Gate Bridge. Bye-bye, moonlit night. Bye-bye, Adrienne.* I refocused. "So spill."

Instead, he faced me. The concern in his face made me wonder if he'd glimpsed Armageddon outside. Nothing else could have made Danny look so . . . *tender.* Even *with* his rampaging beard stubble and tattoos.

"Have you been sweating?" he demanded.

"Sweating?" I crossed my arms. "That's a new kink you've got there. You like a little Slip 'N Slide action these days?"

Impatiently, he crossed the plush carpet. He stuck the back of his hand against my forehead. He squinted into my eyes.

"Easy, there, killer!" I joked, giving him a shove. "This routine might work with most women, but I'm not most women."

"You're still shivering. You might be in shock."

The tone of his voice gave me goose bumps. "Maybe. Or . . . ?"

"Or you might be experiencing what Adrienne did tonight."

"What?" No wonder Danny looked tender. He was mentally composing my eulogy. Instantly panicked, I rushed to the mirror. I don't know what I expected to find. Spots, maybe. Hair falling out in formerly ponytailed clumps. Blood gushing from my nose. Something macabre and pandemic-like. Instead, my own ordinary face, a lot paler than usual, stared back. "I *do* feel dizzy."

As I said it, a wave of nausea passed over me. I couldn't believe any of this was happening. Everything felt slightly surreal—the way it did when you've been awake twenty-four hours straight, crossing time zones and getting increasingly jet-lagged.

Except I hadn't been traveling. Not for weeks.

I should have been getting itchy feet just realizing it.

"How much of Adrienne's green juice did you drink?"

I frowned, thinking. "A few sips. That stuff was vile. You know I'm not much for the health-freak routine." I widened my eyes, suddenly catching Danny's drift. "You don't think—"

"Maybe." His stony expression said it all. He did think.

Now I felt *really* woozy. But also hyperaware. I know it sounds weird, but I swear I could feel my pulse. In my ear. *Ugh.*

It occurred to me that *Adrienne* had been conspicuously sweaty earlier. *Uh-oh. If that was one of the warning signs . . .*

"You weren't out there when the shit hit the fan." Danny paced, casting wary glances at the window and door. "I was. The paramedics said Adrienne might have overdosed on something."

Instantly, I was indignant. "Adrienne wasn't on drugs!

She was a nice, hardworking, strawberry-daiquiri-loving woman."

I remembered our chatty after-work drinks sessions. Those wouldn't be happening anymore. I sat on the king-size bed. Hard.

"She was only in her forties," Danny persisted. "And she died of a heart arrhythmia. That's the theory the EMTs were working with, anyway. That doesn't happen randomly."

"A heart arrhythmia doesn't cause someone to bleed all over!" I shivered, remembering the ghastly sight of Adrienne in Nina's arms. I knew I'd never forget it. I'd never seen a dead person before. Now I had. I didn't know how to feel about that.

"No, but an overdose might," Danny said. "Adrienne might have been vomiting blood. That would explain the splatters."

Yikes. He'd accurately diagnosed blood splatters?

"Your life is vastly different from mine. You know that?"

Danny wasn't bothered by my non sequitur. "That could have been Adrienne reacting to whatever she overdosed on. Your body does its best to protect you from your dumbass brain. Like when you go full bore on those strawberry daiquiris and wind up puking your guts out." Still looking tense, he glanced outside again. Evidently, he'd gone into hard-core security-expert mode on me. "Only sometimes the fail-safe doesn't work as designed."

I didn't want to know how Danny knew that. Also, gross.

But he had a point. "You think *I* might overdose, too?"

"Maybe you were supposed to." His gaze turned hard. "Maybe Adrienne got the dose meant for you. Do you have enemies here?"

At his dire tone, I couldn't help laughing. "Danny! This isn't a movie. It's me. At a chocolate retreat. At a chichi resort with its own security force. Nobody tried to overdose me tonight." I gave him a long look. "You're just being paranoid."

He didn't give in. "Did anyone give you a drink?"

I tried to remember. Rex? I shrugged. "Only Adrienne."

Danny made a face. "That disgusting swamp juice?"

Another shrug. "Sometime I *might* get healthy."

"That'll be the day." He flashed me a grin. "You mainline chocolate like it's your job." A pause. "Oh, wait. It is."

"Hey. Chocolate contains valuable antioxidant flavonoids," I informed him. "Cacao is *very* rich in phytochemicals. Those are good for you. They come from plants. Plus, a third of the fat in cocoa butter is stearic acid, which doesn't raise cholesterol levels." Warming up to my lecture, I added, "Chocolate can help with chronic fatigue syndrome, improve arterial blood flow, ease depression, *and* help prevent heart attacks. So, technically—"

Usually, Danny did his best to nod and look interested when I went into professorial mode. Tonight, though, he only seemed worried. That wasn't like him. Nothing ever fazed Danny.

"So, technically, Adrienne should have been *less* likely to die of a heart attack, rather than more," he finished for me.

For once, our synchronicity was scary, not simpatico.

"Well, chocolate isn't wheatgrass and quinoa," I amended, feeling confused. But warmer. And *not* as if I'd just stepped off a Tilt-A-Whirl. My symptoms—if that's what they were—seemed to be subsiding. "But it's not going to kill anyone. Not right away. Plus, Adrienne was trying to be healthy. That's why she—"

"Drank that swamp juice. Just like *you* did. So, again—"

"I'm fine, Danny. I am." I was spooked, though. Seriously spooked. Could someone *really* have overdosed sweet, responsible Adrienne? Or (gulp) me? I didn't think I had any real enemies anywhere—much less in the City by the Bay, among my chocolate peeps. "I'm sure what happened to Adrienne was an accident."

"Maybe it wasn't the juice," he persisted. "Maybe it was something else." He turned to me. "What was she working on?"

A doomed project, thanks to my unfinished report.

Pricked with guilt, I looked away. "Nothing deadly."

"Hayden."

"A line of nutraceutical chocolates." Maybe it was a good thing the official unveiling hadn't happened yet. I didn't say so, though. I didn't want Danny grilling me about my truffle-munching habits. All that caffeine might have explained why my heart had raced when I'd seen Adrienne, though. Why I'd been so chilled. Why I'd been dizzy, too. I didn't want to worry Danny any further, so I shrugged, instead. "More healthy stuff."

"Healthy? Damn." Danny quit pacing. For a nanosecond, his broad, burly shoulders relaxed. He looked nice, even sans suit jacket, in an open-collared shirt. "Why do I feel like packing down a huge double-bacon cheeseburger and fries right now?"

Him and me both. Suddenly, *healthy* felt *deadly.*

"Don't worry. Maison Lemaître specializes in decadence. You missed the all-chocolate English tea this afternoon, but we can still make it to the all-chocolate brunch buffet tomorrow."

He looked skeptical. "Do they serve until three P.M.?"

"Ha-ha." Leave it to Danny to remember my notorious reputation as a before-noon zombie. I only survived A.M. consults by pretending I'd been up all night. There was a reason I was a freelancer who set her own hours. "We should try it tomorrow."

That is, *if* I could behave normally, without collapsing into tears. My emotions were all over the place. I didn't know the status of the chocolate retreat now. It seemed likely that Christian Lemaître would cancel it. That would be the decent thing to do. But Christian was hardly the king of decency.

Danny indulged my non-homicide-related digression with a nod. "Sure. Brunch sounds like a good networking op for you."

I stifled a groan. Danny was more obsessed with growing my business than I was. I chalked that up to his impoverished youth. "It sounds like chocolate-chip scones with chocolate butter to me," I shot back. "Chocolate-dipped strawberries. Chocolate waffles with hot-fudge sauce. And cocoa-nib bacon."

Unbelievably, he made a face. I'd forgotten that Danny didn't share my sweet tooth—or my adoration of chocolate. He preferred things on the savory-salty-hot "blow your doors off" side of the street. Nachos. Hot wings. Sriracha. Vinegar chips.

In critical ways, we were fundamentally incompatible.

Nevertheless, we had a date. For chocolate brunch.

Until then, I'd had all I wanted of analyzing a tragic death. I'd go crazy if I spent all night ruminating over it.

Besides, I was the kind of girl who moved on quickly. The stipulations of my uncle Ross's will ensured that fact for me.

To feel better, I needed to do something besides talk.

"Hey." I gave Danny a poke as he passed by on his next patrol-my-hotel-room round. "Thanks for coming here for me."

He only shrugged. Evidently, I felt mushier than he did.

Probably that was because *I'd* survived a potential attempt on my life tonight. That kind of thing probably wreaked havoc on a girl's sense of equanimity. *If* it was real.

I remained convinced it wasn't. But just in case . . . I figured I needed to take care of a few things. Downstairs.

Without my makeshift bodyguard dogging my every move and asking questions.

The way I saw it, if I could get ahold of some of the things Adrienne and I had both come into contact with tonight (like a few nutraceutical truffles and/or some green juice) and send them to Travis for analysis, I could put my mind at ease. Maybe.

"Seriously, though," I pressed, knowing there was only one guaranteed way to get Danny to quit hovering like a bossy big brother. "Why were you so late getting here? I expected you hours earlier. Then you strolled in, all light-fingered and—"

"Everything looks safe for now," he butted in. "You okay?"

Bingo. He'd reacted just the way I'd expected he would. Danny liked being interrogated about being late (and being skilled at petty thievery) the way I liked wearing stilettos. Meaning, not at all. Not if it was avoidable. It always was.

"I'm fine." It was an effort not to singsong those two little words. Because I had a plan. I needed him to beat it.

"Then I've got a few things to do." He hooked his thumb toward the door, then followed its lead all the way there. Over his shoulder, he tossed me a strangely intense glance. "Okay?"

I hesitated. Just for a second, I understood why women flocked to Danny. All that intensity was probably intoxi-cating—to the right woman, at the right time. But that woman wasn't me. Not then and probably not ever. We both knew better than that.

"You don't have to babysit me, Danny," I told him, meaning it. "I can take care of myself. I dialed up your suit-wearing friend services, not your übermacho security-man services."

I was trying to flatter him with that *übermacho* stuff. He didn't bite. He only studied the suit jacket he'd hurled at me for warmth in the stairwell, now snuggled securely around me.

"Keep the jacket," Danny said, then he was out of there.

The moment the door closed behind him, I shrugged out of his jacket, dropped it like it was hot, and got on my feet.

A quick trip to the window told me the retreat attendees had scattered, just as Danny and I had. They milled around the grounds of Maison Lemaître, talking in clumps of three or four. Some headed toward the discreet lobby bar. A few waited to retrieve their rides from the valets. It was evident that the welcome reception—which had run late, anyway—had broken up.

As soon as the coast was clear, I headed out myself.

Adrienne's death probably *had* been a heartrending accident, I told myself as I crept downstairs again. It had probably been a case of bad timing writ large. Whatever undiagnosed ailment Adrienne had suffered from—a heart murmur, a blocked artery, or something just as dire but unknowable—it had come up against the stressful, super-long Lemaître welcome reception and just . . . *popped.*

I really, *really* needed to avoid stress in my life.

I couldn't shake the uncomfortable feeling that the whole thing might have been avoidable, though. It was that feeling that prodded me along the empty Maison Lemaître service hallways after getting Danny to scram, listening for potential homicidal maniacs even as I told myself I was being ridiculous.

Homicidal maniacs were probably quiet types, anyway.

Wasn't that what the next-door neighbors always told the media? *Sure, he turned out to be a machete-wielding lunatic,* they'd say on camera for the local evening newscast. *But he seemed so nice! He kept to himself most of the time, really.*

Hoping that "most of the time" encompassed the hours between eleven-fifteen and midnight, I glanced at my cell phone. I gripped it in my fist like the lifeline it was, just in case I needed to call for help. I wasn't one of those daffy sorority girls in a slasher flick, heading down to the killer's basement lair in my lingerie. I was taking all the necessary precautions. All I wanted was to find my abandoned glass of green "energy" juice—aka the potential murder weapon du jour.

In my imagination, my juice had already morphed into a glass full of deadly toxic waste. I couldn't just leave it there, neon green and pulsing, waiting for its next hapless victim.

You know, just in case.

Just in case someone really *had* tried to kill me.

Trying to laugh off that overly dramatic idea, I squared my shoulders and pushed through the double swinging service doors into the ballroom-adjacent kitchen. Being there gave me the willies all over again. Inside, it was quiet and deserted. The worktables still stood cluttered with chocolate, knives, whisks, and bowls. It felt inhabited with the ghost of Adrienne past—a woman who'd been lively (if anxiety ridden), generous (if a little lonely), and far, *far* too young to die the way she had.

I guessed the police or Maison Lemaître security personnel or someone had shooed away the staff before they could clean up. It was almost as if Adrienne would rush in, hands aflutter and blond curls flying, to grab another tray of gilded truffles.

Spotting those platters full of gold-leafed nutraceutical chocolates, I strode straight toward them. A hasty head count told me they'd been left safely untouched—even, surprisingly, by Christian Lemaître. I guess he hadn't needed a caffeine buzz to greet his adoring public earlier? I knew he'd had access to the truffles. I'd run into him while fleeing the crime scene.

No, *scratch that*. Danny and I hadn't been fleeing. Had we?

Nope. No way. Not wanting to think about that, I grabbed one of the third-size stainless-steel hotel pans from a nearby rack. Familiarity with a professional kitchen has its perks; I knew the perfect pan—roughly the size of an A4 sheet of paper, if paper could be two-and-a-half inches deep—to dump all the caffeine-laced nutraceutical chocolates into with no spillage. I banged the pan on my hip like the waitress I was for a while (at a café near the Leidseplein in Amsterdam), then looked around.

Next up: killer green juice. Okay. I couldn't remember where I'd left my glass, so I mentally retraced my steps. First, Adrienne had filled both our glasses. I located the carafe she'd used to pour that swampy green slush, but all it held now were streaky remnants smudged with mashed-up kale leaves. It looked even more revolting than before. Maybe in the ballroom itself?

I had to focus, but the events of the day were getting to me. I still felt jumpy. Also, much too aware of every sound. The industrial flooring made my sneaky footsteps seem way too loud. If anyone found me there, I'd have a hard time explaining why I was looting the resort's kitchen. Partway to the other set of double swinging doors, I heard the walk-in refrigerator's motor kick in. I recoiled and walked faster. I was scaring myself now.

Calm down. Hauling in a deep breath, I headed onward. At the last second, I remembered the anhydrous caffeine.

It was still in its tiny plastic Baggie near the scale. I doubled back and snatched it, just to be safe. I didn't want it falling into the wrong hands. Adrienne and I had studied how to use the stuff; other employees who might turn up to work in the kitchen wouldn't be so well informed. If they decided to add a haphazard scoop to their A.M. java, the results could be lethal.

Brought up short by the realization, I stared at the Baggie. The caffeine powder *looked* harmless enough—

except for the warning, printed in microscopic eight-point type on a label stuck to the bottom edge of the bag, warning against overdose.

Given the circumstances, that Baggie might as well have been a loaded gun. My whole body went numb. For a second, all I could do was gawk at it. Then, newly freaked out, I shoved the caffeine powder into my hotel pan and kept going. I reached the other set of swinging doors and turned my back to them. Like the off-duty restaurant rat I was, I pushed my way through on the right side. The door swung into the ballroom without a sound.

Unfortunately, I couldn't say the same thing for me.

I turned around and started shrieking. Because, on the other side of the doors, a man was there waiting for me.

Lurking, you might say. Quietly. Threateningly. *Knowingly.* Recognizing him, I wanted to groan. "Danny! What the hell are you doing here?" I yelled . . .

. . . mostly in a whisper. Because, you know . . . *murder.*

"Are you trying to give me a heart attack?" I hissed.

That gaffe silenced both of us. *Whoops.* I couldn't believe I'd accidentally been so insensitive. It was funny the things you noticed when one of your work pals had died just hours ago.

My grim-looking friend crossed his arms. In the shadowy ballroom, littered with napkins and wineglasses and round tables still set with tablecloths and abandoned dinnerware, Danny gave me a perceptive look. "Did you really think I bought your get-lost tactics upstairs? I knew you wouldn't be able to resist."

Flustered and feeling as if I might keel over any second, I clenched my hotel pan against my hip. Its stainless-steel edge bit into my fingertips, grounding me. Details tended to do that.

That's why I'd needed to get out of my head and into motion earlier. Too much sitting around—too much thinking—and I'm like a Labrador Retriever at a park full of flying tennis balls. I don't know where to go first. But moving on . . . that's my oeuvre.

"Caught me," I joked. "I needed a nosh, and there was all this chocolate, just waiting for me down here. Guilty."

"I knew you wouldn't be able to resist having a look around after everything that happened," Danny clarified, coming closer in the shadows. The security lights brightened the ballroom's corners—and did a pretty spectacular job of highlighting his squared-off jawline, too. For a one-time thug, he cleaned up nicely. "You like knowing the *hows* and *whys* of things, Hayden," he told me. "Including *this*. That's why you're so good at your job."

He was right. I appreciated details and relished a chance to troubleshoot. But I'd rather have been plunked down in the middle of the *chupinazo* in Pamplona wearing fire-engine red than admit it just then. A running bull didn't sound that bad next to Danny in this moody mood of his. How had he beaten me there?

I laughed and got down to the point, raising my chin for added moxie. "That doesn't explain what *you're* doing here."

"I'm here because you're here." *Dummy,* his tacit but affectionate connotation added. "Do you think I was patrolling your hotel room just for shits and giggles? You're in danger."

"You're too suspicious. Your security work is getting to you." I strode onward, looking around for my lost green-juice glass. With my free hand, I pantomimed holding it, trying to jog my memory. I'd had it when Adrienne and I had left the group photo session. I *hadn't* had it when I'd spotted Rex smarming it up near the ladies' room entrance. Sometime between those two events, I must have set it down. "Lighten up, Rambo."

"What are you looking for?" Danny asked.

His tone suggested he already knew. Damn him.

I raised my chin a notch higher. Pride. Again. "My juice glass. I was worried it might fall into the wrong hands."

Hearing myself, I squashed another impending groan. *Fall into the wrong hands?* Really? Now who sounded paranoid?

"It's already taken care of."

"How could it be? Obviously, no one's been here to clean up this place." I kept looking. "I hope no one else picked it up."

"It's not here." Danny kept watching me, wearing the inscrutable expression he'd patented for his clients' benefit.

But I wasn't one of the corporate whackos or scaredy-cat actors he escorted to public appearances. He wouldn't need that mean face *or* a skeleton-style, two-way radio earpiece with me.

I rounded on him. "Are you trying to tell me you took it?"

"I'm telling you it's not here anymore. *You* shouldn't be, either." His gaze dipped to my truffle cache. "Chocoholic."

"Dictator."

"Control freak."

"Oh yeah? Takes one to know one."

With that juvenile rejoinder, Danny grinned and slung his arm around my shoulders. I knew he was worried about me.

But too much intimacy could only lead to trouble. I ducked away from his sheltering muscles and gave the ballroom one final sweep. Then the patio. "How come there isn't any police tape?"

"Because this isn't a crime scene. Adrienne overdosing is sad, but it's not illegal." Danny waited a beat. "According to Nina, the police think Adrienne had too much of the powdered caffeine she was using for some new line of Lemaître truffles."

Pointedly, he *didn't* lower his gaze to my pile of chocolate. He was too smart for that. He kept his attention locked on my face, instead. "Do you know anything about that?"

"I don't discuss my consulting work with nonclients."

"Then Lemaître *is* your client." Oh, man. He beat me anyway. "You didn't say. When you dangled this trip my way, you only said you'd been invited to the retreat and needed a plus-one."

"I had. I did. And I'm still not saying."

His face tightened. "I'm not at your beck and call, Hayden. I deserve to know everything. Especially now."

Ugh. Not this. Not tonight. At the best of times, Danny had a bad attitude about my life, my wealth, and his place in both. I hadn't inherited until after we became friends. My undeserved fortune was awkward for both of us. I preferred ignoring it.

Purposely, I swung off-topic. "You saw Nina?"

A nod. "She was locking up when I came downstairs." For a second, Danny's expression became almost soft. "She's really broken up. She tried to save Adrienne. I know what that's like."

I knew he had to be referring to the dicier side of his life—the side he kept hidden from me. "You like redheads, huh?"

He jolted, then grinned. I think he was grateful for the reprieve. We both knew I was only needling him about Nina.

"She's married," Danny said—meaning *it's a no go.*

I nodded, not surprised he knew. "Her husband is a CPA, I think." I adjusted my hotel pan of chocolates, then headed to the kitchen while it was still *my* decision to do so. "I'll have to ask her for tips on dealing with numbers guys. Like Travis."

Danny made a face. He and my sexy-voiced keeper didn't get along very well. Unlike me, they'd even met once or twice.

"*I've* got a tip for you." Danny caught up to me at a loping jog. I didn't usually get a head start with him. "Learn to use some bookkeeping software. You won't need that nerd anymore."

I laughed. "I'll *always* need Travis."

Danny grumbled. "What you need is a less deadly workplace."

"I need a good night's sleep."

"I need a snack." He made a play for the gilded truffles.

With effort, I managed not to slap away his hand out of fear that he'd drop dead after one bite. But Danny saw. He knew.

Pursing his lips in thought, he pulled away his hand.

Maybe the police hadn't classified Adrienne's death as suspicious—but Danny obviously had his doubts. More and more, so did I.

All the same, he laughed, taking both our minds off that worrisome thought. "As if I'd waste time with chocolate."

"Hey! Don't bad-mouth my specialty. That's sacrilege."

In the hallway, we fell into companionable silence. Up the stairs, we kept perfect time. At my room, *I* produced a keycard.

I waggled my fingers at him. "You might as well give me yours, too," I said. "You're not going to need it anymore."

"When I'm sure of that, I'll hand it over." Then Danny swaggered over to the door of the adjoining room, stuck in his keycard with nimble pickpocketing fingers, and waved good night.

I didn't think I'd sleep much, but I was going to try.

Chapter 5

The interesting thing about chocolate is that, like people, it can take on so many personas. It can be sugary or savory, sweet or bitter, white or dark or milky brown. It can be whipped into an airy mousse, baked into a dense brownie, or drunk straight. It can be served hot, cold, or somewhere in between.

At Maison Lemaître's famous all-chocolate brunch, almost all of those chocolate iterations were on offer. I intended to try every last one of them before I skipped San Fran. After all, it was my professional duty. Besides, I was owed *some* recompense for dragging myself out of bed near dawn on a non-workday.

It was so early, I'd barely perused the buffet so far. But the lush scent of cocoa butter drifted up to me anyway from the five-spice drinking chocolate I'd ordered as a wake-up jolt for my taste buds. Coffee was nice. Essential, even. But chocolate was *le meilleur*. Fortunately, I had room in my life for both.

Just like I had room in my life for Travis *and* Danny.

"You know," I told the latter as I slumped at an outdoor patio table with him, wearing sunglasses and a haphazard bun (the most effort I'd been up to expending on my hair after tossing and turning all night), "the thing about brunch is that it's *brunch*. It's supposed to come *later* than breakfast. *Between* breakfast and lunch. That's the whole idea. Because people sleep in."

He sat uncommunicatively across from me, arms and legs spread in full command of his ironwork patio chair, gazing across the resort's manicured grounds. I was undeterred, though.

"Speaking of my hotel room—where I'd *rather* be snoring right now," I went on, trying not to wrinkle my cotton skirt, tank top, and Edinburgh cashmere sweater as I dug around in my handy crossbody bag, "did you get one of *these* in yours?"

I slapped the flyer (for lack of a better word) I'd found under my door that morning onto the table. Danny glanced at it.

THE LEMAÎTRE CHOCOLATES FAMILY REMEMBERS ONE OF OUR OWN, it read in flowing faux-calligraphy script across the top of its heavy cardstock. In the middle was a photo of Adrienne, taken sometime during the scavenger hunt yesterday. At the bottom, it read, IN MEMORIAL: ADRIENNE DOWLING. PLEASE JOIN US TODAY TO CELEBRATE HER LIFE.

"'Join us'? That's *it*? After everything that happened to Adrienne?" I smacked my hand on the table, making the Bernardaud china, fancy cutlery, and glassware jitter. "We were all going to be 'joining' one another for the retreat's opening session, anyway." I nodded at the identical time shown. "Lemaître isn't canceling the retreat. They're shoehorning in a memorial service for Adrienne, instead. Then I guess it'll be business as usual."

"So? That's a nice gesture. The show must go on, right?"

"Not like this, it mustn't." The whole thing struck me as a little heartless. Didn't *anyone* want to mourn Adrienne? I knew she'd been single. She'd lived alone. She hadn't even had pets. She'd never mentioned having any family living nearby, either—not to me—not during the three weeks we'd spent hanging out together. Still, *this* took the cake. "The chocolate business can be cutthroat sometimes," I acknowledged to Danny, "but come on!"

"They didn't have to do anything at all." Danny eyed the adjacent buffet with undisguised skepticism. How could he not be tempted by caramel-mocha pancakes and cocoa whipped cream? "It's in Lemaître's best interest to downplay what happened."

"It would be in their best interest to *find out* what happened," I argued as a few retreat goers meandered onto the patio and chose tables nearby. "*Exactly* what happened."

"They already know what happened." Danny's opaque gaze met mine. "So do you. You just don't want to admit it."

He had to be referring to the official theory that Adrienne had overdosed on something. Stubbornly, I remained silent.

Too late, I realized I was playing right into Danny's hands. "Companies don't want it known they're employing druggies, especially ones who OD on the job," he reminded me, graciously refraining from dishing out an *I told you so.*

"Adrienne wasn't a druggie!" Exasperated, I shook my head. I wasn't naïve. I knew restaurant kitchens had their share of users—chefs and line cooks who snorted something here, drank something there, and smoked something after every shift. But Adrienne hadn't been a hardened grunt on the line. "Maybe she OD'd," I admitted, "but if she did, it was an accident."

"Most overdoses are." Danny's gaze looked flinty.

Uh-oh. I'd slipped into a place he didn't like discussing.

I left that touchy subject for now and frowned again, still irritated, at the memorial flyer instead. It wasn't far removed from the consumer come-ons that auto sellers and dry cleaners bulk-mailed to their "valued customers" every week, right alongside the supermarket circulars. Didn't Adrienne deserve better than the treatment given to two-for-one manicure specials?

This had to be Christian's doing, I knew. He'd assembled his cronies for the retreat and didn't want to let them go. Not even in the face of potential poor publicity for his company.

Not surprisingly—given the stature of the retreat attendees and Lemaître Chocolates' longtime contributions to the San Francisco area—Adrienne's death had received media attention already. The complimentary newspaper I'd received outside my door this morning had contained a short article about her death.

It hadn't offered any insights aside from the standing accidental-overdose theory. Despite that fact, I'd scoured every word. I'd welled up at the memories it had provoked, too.

Then I'd dried my tears, thrown on my best somber attire (something I hadn't worn on my most recent trip to Brazil, since black attracts the sun's heat *and* pesky mosquitos), and come downstairs to the (then) unoccupied patio for daybreak brunch.

Now it was getting busier. The low hum of conversation combined with the discreet clank of cutlery, joining the scents of coffee, orange juice, and pervasive chocolate. I wish that familiar, beloved chocolaty smell cheered me up a bit more.

"They could have at least found a nicer photo of her." Grumpily, I studied it. "Adrienne looks totally flustered here."

"She did in real life, too. Pictures don't lie."

Danny's attitude was an anathema to me. *Of course* pictures lied! Otherwise, there was no explanation for the assorted snaps of me, all around the world, looking like a coked-up Teletubbie.

Before I could say so, though, Danny waved at someone.

When I craned around to see who, squinting past the patio's topiaries, flowers, tables, and extravagant ultra-chocolate spread, I almost spit out my last sip of nutmeg-y, gingery, star anise-y drinking chocolate. I swiveled again. "Nina Wheeler?"

"Be nice," Danny grumbled. "She's having a hard time."

"But she's *married*!" I reminded him, having difficulty reconciling this touchy-feely side of my taciturn friend. I knew he had a strict hands-off policy when it came to other people's wives. Yet Nina clearly seemed to expect to see him. Had she and Danny arranged something last night? I wondered. "*You* can't—"

"Comfort her? *I'm* not going to. *You* are." Danny stood.

While I processed that, he greeted Nina with a sort of lazy chivalry. I was fascinated by watching the two of them together. Honestly, I was touched, too. No kidding. I liked thinking that Danny had gone out of his way to help Lemaître's PR exec—until I remembered that he'd volunteered *me* for the job instead.

Irked, I flagged down a server for a chocolate refill.

Nina turned to me, tremulous and delicate. With her blazing red hair, slight frame, and businesslike attire, she looked like an exotic bird—one that hadn't slept well, if at all. Those were serious shadows under her eyes. You could have driven a truck into the hollows beneath them. Despite her flawless makeup job (one whose expertise escaped me, Miss Chapstick and Maybe Mascara), her cheek sported a single, obvious pillow crease. For whatever reason, that one detail made my heart go out to her.

"Have a seat, Nina," I invited. "Won't you join us?"

Maybe I could peer-pressure Danny into caving in.

Or not. "Not me. Sorry." He held up his phone. "Emergency."

Liar, I mouthed to him as he took off and Nina sat. But

by then, I was stuck, exactly the way he'd intended I would be.

For all I knew, Danny was off to score a salty, fatty, junk food-y Egg McMuffin and hash browns. That was more his speed, anyway. Me, I'd started considering attacking the buffet in earnest. A girl needed sustenance, right? *Chocolate* sustenance.

"Thanks, Hayden." Nina flicked an errant strand of hair from her eyes with shaky fingers. Her gaze darted around the patio, then settled on me. "I just wanted to touch base with all the attendees. Make sure everyone is okay. Because there's nothing to be afraid of, you know. Last night was awful, of course, but it was a complete aberration. At Lemaître, we—"

"Are *you* okay?" I interrupted, frowning with concern. She was obviously under a lot of stress. I didn't want Nina keeling over, right there beside the buffet station featuring chocolate fondue, brioche croutons, and fresh strawberry skewers. I'd had enough tragedy for one lifetime. "This must be very difficult for you. I don't imagine Christian is a very forgiving boss."

"Christian is a brilliant and accomplished man." Her words sounded rehearsed—especially since that particular man hadn't given a single day off to the only employee who'd tried to help Adrienne last night. But then, Nina was a *PR* exec. Her job was to smooth over any disruptions and make Lemaître look good. "He wants everyone to know how truly sorry he is about Adrienne."

With a sob, Nina broke off. Seeming appalled by her own lapse in politesse, she clenched her hands. She looked away.

I couldn't help feeling affected by the obvious difficulty she'd been having. And still was. "Look, you don't have to put on a brave front with me," I assured her. "I know you did all you could last night." I tried not to think of any specifics. "Adrienne must have been glad to have a friend by her side."

As I fumbled for a polite way not to bring up any morbid details, Nina nodded. "I did try to help her. I called for help as soon as I realized something was wrong! But it was too late."

Nina went on to describe how she'd found Adrienne vomiting blood . . . inadvertently lending credence to Danny's overdose theory. She described the same kinds of sweaty, chilled feelings *I'd* experienced . . . accidentally lending a sense of terror to *me*.

So much for omitting any morbid details. I got the impression Nina needed to talk, though. So I listened. Still, the whole exchange was pretty awkward. I didn't know Nina very well. Plus, her skittish gaze kept jerking around the patio as she spoke, as though she needed to get busy with something else—probably reassuring all the other retreat attendees of Lemaître Chocolates' undying concern for their well-being. One by one. For that personal touch. I knew what a taskmaster Christian could be. Which reminded me, unhappily, of my overdue report.

Ugh. When was I going to find time to finish it?

Prompted by the anxiety that thought provoked, I glanced again toward the all-chocolate buffet. *Speak of the devil.*

Christian Lemaître had arrived, wearing a "business casual" getup composed of gray trousers, mauve oxfords, and a pink pique polo with the collar turned up. Very "Preppie Meets Eurotrash."

His whole look sported that distinctive sheen that only gobs of money could provide—of course—along with a fat gold Rolex. For all his faults, Christian had taken an outdated, dying company and turned it into a screamingly profitable one.

One that was going to do even better, with my expert help.

Back to Nina. "Were you and Adrienne close?" I asked. I faced her fully, feeling guilty for woolgathering.

"Yes, we were. Very." The PR exec gave me a weary smile. "Before the changeover, a lot of us were close. We lost so many people, unfortunately." She had to be referring to Christian's takeover of Lemaître, when he'd ousted his kindly (horny) uncle, Bernard. "But that's business, isn't it? It's all for the best."

Frankly, that speech sounded pretty rehearsed, too. But I couldn't fault Nina for giving it. She had a job to do, just as I did—and that job *wasn't* gorging on *pain au chocolat,* the way I'd been considering doing ten minutes ago. Despite that fact, though, Nina did accept a demitasse cup of drinking chocolate from the server. We listened as he outlined the buffet by rote.

Kindly, Nina didn't point out to that nervous-looking waiter that she, as a Lemaître exec, knew everything there was to know about the all-chocolate buffet, down to the last muffin.

My estimation of her went up a notch. People who are kind to wait staff get the thumbs-up from (former wage slave) me.

After he nodded and left, Nina's gaze fell on the flyer about Adrienne's memorial service. I'd left it between me and Danny during my tirade. "Ah. You're coming today, aren't you?"

"Nah." I shrugged. "I'm jetting off to Barbados, instead."

She gawked. I felt bad for being flip. What can I say? I sometimes go glib under pressure. Comforting someone you barely knew *was* pressure. I couldn't believe Danny had stuck me here.

"Kidding." I noticed Isabel and Bernard had arrived, too.

"Of course." Nina's composure returned. "The memorial

service was a last-minute thing, I'll admit. But Adrienne deserves to be remembered somehow. The police don't know how long it will take to find any relatives and notify them." She gave a rueful head shake, then touched the flyer. "Graphic design isn't my forte. After I finished dealing with the police and locking up the ballroom, I was up all night doing the layout."

With new insight, I looked at it again. Suddenly, it didn't seem so heartless after all. Also, Danny's championship of Nina was starting to make more sense. *That's a nice gesture,* he'd remarked earlier in her defense. Maybe because he *did* like Nina.

"It's very thoughtful," I said. I couldn't help it.

Far be it from me to kick a PR flunkey when she's down.

"Thanks." Nina brightened. "Now I have to make my rounds. Thanks for the company, Hayden. I hope you *will* stick around."

As I cracked wise about my gridskipping ways (some people never learn, okay?), Nina absentmindedly gathered her clutch in one hand and my demitasse of drinking chocolate in the other.

"Whoops!" I caught her before she made off with it. I gave her an apologetic gesture. "It looks as though we have something in common," I said. *Something besides being the only two people who want to honor Adrienne.* I was starting to like Nina more by the minute. "We both ordered the same drinking chocolate."

Mutely, she gazed down at her cup. In her grasp, it clattered against the saucer. I wondered if she'd ever calm down. Poor Nina. *She'd* need to go to Barbados after this event.

"That cup's mine," I clarified, reaching for it.

"Oh!" She laughed. "They look identical, don't they?"

As she switched cups and then waved good-bye—off to

chat with other retreat attendees—I frowned at my cup. It *did* look the same as Nina's. Just the same way Adrienne's green juice had looked the same as mine had last night. We'd *both* set down our drinks during the photo op. *Was I in danger?* If Adrienne had accidentally served herself *my* drink after retrieving them . . .

She might have died in my place, just as Danny had surmised. With new concern, I examined the patio full of people.

Nobody appeared the least bit sinister. Of course.

Well . . . except Rex Rader. I expected him to look creepy. But even the Melt CEO had toned down the smarm-and-charm routine in the wake of Adrienne's death. I noticed him leave the buffet with an empty plate in hand, approach Nina, and lower his head to speak with her. Rex put his free hand gently on Nina's arm.

His face looked somber, his demeanor attentive. Obviously, he'd noticed Nina's distress, too, and was trying to help.

Given that, it was tough to hold a grudge against the guy.

Sure, Rex had propositioned me (multiple times), but that wasn't a crime. If it were, two-thirds of the male populations of Italy, France, and Spain would be incarcerated. Besides, Rex *had* sacrificed the streusel-topped chocolate-chip coffee cake he'd been eyeing in order to help Nina. That went above and beyond.

Wow. Was I seriously thinking nice things about Rex?

Just as I realized it, he caught me looking at him.

He started. He glanced at Nina—who was talking to him—and frowned briefly. Then Rex held up his hand to me with his thumb and forefinger extended. Cheekily, he mouthed, *Call me.*

For an incentive, he waggled his eyebrows. Then he slid his gaze down my tank-top-covered chest, over my skirted hips, all the way down to my bare legs. It was an unequivocal ogle.

For a *very* physically gifted man, Rex was surprisingly

inept at reading people. I was sorry I'd softened toward him, however briefly. I slung on my crossbody bag, signaled for the check, then scrawled my name and room number on the printout.

Suddenly, sadly, I didn't have an appetite. Not even for chocolate. Not even for white chocolate bread pudding and cacao beignets. *That's* how I knew I had to do something—something to reassure myself that (A) I'd never have to consult for a creep like Rex Rader, and (B) nobody at the retreat was a murderer.

Because if they were—and they were after *me*—how could I be safe? Ever? Several of the most prominent chocolatiers in the world were in attendance at the Lemaître retreat. So were a number of other industry insiders. These were my colleagues. If one of them wanted me dead, it was better to find out *now,* while my guard was up (and Danny was on hand for backup) rather than later, when I was blithely doing something like troubleshooting chocolate praline macaroons for Ladurée in Paris or attempting to improve those delicate, irresistible (but tricky) chocolate-hazelnut Kinder Bueno bars for Ferrero in Villers-Écalles.

Scratch that. Just forget I mentioned any names, okay? For the record, I'm *not* confirming I've consulted for any big-time chocolatiers. Name-dropping isn't cool, anyway. Moving on . . .

I'd start, I decided, by casually chatting with all the principal players. Just to reassure myself that nobody else found anything suspicious about the situation with Adrienne. Just to make sure that I could move on safely. After that . . .

. . . I'd write my report. *Definitely.* No question about it.

* * *

But first, I decided as I ducked through an ironwork arbor bordered by flowering azure wisteria vines and then headed toward Maison Lemaître's main building, I'd call Travis.

I needed to check in. Also, it would be nice (aka reassuring) to hear my advisor's sensible (aka distractingly sexy) voice over the phone line. Besides, it would be smart to check my financial situation. As far as I knew, I'd been sticking with the kooky requirements of my uncle Ross's will—the stipulations necessary to guarantee myself an income stream.

But what if I wasn't? What if I hadn't? What if my inheritance had crashed overnight? There would be no sense getting all principled about not working for Rex Rader if I *had* to do it to stay afloat. Things changed. Stuff happened.

For instance, Adrienne probably hadn't expected *not* to wake up today. That meant time was short. I don't know if my friend's untimely death had me feeling my own sense of mortality more intensely than usual or what, but all at once I *needed* to talk with Travis. Not because I doubted his financial acumen in managing things for me (because that would have been folly, plain and simple). The man was a genius. But just because . . .

I couldn't think up an excuse. Not under pressure with no all-chocolate breakfast goodies to fire up some neural circuits.

Fine. I craved the sound of his voice. Okay? Happy now?

Feeling a rush even as I pulled out my phone, I got ready to dial. I'd tell Travis I'd read an actual *paper* newspaper that morning, I decided. An old-school guy like him would probably be impressed by something so ridiculously traditional. Even a loosey-goosey type like me could tell that getting the news courtesy of Twitter hashtags probably wasn't super responsible.

My phone started ringing . . . just as someone tapped my shoulder.

I must have jumped six feet in fright. LeBron James had nothing on me. Heart pounding, I whirled on the resort path.

Bernard Lemaître stood there, twinkly-eyed and exuding concern. Being scared of him was like having a Mr. Rogers phobia. It just didn't make sense. I gave a repentant grin.

"Mr. Lemaître! You startled me." I stowed my phone.

Nothing less would do when the patriarch of chocolates came calling. Travis could wait. I'd been tapped by the king.

"I'm sorry about that, Ms. Moore." Bernard frowned. "Ms. Mundy? Ms. Mundy Moore?" He chuckled. "During the scavenger hunt yesterday, our conversation was mostly limited to 'I'm coming!'"

Oh yeah. That was because I'd been trying to roust him and the missus out from whatever hidey-hole they'd sneaked into to make out, I recalled. That made seeing him now a bit awkward. At his (likely unintentional) double entendre, I think I blushed.

"It's sweet that you and Mrs. Lemaître are so in love," I told him, offering a handshake. His clasp was dry and firm, full of surprising vigor for a man his age. "Hayden will be fine."

"All right. Hayden." Bernard glanced back toward the patio. It occurred to me that he must have left Isabel. I hoped she wasn't performing an impromptu striptease. He probably was, too. "I'm sorry to bother you, but I wanted to ask you something."

"It's no bother at all!" He was such a gentleman. I could

see why the people of the Bay Area—especially kids—loved him.

I resented Christian all the more for pushing him out.

"But first . . . you weren't leaving, were you?" Bernard gestured toward the path I'd been on. It led through the grass, past some pink floribunda roses, then circled a tinkling Italianate fountain before angling toward the valet stand. "We need you."

Technically . . . they did. The company's latest pet project—the nutraceutical line—was a disaster. The alternative approaches I had in mind for my report would ameliorate that problem and open up new markets for Lemaître. But I'd been under the impression that Christian had hired me mostly in secret. So I was surprised to hear Bernard be so open now about my consulting mission.

I hoped he didn't ask me about Adrienne's caffeinated truffles. I wasn't 100 percent on my game so early in the morning. Plus, I didn't want to turn over those bittersweet (potential) killers to anyone yet. They were hidden in my room, along with Adrienne's packet of anhydrous caffeine.

"No, I'm not leaving," I assured him. "I'm just enjoying the grounds. You really have a breathtaking spot here."

Bernard nodded. He inhaled, taking in the sparkling water views. "Christian is a brilliant and accomplished man."

Okay. *That* was just eerie. Those were exactly the same words Nina had used to describe her boss. *Exactly the same.*

"You must deserve some of the credit too," I pushed, wondering why he didn't have *any* animosity about being ousted.

But Bernard only shrugged. "I'm happy where I am. Which is why I wanted to talk to you." He leaned nearer, offering me a whiff of old-fashioned aftershave. He must have worn it for Isabel. That was sweet, too. "Nina asked me to talk at the opening session today—to give a eulogy, of sorts, for Ms. Dowling. But I'm not sure that would go over altogether well."

"Why not?"

He flinched. Too late, I realized I'd stepped in it.

After a brief hesitation, Bernard confirmed my blunder. Maybe I ought to have known his secret already? "Especially with Mrs. Lemaître," he said gently. "She's a bit . . . possessive. Hearing me speak about Adrienne, especially in the glowing terms she deserves . . ." Bernard broke off. "I just couldn't say no to Nina. And I *did* know Adrienne quite well. But after some thought—"

Aha. "Enough said." I held up my palm, embarrassed for both of us. A man like Bernard shouldn't have had to make excuses for his wife. "I'd be happy to"—*keep you out of the doghouse*—"say a few words about Adrienne today. Don't worry about it at all." I could see how Nina's PR-stoked dynamism could steamroller poor Bernard. "I'll keep it on the down-low, too. With Nina."

The stark relief on his face surprised me. Was Bernard serious about Isabel being jealous of a deceased employee?

I knew jealousy was a largely irrational emotion. But *really*? Isabel was a (stunning) former lingerie model. Could she truly have considered a dowdy (older) chocolatier like Adrienne to have been a rival for Bernard's affections? If so, how far would she have gone to eliminate that potential rival?

Far enough to kill her?

There'd been no love lost on Adrienne's side of the equation, either, I mused. Who knew what had gone on between her and Isabel before I'd come on the scene? My friend's disparaging remarks about Bernard's wife at the scavenger hunt had been the snarkiest things I'd ever heard her say. If there was some kind of bad history among Adrienne, Bernard, and Isabel . . .

But that was crazy. Who was I, the new Miss Marple? I didn't need suspects and theories and wild suppositions. I was seeing ghosts. What I needed, just then, was a proper eulogy.

Because Adrienne deserved it. Because I'd made a promise.

Because it was, in all honesty, the least I could do.

At that, a fresh wave of melancholy struck me. I fidgeted (hey, maybe an attack of dancing feet could save me?), then leaped onto the first diversionary tactic I could think of.

"How long did you know Adrienne?" I asked Bernard.

In the pause that ensued, I realized that I couldn't remember seeing him (or Isabel) during the mêlée last night.

"A few years," Bernard confided, his gray hair ruffled by the breeze. "Adrienne used to work for one of my charities. Christian persuaded her to work directly with Lemaître, instead."

He'd poached her, was what Bernard meant, I figured. But bonus points to Adrienne. She'd done charity work, too? The world really needed to quit thinking of her as a druggie.

At the end of that tangential thought, I glanced back at Bernard. He looked . . . wistful. He was probably a sentimentalist.

"Well, Adrienne was very talented. I can vouch for that."

"She was." Bernard cleared his throat. "Very talented."

I was making the king of chocolate cry. Nobody wanted to hire a chocolate whisperer who made people cry. What was the matter with me, grilling Bernard like this? Next I'd be asking . . . "Did you have a few final moments with her, at least?"

I barely murmured it. But Bernard heard me. He frowned.

"I'm afraid I was with my wife at the time." Frostily,

Bernard glanced at his watch. It was much less ostentatious than his nephew's. "Speaking of the time . . . I have to run. Thank you for your help, Hayden." He shook my hand. "Enjoy the retreat."

That sounded, chillingly and finally, like a good-bye.

Had I just committed career suicide by offending one of the most important people in the chocolate business? I hoped not.

Before I could decide, Bernard was striding back to the patio, back to the all-chocolate buffet, back to his jealous (much younger) wife. He moved with all the strength and purpose that had enabled him to haul me away from the scary ridge's edge during our scavenger hunt yesterday. If Adrienne had been killed in a more physical way, I mused, and I were a more cynical type . . .

Well, I'd have to say that Bernard could have done it.

But that was insane. Bernard Lemaître was a well-respected chocolatier and businessman . . . and a beloved city figure, too. He'd just asked me to make sure Adrienne was honored later today.

How secretly evil could Bernard possibly be?

I wasn't there to pinpoint suspects and assemble alibis, I reminded myself staunchly. I didn't know anything about that stuff. I didn't want to, either. I'm a get-in-and-go gal. That's it. I've got no expertise that doesn't pertain to chocolate, traveling, or knowing how to get people to cozy up to me in a heartbeat. For whatever reason, strangers are happy to dish to me about their problems, challenges, and new ideas. That's how I stumbled into my unconventional job in the first place—not to mention innumerable conversations on planes, trains, and city sidewalks all across the world.

I guess I have "one of those faces" or something.

But my *tell me everything* face was no help to me now. Not with the day I had ahead. Shaking my head over

Bernard's abrupt departure, I fished out my phone again. Within a few impatient steps (mine), Travis's sexy rumble came over the line.

"Hey, hot stuff!" I felt enlivened already. Moving on (and talking to my travel-phobic financial advisor) tended to have that effect on me. "Here's a new one for you—got any tips for improvising a eulogy? Because I'm on the hook for a doozy in about half an hour." I hauled in a breath, then gazed toward the rocky nature trail in the distance. Was that *Danny* running along the ridge? Had he foregone junky fast food for *exercise*? No way. Deliberately refocusing, I exhaled. "It's got to be good, too."

"Come on now, Hayden." Travis's voice was like butter on toast. Hot fudge on ice cream. Crème fraiche on old-fashioned molten chocolate cake. It was *meltingly* good, is what I'm saying. "*Everything* I do is good. Give me all the details."

Grateful for his help, I did exactly that.

Chapter 6

After the chocolate retreat's opening session-turned-memorial service (the hybrid nature of which still rankled me), I needed to get away. The ballroom where the session was held felt too packed, too corporate, and too reminiscent of the ballroom from last night. Plus, sitting still was getting to me.

I stretched my legs with a walk to the resort's swimming pool. Because most of the retreat's attendees had stayed to network after the opening session, the place was tranquil. It was also luxurious. The pool boasted clear sky blue waters; the impeccable landscaping, comfortable lounge chairs, and lavishly outfitted cabanas surrounding it promised to pamper. Each cabana held its own stock of signature Lemaître chocolates. On the menu at the adjacent outdoor bar were cocoa martinis, cacao-mint mojitos, and chocolate porter. I was supposed to be networking. All I wanted to do was kick off my shoes and forget everything.

It was probably too early to get boozed up. I'd be lying if I said I didn't consider it, though. It had been a stressful day already. My eulogy had gone over well. So had everyone else's.

Unbeknownst to me (and apparently Bernard), Nina

had hedged her bets when it came to remembering Adrienne. My tribute had been preceded and followed by fond remembrances from several Lemaître staff members, including Nina herself and (gallingly) Christian. Even Isabel had raised her Bloody Mary in a toast.

So much for Isabel harboring undying resentment toward her supposed rival, I mused now as I *did* toe off my shoes. So much for Bernard's eulogy to Adrienne being indicative of them having had any kind of special relationship, too. I bent to scoop up my flats, enjoying the familiar, faraway sounds of the Maison Lemaître kitchen staff preparing for service. So much for Adrienne not being remembered if *I* didn't help make it happen.

Bernard and I had both overestimated our own importance.

Theoretically at least, the rest of my morning was loose. Attendees were supposed to make business connections, taste chocolates, and sample the cacao-themed spa services. The event was really one big ego stroke for Christian, who got to host the whole shindig *and* take credit for all Lemaître's success, while Bernard was shunted to the sidelines of the company he'd built.

I couldn't be *too* disapproving of Christian's tactics, though. If Bernard wasn't bugged, why should I be? Besides, I was there because *I* wanted to benefit, too. That's why I'd accepted Christian's invitation—the deferred deadline on my report was just a bonus, though he seemed to have recanted that offer. I have an admittedly prestigious list of satisfied clients to my credit, but I can always use more.

Speaking of which . . . on the phone, Travis had confirmed that my financial situation was holding steady. Just like he was. Meaning, I *didn't* have to take on a sleaze like Rex Rader as a client. So part A of my two-part A.M. resolution was taken care of. As far as part B went . . . well, in the sunshiny light of another northern California morning, making sure that none of my fellow attendees was a crazed murderer seemed like a nonissue to me.

At least it did . . . until Christian Lemaître sneaked onto the pool deck beside me, tapped me on the shoulder, and smirked.

He might as well have stabbed me. I jumped that high.

"If you've got time to resort, you've got time to report," Christian gibed. He gave a tsk-tsk. "Don't you have work to do?"

I felt like Adrienne being badgered by him at the scavenger hunt. Heart pounding with pointless alarm, I shook my head. "I'm just enjoying Maison Lemaître," I told him. What was with the Lemaîtres following me today, anyway? "As a retreat attendee."

Christian narrowed his eyes. As dirty looks went, his was second only to the doozy he'd aimed at Adrienne when he'd found her hunting chocolate-themed clues instead of molding truffles.

It occurred to me that he'd seemed to have a beef with Adrienne, too. Just the same way Isabel Lemaître had. Had Christian's issue with Adrienne been *deadly serious,* though?

"I didn't invite you so you could skulk off alone," he said, giving nothing away except his usual autocratic attitude.

"I didn't come so I could be hounded." The amended deadline for my report was still a few days away. I had plenty of time.

"You're supposed to be networking," Christian pushed, checking his watch. "What are you doing out here at the pool?"

I thought about it. "Taking up Olympic diving?"

He wasn't amused. "I want you to be *seen,* Hayden."

"*You've* obviously 'seen' me 'skulking,'" I shot back,

not content to be his trophy. I might have mentioned before that I don't like being bossed around. If I haven't . . . I don't. Especially by a dictatorial type like Christian. "What's the problem?"

He compressed his mouth, looking annoyed. If Christian *was* a secret murderer, it occurred to me absurdly, then I was an idiot to get on his bad side this way. What was I thinking?

The man was going to write me a paycheck within days.

"I'm sorry," I amended hastily. I considered myself pretty brave—but not pointlessly stupid. "I'm being confrontational. I don't mean to be. I guess we're all still upset about Adrienne."

Christian gave me a noncommittal glance.

"I understand you'd known her longer than most people at Lemaître," I went on (knowing when to quit has never been my strong suit), "since you recruited her from Bernard's charity?"

But this time, Christian laughed. "*That* sorry excuse for a tax write-off? I can't believe my uncle still talks about it."

I have to say, his answer didn't give me the warm fuzzies. What kind of guy dissed charities? And his kind-hearted uncle?

I didn't believe for one second that Bernard had calculatingly established a charity for its tax advantages.

"He sounded proud of it," I said. "What's its mission?"

"Officially? Offering training in the culinary arts to at-risk high-school students." Christian made a face. "In reality? Adrienne was wasting her time in that dive."

"You saved her, then. She must have been grateful."

Christian scoffed. His face turned unexpectedly chilly.

"Not grateful enough for her *not* to sabotage me," he said.

That was interesting. "Sabotage you?" *Adrienne?* "How?"

"Forget I said anything." Disappointingly, Christian backpedaled just when things were getting juicy. He crossed his arms over his chest, then shook his head. "It'll all be swept under the rug now, anyway. You know how it is when people die."

"Nope. This is my first time. How is it?"

He actually cracked a grin at that. Like I said before, I have a knack for making friends fast. Whether I wanted to stay friends with Christian was debatable. But I was interested now.

"Everyone will forget what Adrienne was *really* like," Christian told me. He looked disgruntled. "What she really did."

"Which was?" At his suspicious glance, I waved my shoes. "Come on. I'm a barefoot chocolate whisperer who's never stayed in the same city longer than a month. Who am I going to tell?"

With a nod that said *you have a point,* Christian relented.

"She was selling secrets—recipes—to a rival chocolatier."

No way. I didn't believe it. "Which one?" I breathed, sounding as giddy as a gossipy girl at a slumber party.

It was a tactic that usually inveigled out secrets pretty effectively. Most people wanted to share. If you're guessing that *gushy* sounds inauthentic on me, you're right. It does. Fortunately, most people don't notice. Unfortunately, Christian did. Either he hated gossip or was smarter than I thought.

"I'm surprised *you* don't already know which one, after all your time consulting at Lemaître," he said. "Your reputation was better than that. I was told you offered a *complete* approach."

Ouch. Way to sucker punch a girl when she already had low blood sugar. Christian was more vindictive than I'd thought. He obviously had no compunction about casually playing dirty.

But where did he draw the line when it came to the employee who'd (allegedly) sold him out? I wondered. If Christian believed Adrienne *had* committed corporate espionage, he might have felt justified in slipping her a deadly caffeine overdose.

You know . . . as crazy as that sounded. And it definitely did.

The thing was, mulling over potential reasons people may have wanted to murder Adrienne was starting to seem more reasonable by the minute. It occurred to me that Christian—almost solely among his staff—knew of the powdered caffeine's hypothetically lethal effect. At least he did . . . if he'd read my preliminary report, which had dutifully outlined its dangers.

I'm a procrastinator, sure. But I *do* turn in detailed work.

"I can always ask Rex Rader," I bluffed. "He'll tell me."

It was a shot in the dark. Although I'd done my share of chitchatting with other attendees, Rex's name came first to mind because he'd been pestering me. But somehow I struck a nerve.

"Talk to Rader, and you'll never work in the chocolate business again," Christian threatened. "Speaking of which—"

"Speaking of . . . which? My imminent blackballing? Or speaking of Rex?" I frowned. "Let's be clear, so I know when to break out my woobie. If you're trying to warn me that *mmm*-Melt is in trouble, I already knew that." *Because Rex tried to hire me.*

Like I've said before, I go glib when cornered. I'd hate to let Christian think he'd cowed me the same way he had Adrienne.

On the verge of saying more, Christian snapped shut his mouth. He looked at me blankly. "Melt is in trouble?"

Was he really so clued-out that he hadn't heard? I knew Christian was ridiculously self-absorbed. But there was garden-variety narcissism . . . and then there was corporate hari-kari.

I decided to school him. "You're not saying it right," I told Christian with a grin. "Try again. mmmm-Melt."

My sexed-up Melt pronunciation didn't even merit a smirk. We'd been becoming such buddies a few minutes ago. On the other hand, we were discussing one of Lemaître's *rivals*. Business was never a laughing matter. Not to men like Christian Lemaître.

"Never mind," he muttered. "This is a waste of time."

He turned to leave. As he did, I touched his arm. For a nouveau riche whiz kid, I noticed, Christian was pretty buff.

If Adrienne had, instead, been pushed to her death . . .

I have to say, Christian could have done it.

"Wait!" I said. "If talking with Rex Rader is the kiss of death to my consulting business, I'd rather skip it." Earnestly, I looked into his eyes. "Help a girl out, willya?"

For a second, he almost relented. I gave all the credit to my bare feet and baby blues. I might not spackle on L'Oréal on a daily basis, but I do like to rock a slamming pedicure. Maybe Christian had a foot fetish, because he leaned even nearer.

"I almost forgot to mention," Christian said coldly. "I want that notebook Adrienne gave you. In my hands. Today."

Her notebook? I'd thought he hadn't seen that exchange outside on the Maison Lemaître grounds. I remembered Adrienne handing it to me, looking panicky, warning me that she couldn't allow Christian to have it—telling me she had to keep it safe.

Was there more to that notebook than chocolate recipes?

"You must mean my report," I bluffed. "It's coming up."

I didn't want to betray Adrienne's trust by doing anything else. She must have given that notebook to me for a reason.

She must have *brought it with her* for a reason. But why?

Luckily, Christian didn't push me any further. "It's company property," he said. "I want it." Then he gave me another smirk, popped his "where's the kegger?!" pink collar at a sharper angle, and headed back inside to rejoin the retreat.

After my showdown with Christian, I felt pretty shook up.

I didn't think he had deliberately hurt Adrienne. He might have *wanted* to hurt her, but I didn't think he *had*. Not once I had a chance to consider things rationally. Because, after all, Danny and I had run into Christian coming out of the ballroom kitchen ourselves. Since I had to trust my own eyeballs, Christian Lemaître had about as rock-solid an alibi as anybody could have.

Unless he'd overdosed Adrienne and then doubled back to the kitchen to look especially guilty, I reasoned, he was clean. Spiteful and overbearing, but clean . . . aside from those incriminating fingerprint-size chocolate smudges I'd noticed on his shirtfront last night, that is.

Adrienne had had chocolate on her fingers while working, I knew. Nobody dipped truffles without making a minimal mess. She'd been wearing foodservice gloves, of course. But if she'd had to physically ward off her killer, that struggle would have left evidence. Evidence similar to what I saw on Christian.

Then, too, Christian *did* look guilty for another reason, I mused as I left the pool area. He'd been constantly pressuring

Adrienne to work faster on the nutraceutical chocolates line. What if he'd tried to goose her performance by scooping extra caffeine into her "energy" drink? He didn't have to have meant to kill Adrienne, I reasoned, to have done it accidentally.

So far among my informal suspects, I had to count Mrs. Green-Eyed Monster, Isabel, and Mr. All-Business, Christian. As I bounded across Maison Lemaître's grassy grounds sometime later with a spa menu in hand, I was forced to add a third suspect. Because while passing by the fountain, I glimpsed the same reporter Rex Rader had been feeling up at the welcome session last night. She was perched on the fountain's Italianate stone, beside her former paramour, holding a cell phone in his face.

In case this was something kinky, I didn't want to linger.

"What do you say to those people who claim there was bad blood between you and Adrienne Dowling?" the reporter was asking. Firmly. "After all, you *did* reportedly threaten her."

Intrigued, I slowed down. Casually, I looked back.

Rex appeared trapped. I guessed the phone was recording.

"Aw, baby, be reasonable." He wiped sweat from his handsome temple, then attempted a smile. "You said you'd write a profile of me for your magazine—not come at me with a hatchet job."

Aha. An advantageous profile would explain Rex's interest in her—and hers in him. She looked young enough to be a junior reporter or even an ambitious intern out to make a name for herself at a publication like *Chocolat Monthly.* Which only made Rex seem twice as shady, in my book, for pursuing someone so young. He'd probably thought he could take advantage of her naïveté.

It looked as though she had the upper hand now.

"I *am* profiling you for my magazine." The reporter held her phone closer. "To prepare for that profile, I did some research. That's how I found out about your ongoing issues with Adrienne."

"I had hurt feelings, that's all," Rex explained. "Adrienne had just turned down a job with Melt. A *good* job. I saw Adrienne at an industry function and went off on her. I shouldn't have done it. But she should have taken that job!" At a grumble, he added, "At least nobody *dies* while working at Melt."

A job? With Melt? I hadn't known about that. Curious, I ducked behind the wisteria-covered arbor I'd passed through earlier. From my vantage point, I could hear everything.

"She did more than turn you down for a job, though, didn't she?" the reporter asked. "Wasn't there more to it than that?"

Even more curious now, I wondered what more there could be. I envisioned Adrienne putting axle grease in Rex's hair gel, kneeing him in the groin, or swapping his daily truffles for "chocolaty" laxatives—understandable impulses, all of them.

"At the same function," Rex conceded, "Adrienne took a few jabs at Melt. A few *very public* jabs, saying our new Criollo-bean chocolates were really made of mostly Forastero beans."

"Were they?" the reporter asked. "Maybe you made a mix with hybrid Trinitario beans?" she suggested, obviously leading him.

Most likely, she knew the same thing I did—that extra-pricey Criollo beans (grown mainly in the Caribbean and Central America) make up less than two percent of the world's cocoa. It was unlikely Rex could afford to use them exclusively at Melt.

"Beans are beside the point," Rex evaded. "Some important people were listening when Adrienne mouthed off that night. We took a hit on orders at Melt. But so what? We're still here."

They were, I knew . . . but maybe not for long. Rex had seemed downright desperate when hitting me up for help yesterday.

Undoubtedly, hiring a skilled chocolatier like Adrienne would have improved Melt's business prospects and growth. But if instead she'd done all she could to torpedo Rex's chances . . . Well, I have to say, he could have wanted her dead.

"I heard Melt was *still* struggling," the reporter pushed.

Rex wiggled his fingers through his dark, curly hair. He gave a grin. "Have you looked at our portfolio? We're booming!"

His gregarious tone didn't fool the reporter into dropping her line of questioning. She continued in a more intimate tone that was probably supposed to invite him to confide in her.

I was busy being reminded of the portfolio Rex had pushed on me yesterday in the hallway. I hadn't examined it yet. I'd been planning to overnight it to Travis for further analysis.

"Look, I know I said I wanted us to help one another," Rex was saying when I tuned in again, "but that's enough for now, okay? You weren't this interested in *talking* to me last night."

His lascivious tone made his insinuation plain. *Yuck.*

"Last night, I couldn't find you to talk," the reporter said crisply. "I ducked into the ladies' room, remember?" She must have come in there right after me, I realized. "When I came out, you were no place to be found. You ditched me. I bet you're sorry for that now, though, aren't you?"

That was interesting, I couldn't help thinking. Not that the reporter had apparently decided to exact her revenge for Rex ditching her by penning a negatively slanted article, but that Rex *also* had been unaccounted for during last night's tragedy.

Suddenly, I realized they'd both quit talking. *Uh-oh.*

I peeked out from behind the wisteria. Rex and the reporter were both staring at me. Pointedly. I waved and headed onward.

The spa awaited—and so did about a million more questions.

———

Faced with what amounted to a steaming hot tub full of chocolate pudding, most people would have grabbed a spoon. I grabbed my plush spa-issued robe instead. Then I dropped my robe onto a waiting hook and (dressed in a spa-issued tankini swimsuit for modesty), I got right in. Instantly, the warmth of Maison Lemaître's signature hot-cocoa mud bath enveloped me.

Ah. My tense muscles turned to fondue on the spot. My nose filled with the familiar scent of chocolate—albeit chocolate infused with subtle mineral undertones due to its springwater base. The mud bath felt . . . weirdly good. Weirdly, because mud (even chocolate-laced mud) was a lot thicker than the water you'd find in a typical hot tub. Weirdly, because I wasn't alone.

That made the groan of pleasure I let out as I sank deeper doubly embarrassing. But I decided to roll with it, anyway.

"Ah!" I said, really committing this time. Never let it be said that Hayden Mundy Moore did anything halfway. "Amazing!"

"All our guests really enjoy the hot-cocoa mud bath." The attendant set down a fresh pile of fluffy, mocha-colored towels on a bench near the adjacent pristine-tiled shower stalls. She smiled at me. "Remember not to stay in for too long, though."

The spa goer beside me—a woman with a wrapped-towel turban on her head—gave a languid wave. She didn't open her eyes.

I recognized her, though. Isabel Lemaître. Topless. Of course. It was as if Bernard's wife was allergic to clothes. Not that she wasn't mostly (and artfully) covered with creamy, chocolaty hot-cocoa mud bath goo; she was. I was grateful for that, too. I'm no prude, but after so many years traveling, I can be pretty chameleonlike when it comes to fitting in. I didn't think it would help grow my consulting business if I gallivanted around topless. Or maybe it would, I mused. *Hmm . . .*

"Don't crush our groove, Britney," Isabel said in a world-weary, accented voice. "What's the worst that could happen?"

"Well, technically, staying too long in a hot environment can cause fainting due to heat exhaustion," Britney recited. "It can overstress the heart or induce very severe dehydration."

"Aren't you charmingly earnest?" Isabel opened her eyes. She raised the champagne flute she'd left on the edge of the sunken tub. "That's why we have these. Another choco-mosa?"

"Right away, Mrs. Lemaître." Britney rushed to collect her empty glass. She paused near me. "Would you like one, as well?"

I shook my head. I was there to de-stress, not to become one with the hot-cocoa mud bath. One death by chocolate was more than enough for a single resort stay. If I tried that revamped house mimosa—a mix of champagne, orange juice, and a splash of chocolate liqueur—I'd be done for. "Not right now, thanks."

"Hayden! Is that you?" Stirring herself enough to recognize me at last, Isabel gave me a warm smile. "How are you?"

"Hot. Muddy." Lazily, I raised my arms. "Limp."

"Sounds like my husband. Thank God for ED drugs."

I really didn't want to think of Bernard in that way. I focused *very* hard on the spa's serene New Age background music.

"He's gotten *so* much more fun since retiring, though," Isabel went on as Britney left the tub area. "Soon we'll be enjoying the life I *thought* we'd have when I married him."

"What life is that?" I asked, wondering if I should invent an excuse to bail out on my hot-cocoa bath. I liked it, but it might not be smart to go hot-tubbing with a prospective killer.

"Traveling. Shopping. *Enjoying* one another!" Isabel said with an enthusiasm that was infectious. She didn't *seem* capable of murdering Adrienne in a jealous rage. "Pampering Poopsie."

I blinked. "Poopsie?"

"Our adorable baby girl." Beaming, Isabel nodded to the other side of the tub's edge. "She's having a nap right now."

Expecting to see a *very* unfortunately named infant, I glimpsed a Yorkie instead. It was snoring atop a tasseled silk pillow. *Poopsie.* I melted. I couldn't help it. I *love* dogs.

I've always wanted one. With my globe-trotting lifestyle, though, canine companionship just isn't practical. Not for me.

"Aw!" I squealed—and this time, my girlishness was genuine. What can I say? I'm not *all* coolness and procrastination. "She's adorable." I wanted to squeeze Poopsie with glee. "So cute!"

"She goes everywhere with us," Isabel confided, casting the snoozing Yorkie a fond look. "Bernie got her for me."

How nice. "That was thoughtful of him."

"Yes, it was. Mostly. I needed company back when Bernie was running Lemaître." Isabel looked troubled. Her face sort of . . . *hardened,* similar to the way Bernard's had done on the ridge yesterday, after Isabel had cooed about him always "being so good" to her. He'd looked, I remembered, oddly guilty.

Just then, so did Isabel. I didn't know why.

But it probably wasn't remorse over committing a murder, I assured myself, feeling hot-cocoa mud squelch between my toes. I just couldn't bring myself to believe a dog person would do that. I know that sounds crazy. But I trust my instincts.

"He surprised me with Poopsie right after his affair," Isabel went on lightly. "But you know. Things happen. I'm over it now. I'm French! I'd be bored if Bernie was true to me."

His affair. Just like that, Isabel confirmed that her husband had cheated on her—just not with whom. I was dying to know, although she sounded pretty blasé about it. I can't say Isabel's attitude surprised me, given her overall demeanor—and her comfort level with nudity. Clearly, she wasn't hung up on American societal norms. Those didn't sound like the rantings of a possessive wife to me, either. On the other hand, that didn't mean that Bernard didn't genuinely have a guilty conscience.

Maybe he'd decided not to eulogize Adrienne because he'd been afraid he'd say something insensitive. He wouldn't have been the first man in history to overcompensate for infidelity.

The idea still boggled my mind, though. Bernard . . . and Adrienne? Why hadn't she told me? How many secrets had she had, anyway?

Already, I knew about her chocolate development

notebook. Her (maybe) affair with Bernard. Her (likely) feud with Rex.

I couldn't honestly fault Adrienne for disliking Rex, though. For my money, he was the front-runner in the who-might-be-murderous sweepstakes currently playing out in my head. He was desperate. And motivated. That meant he could have hurt Adrienne. Isabel, in contrast, seemed way too frivolous to plot anything more devious than snaring another choco-mosa. She'd been knocking back Bloody Marys at the memorial service, too. Not to mention choco-late martinis at the reception last night.

Maybe, it occurred to me, Isabel wasn't all *that* care-free. Most people didn't drink to excess for the sheer fun of it.

"You are surprised by my blunt talk?" she asked, watching me. For a second, she seemed completely sober. Also, beautiful. Not even rampant tipsiness could mar her modelesque good looks.

She and Rex Rader would have made stunning, vacuous babies together. They should have been a couple, not her and Bernard.

"Well," I hedged with a grin, "I wasn't expecting to get a hot-cocoa mud bath *and* juicy gossip. You caught me off guard."

"I have that effect on people," Isabel said. "I don't mind Bernie stepping out on me, because now *I'm* not obligated to be 100 percent faithful to him, either. Fair's fair." She gave me a mischievous wink. "I'm having a workout after this—my third in two days. Bernie thinks I'm training for a modeling comeback, but that's not it." She paused to drag one hand free from the mud. "Have you *seen* the personal trainer here?" She fanned herself, slopping mud all over the tile. And me. "He's *hot.*"

"Really?" I shook my head to dislodge a stubborn cocoa

clump. "I'll have to make an effort to shape up while I'm here."

"Right? Who doesn't like having a sexy man's hands all over them?" Isabel grinned. "It's important to have correct form."

"That's true." I glanced over at napping Poopsie, feeling my heart expand at the sight of that little dog. If I ditched my sole suitcase and carried only my duffel, I could bring a small pet carrier on my travels. "If *my* millionaire husband had an affair," I cracked, setting aside that idea for now, "I'd want a lot more than a dog in compensation, though. Even a cute one."

This time, Isabel looked surprised. Then she grinned.

"I just might get more," Isabel confided. "From Hank."

The resort's personal trainer, I surmised. *Hubba-hubba.*

"Now that I don't have any more *boring* 'getting to know you' games to do, that is," Isabel specified, rolling her eyes. "Ugh. That scavenger hunt yesterday was a real yawn!"

"I don't know," I joked. "You seemed to liven it up okay."

She laughed. "I'm trying to persuade Bernie that there's life outside Lemaître. I've almost cracked him."

I inhaled chocolate. "I thought Bernard was retired."

"He is," Isabel confirmed, "but the business still has first place in his heart. Just look at the way Bernie came running when Christian invited him to make an appearance at the retreat!" She accepted a fresh choco-mosa from Britney. "Bernie just can't quit. He *has* to have a hand in Lemaître Chocolates."

"That would make traveling tough," I agreed.

"Try impossible! I tried to persuade him to come with me on holiday to our palazzo on the Amalfi Coast last month, and he turned me down flat. I'm almost at the end of my rope."

I could understand that. "I *love* Italy," I told her.

That launched us, effortlessly, into a conversation about traveling. We bonded instantly over our shared love of being on the move. Neither of us understood homebodies; both of us were multilingual—Isabel *much* more so than me, of course. I've picked up a few bits and pieces over a nomadic lifetime. She'd attended the best schools in France, Switzerland, and "memorably" Greece, then spent almost a decade modeling in international locales.

If I wanted to continue nosing into part B of my resolution, I realized, I'd never have a better time than this.

"I feel bad talking about all these fun things, though, after what happened to Adrienne," I confessed truthfully. I looked away. "Do you really think she overdosed on something?"

"Maybe that green slop of hers was deadly," Isabel joked.

She seemed completely unbothered by the subject of her husband's (rumored) mistress. A little crass, too, to be honest. But that was almost refreshing. I looked at her more closely. I have to admit, I wanted Isabel to be innocent. I liked her.

"Maybe someone *made sure* her green juice was deadly."

"Yes!" She blinked at me, seemingly enthralled by the idea. "My money's on Rex Rader." Emphatically, Isabel nodded. "With Adrienne out of the way, he'd have a straight shot at Bernie."

That was unexpected. But if Rex wanted Bernard, didn't that mean he'd have to get *Isabel* out of the way? I was baffled.

That had been happening to me a lot lately. It wasn't fun.

"But Bernard's not gay," I protested. "Is he?"

Neither was Rex, as far as I knew. He certainly gave a convincing impression of being relentlessly into women only.

Isabel laughed. "Not *that* way!" Her amused gaze met mine. "I mean, now Bernie and Rex can rekindle their relationship. Not that I *want* them to. Not now, when I'm just making progress. If the two of them hook up again, I'll never get Bernie to retire!"

I paused. Maybe we were having a language-barrier issue. "I'm afraid that all sounds like one big euphemism to me."

It sounded, more accurately, as if Bernie and Rex were going to go hot and heavy the first second they had a chance.

"Oh, I forgot." Isabel sipped her choco-mosa. "You're new around here. You don't know all the history." She stretched her leg out of the hot-cocoa mud bath, then rotated her slender foot. I'd swear she admired it, too. For a good few minutes.

"The history?" I prodded. Well, wouldn't you?

"Bernie used to mentor Rex, back in the day," Isabel confided. "The two of them were as thick as thieves. Then Rex decided to strike out on his own, Christian came along and booted Bernie out, and everything fell apart." She pouted. "I'm sure Bernie met with Rex on the sly last night. I think he wants to bring him into Lemaître to re-place Adrienne. They *will* need a new head chocolatier im-mediately, and Rex *does* know all the ins and outs of Lemaître. But I want Bernie to *retire*! If he doesn't, I swear I'm going to have to do something *drastic*!"

Her overly dramatic tone rang alarm bells in my head. But frankly, my head was so full of new information just then that the warning barely registered. Bernard's former mentorship of Rex meant, I realized, that Rex would have had a good reason to get Adrienne out of the picture. If she was gone, he must have known he'd have a chance to return to Lemaître. With Melt on the skids, he might have wanted to, too. There was just one hiccup. . . .

"But Christian runs Lemaître now," I said.

"Bernie thinks he can win over his nephew by fixing

this new 'problem' for him." Isabel rolled her eyes. "Even dead, Adrienne is messing things up for me! I can't catch a break."

I guessed that meant Adrienne *had* been involved with Bernard. Isabel's lament was as good as an admission.

"Yes," I said. "Her death must be very difficult for you." I was being sarcastic. But Isabel didn't get it.

"It is!" she wailed. "I just want my Bernie back!"

But I'd already moved on. Because if Bernard saw Adrienne's death as a way to get on Christian's good side, that meant that I had to add *another* player to my roster of potential suspects: Bernard Lemaître. He was strong, motivated . . . and maybe ruthless?

Nah. I just couldn't believe it. It seemed more likely that Isabel *wasn't* as nonchalant as she seemed to be when it came to her philandering husband and his mistress. Could Isabel's blithe attitude be a front, after all? I glanced at her to decide.

She waved back, obviously blotto. She seemed *much* too drunk to scheme. On the other hand, I was apparently not the world's most perceptive observer. I'd actually bought into her and Bernard's lovey-dovey routine yesterday—hook, line, and sinker.

"So, you think Bernard and Rex were meeting last night?" I asked, careful to keep my tone light. Hoping to distract Isabel into letting down her guard, I made a move toward the tub's edge. "Where were you during all this? You weren't invited?"

Feeling stealthy, I tried to boost myself onto the edge of the tub. Coolly. The way a "good guy" cop would have done while interrogating a suspect. But the hot-cocoa mud was too slippery for the casual maneuver I had in mind. I slipped instead.

Helpfully, Isabel gave me a boost from behind. But she

pushed too hard. One minute, I was almost perched on the tub's edge. The next, I was flopping face-first onto the floor. Hard.

Ouch! Feeling my elbow and knee crack on the tiles, I grunted with pain. It radiated outward. I closed my eyes.

"Hayden!" Isabel yelped, sounding fuzzily contrite. "Are you okay? I'm so sorry! I didn't mean to push you so hard."

"That's okay." Gingerly, I got to my feet. The slick tiled floor was splattered with hot-cocoa mud—remnants of Isabel's exuberant European gestures earlier. If I wasn't careful, I'd take a header straight back into the tub. "I'm fine."

"I guess my workouts with Hank are working!"

"I guess so." Her helpful shove *had* felt surprisingly forceful. Ruefully, I studied the tub. "I think I've had enough hot-cocoa mud bath for one day, though. I'm going to clean up."

I still wanted to check with Britney or someone else at the spa café to find out what Adrienne had eaten and drunk there yesterday. Maybe I'd find something that *didn't* point the finger at someone employed in the chocolate industry. I hoped so.

"Well, we'll have to do this again sometime," Isabel said.

"I'd like that." We made arrangements to meet at the spa in a couple of days. Then, dripping hot-cocoa mud bath goop, I limped toward the shower stalls. Those rainfall showerheads and secondary water jets looked pretty good to me right about then.

It wasn't until I was already cleaned up and hobbling my way back across Maison Lemaître's grounds (my banged-up knee *really* hurt) that I realized . . . Isabel had never answered my last question. Where *had* she been last night when Adrienne had died?

With no other logical choice, I reluctantly bumped Isabel Lemaître a few notches higher on my list of potential murderous lunatics. For a lot of reasons, I have to say, Isabel could have done it.

The trouble now was . . . how to prove it?

How to prove any of it?

I was no good at subterfuge. My pratfall out of the hot-cocoa mud bath had demonstrated that. From here on out, I told myself, I'd do better just to be myself, with no pseudo "good cop" interrogation tactics to get in my way. Otherwise, I realized with a chill, *I* might be the next person getting an unwanted ride from Marin County to the morgue across the bay.

Chapter 7

I didn't come up with any answers right away. That's because even as I was limping along the path toward Maison Lemaître's main building, mentally devising an outfit for that evening's cocktail party, I heard someone shout my name.

I turned. Nina Wheeler emerged from a resort side door and headed toward me at a nervous trot, carrying her clipboard.

"I've been looking for you," she said. "I was worried!"

She looked it. Her face seemed even ghostlier than it had that morning. "You should go home, Nina," I blurted, unable to keep a note of concern from my voice. "It's been a long day."

Someone had to worry about *her,* after all. Besides, if Nina never saw her number-crunching CPA husband, how could we bond over figuring out how to deal with our mutual numbers guys?

I tried, but Travis wasn't the easiest guy to get close to. So far, he was the only person who'd ever resisted my charms. He'd revealed only the bare minimum of personal info to me—while having *all* the skinny on me, my plans, and my financial life.

It was driving me crazy. It had been for a while now. Ever since Travis had taken over for his stodgy predecessor.

"I'm fine!" Unconvincingly, Nina waved off my concerns. Her hand shook. She lowered her voice. "I just wanted to warn you to steer clear of Isabel Lemaître for the next day or two."

The hair on the back of my neck prickled. I swear it did.

"Why?" I asked. My voice *may* have squeaked a little.

I'm strong, but I'm not Wonder Woman. Given Adrienne's death, it seemed prudent not to tempt fate too hard.

"Isabel saw you and Bernard talking this morning." Nina leaned nearer, clutching her clipboard to her chest. Her anxious gaze probed mine in the waning daylight. "She confronted him when he came back to the patio for the brunch buffet."

"Confronted him?"

"Flipped out is more like it," Nina told me. "She'd already had a Bloody Mary or two by that point." I knew that much was true; I'd witnessed it myself. "And, well, you might have noticed that Isabel is *really* possessive about Bernard."

Confused, I angled my head. My own experience with Isabel contradicted that. Yet Nina was the second person to say so.

Who was I supposed to believe? I liked Isabel. But I liked Nina and Bernard, too. I couldn't make up my mind about anyone.

"I'd be wary if I were you," Nina went on somberly, making my mistrust seem reasonable. "*Especially* if Isabel thinks you're after Bernard. If you two run into each other before she has time to cool off, I'm afraid she might cause a scene."

Suddenly, it all made sense. I couldn't believe I'd overlooked the obvious. "You're worried about the retreat."

"Of course I am! Handling events like this is one of

my specialties." Nina's gaze softened. "But I'm worried about you, too. Speaking of which—what happened to you? Are you okay?"

Her gaze dropped to my knee. Britney had insisted on helpfully bandaging it for me . . . right after letting me know that Adrienne had had green tea, cacao-crusted salmon, and wakame salad with yuzu vinaigrette at the spa café yesterday.

"I'm fine." I decided a diversion was in order, before I was forced to admit I'd already run into Isabel Lemaître— and had a banged-up, bruised elbow to show for it, too. I'd really hit the tiled floor hard. "Are you going to the cocktail party?"

"Yes." Nina perked up. "Will Danny be there?"

"I don't know." It was the truth. It was also convenient. I didn't want to aid and abet my pal's potential philandering with a married woman—no matter how eager that woman was to join him. "I'm headed upstairs soon. I'll probably see him shortly."

"I saw him running on the ridge earlier." Nina hugged her clipboard, looking dreamy. She sighed. "He looked really . . . fit."

Then I *hadn't* imagined it. Danny *had* been exercising. On purpose. Just the way Travis (a marathon runner and swimmer) often did—only to have Danny razz him mercilessly about it.

This was going to be fun. I couldn't wait to see Danny.

"Oh yeah? Who looked fit?" Rex Rader jogged up, obviously having overheard the end of our conversation. "Huh? Who did?"

He panted and kept on jogging in place, looking expectantly from me to Nina and back again. I didn't know how he'd sneaked up on us. He wasn't exactly a diminutive guy. He was six feet tall and almost two hundred pounds, easily. He panted again.

"You did, Mr. Rader," Nina said smoothly. "Hayden and I were just here admiring your approach as you ran up to us."

Rex beamed. He puffed out his chest. "Really?"

No, not really, you nincompoop! I wanted to yell.

But Nina was far more tolerant than I was. "You have very impressive endurance. No wonder you're so successful."

Rex's formerly careworn expression vanished. He looked as though he might explode with glee. Nina was a miracle worker.

After his showdown with that reporter, I supposed, Rex probably needed a dose of positivity. But couldn't he have been just a *little* less icky in his approach? Just 10 percent or so?

Also, Nina was a much more skilled liar than I'd thought she was. That was surprising—until I realized that she probably felt she owed Rex one for cheering her up earlier. That made sense. Besides, wasn't PR one colossal con game, anyway? An ability to schmooze probably came with the clipboard.

Speaking of which . . . Nina consulted hers. "Well, I'm off to make sure the setup is done for the cocktail party! Bye now."

She waggled her fingers and headed off. Naturally enough, Rex ogled her as she did. He was really a beast. I didn't notice for a second, though. I was busy wondering . . . *if* Isabel really was the insanely possessive type—and she'd freaked out after learning Bernard had spoken to *me* earlier—could she have tried to get revenge on me just now? Had her "helpful" push been on purpose?

I shivered just thinking about it. So far, all signs pointed to someone possibly wanting Adrienne dead . . . not me. But that wasn't as reassuring as you might think. Especially since I now felt *more* clueless about all the maneuverings at Lemaître, rather than *less*. However you sliced it, one murderer on the loose was one murderer too many. I was starting to wish I'd skipped this industry powwow altogether. But I couldn't leave now. Not before I had a lot more answers than I did so far.

"So, hey, Hayden." Rex broke into my thoughts with a remarkably (for him) low-key voice. "About earlier . . ."

He had to mean the conversation I'd overheard. I didn't want to go into it. I felt embarrassed for him *and* for me.

I'd never eavesdropped in my life. What was wrong with me? The tragedy with Adrienne was making me do things I otherwise would never have done. Such as continue chatting with Rex.

"Forget it ever happened." I raised my palm, hoping he wouldn't argue. "I will, too. It's been a long, weird day."

"I meant earlier *yesterday*." His tone turned icy. "When I gave you my portfolio. I'm going to need that back. ASAP."

You guessed it. He actually pronounced "ASAP" like a word. He was back to smarmy again. "Need it back? Don't you have spares?"

"Not with me." Around us, the landscape lighting suddenly switched on, illuminating his face more clearly. He seemed . . . kind of menacing, to be honest. "Anyway, that's not the point. I want it back because I won't be asking you to consult for Melt anymore."

"You're withdrawing your request?" I was taken aback. Honestly, I was a little offended, too. What did it say about me if a lowlife like Rex didn't want me?

Hands on hips, he nodded. Sweatily and breathily.

Knowing Rex, he probably thought he was charming me.

"I've decided to go in another direction," he said.

I remembered Isabel's idea that Rex and Bernard were working on bringing Rex to Lemaître Chocolates. For all I knew, they were plotting to overthrow Christian—which would explain why Bernard hadn't seemed more bitter about being forced out.

He knew he'd be getting the last laugh. Nodding at Rex, I said, "You don't want any proof around that you approached me."

"That's about the size of it." He jogged again. "So?"

"So I don't have your portfolio with me at the moment."

He waggled his eyebrows. "We could go up to your room together. To retrieve it. *Together.*" More waggling. Gross.

"That won't be necessary." I paused, unable to resist stirring the pot. He *had* provoked me. Bad idea. "If you'd prefer, I could deliver your portfolio directly to Christian."

Rex narrowed his eyes. "Why would you do that?"

"Or Bernard?" I pressed, hoping to catch a telltale glimmer of guilt. Admittedly, I was living dangerously. I knew I ought to be wary of Rex, given what I knew about his possible homicidal tendencies toward Adrienne. But wariness was tricky to sustain when he was so cartoonishly over-the-top all the time. I couldn't help feeling that if Rex wanted to kill someone—and successfully pulled it off— he'd get caught. Because he'd feel compelled to brag about it afterward. "Would that be better?"

"I'm not following you," Rex said, frowning more deeply.

His confusion seemed genuine. That confused *me.* A lot.

Had Isabel been wrong (or lying) about Bernard's possible meeting with Rex? Or was Rex a lot smarter than I thought? Was he smart enough to cover his tracks until the deal was done?

Sure, Rex had (allegedly) threatened Adrienne . . . *if* the rumors about him were to be believed. (I still wanted to check on them myself.) I didn't trust secondhand information. But one careless threat didn't mean Rex had purposely overdosed Adrienne. Did it?

Feeling hungry and reckless, I decided to go for broke. You would think it would be impossible to be *starving* at a resort that specialized in chocolate, but I was. I needed chow. Stat.

I was going to have to settle for answers, though.

"I just thought you might be planning to use your portfolio as a résumé." I shrugged, watching Rex closely. "In case you wanted to go for Adrienne's old job at Lemaître Chocolates."

"Why would I do that? I have my own company to run."

If he was hiding a secret scheme, he was very good at it.

"Because Melt is in trouble," I said. "Otherwise—"

"Who told you Melt is 'in trouble'?"

His sharp tone rattled me. "You did. By trying to hire *me*. I'm a troubleshooter." Everyone knew that. "I fix problems—"

"*And* innovate," Rex interrupted, noticeably short on patience. "I came to you because I want to keep Melt on the cutting edge of chocolate, not because I need damage control."

I didn't believe him. The evidence didn't add up. "Okay, well . . ." That still didn't explain why he'd declined my services. "How has that changed in the past twenty-four hours?"

"I don't have to explain myself to you." Rex jerked up his chin, deliberately staring down at me. I'm not small by any stretch, but his stance made me feel petite. Plus, threatened.

Surrendering, I held up my palms. "You're right. You don't. It's none of my business. I'll return your portfolio. Consider it done." *Right after I have a thorough look at it.* "Okay?"

Rex gave a grudging nod. Then: "You're sexy when you're feisty."

Ugh. Evidently, *nothing* dampened Rex's libido. If his hypothetical killer impulses were half as strong as his sex drive was, Rex would be the most go-get-'em murderer *ever.*

On that thought, I decided to dash. The breeze from the Marin Headlands had turned brisk, ruffling the white blossoms on the nearby Callery pear trees and raising goose bumps on me. I'd left my cardigan in my room before heading to the spa, but now I regretted that decision. That was northern California weather for you—as changeable as the many moods of Rex Rader.

"Just rein it in, Rex. It's *never* happening between us."

Before he could argue, I gave him a head shake and turned back to the path, headed toward Maison Lemaître's lobby. If Bernard intercepted me halfway there, I realized wryly, I'd be four-for-four in running into my theoretical suspects today.

I hoped that didn't happen. *Me* plus *low blood sugar* plus *too many murder theories* equaled *one seriously sour attitude.* If anyone came between me and the boost I intended to get from raiding the all-chocolate happy-hour spread that Lemaître put out every day in the lobby bar, things were liable to get ugly.

In the end, not surprisingly, Bernard *did* show up to waylay me. But he waited until I had a glass of ruby port and a plateful of chocolate-themed tapas in hand, so the situation wasn't as unpleasant as it could have been. Embarrassingly, though, I'd just shoved an entire diminutive sourdough crostini (topped with melted chocolate, a sprinkle of crunchy *fleur de sel,* and a fruity drizzle of Paso

Robles olive oil) into my mouth. So the timing could have been better overall.

That crostini was *delicious,* though.

"Hayden!" The chocolate patriarch surprised me as I slid into a comfy, high-sided leather banquette, chewing while balancing my plate. "You're just the person I wanted to see."

I couldn't imagine why that would be. We hadn't exactly left things on the most gracious footing that morning. That was my fault, though. I'd overstepped. Wishing I didn't have chipmunk cheeks stuffed with crostini, I nodded at Bernard.

For lack of a verbal greeting, I patted the banquette, inviting him to join me in my secluded, dimly lit corner of the crowded lobby bar. I'm no fool. Being on friendly terms with the man who'd made artisanal chocolate a household essential (breaking Hershey's nearly century-long stranglehold on the hearts and palates of Americans) could only be good for me.

Besides, I liked Bernard. Even knowing he was an adulterer and possible conspirator with Rex, I did. Because I *didn't* like Christian. Anything that upset his apple cart was okay with me.

Besides, I had to acknowledge, being married to a high-maintenance type like Isabel probably wasn't a walk in the park. If Bernard had gotten intimate with Adrienne, it would be understandable. My chocolatier buddy had been warm, intelligent, and overwhelmingly giving. Those weren't Isabel's high points.

Not that I'm excusing infidelity. I'm not. Let's just say I was relaxing my ordinarily high standards (see my three ex-fiancés for more details) when it came to Bernard and Adrienne.

With a heavy exhalation, Bernard joined me. In fact, he all but cornered me between him and the wall. With the high tufted back of the banquette on the other side, we were *very* cozy.

The hubbub of the bar washed comfortingly over me as I chewed madly, finishing the last of my crostini. I liked being in the midst of things, yet apart. I guess I'm an observer at heart—one who was currently being squished by Bernard's butt.

Subtly, I wiggled to make room for myself. No dice.

Well, he probably wouldn't linger. Not if doing so would mean incurring the wrath of Isabel. From all indications, the grapevine was alive and well at the retreat. She'd find out.

"So, how are things coming along with the police?" Bernard asked me, eyeing my overstuffed plate of tapas. "Did they locate Adrienne's next of kin yet? Do they have leads on her death?"

Befuddled, I stared at him. He stared back, his kindly expression firmly intact. His eyes looked a little hazy, though.

Was Bernard . . . *senile*? He seemed to have confused me and Nina. She was the one who'd been dealing with the police, with all the details, with collecting Adrienne's personal effects. Not me.

I didn't want to embarrass Bernard. So I shook my head. "Not yet." I was going to hell for misleading him. "Sorry."

I swilled a mouthful of my port, then bit into a sizzling bite of *patatas bravas*—served in this instance with a fiery chocolate mole sauce—while surreptitiously examining Bernard.

If he *was* suffering from some mild form of dementia, it occurred to me, his being forced out of Lemaître made a lot more sense. So did Isabel's joke about Bernard needing erectile dysfunction medication. Maybe I'd been too harsh on Christian.

Nah. That was impossible. Christian was a tool.

"It was a lovely memorial this morning," Bernard went on. Tears glimmered in his eyes. With an unsteady hand, he brushed them away. He sighed. "Poor Adrienne. I'm going to miss her."

"I am, too." I felt awful for him. I touched his hand.

It felt papery with wrinkles. But strong. He clutched me.

He clutched me a little too hard, in fact. Confused, I tried to pull away. But Bernard held fast. What the hell?

"Don't let your feelings get the better of you, though, Hayden," he said in a clear, rumbling voice. His hand squeezed painfully on mine. "Nothing good can come of that. *Nothing.*"

Was Bernard *warning* me? Disturbed, I pulled away.

"I'm *not* going to just forget Adrienne," I told him.

Maybe it was the port I'd swigged. Or maybe I was just being stupid. But I didn't want to back down. Not about this.

My friend deserved better than that.

"Everybody has to forget sometime!" Bernard announced cheerfully. Then, ominously, "The sooner, the better, in your case." He nodded at my plate. "Try the *alfajor de chocolate* next," he advised. "Adding bittersweet chocolate to Argentinian *dulce de leche*"—Bernard kissed his fingers—*"exquisito!"*

Then he chuckled and slid out of my banquette. He was gone before I could be sure I hadn't imagined him. My still-aching fingers were a reminder that Bernard's threat had been real, though. If he *had* been warning me to quit asking around about Adrienne's death . . . well, it would fit right in with the way he'd gone all frosty on me this morning when I'd asked if he'd had a few final moments with his former mistress. On the other hand . . .

Bernard had seemed convinced, for a moment there, that I'd been *Nina.* So maybe his grasp on current events wasn't quite as razor sharp as it should have been. Plus, I'd glugged at least half a glass of fortified port while filling my tapas plate.

I wasn't the most reliable judge of lucidity just then. *Me,* plus *a peculiar day,* plus *high-proof port on an empty stomach* . . .

Deciding that being safe was better than being sorry, I finished my port, spooned up my thimble-size portion of rye-infused chocolate *pots de crème,* then reached for my cookie.

It was the *alfajor de chocolate*—the chocolate-covered double-decker treat sandwiched with burnt caramel—that Bernard had recommended. While an upscale Oreo probably wouldn't kill me, in light of recent events, I opted to skip it.

If I was imagining the threatening look in Bernard's eyes, I was going to regret passing up that *alfajor,* I knew. I'd done some consulting with Maison Lemaître's head pastry chef as part of my assignment; I knew she was incredibly skilled. But thirty minutes later—after chatting with a few more retreat attendees as I left the lobby bar—I was back in my hotel room and too busy getting ready for the cocktail party to get too caught up in missed opportunities . . . even one-of-a-kind chocolate-themed ones.

I was flipping through Adrienne's handwritten notebook, rubbing my fingers over chocolate splatters and trying not to think too hard about missing the woman who'd made them, when someone knocked on my door. With a twitch, I looked that way.

My blood pressure skyrocketed. I told myself the jumpiness I was feeling was only excitement, then marched to the door.

When I opened it, Danny scowled at me. "At least look

through the peephole next time, dummy. Do you *want* to get strangled? Knifed? Beaten? Shot? Pushed out the window?"

"Your imagination is terrifying." I stepped aside as my broad-shouldered friend strode in. His warning jolted me, though. Ordinarily, as a woman traveling solo, I was a *lot* more cautious than this. I shut the door, taking absurd comfort in its solid autolocking *clunk.* "I knew it was you, Paranoid Pete."

"It's not paranoia when people are dropping dead."

"One person." As distressing as that was. "Not me."

"That's because *I'm* watching over you." Danny prowled the corners of my deluxe room. He nudged aside cast-off clothing choices (basically my whole fits-in-a-suitcase wardrobe, which I'd been mixing and matching), peeked under the bed, looked out the window, and checked the armoire. I thought he might nose into Adrienne's notebook, which I'd left conspicuously open on the pillow-piled bed, but he didn't. "You're a slob, Hayden."

That was it. No concerned "Are you okay?" or "Did Bernard Lemaître just go cuckoo and possibly threaten you?" Just "You're a slob, Hayden." As if I didn't know that already. As far as I'm concerned, a certain amount of clutter makes impersonal spaces (like hotel rooms, train compartments, and yurts) feel personal.

"Nice to see you, too." There was no time like the present for a little tit for tat. "Did you have a nice workout?"

Danny's gung ho *Booya!* attitude ground to a halt. I could have sworn a flush climbed his cheeks. His nonstop beard stubble made it hard to tell. As far as I knew, he never got flustered.

Just then, I was on a mission to change that. Dressed up in my flat strappy sandals, bare legs, my ex's silk button-up shirt partnered with a chunky belt (which officially made it double as a breezy minidress, in my book) plus a tangle of silvery chains sparkling at my décolletage, I kept at him. "I knew your fast getaway at brunch seemed suspicious this morning." I could barely keep up my (admittedly nonexistent) poker face as I added mildly, "Who knew you were aching to feel the burn?"

My reference to Danny's physical exertion made him groan. He paced, never content (like me) to stay in one place too long.

"I 'got away' at brunch so you could network," he said.

"Nice try. But I can network with *you* present."

"I figured Nina would open up to you more alone."

"That's very generous of you. Pump any iron lately?"

I had no intention of letting this slide. Not after the hard time Danny had given Travis about his "health freak" ways.

Privately, I enjoyed thinking about Travis getting his workout on. I might have never met my financial advisor in person, but that hadn't stopped me from imagining the way he'd look, all slick and muscular from the pool. With a calculator.

What can I say? My imagination has its quirks.

"I knew you'd do this," Danny complained. "*That's* why I didn't tell you." With a grin, he gestured at his rugged build. "You didn't think all *this* happened by accident, did you?"

"I thought it happened courtesy of beer and hot wings," I deadpanned. "Apparently not. That was just your cover story."

"Okay, you've had your fun. Just let up, okay?"

As if *that* was going to happen. I had him on the ropes now.

"Maybe it's something in the water around here," I mused, pretending to consider it. "I saw Rex running earlier, too."

"Not on the ridge, I hope." Danny surprised me by

speaking seriously. "I doubt he's got the stamina and agility to navigate that rocky path. One wrong step, and it's a long way down."

"Right. Just because he's not *you,* he's a crash test dummy waiting to happen? He's not that much of a buffoon."

Except he was. *What was I doing? Defending Rex?* This had gone too far. I outfitted a clutch with necessities from my trusty crossbody bag, intent on finishing my prep for the party.

"I mean it," Danny insisted. "Maison Lemaître ought to fence off those bluffs. Or at least post warning signs."

"Spoken like a true security expert." I primped. "I didn't think resort liability issues were your area of expertise."

"There are things," Danny said, "you don't know about me."

I wanted to keep needling him about "feeling the burn." But that was too good an opening to pass up. "Such as why you were late getting here? Why was that, anyway? Care to share?"

"Nope."

"Let's give it a go, anyway."

"Fine." Danny eyed me with reluctance. He turned his back to me, looking out at the enviable view. "One of my buddies was just paroled. I'm letting him crash at my place. He got held up, so I caught a later plane. Now I'm here. End of story."

"Danny!" I protested, having visions of him coming home to an empty apartment—one devoid of pawnworthy TVs and accessible cash. "You told me you were going to quit hanging around those people!"

"'Those people' are my friends." His face looked stormy as he turned again. "Just like you are. I like problem cases."

His knowing grin as he added that last bit put me on

edge. *I* wasn't a problem case. Not when it came to him, at least.

"But now that you know about that," he added before I could set him straight, "I might as well tell you about Rex Rader."

I was duly baited and switched. "What about Rex Rader?"

"Well, you know how I found his wallet yesterday?"

I bit my tongue so hard, I could have added a DIY dumbbell piercing and called it a day. Not that I don't have a piercing or two. I do. But I'm certainly not telling you where they are.

"I asked one of 'those people' to run financials on Rex."

I knew what he was saying. Danny had used his underground connections to find out more about Rex Rader. He'd leveraged the contents of Rex's stolen wallet to investigate the Melt CEO.

"You shouldn't have done that," I told him.

"Why? Because you were going to ask Travis to do it?" Danny shook his head, typically cocksure. "My way is faster."

I shouldn't have endorsed his tactics. Not even obliquely. But I just couldn't help it. "What did you find out?"

"That Melt is going down fast. That Rex is up to his manscaped eyebrows in personal debt. That he *needs* a fix."

"That fix was supposed to be me, I thought." I told Danny about my run-in with Rex, then gave him a roundup of the day's events. Bernard, Christian, Isabel, Rex, Bernard *again* . . . all of it. I needed to get it all out with someone I trusted. "I had no idea there were so many things going on behind the scenes here."

"Every place has its conspiracies." Danny didn't seem daunted. In contrast, everything sounded twice as unbelievable to me. "Usually, money is at the root of everything."

"I have to involve Travis, then! He'll know what to—"

Do, I meant to say, but Danny cut me off before I could.

"You can't." His voice was rough. Suddenly, he looked *really* intense. "If you do that, you know what he'll do."

"Find out more details for me? *Legally?* Ooh, scary."

"He'll pressure you to settle down. To be safe"—Danny made scornful air quotes around the word—"*his* way. You'd hate that."

I didn't say so, but a teeny-tiny part of me—the part that yearned for an Irish setter and a place to keep doggie chew toys for more than a month at a time—actually kinda *liked* the idea of settling down. But that was impossible. So it didn't merit thinking about. Wanting distraction, I shrugged. I grabbed the Maison Lemaître body lotion from nearby, propped my foot on the upholstered divan, and smoothed some on. *Hmm.* I still needed to pitch Christian about refining the formula. The whole "orange Kool-Aid meets Yoo-hoo" vibe was a turnoff in toiletries.

I caught Danny watching me and stopped short. Too late, I realized I'd hiked up my shirtdress to a nearly indecent degree. I'd known Danny so long that sometimes I forgot he wasn't one of my girlfriends getting ready for a ladies' night out with me.

"At least no one wants to off me so far." I laughed, then rubbed the remaining lotion onto my hands. "No enemies here."

Danny appeared skeptical. "Are you sure? Think harder."

"Hey! Are you insinuating that I'm an airhead?"

"No. But *you* don't specialize in eradicating risk. *I* do. The first step is always reconnaissance, so let's go deeper."

He wouldn't be satisfied until I cooperated. So I did.

"Okay. Well, I *do* sometimes meet a few unsavory characters during my consulting gigs," I admitted. "Occasionally, I'm offered a bribe to wreck a competitor's product line. Sometimes I refuse to work with someone, and they get touchy about it."

"'Touchy'?" Danny gave a formidable frown. "*Touchy,* how?"

I shrugged. "Raised voices, maybe. That's all. I keep a low profile, remember? I'm good at smoothing things over before they get out of hand. Believe me, I'm aware of the fact that by helping some companies, I might inadvertently hurt others. It's business. It's occasionally pretty cutthroat." My gaze dropped to Adrienne's notebook. I wondered who she'd been selling secrets to. "It's not just cocoa beans and conching machines. There's creativity involved in chocolate making, too. It won't be easy to replace someone like Adrienne. She was talented."

"Then her notebook is valuable?" Danny inferred.

I nodded. "To the right people, it is. You'd have to know how to use it." I thought about the notes and formulas inside, some of which had been revelatory even to me. "But if you did, you'd be willing to do a lot to get ahold of it, for sure. It would be the next best thing to having Adrienne on payroll."

I still didn't know how I was going to delay giving it to Christian. As Adrienne's employer, he had a legitimate claim on her work. But going against her wishes rubbed me the wrong way.

"Then I could sell that thing"—Danny nodded dubiously at Adrienne's chocolate-smudged notebook—"for big bucks?"

"Theoretically, sure. But that doesn't explain where *I* come in." Except that Adrienne had given it to me. "Or why someone would want to kill her. Except maybe to avoid paying Adrienne her asking price for it?" I sighed. "Maybe I'm blowing all this out of proportion," I told Danny. "Maybe it's nothing."

"Do you feel like it's nothing?"

Reluctantly, I shook my head.

"Then it's probably not nothing."

I sighed. "Let's just go to the party and forget about it."

But Danny was having none of that. Not yet.

"Soon," he promised. "But first . . . let's go over this again."

He'd always been slightly more disciplined than I was. In this case, that was probably a good thing. For my own well-being.

Together, we ran through what we knew so far. We knew that Adrienne had had a fling with Bernard. That she'd (reportedly) been selling secrets. That Christian had wanted to make her pay for her sabotage and/or had accidentally "hurried" her chocolate making too aggressively. That Bernard was either doddering or evil or (maybe) both at once. That Isabel was either maniacally possessive or totally carefree, my ideal travel buddy or my pushiest (literally) spa-going nightmare. We knew that Rex Rader had a lot to gain from Adrienne's death . . . and that he'd lied about Melt being prosperous. (I trusted Danny's source more than Rex.)

Just then, my money was on Rex being the most murderous.

"I'm not sure this helps," I admitted after our impromptu analysis was finished, "but I do feel better sharing with you."

"Yeah. I knew you would." Danny gave me a look that recalled all our barhopping days, our nights discovering indie bands, our longtime friendship, and our sometimes precarious efforts to keep that friendship (mostly) platonic. We were only human. For a while, we'd been too clueless to take reasonable precautions. "You'll feel even better after you hire my security services," he said next. "I'm not budging till you do."

I laughed. "Come on, Danny. I'm fine. Really!"

"You're wealthy enough that my salary won't make a dent."

Uncomfortably, I realized that was true. It would have been churlish of me to argue with him—and stupid of me to refuse. People paid big bucks for Danny's freelance security expertise. He'd dropped everything to attend the chocolate retreat with me. I owed him. We were both cognizant of the background details.

I nodded. Once. That's it. And that's how Danny Jamieson became my official (off-the-record) bodyguard. For the moment.

With that decision, I ran out of reasons not to look into Adrienne's untimely death. For better or worse, I realized as we finally headed downstairs to the cocktail party, I was committed to investigating further. But at least Danny would have my back while I did—just in case *I* was the one who'd been meant to die.

Chapter 8

When I tell you I was blindfolded, you're going to think I was up to something perverted. When I add that I was being watched by hundreds of people while blindfolded, you're going to think I was doing something *really* deviant. When I specify that *all* my senses were intimately involved in that activity . . . well, let's just end the analogy right there. This wasn't *Fifty Shades of Grey* territory, and I wasn't doing anything remotely shady.

Instead, I was appearing as an expert panelist on Lemaître Chocolates' "Name That Chocolate!" It was a game-show-inspired session that had been planned by Nina, cunningly designed to highlight all the most self-aggrandizing chocolatiers present.

Oh, and *me,* too. I was appearing among them.

I'm not much for self-promotion. I can't be. The name of my game is discretion. I can't very well shout from the rooftops about the famous chocolate companies, restaurants, and fine-food purveyors that have had their big-time goofs corrected by me. That would be a recipe for nonreferrals. Mostly, I do my job and then keep my mouth shut, trusting word to get out when it needs to.

It works, too. That's why you won't see me taking out

ads in trade press outlets or (God forbid) Tweeting about my know-how to any schmo who'll listen. I don't have to. One way or another, people who need my help find a way to throw out a Bat-Signal, then I come and magically make everything better.

Today, though, Nina had begged me to join the panel. Armed with both her phones, a headset, and *two* fresh clipboards, she'd cornered me after a tasty breakfast of cocoa-hazelnut granola and a gallon of coffee (these early mornings were killers, no pun intended) and applied her best PR mojo to the task. Not that any persuasive machinations were necessary. I'd taken one look at Nina's noticeable new (and unfortunate) stress-related eye twitch and agreed to get my taste test on for the public.

The whole endeavor had two parts. First, a chocolate tasting featuring multiple rounds, with one panelist being eliminated after each round. Second, a wagering component that enabled retreat attendees to "sponsor" the panelist of their choice. The whole endeavor was meant to funnel donations toward Bernard Lemaître's culinary arts charity—which I still refused to believe was a tax dodge. There were several disadvantaged high-school students in attendance at Maison Lemaître to enjoy the spectacle. I'd spoken with a few of them beforehand. They'd impressed me with their diligence, curiosity, and enthusiasm.

I wished I could say the same thing for my fellow panelists. Six rounds in—*sans* blindfold now—I was feeling the pressure. Not because anyone intimidated me—just because no one else seemed to be taking the job at hand very seriously (so far). Didn't they realize there were donations at stake? *Kids' futures?*

With my footloose ways, I'd probably never have any kids of my own. So I did my best to buckle down on behalf of everyone.

The accoutrements of each round were a nameplate

(mine read HAYDEN MANDY MORE, a classic but typical gaffe), a glass of room-temperature sparkling springwater (it couldn't be cold, or it would obliterate the temperature-sensitive qualities of the cacao), and a stack of bland, palate-cleansing water crackers.

You might think that tasting chocolate is a dream job. You wouldn't be far off. When I'm focused on a nice French *mendiant* studded with dried figs and almonds or a plain *tablette* of 73 percent dark bittersweet, my monkey mind finally shuts up. Everything falls away. All that exists is me and the *Theobroma cacao.*

Tasting chocolate—even publicly—is the closest I ever come to achieving nirvana . . . at least outside of the bedroom, that is. It's the only time I'm not thinking about *anything* else.

I was looking forward to shutting out the crowd and getting in the groove as the next volunteer charity student made his way down the panelists' table, carefully distributing silver-domed trays of chocolate samples—each of which had been donated by a different company or artisan. I transferred my attention from the thronged ballroom to the shiny challenge in front of me.

Already, we'd been through simple *carrés*—bite-size squares—of varietal chocolates, which presented minimal challenge to a knowledgeable taster. Now we'd progressed to truffles. They were more complex and subsequently harder to evaluate. A hush fell over the retreat attendees as we prepared to do exactly that.

Nearby, Rex's (least favorite) reporter did a roadie walk toward the stage. Partially hunched, she snapped a flash photo.

Apparently, our antics were being documented for *Chocolat Monthly.* I hoped my hair looked good. At least I wasn't wearing chef's whites and a pair of kitchen clogs. My navy wrap dress was crushable, packable, hand-washable, *and* reasonably chic.

"All right, panelists! Get ready!" Nina strode the length of the panel, acting as volunteer emcee. Her clip-on mic made her voice boom through the ballroom. "Time for another round!"

I'd be lying if I said anticipation didn't buzz through the place. Everyone on the panel was a professional. Screwing up would make any of us look bad. I wanted to ace this.

I glanced sideways. Remaining on the panel with me were Rex Rader, a rep from Torrance Chocolates, someone from a cocoa bean supply company, and Christian. (That's right—just as with the scavenger hunt, he'd joined his own challenge.) The five of us were instructed to lift the silver domes of our samples.

As I did, the lush scent of chocolate struck me. Hard. I knew better than to be seduced right away. There was a protocol here, starting with evaluating the chocolate's appearance. It needed to exhibit a shiny gloss, which indicated good tempering. It needed to display a nice color—although contrary to popular belief, darker chocolate isn't necessarily better; some very good cacao beans are quite pale. If it was a bar (or slender French *bâton*) of chocolate, it needed to demonstrate a clean snap when broken in half, with no discernible bending or crumbling. That meant the sample had a proper cacao content.

After I'd evaluated the appearance and snap, *then* it was finally time to contemplate the aroma. It's always seductive, but it's never simple. Not for me. Whether in a varietal or a cuvée, it should be possible to pick up notes ranging from floral to fruity, smoky to spicy, malty to earthy to herbaceous.

Just like wine, each chocolate carries a unique fingerprint. Fortunately for me, I'd learned to ID several.

Today I was under the microscope. That meant I wanted

to really excel. So while my fellow panelists bit right into their samples, trying to beat the game clock, I picked up my knife and carefully bisected the truffle I'd been given. I studied it. With bars, it's possible to evaluate the chocolate's grain—the pattern of crystallization that develops among the components of cocoa butter, cocoa liquor, and (sometimes) sugar. With truffles, though, the chocolate coating isn't thick enough for such intricacies. All I wanted to do was release more aroma.

Inhaling it (but not necessarily expecting to taste its constituents in the finished truffle), I cut off a diminutive bite. I let it melt on my tongue, checking that it liquefied appropriately. Some of the chocolates we'd tried had tasted flat—probably due to an omission of vanilla, misguidedly intended to enhance the chocolate's bitter notes—but this one didn't. It melted like a dream, tasting of berries and spice.

In that melting bite, I experienced the stars of the show: mouthfeel and taste. Playing it safe, I chewed my next bite. The flavor was complex, the aftertaste clean, the finish long.

You may have had chocolate that's waxy, gritty, or grainy. That means it's cheap, old, or both. This truffle was neither.

I punched my buzzer. (Yes, we each had one; however cheesy, it was all for the sake of charity.) "Cacao from Colombia. The Chucureno region. Light roast." That made it trickier. "With a filling of lime-infused ganache lightened with *cajeta.*"

Nina's eyes lit up. "Right again, Hayden!"

The other panelists groaned. Have I mentioned that this was a timed session? Whoever got the right answer first won the round—and kept the attendees who'd sponsored them paying up.

I was safe again. The same couldn't be said for Rex,

though, who—according to the rules—was eliminated. He had the fewest sponsors paying for him, *and* he hadn't identified the chocolate sample in time. He tossed me a hostile look, then took a seat in the audience. I felt his animosity radiating toward me.

With only four of us remaining, the audience's interest was increasing. Another of the volunteer students circulated among them with labeled and branded promotional samples of curry and basil truffles from a New York confectioner, each enrobed with a hand-ground mortar-and-pestle bittersweet couverture. I saw Danny shake his head to (unbelievably) pass on one. Cretin.

Catching me watching, he made a face. I noticed he was seated next to the *Chocolat Monthly* reporter. She'd angled her whole body toward Danny with interest. If he wanted, he could really clean up at the retreat. First Nina, now . . . I really needed to learn the name of Rex's nemesis. Maybe after the panel.

First, there was another sample to taste. Nina amped up the attendees' enthusiasm with an anecdote about Point Reyes—a scenic area nearby—encouraging them to visit after the retreat was finished. (I wondered if the California tourism board had sponsored her emceeing gig.) While we panelists chewed unsalted crackers and sipped sparkling water to prepare, more silver-domed trays emerged from the ballroom kitchen. My mouth watered.

I lifted my tray's dome. Greeting me, atop a paper doily, was another chocolate truffle. Its surface was milky brown, dusted with vibrant, almost neon green particles. Its interior, when I cut into it, looked like vanilla cream. I knew it wasn't.

At an event like this one, nobody was trotting out a sample that could have been crafted at an old-timey seaside candy shop.

While I was still tasting, the supplier smacked her buzzer.

"I'm detecting . . . tangerine!" she said, nearly on her feet with zeal. "Hints of cedar . . . raw sugar . . . it's Ecuadorian cacao!"

Nina shook her head. Automatically, so did I.

"Venezuelan," I identified, "from the Sur del Lago region. Another light roast." I gave her a sympathetic look. "The matcha dusting and Camembert filling are probably throwing you off."

I felt rushed making the assessment, but the retreat attendees were impressed, anyway. An approving murmur swept the ballroom. I don't often receive public recognition for my work, so I appreciated the approval—until the cocoa bean supplier shot me a disgruntled glance and left the stage. If looks could kill, I'd have been to the pearly gates and back again twice today.

I hadn't come here to make enemies. Couldn't they all just lighten up? I was only serving on the panel as a favor to Nina; I hadn't even had time to collect more than a few token sponsorships beforehand (including one from Danny). Plus, I couldn't help being good at my job. I have a talent for cacao, sure. But it's not as if I can do something *really* crucial, like perform successful brain surgery or pilot a Boeing 747-400.

You've probably guessed by this point that chocolate-industry types can be somewhat tantrum prone. That person in your office who just can't let go of the fact that someone else ate the last "everything" bagel or didn't chip in for the coffee fund? That person would have been celebrated for their "vision" and "attention to detail" in my biz. Creative pursuits tend to reward idiosyncrasies and encourage prima donna behavior. In the world of chocolate, "difficult" is a synonym for "talented."

A subsequent (and straightforward) round of chocolates

paired with liquor knocked out the rep from Torrance Chocolates. Felled by the palate-confusing (but orgasmic) combo of single-malt finish rum plus litchi truffle—which we three dutifully sipped, bit, sipped, and chewed—she left the panel, too.

At least she didn't shoot me daggers on her way. She gave me a bubbly thumbs-up before taking her place in the audience.

It was down to me . . . and Christian Lemaître. Seated *way* down the panelist's table from me, he frowned and cracked his neck like a boxer in the ring. *Oh, brother.* Wanting this over with, I watched the next volunteer student distribute silver-domed samples to us both. No one in the room needed either of the stimulants—theobromine and caffeine—that were naturally present in cacao beans to perk up for the final round. It was *on*.

Refraining from delivering a few *Rocky* air punches, I found Danny in the crowd. I grinned at him. He gave me a somber nod. That grounded me. With a start, I remembered everything that had been going on. Danny probably thought I'd be sniper shot if I won the tasting. He might not be far wrong, either.

But I wanted to win anyway. I *know* I've told you how competitive I am. Plus, once my chocolate sample was unveiled, I forgot anything else existed. All there was, for me, was cacao.

I took my time, examining the sample's appearance, aroma, snap, and mouthfeel. I'd just started on its taste when Christian yelped beside me. He slammed his hand on his buzzer.

"Trinitario beans!" he shouted. "Likely sourced from Venezuela, with Tahitian vanilla and crushed cacao nib filling."

He shot me a triumphant glance. The crowd applauded.

A few people even started gathering their things for the next session.

I held back, though, even as Nina turned expectantly.

"Hayden, if Christian is right, you're eliminated. You don't have enough sponsors to tie the round. But if you—"

"I'm right!" her boss crowed. "This one's easy."

"—*do* have the correct answer," Nina rushed to say, "and Christian doesn't, you'll win the round and the tasting, bringing your sponsors and their donations with you. Well?"

I drew in a deep breath, considering. If Christian was a secret murderer, I probably didn't want to antagonize him.

On the other hand, competitiveness isn't easily squashed. There was no way I was taking a dive. It just wasn't in me.

"Criollo beans," I disagreed, "with a medium roast." I don't know *how* I can detect these specifics. I just know that I can. "Likely sourced from Madagascar. The vodka fragrance and woody notes—the hint of spice and cedar— give it away."

I didn't dare look at Christian. He was probably seething.

At least he was . . . if I was right. I knew I was.

"But the filling—that's the tricky part," I went on. I pointed at it. "Modern palates identify that texture as cacao nibs, but I've got to say . . ." I paused to take another nibble.

"She's cheating!" Christian fumed. "That's cheating!"

". . . *that* tastes like good old-fashioned praline to me." I smiled. "In a world full of habanero-guava chocolate bars and wood-smoke-infused salted ganache, that's . . . perfectly delicious."

Bernard stood amid the crowd. "You're damn right it is!" he yelled, pointing at my truffle. "That's *tradition*, right there!"

Taken aback, I glanced again at the truffle I'd neatly sliced in two. Yep. If you paired those halves and then studied the squiggly swirl on top, it formed a distinctive letter *L.*

Christian had failed to identify a Lemaître Chocolate— one that Bernard had apparently entered in the tasting on the sly.

The crowd realized what had happened at the same time I did. A rumble swept through the attendees. Isabel gave Bernard a forcible yank back into his chair, then gave me an apologetic shrug. She seemed at a loss to explain her husband's outburst. If Bernard had planned this, he hadn't included his wife.

Bernard himself seemed as pleased as punch. He sat there beside Isabel, looking giddy, not talking to anyone. I have to say, his behavior only made it appear more likely that he was suffering from some form of cognitive deterioration. Either that or he really wanted to stick it to his nephew. Publicly.

If getting revenge on Christian was Bernard's goal, though, this stunt was small potatoes. Retaking his own company was going to be the most effective tactic. Maybe, I mused, with Rex's underhanded assistance, Bernard meant to do both?

Glancing at Rex's unreadable face, I simply couldn't tell—not even when Rex got to his feet and left the ballroom. He might have wanted to celebrate Bernard's coup in private. Or he might have been annoyed that Bernard had embarrassed Christian.

For all I knew, Isabel was wrong, and Rex was scheming with Christian, instead of Bernard. I would have believed either.

For that matter, Adrienne could have been partnering with Bernard to sabotage Christian . . . and somehow Christian had found out—hence his (brief) tirade to me about Adrienne yesterday.

Danny believed that Adrienne had probably been selling secrets to Melt. But he hadn't known Adrienne as well as I had. I couldn't see her conspiring with Rex.

"I'm sorry, Mr. Lemaître," Nina told Christian in a newly subdued voice. "Hayden is right. I'm afraid you're eliminated."

As far as I was concerned, we both should have been able to identify that chocolate—even to distinguish it from its purer-bred Venezuelan Porcelana strain, which delivered heady (but very different) aromas of butter, strawberries, and cream.

Trying to put aside the tasting now that it was finished, I got up to shake Christian's hand. "Nice job," I said. "I'm sure you garnered more sponsorship votes, anyway, so everyone wins."

At least they would, if he did the right thing and channeled all the donations into Bernard's culinary charity.

Christian didn't see things quite so prosaically. He pointedly ignored my outstretched hand. He humphed, then ripped off his clipped-on mic. "Nobody likes a show-off. *Nobody.*"

Was Christian kidding me? After all the showboating he'd done, now he had the nerve to lecture *me* about hamming it up?

I considered apologizing—just for my business's sake—but Christian stormed off before I could. Left stranded on the panel with a befuddled teenage culinary student and Nina, I smiled.

It would take more than Christian Lemaître's temper tantrum to take down Hayden Mundy Moore. Especially for charity's sake.

"Let's hear it for our host, Christian Lemaître!" I said into my mic, leading the applause myself. "A fine choco-latier, a supporter of charity, *and* a brilliant and accom-plished man!"

I was freestyling, sure, but that last bit came a little *too* easily to mind. Too late, I realized I'd parroted this week's favorite description of Christian—just as Nina and Bernard had. All the same, everyone dutifully clapped. A few quizzical looks did come my way, though. Bernard frowned. Danny squinted at me, obviously lost in thought. Isabel comically rolled her eyes. (I could count on her to lighten the mood.)

Nina rushed to my side to take over the emceeing again.

"We'll be ready for our next session in just a few minutes, everyone," she announced with a vivid smile. Her poise made me yearn, just for a second, to be half as composed. But then . . .

Nina ripped off her mic and turned to me, looking agitated. "Are you crazy? Are you *trying* to get yourself blackballed?"

I laughed. "Christian can't do anything to me." Okay, he could refuse to pay me, but that was actionable. I'd already checked with Travis on that point. "He probably didn't even hear me. Besides, I didn't say anything that wasn't complimentary."

"When Christian's in a mood like that, there's *nothing* that's complimentary enough, believe me," Nina fretted. "It'll take me hours to calm him down. I have so much to do already!"

Full of remorse and hoping to soothe her, I touched her arm. She felt breakable, like a titian-haired china figurine.

"I'm sorry, Nina. I was caught off guard. I don't want to make anything *more* difficult for you." Wanting to make amends, I shook my head. "I'll make it up to you, I promise." I gazed into her harassed but flawlessly made-up face, even as retreat attendees gathered nearby to converse and make plans. "How about if I retroactively sponsor Christian in the tasting? You can make an announcement later that *he* raised the most funds."

At that, Nina seemed minutely cheered. "Really?"

"Of course!" I could afford it, thanks to dear old wacky Uncle Ross. Just as long as I didn't linger. "In fact, I'll match all the sponsorship donations. Let me know how much we raised, and I'll have my financial advisor set up an EFT."

Now she seemed aghast. "You can't afford that!"

"That's up to me and my financial advisor to decide," I assured her. "I've told you about Travis, haven't I?"

I could have waxed rhapsodic about him all day.

Given our busy schedules, five minutes had to suffice.

When I'd finished, Nina said, "He sounds wonderful."

"He is!" I half expected Danny to materialize and argue with me about that, just to be difficult. "You know numbers guys, though," I added with a dose of bonhomie. "They're tough to cuddle up to. How did you get your guy to open up, anyway?"

I was dying to know how to make Travis spill some personal information. All I knew about him were the bare essentials.

Nina gave me a blank stare. "My guy?"

"Your husband? He's a CPA, right? I heard that someplace."

Asking around, I'd learned that Nina's husband had done some impromptu financial advising for the Lemaître Chocolates staff. I was pretty sure Adrienne had mentioned getting advice from him once or twice. He sounded like a stand-up guy—just like Travis.

"Right." Nina tittered, waving her hand to excuse her absentmindedness. "I'm so frantic, I forgot about Calvin. I think I'm already mentally halfway to the kitchen, making sure the preparations are on schedule for tonight's banquet service."

I couldn't imagine being so scattered. My work left me feeling more centered, not less. That's why I liked it. "You need one of Maison Lemaître's spa services. Why don't you sneak away and join me for a mani-pedi later?" I invited. "I hear the cacao nib and espresso bean pedicure scrub is ultrarelaxing."

Inadvertently, my gaze dropped to Nina's fingernails. I was shocked to see that they were gnawed, with chipped polish. On such an otherwise perfectly put-together woman, that was . . .

. . . *endearing.* It was to *me,* at least. As a nonstop traveler, I use shampoo to wash my delicates. I let sunscreen double as moisturizer. I don't wear much makeup. I'd once gone a month without shaving my legs while exploring Mount Esja, near Reykjavik, and I have a serious weakness for hats to hide a bad hair day.

What I'm saying is, I liked that Nina had *one* flaw.

"I can't," she protested, looking flustered. "I have so much to do! The banquet, the rest of today's schedule, more sessions, a trip to the media area, a meeting with Christian—"

Yikes. "Maybe a quick cocoa oil massage, then?"

"Doesn't a 'quick' massage defeat the purpose?"

"Something's better than nothing." I nudged Nina. "Come on. Do it! I'm headed to the spa soon, anyway. I can ask Britney to set up a massage for you." Inspiration struck. "Or, even better, a *couple's* massage! That would be even *more* relaxing, right?"

A frown. "You want us to have a couple's massage together?"

I laughed. "Not *us.* You and your husband, of course."

Nina looked alarmed. "Calvin isn't much of a spa guy."

Maybe she was worried he'd feel out of place. "I can probably get Danny to come, too," I persuaded. If one macho dude agreed to be slathered in what amounted to sweet, slippery, liquefied candy components, another one might, too. "We can relax, the guys can relax . . . *then* you can get back to work."

Nina bit her lip. "You're a bad influence, Hayden."

I grinned. "So I've been told. So? Will you?"

"No." She straightened, then held her clipboards more tightly. "But I *do* appreciate the effort. I really do."

I wasn't ready to call it quits. Maybe I could come at this from another angle. "Is it Calvin's job? Do they disapprove of their CPAs sneaking away in the middle of the day for massages? If so, maybe I can arrange something. My friend Danny's a pretty good forger." He'd let it slip once. "He could probably fake a doctor's excuse with a very high degree of believability."

I was joking, but Nina reacted as if I'd suggested we set fire to Calvin's workplace, rather than smuggle him out of it.

"No one's breaking the law on my account!"

"I know." Immediately, I relented. "I didn't mean—"

"I've really got to run." Nina's terse look cut me off. "I'll let you know how much your generous charitable donation should be." She nodded. "Have a nice time at your next session."

Then she scurried away, leaving me gawking.

Had I really just volunteered Danny's *forgery* services?

Oh, boy. It was a good thing he hadn't overheard *that*.

I hadn't netted any insights about how to loosen up Travis, either. I was batting zero for two. But there was always next time, I told myself as I headed toward the *Chocolat Monthly* reporter to get better acquainted. Whatever her intentions were toward Danny, I wanted to know about them. That was my duty.

Oh, and I wanted to know what she knew about Rex Rader, too. Because if there was anyone better than me at sussing out top secret information, it had to be someone who did it for a living.

Chapter 9

After "Name That Chocolate!" broke up, the ballroom emptied quickly. Retreat attendees scattered to attend workshops, listen to chocolate-industry speakers, and enjoy the spa's chocolate-themed services. Me, I was more drawn to the chocolate-caramel frappes being served out in the sunshine, on Maison Lemaître's grassy manicured grounds, with a fresh bay breeze on the side.

Ah. After stepping outdoors, I stuffed my dorky lanyarded name badge into my bag, then exhaled and tipped my face to the sun. Being stuck inside so much was making me itchy. I guess after so many years spent globe-trotting, I have a hard time settling down unless there's chocolate in front of me. Given my habitual restlessness, it's a wonder I get anything done.

I *had* gotten to know Rex's *Chocolat Monthly* reporter a bit, though. Her name was Eden. She was twenty-three. She was convinced that her story about Rex Rader was going to "blow the doors off" the magazine's staid readership. The trouble was, Eden had confided, her editor had nixed the front-page slot she wanted. She was considering taking her scoop elsewhere.

"There *are* competing media companies here," Eden

had informed me, ambitious and confident. "They'll pay for this."

On a whim, *I'd* offered to pay for it. It was a day made for throwing money around, after all. If I was going to make Travis dig into my coffers for Danny's salary, Bernard's charity, and Nina's forced-relaxation couple's massage (I hadn't yet given up on the idea of treating her and Calvin), I might as well go for broke. What was one more expense on top of everything else?

But Eden had shut me down. "I saw you and Rex together," she said. "For all I know, you want to buy my story to bury it."

"I promise you, that's *not* it," I'd assured her.

But in the end, my offer was a no-go. Half an hour later, I was no closer to learning what Eden knew about Rex's feud with Adrienne than I had been going in—except that it seemed unlikely she would actively conspire with her (supposedly) sworn enemy.

During my efforts, I'd lost track of Bernard. I'd meant to talk to him—in a very *public* place, this time—to discern how lucid he was (or wasn't) . . . and to find out, if I could, if Bernard really *had* had an affair with Adrienne. Verifiably. After all, at this point, I didn't know who to believe. Isabel might have misled me, accidentally or on purpose. I had to know more.

Getting fortified for that effort, I sipped my sweet, frosty frappe while I tromped upstairs to my room. The drinks were courtesy of Lemaître. They were winners, made with quality ganache-based chocolate sauce, house-made caramel, and a variety of milk or coffee bases. The result was somehow indulgent and refreshing at the same time. I couldn't stop drinking it.

Trying to suck up the last delicious dredges, I stopped in the hallway outside the service stairs, then shamelessly slurped. *Yum.* Mission accomplished. Not a drop was left.

Satisfied, I gripped my cup, shrugged my crossbody bag in place, then skirted a parked housekeeping cart. That frappe would have to suffice as lunch, if I was going to have any time in the spa before my next obligations. I wasn't attending the retreat just to schmooze. I intended to enjoy myself, too.

Arriving at my room with visions of warm chocolate-fondue body wraps in mind, I reached inside my bag's outer pocket for my keycard. Then I noticed that my door was already ajar.

Housekeeping, I reasoned, glancing back at the parked cart. No doubt the staff was wildly overworked with the retreat. I knew from experience that it was next to impossible to remove chocolate stains from clothing . . . say, your favorite faux leather moto jacket. Just for instance.

Or, the door could be open . . . because of *Danny.* He still had his copy of my keycard. He probably intended to deliver another personal-safety tutorial—this time, something more hands-on than the recitation of the dangers he'd given me last night after I'd opened the door without looking through the peephole. That would explain why he'd made himself scarce after the chocolate-tasting panel. He hadn't given me that dour look just for kicks. I was willing to bet Danny really *did* think I was recklessly endangering myself.

Well, he hadn't seen anything yet. Buzzing on burnt sugar and caffeine, I slipped inside the slender opening between the door and the jamb, making sure I didn't make any noise. I'm proud to say I succeeded. My plan was to catch Danny off guard.

It wouldn't be easy. But last April in Bangkok, during Songkran (a multiday New Year's festival during which *everyone* gleefully soaks *everyone* with water from buckets, Super Soakers, and anything else at hand), I *did* manage to completely drench Danny. So there was a precedent.

Otherwise, I wouldn't have expected to get the jump on him today.

Hearing shuffling farther in my room, I crept closer. One of my shirts came flying past. It landed on the floor. Weird.

A shoe came next, followed by my (empty) duffel bag.

What the hell? If this was housekeeping service, it was seriously flawed. I didn't mind a little untidiness, but—

More sounds of scrabbling came from within my room. Ahead and to the right. Just around the corner. My heart sped up.

May——had the wrong room? Baffled, I crept back to check.

No dice. The engraved placard read 332. My room. "Huh."

I didn't mean to say it out loud. It was automatic.

The next thing I knew, someone in my room swore. I didn't recognize the voice. I didn't have a chance to. Because the next thing I knew, there was a rush of air behind me . . . then darkness.

I don't know if you've ever woken up on the floor of a hotel hallway—or the hallway of a posh resort, for that matter—but it's a seriously disorienting experience. Opening my eyes, I became aware of several things at once. *Too many* things.

First up, what was I doing on the floor? Next, why did the walls seem to be slanting sideways? Also, who was that beside me? Woozily, I shut my eyes, wanting to block out all of it.

"Hayden." Danny's voice intruded on my bewilderment. I winced at the sound. "Danny? What's going on?"

"I was hoping you could tell me."

There was a smile in his voice. Also, concern. Bravely,

I opened my eyes. I instantly regretted it. Afraid to move, I looked around. Yep. I was sprawled on the floor at Maison Lemaître, half in and half out of my room. Fortunately, there wasn't anybody around. I glimpsed my empty frappe cup nearby, then my crossbody bag, still twisted around me. I clutched it.

"Nothing's missing," Danny said. "Not in there, at least."

"You *searched* my bag?"

"No." He was being unusually patient. "You landed on it."

Fuzzily, I understood. "I prevented a mugging with my knocked-out body as a shield? Nifty. I've been traveling so long, I've perfected the art of unconscious self-defense."

His smile comforted me. "Way to look on the bright side."

"But I'm not lying on top of it anymore." That seemed like a very important point. In addition, I couldn't stop thinking that there was something *significant* I should have remembered. Some . . . *word*? Something I'd heard? I remembered hearing swearing. . . .

Had that been me? Swearing at an intruder?

"I rolled you over to make sure you were breathing."

"Nice." I groaned, envisioning the ghastly scene when he'd found me. "Don't sugarcoat the situation or anything."

"Someone had to do it." Capably, Danny held out his arms. He was good in a crisis. His steady presence calmed me down. "Can you get up?" he asked. "Do you remember what happened?"

"*Should* I get up? What if I'm paralyzed?" Panic gripped me. I'm not ashamed to admit it, given the circumstances. "Ohmigod!"

"You just waved your arms in fright," Danny pointed out.

"I guess I'm not paralyzed then." I risked standing up.

With Danny's help, I shakily got to my feet. "My head hurts."

"It looks as though somebody walloped you pretty good." Danny toed something on the floor. A Maison Lemaître lamp. "My money's on this, since table lamps don't belong in the hall. I'm guessing you hit your head on the floor when you fell, too. Double whammy." He made a face. "I'm taking you to a doctor."

"Someone was in my room!" Hazily, I remembered that much.

"Let's get *you* in your room," Danny urged.

I was glad he was there. "You go check it first."

He gave me a doubtful look. I was adamant.

"If I can't use my personal security guy to pave the way into danger for me, what can I use him for?" I insisted.

"Wait here." Leaving me propped securely in the entryway, Danny went in. I craned my neck to watch, noticing more of my stuff scattered around. I felt creeped out. Violated. Afraid.

I had to take action. I weaved my way in. "Do you see . . ."

Anything? I meant to say, but the sight of everything in my room shut me up immediately. I'm not kidding when I say it was a righteous mess. You know how you see ransacked rooms on TV? Torn-apart drug kingpins' mansions in the movies? That's how my room looked, minus the soundtrack, actors, and moody lighting.

Goose bumps broke out on my arms and legs. "It wasn't you."

Danny, of course, didn't understand about my plans to reenact my watery Songkran triumph. "Of course it wasn't me." He turned to face me, his expression alive with protectiveness. "But I'm going to find out who it was, that's for damn sure."

"No, I mean . . . I thought it was you in here." On

wobbly legs, I came closer. Numbly, I picked up some clothes and tossed them on the bed. At least that felt decent. It gave me the willies to know that someone else had touched everything. "That's why I—"

"*You came in here?*" Danny thundered, uncannily guessing what I'd been about to say. "After *everything* I told you?"

Feeling like crying, I nodded. "It could have been housekeeping. The maids leave the door open. It wasn't stupid."

"It was *very* stupid," Danny disagreed. He surveyed the damage with his hands on his hips. "Did you see who it was?"

"I heard them. But . . ." I focused. Nada. "I can't remember."

That's being bashed on the head for you. Apparently, it screws with your memory sometimes. I'm not saying I morphed into that dude from *Memento* or anything, but I had a pretty sketchy sense of the past ten . . . fifteen . . . five . . . however many minutes ago.

"Try harder," Danny bit out.

But I couldn't. "Maybe it'll come to me. Later."

Thoroughly freaked, I looked around. I shivered. Then . . . "Adrienne's notebook!" I rushed to my hiding place.

Of course. It wasn't there. I smacked my forehead.

Pain ricocheted through my skull. Whoops. First my bum knee and bruised elbow, now my banged-up head. If I made it out of San Francisco in one piece, it would be a miracle. I sobbed.

Adrienne had given me that notebook to keep safe. Now I'd failed . . . at the very last thing my friend had ever asked of me.

It had felt *so* important to protect it. For Adrienne.

"Hey, hey." Danny came closer. He put his arms around me. He patted me extra gently. "Easy, there. You're pounding on one of my favorite people, and she's hurt right now. Settle down."

"I can't!" I sniffled. "I lost it!" I gestured to my most reliable hiding place. "I left it where *no one* else could find it, in my *best* hiding place of all, the one that *never* fails—"

"Inside the torn bottom lining of your wheelie bag?"

I gawked at him. I nodded. "The frame hides lumps."

That niche had seen me through Vietnam, Mexico, Belgium, and countless other international locales. It was rock solid.

"Yeah." Danny looked away. "It's not that secure."

"Well, I can see that *now*!" I wriggled out of his grasp, then paced away. "At least the nutraceutical truffles are safe," I reflected. "I sent them to Travis for analysis, to try to find out if any of them contained enough caffeine to—" *Kill Adrienne.*

Danny didn't let me say it. He crossed his arms. "Travis?"

"He's got guys, too. Just like you. Guys who know things."

"Yeah. Line-item deductions and interest rates."

"I trust Travis. He's the one who hooked me up with an expert on anhydrous caffeine in the first place."

The merger of pharmaceuticals and chocolate had been new to me. I hadn't wanted to wade in without assistance on hand. Plus, I'd gotten a long, sexy chat with Travis out of the deal.

Mindlessly, I went on tidying. Doing something—anything—felt better to me than standing around, dizzy and scared.

"You should have trusted *me*." Danny's voice followed me. There was a pause. "Adrienne's notebook is safe. I have it."

"*You* have it? Are you sure?" I didn't know whether to

be relieved or annoyed. I settled for argumentative. "What for?"

"For keeping it out of the wrong hands," he told me, already (sort of) earning his new salary. Given a choice, I would have preferred he protect *me,* but I was in no position to split hairs just then. After all, I *had* technically blundered into danger moments ago. "If it's as valuable as you say it is, I figured someone would come after it. Sooner or later."

He was right. In a way, maybe this had been inevitable.

"We're switching rooms," Danny announced. "Right now."

"No." I frowned. "I'm not just running away!"

"*Or* you're running away," he bargained. "Solid idea."

I can't say I wasn't tempted to leave. I was.

I had the means, the motive, and (now) the opportunity to call it quits on the chocolate retreat and save my skin. Believe me, I *wanted* to live to fight another day (and taste another devil's food cake with vanilla Swiss buttercream). But someone had just rifled through my stuff, clobbered me on the head, and left me for dead in a hotel hallway. Before, this whole situation had been troubling and confusing. Now it was personal.

I might not have been ready to leave Maison Lemaître after my room was looted, but I *was* ready to unwind with that warm chocolate-fondue body wrap I mentioned before. Especially after Danny sternly marched me down to see the resort's on-call physician to have my head examined (let's just skip the obvious joke here), only to learn I had a concussion. It was supposed to clear up with rest and time. In the meantime, I'd been told I could expect headaches (check), dizziness (not anymore, thanks), trouble sleeping (I hoped not), mood swings (what else is new?), and, uh, one more thing. What was it? Oh yeah. Memory problems.

Double check mark on that one, as it turned out. I still couldn't remember . . . *something* about what had happened right before I'd been hit. The doctor had warned me to guard against repeated concussions. I'd let him know I'd do my best not to get walloped by surprise anytime soon, then I'd beat it out of there with Danny in tow, frowning at me. It had become his new default. But I guessed a guy didn't get to be a professional security expert without being able to foresee every possible (grim) scenario. I figured Danny was probably preoccupied with thinking up ways I might wind up dead. It was possible I'd scared even *him.* It couldn't have been fun for him, I knew, to have found me that way. He must have thought, for a second, that I was dead, too.

Not that Danny would admit as much. He was way too tough for that. So, with the doctor's visit duly completed, I decided to . . . Wait, where am I? (Just kidding. You've gotta laugh, right?)

I was still scared, but I wasn't scared *away,* if you catch my drift. It would take more than messing up my stuff—as unsettling as that had been—to make me abandon ship and leave.

On the plus side, it was unlikely my room had been searched at random. That meant I had *something* someone wanted. Since I'd taken only Adrienne's notebook, Rex's portfolio, the (maybe lethal) nutraceutical chocolate samples, and the tiny Baggie of anhydrous caffeine Adrienne and I had used, I figured that meant there was more going on with *someone* at Lemaître than I knew.

Christian wanted Adrienne's notebook. So did whoever she'd been conspiring with. Rex wanted his portfolio. So might one of his competitors—because, after all, Melt had made a name for itself by becoming San Francisco's "modern" chocolatier, right about the time that Christian had taken control of Lemaître. In a business like mine, intel is always valuable. Then there were the caffeinated chocolate samples . . . but I didn't know who'd want them. A die-hard chocolate fanatic, maybe? A hungry house-keeper?

Neither of those categories of people would ransack my room and then bludgeon me to get away with truffles—especially not when there were chocolate samples at every retreat session and more chocolates being given away (like my delicious frappe) on the resort's grounds. Nothing made sense. Too concussed to trust my own judgment about things for a while, I swapped my stuff with Danny's, then sensibly moved into his (militarily tidy) room next door. He took possession of my (now tainted) former room, moving with an ease that confirmed that Danny packed as lightly as I did. We were two peas in a pod.

With that done, feeling more secure, I picked up the spa menu card, gazed at it . . . and realized there would be no decadent spa treatments for me today. Not now that I'd spent my precious free time unconscious on the hallway floor and/or being scrutinized by the resort's physician.

It was almost time for the banquet being held that evening to honor chocolate-industry leaders. There was a reason Nina had been preoccupied arranging it, I knew. The event was being held picnic style, outdoors on the Maison Lemaître grounds, at twilight. From my window, I could already see tables being set with snowy tablecloths. Resort staffers arranging strings of lights and freestanding torches. Other employees setting up a temporary dais for the guests of honor.

The overall effect was already impressive, and it wasn't even finished yet. Further meticulous preparation was needed. Otherwise the fête couldn't work its necessary magic—which was, of course, making Christian (and Lemaître Chocolates) look *good.*

Traditionally, I'd learned, the banquet was a highlight of the annual retreat—the time when Christian typically unveiled new products and innovative flavors. The banquet had to happen early enough that the attendees could buzz about whatever the "it" chocolate of the moment was . . . but late enough that no one would be tempted to start nitpicking the specifics. Thus, it was taking place *now,* smack-dab in the middle of the retreat.

As marketing strategies went, the banquet was effective. So, I had to admit, was Christian. He'd almost single-handedly led Lemaître to shed its dowdy image and emerge a chocolate superstar. If there'd been a Steve Jobs of truffles, it would have been Christian. . . . And speaking of truffles, I'd expected him to ask me about the nutraceutical samples Adrienne had made—if not earlier, then certainly now. It was likely that he'd remembered their *non*debut, so I'd thought he might decide to introduce them that evening, instead. To my surprise, he hadn't.

Unless *he'd* broken into my room to find them earlier . . . and had been disappointed in his search, of course.

More likely, Christian had opted (wisely) to play it safe, I mused as I performed a few touch-ups in room 334's bathroom mirror. After all, if those gilded caffeinated truffles *had* accidentally caused Adrienne's death, it would be a colossally bad idea to serve them to a couple hundred people tonight. Even Christian had to recognize when common sense should prevail.

Except when he didn't. Because as I was wrestling with my hair, trying to achieve something fancier than a ponytail (since I didn't have too many clothes to work with in my vagabond's existence), I heard a knock on the door of the room next door.

That was Danny's room, my (old) room. Intrigued—

and, frankly, picturing a clandestine visit from Nina and/or Eden—I quit futzing with my hair and listened. Nina and the *Chocolat Monthly* reporter had both been giving Danny the eye during "Name That Chocolate!" I hadn't noticed Danny returning their interest, but my old pal was pretty stealthy. When we were together, I *never* (for instance) caught him checking out another woman—but I knew he *had* to be doing so. What red-blooded guy didn't? I liked to think Danny was just being respectful (unlike Rex), but I knew he had (shall we say) *needs*. Would he opt to satisfy them with the fresh—but overtly conniving—reporter or the married woman?

I hoped neither. Just because Danny could do better. But on the other hand, I could have used some garden-variety scandal to liven up my mood. The painkiller I'd taken earlier had worked to crush the aches in my knee and elbow, but it was scarcely making a dent in my headache. Wincing at the pain, I listened closely.

Christian's loud voice made me recoil in surprise.

"Where is Hayden?" he demanded to know. "I need her!"

Frustratingly, everything went quiet. I could *almost* make out a murmur—probably Danny cutting short Christian. Then . . . "If she's double-crossing me with the information she's gathered for her report," Christian said next, sounding loud and vindictive—and maybe drunk, too—"I *swear* I'll make her—"

Another murmur. Danny didn't need to yell to get attention.

Apparently, Christian didn't need *real* evidence of treachery to accuse someone of it, either. That detail put a serious dent in his accusations about Adrienne's "sabotage." On the other hand, an out-of-control guy making threats not long after a murder? That guy looked pretty guilty to me.

"She owes me that report!" Christian protested next,

his voice muffled by the walls between us. "I want it. Tomorrow!"

Inwardly, I groaned. My written consulting reports were the bane of my existence. I loved doing the work necessary to gather the information. I did not love cataloguing every detail of it.

This time, at least I had good reasons for procrastinating. Also, it wasn't due yet. Why was Christian pressuring me?

As quickly as it began, Christian's encounter with Danny ended. Danny said something else—probably something unprintable about Christian's rampant Napoleon complex—then shut the door.

I was still crouched in a ready-to-eavesdrop position when Danny arrived in my room, courtesy of his spare keycard. (He seemed to have multiples.) He came straight to the bathroom.

"Oh, hi! Am I that obvious?" I asked, pretending to mess with my hair again. For added veracity, I'd even had the foresight to stick a bobby pin between my teeth. I arched a brow. "Exactly how did you know you'd find me in here primping?"

Danny grinned. He leaned in the doorway, watching my efforts with shrewd eyes. "I knew you'd be here because this is the best place to listen in on my conversation with Christian."

"Your what?"

He laughed, not buying my wide-eyed, born-again naïveté. "I'm pretty sure he thinks we're having a hot and heavy fling."

"Well, of course. Why else would you be in *my* room?"

Except the obvious—security detail. I was happy to let Danny play decoy, though. After discussing it, we'd opted not to report the break-in into my room—or our subsequent decision to swap room assignments. What was done, was done, anyway. Whoever had searched my room hadn't taken anything, and I didn't want to waste time giving the Maison Lemaître security (or the police) the same *non*-information I'd given Danny. Besides, now I had Danny for protection. He'd sworn to stick close by me.

As proof, he'd outfitted himself appropriately. I examined his outfit for the banquet. "A suit, huh? Nice. But no tie?"

He touched his collared shirt, inadvertently calling my attention to the muscles beneath. "Guys like me don't own ties."

"Surely you need one for all those premieres you go to?"

But Danny didn't want to talk business. Not then. "You must have heard—Christian wants your report. Are you late again?"

"You make me sound like you," I hedged. *There.* Hair done.

I applied some lip gloss while Danny watched me amusedly. "You probably shouldn't antagonize Christian. He hired you."

Have I mentioned that Danny is *very* interested in growing my business? "Don't worry," I assured him, shimmying past to grab my clutch. "Even if my consulting tanks, I can pay you."

That was the wrong thing to say. Danny didn't like talking about my newfound, undeserved wealth. You know . . . unless he was pushing me to spend some of it on hiring his security services.

It occurred to me that I still needed to call Travis.

"Are you ready yet?" He followed me. "You look ready."

I was. I sighed. "Do you think anyone would notice if I skipped this shindig and went to the spa, instead?"

"Hey, for all you know, *you're* being honored tonight."

I didn't think that was likely. I essentially worked under-cover. "Hey, I must be having one of those cognitive lapses the doctor mentioned," I teased as I double-checked my keycard. "Because I think you just complimented me."

"Don't get used to it." Danny opened the door. "Try not to concuss yourself walking out the door this time, you klutz."

Both of us knew that wasn't what had happened. But it made me feel better to pretend I *hadn't* been targeted hours ago.

Besides, that was more like it. "Anything you say, boss."

Then we headed downstairs and got ready to hear speeches.

You know how awards shows sometimes "play off" the winners in the middle of their acceptance speeches? Generally, I hate that. I *like* hearing ordinarily restrained professionals gush about their spouses, directors, cast mates, agents, and caterers. But at the Lemaître Chocolates banquet, I found a new appreciation for cutting those speeches short. Because if you *weren't* one of the afore-mentioned spouses, directors, cast mates, agents, or cater-ers, I learned at sunset while seated at one of those long, luxe tables in the green, lush surroundings of the resort's grounds, then listening to tipsy, teary-eyed types ramble on about chocolate and "excellence" was *boring*.

Drifting away from the tedium, I let my gaze wander, appreciating all the effort that had gone into staging the event. Nina had done a spectacular job coordinating things. You would never know she'd had cause to stress out about it. The food had been divine. The drinks had been delicious. And the dessert . . . well, it went without saying that triple-chocolate mousse torte with boozy Armagnac whipped cream and candied orange peel was out of this world. Sated and slightly sleepy, I listened to the Torrance Chocolates rep accept a "renaissance" award. She managed to thank her boss, her boss's wife, her boss's father—pretty much anyone related in any way to her boss.

So far, Torrance Chocolates sounded like a lot friendlier place to work, I couldn't help thinking, than Lemaître did.

A breeze ruffled the tablecloths and threatened my hair. I tried to nudge a stray dark strand back into position, feeling grateful for the rapidly fading twilight and the flattering torchlight—which was doing an excellent job of hiding the hasty efforts I'd made getting ready. Away from the tables full of attendees, additional lights glimmered among the tree branches.

Far across the grounds, the Golden Gate Bridge arched over the water. Its cables and towers were illuminated to highlight its Art Deco features and famous International Orange paint color. The air smelled sweet with chocolate and redolent with flowers. It was warm. I was secure with Danny beside me. I hadn't received an industry award, but in that moment, I didn't care. Lulled by all the speeches, the fine food, the overflowing wine, and three kinds of chocolate, it seemed to me that I might have imagined everything—Adrienne's death, my own amateur poking and prodding among my informal suspects, even my concussion.

Then, a few awards (and subsequent speeches) later, Bernard took the stage and blew my newfound equanimity to smithereens. It started off mildly. Accepting an "initiator" award, the gray-haired Lemaître Chocolates founder beamed out at the audience.

"First, I'd like to thank everyone for coming tonight."

Uh-oh. Stifling a yawn, I prepared for the worst. Usually, when someone led off with "first," it meant they intended to go on. And on. *And on.* Plus, Bernard had that faintly hesitant cadence to his voice that the elderly—and probably the more deep-thinking members of society—sometimes had while winding up for a good, long rumination. We might be here awhile.

Surreptitiously, Danny nodded at one of the servers— an attractive blonde—signaling for another Guinness. I silently requested more wine. As usual, we were on the same wavelength.

"Especially my dear nephew, Christian," Bernard was saying when I tuned in again, "who kicked this doddering old fool out of his comfort zone and into a new life." He gave his trademark twinkly-eyed grin to the attendees. "I'm grateful for that."

He went on to natter about the subjects of chocolate, being on morning television in the '80s and '90s, and the challenges of marriage. Around me, people shifted. Bernard had officially entered the "play-off music" zone. But no one would have dared.

I reminded myself that this man was the patriarch of modern chocolate making as we knew it. It was because of people like Bernard that I have a thriving industry to work in at all.

"So I'd like to dedicate this award," Bernard droned while servers circulated, delivering drinks at double speed, "to the woman who helped me see all that. The woman who *changed* me. . . ."

I swear, my head nodded drowsily. I wasn't proud of it, but it happened. Given what I knew of Isabel's disgruntlement with her marriage, I wasn't buying Bernard's blissfully wed routine.

Curiously, I glanced toward Bernard's just-vacated seat, wondering how Isabel was taking all this. She wasn't there.

In her place, Eden from *Chocolat Monthly* was seated. *Huh?* Maybe she'd decided to broaden her article's scope.

"So *this* is to you." Bernard lifted his award. Atop its

gilded pedestal, a crystal cacao bean gleamed. Choked up, Bernard added, "Wherever you are!"

Awkward. Now other attendees had noticed that Eden was *not* Isabel. People began murmuring. Danny glanced at me. I shrugged.

I might not have jetted off to Barbados myself, but I wouldn't have been surprised if Isabel had. Right along with Poopsie. I'd miss that little Yorkie. And her keeper, too.

"I don't know why you had to leave," Bernard wheezed, "but I'll never forget you! Never! No one will ever know what you meant to me." He gave an enormous sniffle. "But I will! I'll—"

He broke off, sobbing as he clutched his award to his chest. Galvanized by his emotion, everyone stared silently.

Discreetly, Nina hustled to the microphone. She took Bernard's arm, then murmured something to him. He nodded.

I glanced again toward Isabel's vacant seat. Why hadn't she come tonight with Bernard? I hadn't noticed her missing earlier, but I'd been a little out of it (thanks, concussion!). It looked as though a new dose of drama had shaken up the retreat, though.

I didn't seriously think Isabel had refused to come see her husband fêted. Maybe she'd simply been too hungover to attend?

"Bernard Lemaître, everyone!" Nina's voice burst through the sound system. "Your inaugural 'initiator' award winner!"

Looking uncomfortable, Christian stood to applaud. So did the Torrance Chocolates rep, a bean supplier, and others from my panel. Danny stood, too, inciting our whole table to rise.

By the time Bernard weaved past (tipsily or senilely, I wasn't sure which), he was making his way through a standing ovation. Everyone around me clapped. I did, too.

It was a beautiful moment, seeing a mainstay of my industry honored in that way. Seeming touched, Bernard smiled, still led by Nina.

When he reached *me* amid the applause, though, he veered away from the PR rep. Suddenly determined, he grabbed me.

"*Don't* forget Adrienne!" Bernard told me intently. "Don't forget! Remember her the way she was—the way she *really* was."

His gravelly voice and grave tone raised goose bumps on my arms. His hazy, pain-filled gaze penetrated mine. I didn't know if Bernard was suffering from dementia or not. But in that moment, it was clear to me that he was suffering from grief.

The question was . . . was Bernard mourning the (apparent) loss of Isabel? Or the loss of Adrienne? *Had* they been involved?

Before I could say anything, Nina led Bernard away. She was obviously controlling the situation before it could get any more out of hand. I had to admire her quick thinking. Thanks to her (typically) dedicated efforts, though, Lemaître Chocolates' founder was gone . . . and so was my chance to find out more.

After all the spectacle, however, I felt more lively than I had since before having my head smashed. That was a plus.

I poked Danny. "Hey, you wanna get out of here?" I asked.

He jolted, startled out of what he'd been doing—which was checking out the dishy blond server I'd noticed earlier. "Huh?"

"Never mind." It was obvious he had another one on the hook. I wasn't sure how he . . . *Nah, scratch that.* I knew how he did it. "I just wanted to tell you you're officially off the clock."

"Says you." He swerved his gaze to me. "What's up?"

"The banquet's breaking up." *And I want to find Isabel.* I had to know more. "I think I'm going to go for a walk."

"Not without me, you're not."

And that's how I got six-feet-plus of masculine company for my next excursion onto Maison Lemaître's darkened grounds—and accidentally foiled Danny's latest hookup plans in the process.

This new arrangement of ours might have its complications, I realized as we walked. I didn't want to get in the way of Danny's freedom. But I didn't want to wind up dead the next time somebody set their sights on something I had in my hotel room, either . . . *or,* it occurred to me as I remembered Christian's earlier visit to my (former) room, something I *didn't* have anymore.

I fished out my phone and dialed up Travis. Danny sauntered a few feet away, looking attitudinal. For the millionth time, I wished the two of them got along better. As the phone rang, I looked across the bay at the twinkling lights of San Francisco.

I could have been happy here, I thought. Minus the murder.

"Hey, Travis!" I felt a rush of well-being as the phone connected and my financial advisor's rumbling voice came over the line. Thrillingly. "What are you wearing right now?"

He chuckled. I won! Right away, I'd made him laugh.

"You never quit, do you, Hayden?" Travis asked huskily. Was I dreaming, or did he sound happy to hear from me?

I cradled the phone, picturing him. Sort of. In my imagination, Travis was *hot.* Hot in a way that corporate headshots and social media pics couldn't have begun to capture—not that he'd allowed any of those to become public. (Yes, I'd snooped.) "Not if I can help it."

"Well, I'm afraid there's one thing you might want to consider giving up on," Travis said crushingly. I caught sight of Danny watching suspiciously. He didn't trust Travis's no-punches, no-rap sheet, no-parolees approach to life. "Your retreat. I don't think you should stay in San Francisco."

I didn't say anything—but I did shoot a concerned glance at Danny. Apparently, he was prescient, because he'd predicted this outcome earlier. Travis *did* want me to quit gadding around.

Didn't Travis know how much gridskipping meant to me? I'd grown up rough-traveling the world with my (similarly) adventure-loving parents. Thanks to them, I'd been filling out supplemental passport pages at a comically early age.

Thanks to them, I knew there was no point getting comfy.

But Travis wasn't aware of my ancient history—or he didn't care. That was a number cruncher for you, I guessed. Either things added up . . . or they didn't.

"I got the results of your truffle tests today." Travis paused. His voice lowered with authority. "We need to talk."

Chapter 10

"That's right. We do." I jumped in before Travis could deliver whatever bad news had him sounding so ominous. "I'm going to need to make some changes to my cash outflow." I told him about Bernard's charity and my offer to match all of today's donations to it. That went off without a hitch. "And my budget."

Travis gave a sexy *"go ahead"* rumble. So I did, watching as Danny put his hands on his hips and strode a few feet away. He might as well have been wearing a NO MONEY TALK T-shirt instead of a suit, because his demeanor made it plain that he didn't want to listen to me dole out my unanticipated fortune.

"I'm hiring Danny," I told Travis. "For security."

A pause. Then, "See, *that's* why I wanted to talk."

I'd anticipated some pushback. Here it was. I drew in a deep breath. "Look, I know you and Danny don't get along—"

"I'm not much for prison pen pals."

"—but he could be really useful to me here. It's done."

I'd be lying if I said I wasn't worried about how Travis would react. I wanted to stay on friendly terms with him. Danny was one of the few sticking points between us. But

I wasn't prepared to budge on the issue of one of my oldest friends.

In the distance, the lights of Maison Lemaître shined into the darkening evening. I glimpsed people milling around near the banquet picnic area. They seemed very far away now. Nearer to me and Danny, the resort's outbuildings and luxurious private cabins stood at moderate distances from one another, mostly deserted now because of the retreat's goings-on. Farther out, the waters of the bay shimmered in the glow of the city lights.

Travis heaved a sigh. "You know I can't stop you from spending your money however you want, but is this wise?"

"Why wouldn't it be wise?"

"Should I read you Danny's arrest record?"

"That's ancient history." Not far from me, I saw Danny. His shoulders looked tense, his face stony. "You don't know him."

"I know that you feel you're in danger there."

Travis was right. I frowned. "Not if I have Danny!"

"Maybe even *if* you have Danny." Travis went silent. Maybe he was sipping cognac in his high-tech office. Maybe he was loosening his silk tie. Maybe he was picturing *me,* too. "I don't want to argue with you, Hayden. But I think you should leave."

"And go where? Home?" I did my best to laugh off Travis's slipup. "We both know I don't have one of those. Not really."

"You could stay here. With me. Until you make other plans."

Struck speechless by that, I went still. I couldn't help wondering what it would be like to bunk down at Travis's place. Everything would probably be clean, expensive, and ridiculously organized. Plus, I could make Travis read aloud to me daily.

I got shivers of anticipation just thinking about it.

Which was enough to tell me I had to refuse. "Thanks, but no thanks. I'm fine where I am." Which was on the move, sooner or later.

"Are you? You don't usually call me out of the blue."

"I'm not calling you out of the blue. I'm calling you about *business,*" I reminded him, omitting my constant yen to hear his sexy voice. "The charity donations. Plus, Danny's salary will—"

"You sound stressed," Travis interrupted in a husky, inviting tone. "Why don't you tell me what's been going on?"

Given that bedroom voice of his, I wanted to, but I refrained. "I'm fine."

"Are you?"

"Of course." Automatically, I dug in my heels. I don't like being told what to do, and I felt another big, fat *"Here's what you should do"* coming my way. I hadn't even told Travis about my room break-in (or my concussion) yet. Maybe I just . . . *wouldn't.*

The fact that I was considering leaving out those details concerned me. It was possible that finding out if someone had purposely overdosed Adrienne meant more to me than I was willing to admit.

"Even though you overnighted truffles to me to ID as a possible *murder weapon,* you're still fine?" Travis pushed.

"I didn't say 'murder weapon,' per se," I objected.

"You didn't have to. Hayden . . ." Travis broke off. I pictured him pacing, all lean and muscular, in his imposing office. "It's obvious something bad is going on there at Maison Lemaître."

"Were the truffles toxic or not?" I asked. "Could one of them have killed Adrienne?" I *had* told Travis about her death.

Typically, Travis set aside his personal feelings long enough to deliver the goods. He was a pro. "No. The levels of caffeine weren't high enough to cause an overdose.

Adrienne would have had to eat dozens of truffles for problems to occur."

"Good. Then I'm home free." I shrugged, trying to loosen up my suddenly tense shoulders. "Well, have a nice night, Travis."

"That's not all." His tone brooked no argument. Evidently, when pushed, Travis could be a tough guy. I kind of liked that. He was hot when being commanding. "About Danny—don't you think it's convenient that he showed up there with you, right when everything fell apart and you needed security?"

I understood what Travis was driving at. I resented it.

I glanced at Danny. "It's not like that. I asked him here."

My pal's ears perked up. He looked straight at me.

"Danny could benefit enormously from you," Travis insisted, his voice raspy with urgency. "Isn't it possible he's making it *look* as though you need a bodyguard, when you really don't?"

That whole idea was preposterous. Offensive. Prejudicial. As a general rule, I'm not the biggest fan of reformed criminal types. But I *am* a fan of one of my oldest, closest friends.

"I'm going to pretend you didn't just suggest Danny is playing me," I said, getting more annoyed now. "He's not."

"How do you know he's not? It's all pretty coincidental."

"A woman died!" I told Travis, clutching my phone with a suddenly shaky hand. I didn't like arguing with him, but I had to. I'm loyal. Nobody was bad-mouthing Danny. "He didn't kill Adrienne. He didn't break into my room. He didn't clobber me—"

"About that," Travis broke in. "Did you really think I wouldn't see the doctor's bill come through today? We're not living in the Dark Ages. Financial transactions are immediate. You should have told me." He gave a growl of frustration—a *seductive* growl of frustration. Damn him.

"Come on, Hayden. It's me. I'm Mr. Attention to Detail. Just listen to me for once."

"I'm fine. Just concussed. Thanks for asking, though."

"Don't be like that," Travis urged. I was already softening when he added, "*Don't* hire Danny and *don't* stay there."

His know-it-all tone finally got the better of me. I might go all gooey for Travis's voice sometimes, but I never lose my wits altogether. I hadn't called him just to be bossed around.

"If I don't need a bodyguard—according to you—then I don't need to leave, do I?" I shot back. "Problem solved."

I was really feeling shaky now. I didn't know if it was arguing with Travis that was affecting me or my concussion. This might have been one of those mood swings I'd been warned about.

"Look, Travis." I relaxed my tone. "I'm sorry. I don't mean to take everything out on you, but I *do* have a minor head injury right now—and I think you're being just a little bit irrational on the subject of Danny. Just the way you've always been."

I wished again I knew why they didn't get along. I was about to ask Travis—one more time—when Danny strode closer.

He grabbed the phone. "Hayden has to go. Bye, Harvard."

He hung up. He seemed to seriously contemplate throwing my phone into the bay, too. Defensively, I snatched it from him.

"I was still talking to Travis! What is *wrong* with you?"

I was too dumbfounded even to lecture Danny about his habit of using pejorative nicknames for Travis. At least "Harvard" was printable . . . unlike some others. It fit. Travis was an alumnus.

Danny compressed his mouth. "He was upsetting you."

So was Danny, at that moment. Because I couldn't help

thinking . . . wasn't this *exactly* what he would have done if he *had* been trying to con me into hiring his security services—and now knew that Travis was throwing a monkey wrench into his scheme?

Maybe Danny and Travis didn't get along, I mused, because Danny wanted to swindle a fortune from me . . . and Travis wanted to stop him. But that was crazy. I would have given Danny just about anything he wanted. He didn't have to trick me to get it.

"Hey." Companionably, I prodded his shoulder. "You know I've got your back, right? What's mine is yours, and all that?"

Darkly, Danny gazed out toward the bay. "Yeah," he finally said, not looking at me. "But it's not, is it? Not really."

I didn't know what to say to that, so I stayed mum.

The silence stretched between us—me, feeling upset over my skirmish with Travis, and Danny, obviously in a brooding mood.

We needed to move on. At least now I knew that Adrienne hadn't been overdosed by her truffles. That was progress. As for the rest of the information I needed, it was somewhere nearby.

I started walking. Casually, I asked, "So . . . any idea where Isabel and Bernard might be staying while they're here?"

Most likely, I knew, Maison Lemaître had a penthouse suite on the top floor. Even more likely, Christian had claimed it.

Danny gave me a long look. "As if you don't know. You've been purposely meandering toward it all this time."

I hadn't been, but I didn't want to disillusion him. If Danny wanted to think I was some kind of sleuthing savant . . . why not? "Just for argument's sake?" I pushed. "To test you?"

He relented. "One of the cottages." He pointed. "That one."

I headed that direction, leaving Danny to trail me, trying not to wonder *too* hard how he knew everyone's room assignments.

A few minutes later, my knee had slowed me down and Danny had overtaken me. I looked at his back as we neared the cottage where Isabel and Bernard were staying, unable to stop wondering . . .

If Danny still had one foot in his shady past (and he did, as evidenced by his parolee pal, his unconscionable lifting of Rex's wallet, and his later profiling of that wallet's pilfered contents), then who was to say he *wasn't* pulling a con on me?

Nothing, that's what. Nothing except my intuition— which pinged madly as we reached the cottage and saw lights inside.

In the window, Isabel appeared. I stopped near a bush.

"Hey." Danny looked over his shoulder, obviously mystified. "What are you doing? I thought you wanted to talk to Isabel."

I did. I'd told him about my thoughts during Bernard's award acceptance speech—about wondering where Isabel was.

Now I knew. But she wasn't alone. Even as I bit my lip, another figure appeared. I could only see him from behind. But judging by his dark curly hair, he wasn't dear, graying Bernie.

I had a sinking feeling it might be Hank, the resort's personal trainer. Isabel *had* mentioned she might "get more" from him. She probably hadn't meant an effective triceps workout.

"She looks busy." Indecisively, I lingered. Coming there

had seemed like a perfectly innocuous idea . . . when I'd conceived of it. Now that I was there, though, I had my doubts. Should I really be poking into Isabel and Bernard's private life? Or Hank's? He could probably be fired for consorting with Isabel.

"Look, either talk to her or don't," Danny said. "Just know that I'm blowing off something else to be here with you."

The blonde from the banquet. Duly poked, I took a step.

Raised voices came from inside the cottage. I stopped, then cast a quizzical look at Danny. He'd heard them, too. In unspoken unison, we ducked behind the bush I'd stumbled upon.

"You should have said so the other night!" Isabel yelled, sounding intoxicated (and infuriated). "I wouldn't have wasted all this time with you!" In the window, she gave the man a shove. "I missed a good opportunity tonight, thanks to you."

Beside me in the sheltering darkness, Danny quirked his mouth. "Missed opportunity, huh? Isabel and I have something in common."

"Shush!" I kept still, listening harder. I could almost make out the man as he turned. He left the curtainless window before I could positively ID him. I know I shouldn't have been snooping at all. It really wasn't like me. But if I was going to, I reasoned, I might as well do a thorough job of it.

"Fine!" Isabel's shrill voice came next. "Just leave!"

There was another indistinct voice, too low to make out.

Then the cottage door smashed open. Danny and I flinched.

Rex Rader appeared in the doorway, agitated and mussed up.

He pointed at Isabel. "Don't even *think* about telling him!"

"You either!" Isabel jerked up her chin. "Don't you dare!"

Meanwhile, I was pretty busy boggling over the idea of the two of them together. As a couple. Isabel . . . and Rex? *Really?*

Given their mutually unkempt appearances, it looked as though they'd spent much of the award ceremony getting frisky here in Isabel and Bernard's cottage. It occurred to me that I couldn't remember having seen Rex at the banquet earlier—but that didn't mean he hadn't been there. I'd been distracted.

A concussion did *not* do wonders for your critical thinking skills, I was learning. Not to mention your sense of equability. Travis had only been asking questions. Looking out for me. That was his job. It hadn't been fair of me to attack him for it.

While I was contemplating the sorry state of my gray matter, Rex swore and stomped off. He strode in the opposite direction from my hiding place, audibly muttering in the darkness. From her cottage's porch, Isabel watched him leave.

She slurred a swearword in French, then slammed the door.

Something about her use of that expletive niggled at me. It reminded me of . . . *something* I'd lost track of after my headache had started. Which, speaking of, I wished I had more painkiller for.

"Well," Danny prompted dryly, "here's your big chance."

He nodded toward the cottage. Inside, probably, Isabel was still fuming. Confirming as much, I heard something smash.

A second later, Isabel burst through the doorway, looking terrifyingly like a woman about to embark on a rampage. I thought better of my nascent plans to innocently question her.

In fact, if Rex had been a meeker type—more like Adrienne—I would have been worried about his well-being in that moment. I didn't ever want to be on Isabel's hit list, that was for sure. It was a good thing I wasn't personally into lingerie models.

"Nah." Casually, I waved off the idea. "We can chat later."

Wisely, Danny and I crept away and made our escape.

I was still sacked out in bed—with a long-warmed-over ice pack on my forehead and Rex's Melt portfolio still open on the other half of my king-size mattress—when Danny awakened me.

At least he did so relatively civilly, by waving a coffee under my nose. "Hey, bedhead. Time to rise and shine."

Reflexively, I put my hand on my disheveled hair. "This is a very stylish look," I argued. I dragged off my spent ice pack and opened my eyes to see my pal standing beside my bed wearing track pants and a T-shirt. Maybe sneakers, too. I couldn't see his feet. "Unlike your ensemble, I might point out. Have you been *exercising* again? On purpose?" I made a face, groggy and confused. "Did somebody kick sand in your face at the beach or something? What's with the get-fit routine, all of a sudden?"

"*I* haven't been exercising, but *we're* about to," Danny informed me. He shoved a banana at me with his other hand. "Eat this. Drink that." He nodded at the coffee. "Let's get going."

Blearily, I surveyed the so-called "breakfast" he was offering. "Thanks, but chocolate chip waffles sound better."

"If we're going to stick together, we have to stick together," Danny pushed. "I'm going for a run this morning. That means you are, too." With a yank, he pulled off the comforter.

"Whoa!" I clutched its luxurious puffiness, sending Rex's portfolio papers flying. I kicked my legs, seeking cover. I didn't sleep naked, but my habitual frayed long T-shirt didn't provide much decency, either. "Just go! I'll join you later."

Danny disagreed. "I can't leave you here alone."

"Sure you can." I gestured. "I'll pay you to leave."

Danny's face hardened. "Never mind. I think I just quit."

He strode away, taking the delectable scent of coffee with him. I didn't think he was serious—until the door slammed shut.

Alarmed, I sat bolt upright in bed. I blinked at the door.

Any second now, I figured, Danny would come back. *Ha-ha! Fooled you!* he'd say. Then we'd laugh . . . and we'd have to jog. *Ugh.*

I wasn't supposed to exercise, anyway. Hadn't the Maison Lemaître physician said no exertion? I had an ironclad excuse.

That didn't make me feel any less awful about what I'd said to Danny just now, though. *I'll pay you to leave.* What was the matter with me? I couldn't keep pulling rank on him with my fortune.

In my own defense, though, it was roosters' happy hour outside. Anyone who woke me up that early and expected coherence didn't know me at all. I'm a late-night girl, not an up-and-at-'em type. For as long as I'd known him, Danny had been the same.

But maybe I didn't know Danny as well as I thought I did. Maybe Danny had changed. Shaken by that thought, I frowned.

Nope. I wasn't that fickle, I reminded myself. Unlike Travis, I *believed* in Danny—despite his disreputable past.

Trying not to think about the fact that I was now on the outs with *two* of the most important people in my life, I leaned over and started corralling fallen papers. Some were on the carpeted floor. One had drifted beneath the nightstand. Most were scattered atop the comforter. I stuffed those I could reach into Rex's portfolio, feeling put-upon. On the bright side, I tried to tell myself, at least I wouldn't have to argue with Travis about hiring Danny anymore. Not if Danny had already quit. Similarly, I didn't have to sweat mollycoddling Danny, because by the time I saw him again later, he'd be over it.

Danny wasn't the kind of guy who held a grudge.

"I'm the kind of guy who gets even," he'd joked to me once.

But now, that joke held a new (and unwelcome) significance. Was it possible that Danny secretly resented my inheritance?

He certainly seemed to feel that way sometimes. It was uncomfortable. Yet . . . a handwritten scribble on one of the fallen papers caught my eye. I must not have noticed it last night as I'd attempted to gather espionage clues by analyzing Melt's portfolio. It looked like . . . chicken scratch. I squinted and leaned nearer.

Christian is a brilliant and accomplished man, I read.

Startled, I dropped the paper. What the . . . ?

Heart pounding, I looked again. Closely. There was no question about it. In the same handwriting I recognized from Rex's smarmily scrawled *Call me!* (and phone number) on the inside of the portfolio, Rex had written . . . *exactly* the same thing that Bernard and Nina had said to me about Christian. The same thing that *I'd* said about him after "Name That Chocolate!"

I'll admit, I thought it was super weird. There had to be an explanation for that stilted phrase, I knew. But what?

Wanting answers, I slid out of bed and got dressed, opting for the closest thing I had to workout gear—an upscale sweatshirt from a Parisian boutique, a pair of shorts, and my Chucks. I wanted to find Danny and apologize. After some water and a bite of Danny's forgotten banana, my headache was gone, but I still felt fuzzy about yesterday. Except about one thing . . .

Travis answered on the first ring. Sleepily. "Hayden." He cleared his throat. Sexily. "Is everything all right?"

If anything, my buttoned-up keeper sounded even huskier and more masculine first thing in the morning. *Wowzers!* I swooned.

You know, *repentantly.* "Do you sleep naked, Travis?"

"Everything *is* all right," he judged. I'd swear he smiled.

"It is if you'll accept my apology," I told him. "I'm sorry about last night. I want to go ahead with hiring Danny—but I'll give you full 'I told you so' rights if I turn out to be wrong."

"Wow, that's big," Travis rumbled. "Especially coming from you." There was a pause. "Do you want to know my counteroffer?"

Of course he had one. "Nope. I'm not open to bargaining."

"Well, I've got to admire your loyalty, then." The phone rustled against something. I wondered if he was in bed. I could certainly *imagine* Travis in bed. "Okay. Apology accepted."

With that, blissfully, I was ready to start my day.

On my way downstairs to see if any of the Maison Lemaître staff were even on duty so early in the A.M., Nina intercepted me.

More accurately, she scared the bejeezus out of me.

"Hey, you!" The PR rep popped into the (usually deserted) service stairwell I'd taken to using, coming from within Maison Lemaître's labyrinth of back rooms and staff-only areas. "You're up early!" She eyed my shorts,

Converse, and couture sweatshirt. "I was going to look for you later. Got a minute right now?"

"Actually . . . I do," I told her. I remembered that inexplicable scribble on Rex's portfolio page and decided I might as well start digging right away. "Do you remember telling me the other day that Christian is 'a brilliant and accomplished man'?"

Nina's smile remained bright. "Yes. So?"

Clearly, whatever behind-the-scenes subterfuge I'd been imagining lay behind that affected phrase was only in my mind.

"What does it mean?" I asked, feeling slightly silly. "Why use those *exact* words?" I paused. "Bernard used them, too."

"So did you," Nina pointed out, checking her phone.

That was true. "I know, but . . ." *But I thought they might have an ominous meaning.* "Oh, never mind. I'm being absurd."

"Yes, but that's *good*!" Nina said perkily. Now that the awards banquet was finished, her stress levels seemed to have ratcheted down a bit. "That means that now I won't feel so goofy telling you *my* news." Nina leaned nearer. Then, confidingly, she added, "It's not the least bit professional, either!"

Touched by her gleefulness, I smiled. "Good for you! And . . . ?"

"And Calvin and I can join you and Danny for that massage!" Nina's voice echoed in the chilly, concrete-walled stairwell. I was reminded how my own voice had echoed similarly when Danny and I had taken to the back stairs on the night Adrienne had died. "I spoke with Calvin, and he was up for it, after all."

"That's great." Warmly, I touched her arm. Given the mess I'd made of my friendships lately, it was heartening to know I wasn't a total screwup. I *did* still know what made people happy. Speaking of which . . . "I'm on my way to see Danny. I'll tell him."

Enlisting him for a compulsory couples massage—even one that featured fragrant warm cocoa oil—wasn't exactly an olive branch. But I had game. I knew how to persuade him.

It could have been worse. It could have been a mani-pedi.

"It probably won't be until closer to the end of the re-treat," Nina warned me. "I'm still swamped at the moment."

"No problem." I was disappointed that my supposed superclue hadn't amounted to anything. After a few moments' chitchat, Nina and I said good-bye. I couldn't linger. After all, Travis wasn't the only man in my life I wanted to make my apologies to.

"Oh, and that phrase?" Nina stopped on her way upstairs. I was headed down. "It's Christian's new 'power phrase.'"

"'Power phrase'?" I couldn't help guffawing. Nina did, too.

"He wants it to sound natural. I guess I blew it on the delivery," Nina confided. "*Please* don't tell him I told you."

"I won't," I swore. I liked bonding with Nina. She understood me. She was even *more* beleaguered by Christian's idiosyncrasies than I was. "Cross my heart and hope to die."

Whoops! I think both of us shivered. It was funny how glib sayings had a lot more bite when there'd been a real murder.

Or an accidental overdose, I allowed. But I didn't think the police were right about their official "accidental death" ruling. Not given all I'd learned.

"Hope not!" Nina said sunnily. "Take care!"

Then she whirled up another flight of stairs, opened one

of the staff-only doors, and vanished from sight, leaving me alone.

In the deserted stairwell, I shivered. Time to get moving.

By "get moving," of course, I meant *running*. Probably at speeds a turtle would be ashamed of. Since I didn't get much exercise beyond wrestling with industrial mixers, hauling bags of sugar, and chopping chocolate blocks into submission, I knew I wasn't exactly at Olympian-level fitness. I could probably use some help—especially if I wanted to keep doing my chocolate-intensive job while still fitting into my favorite pants. So I emerged from the resort's lobby onto the grounds, inhaled deeply of the fresh springtime California air, and looked for Danny.

A jog wouldn't be that bad, I told myself. My headache had gone, so I was probably cured of my concussion. I'd take it easy. I'd do what Danny wanted to do for a change—the better to make amends for my thoughtless comment earlier—*then* I'd make him go get some of those chocolate-chip waffles with me. With hot-fudge sauce. And cocoa whipped cream. And a strong black coffee.

No sugar in that coffee, of course. I was getting healthy.

Grinning at my own well-developed ability to mislead myself, I shaded my eyes with my hand and scanned the ridge.

I couldn't tell if Danny was there . . . but several other people were. Two uniformed EMTs. Two police officers. And . . . Christian?

Given the flashing lights on the SFPD patrol car that I belatedly noticed parked on the landscaper's path a short distance away from the ridge trail—right next to an ambulance—something serious was going on. I started walking toward the ridge, squinting harder as I tried to pick up more details.

The EMTs knelt, examining something. I was still too far away to discern what it was. Growing concerned, I moved faster.

Someone shouted to me from the grounds—Eden from *Chocolat Monthly,* I thought—but by then, I realized the EMTs were moving a limp body from the ground onto what looked like a waiting scoop stretcher. A few moments later, they lifted the stretcher.

Whoever they'd put onto it didn't move. *Danny?*

I knew he'd been headed for a run. If he'd gone to the ridge trail again . . . Engulfed in panic, I started running. I didn't care if I jostled my brain or wrecked my gimpy knee permanently. I had to keep going. I had to know if something had happened to Danny.

Staring fixedly at those EMTs as they carried the stretcher to their waiting ambulance, I tripped on something. I kept going. I was close enough now to see the police officers' faces as they looked at me; close enough to see Christian's stricken expression and shaking head. It seemed completely likely that my heart would burst with fear. It *couldn't* be Danny. It couldn't.

The morning breeze chilled my legs. I felt dewy grass whisk past my ankles, dampening my shoes. Far below the ridge I was cresting, the bay water swirled against all those spiky rocks.

I pictured them as I reached the top of the ridge, then veered down the trail. I'd almost fallen onto those rocks myself. I could imagine too well what that descent would feel like. I didn't want to picture Danny's lifeless body on those rocks, but I couldn't help it. Had I distracted Danny too much? Had he left the resort—still steaming from our tiff—and fallen?

My knees felt rubbery. I followed the EMTs, my chest heaving with harsh breaths. Efficiently, they reached their ambulance and loaded the stretcher inside. By the time I made it to their position, gasping for breath and shaking with fear, one of the EMTs was swinging shut the door. I couldn't see inside.

The other EMT got in. He didn't turn on the siren.

Oh, God. Oh, God. Oh, God. My mind was a litany of jumbled fears and pleading as I grabbed the closest emergency worker.

"What happened?" I asked. "Is he going to be okay?"

The EMT looked startled. He shook his head, opened his mouth to reply—and then Danny strode in between us. He grabbed me, offering a curt wave to the EMT. "I've got this. Thanks."

His air of authority startled me—but not more than *he* did.

Wordlessly, I threw my arms around him. I might have cried a little. I *definitely* got shaky—and I definitely did my best to bear-hug Danny into not ever getting away from me ever again.

In my arms, he stood like a boulder, stoic and still. The ambulance drove away, crunching gravel beneath its tires. Its ordinary fading engine noise sounded extraordinary and surreal. So did the birds chirping in the trees. And my own heartbeat.

"I thought it was *you*!" I cried with my face in Danny's T-shirt. I balled up fistfuls of cotton from his back, clutching him harder. He felt completely hard all over. "Where were you?"

Danny shrugged. He dislodged my arms from around his—I'd pinned him pretty good—and then stepped back to establish a few inches of breathing room. "I doubled back to go get you."

Aw, he hadn't wanted to go on without me. He hadn't wanted to leave things between us on a bad footing. Now I *really* felt like crying. Sniffling, I nodded. "You doubled back . . . and that's when you decided we should apologize and be friends again?"

Danny looked puzzled. "No, that's when I noticed the body at the bottom of the ridge." He nodded toward the SFPD officers and Christian. "I sure as hell wasn't going to apologize. Not when you were wrong." His *you must be kidding* look washed over me . . . but I'd swear he seemed glad to see me. "You're so sappy." He cracked a grin. "You should have seen your face. It was as if someone had just shredded your passport, right in front of you—"

"Hey. I *need* that thing." Just as I needed him.

"—and you were going to *kick their asses* for doing it." Danny shook his head, seeming to marvel at me. Not that he would. "You're kind of formidable sometimes, you know that?"

"I'm kind of a jerk sometimes, I know *that.*" Full of relief, I stared at his shadow-bearded face. "I'm sorry, Danny."

He knew what I was talking about. He glanced away, silently watching the police officers and Christian. Then he nodded.

Danny slung his arm around my shoulders. He turned us both toward the ridge, then squinted upward. "See what happens when you don't go running with me?" he asked. "Next time, just come."

I gave a choked laugh. "Next time, I will." I fell into step beside him as we ascended the ridge. Looking at the SFPD officers talking with Christian, I remembered what had drawn me to gallop across the resort's grounds in the first place. "Do you know what happened? Who was it at the bottom of the ridge?"

Danny took away his arm. "It was Rex Rader."

"*Rex?*" I stopped cold. "Are you sure? Was he—"

"Dead? Definitely." Danny kept walking, forcing me to trot to keep up with him. "For several hours at least, judging by the condition he was in when I finally spotted him down there."

I shuddered, not wanting to think about the details.

I lowered my voice as we approached the group on the ridge. I heard Christian's voice filtering to us on a gust of wind, strident and shaken and slightly defensive. An officer nodded.

I figured I needed to know more. "Do you think—"

"Rex was pushed?" Spookily reading my mind again, Danny nodded. "He could have been. He *wasn't* very well conditioned, though. It's possible he slipped and fell on his own."

I remembered Danny saying that Maison Lemaître should have closed off the ridge trail or posted warning signs. He'd been right. This disastrous outcome was proof of it.

I hadn't liked Rex, but I hadn't wanted him dead.

"Slipped and fell? Seriously? Here at the *'death retreat'*?"

I was trying to take refuge in comforting sarcasm. It was a way of distancing myself from the horror of what was going on. Evidently, my appalled voice carried, because one of the officers broke off from interviewing Christian. He approached me, instead.

"'Death retreat,' ma'am? Can you elaborate on that?"

I quailed. No doubt about it. I'm the type who gets jittery if a police car follows me innocently in heavy traffic. I start sweating when a patrolman parks beside me at the coffee shop. There's something about uniforms, authority, and those damn mirrored sunglasses that makes me feel instantly guilty.

I hadn't done anything. Mr. SFPD didn't know that, though.

"I'm sorry. I was making a joke. I didn't mean anything."

Protectively, Danny took a step closer. His shoulder shielded me from the police officer, making me feel . . . well, "runty" would be the best word for it, I guess. I was nervous, not incompetent. Pulling down my sweatshirt, I stepped forward.

I nodded toward the ridge. "Do you know what happened?"

"We'll know more after we interview you and Mr. Jamieson," the officer said somberly. I realized he must have known Danny's name because Danny must have been the one who'd summoned help. I also realized, frankly, that the officer didn't seem nearly as impressed by my bravado as I was. He pulled out a worn notepad.

"Ah! You have a notepad," I said in a too-hearty voice. "I do, too! Mine's a Moleskine. It's really handy. How's yours?"

My attempt at establishing camaraderie with him fell flat. (Hey, even *I* don't bat .1000 on the whole making-friends-easily thing *all* the time.) And that's how Danny and I wound up being interviewed by the San Francisco Police Department . . . for almost an hour.

Chapter 11

In the end, the police informed us that Rex's death had "probably" been an unfortunate accident. In the absence of any material evidence, they didn't have the impetus or the resources to investigate further. Not even when I reminded the officers (at risk to my own overworked nervous system) that maybe they should check "for tracks."

The officer Danny and I had spoken with had looked amused at that. Evidently, there were *hundreds* of tracks on the ridge, belonging to all the many Maison Lemaître guests who'd traversed that path over the past few days. Sneaker prints weren't exactly the same as fingerprints. Several retreat attendees and staff members were interviewed, but no one had seen anything unusual.

The conclusion was that Rex had gone for one of his usual runs on the ridge, then somehow slipped onto the bayside rocks below. He'd probably been killed, we were told, by a head wound.

I couldn't help touching my own lumpy noggin, feeling lucky that I hadn't been thumped even harder. I'd had the dubious good fortune of landing on a nice, nonjagged hallway floor, with carpeting as a cushion and Danny to come to my rescue shortly afterward. I'd suffered a concussion, but I was alive.

I wished I could say the same thing for Rex. I saw Nina dealing with the police after Danny and I were through, and knew that she probably felt the same way. After all, Rex *had* been kind to Nina at the buffet. Like me, he'd noticed her distress. He'd tried to help her feel better about things. That meant Rex wasn't all bad. He wasn't all smarm. He was . . . *He'd been* . . . a human being just like me, flawed and stressed and trying to get by.

I said as much to Danny. He chortled, then shook his head.

"Rex was our number one suspect in Adrienne's death," my pal reminded me, jerking me out of sentimental "Kumbaya" mode and back to harsh reality. "With him gone, we're back at page one."

Oh yeah. Amid all the turmoil, I'd forgotten about that.

I wanted to continue forgetting about it, too. All at once, I'd had more than enough of danger and death and uncertainty. In the wake of Rex's unfortunate demise, Christian must have felt somewhat the same way, because he showed a little humanity himself and canceled the day's activities.

He did so via Nina, his right-hand gal, of course. After the police finished talking with him, Christian disappeared.

But the antics of Lemaître's (cowardly) leader aside, I felt at loose ends after Rex's death. I knew it was probably shock talking, but I seriously considered leaving San Francisco.

"It doesn't matter," I told Danny, walking back across the grounds after being grilled by the authorities. "I'm starting to think that maybe Adrienne *did* accidentally overdose herself. She was in a dither that night at the welcome reception. She probably went overboard on the caffeine in her green drink, and that's that. Whether she was conspiring to sell

Lemaître's secrets to a competitor or"—I lowered my voice—"having a fling with Bernard, Adrienne is gone now. None of that matters."

I don't know why I thought, ludicrously, that talk of Bernard and Adrienne's torrid (potential) romance deserved *more* discretion than her (supposed) corporate espionage. It just did.

"It matters," Danny said, "because *she* mattered."

He was right. I sighed. "I'm all mixed-up. Sad too."

He looked away. Another man would have tried to comfort me. Danny wasn't like that. He'd already reached his hug quota for the year in a single visit, and it hadn't been a whole week yet.

He cleared his throat. "How about that cocoa oil massage?"

It was the closest he was liable to come to giving me a pep talk. I was grateful for the effort. Also, I was reminded of . . .

"Not today." I had to let him off the hook. I'd told him about my idea to treat Nina and Calvin to a couple's massage, with Danny and me as tagalong incentivizers. "I made spa plans with Isabel today"—*right after she (maybe) gave me a purposely injurious shove*—"and I don't want to leave her hanging."

"After seeing her last night, I wouldn't want to, either."

While Danny grinned over that, we both lapsed into silence. I didn't know what he was thinking about, but *I* was remembering the argument we'd seen Isabel having with Rex. She had, very literally, looked ready to commit homicide on the spot.

Had she looked equally murderous on the night of Adrienne's death? Maybe Isabel really *had* overdosed her rival. Given what Danny and I had seen last night, it certainly seemed plausible.

Then again, *everyone* looked suspicious to me just then.

"Probably," I mused, "Isabel cooled off after Rex left."

"Probably she passed out before she reached him," Danny volunteered, clearly on a similar wavelength as me. He glanced at me as we reached the Italianate stone fountain. "You know how much Isabel knocks back every day. And night. She was loaded."

"Probably way too drunk even to *find* Rex in the dark," I said, "much less confront him on the ridge and push him off it."

We both stared toward the now-distant ridge, considering it. Unfortunately, that scenario felt much too plausible to me.

"After all this, are you sure you want to keep a spa date with Isabel?" Danny gave me a serious look. "You can always say you're too busy writing your overdue consulting report to have someone smear expensive mud all over you."

"It's not 'expensive mud,'" I replied with dignity. "It's a *treatment*. Plus, Isabel doesn't know about my consulting for Lemaître, so I can't use it as an excuse. I was undercover, remember? Besides, my report isn't overdue. Not technically."

Not yet. But I still felt that familiar (unpleasant) twinge of anxiety that always dogged me when I had work left to do.

"All the same . . . ," Danny pressed, not buying it for a minute.

"I'm going. I still want one of those warm chocolate-fondue body wraps." Staunchly, I glanced toward the spa. "You coming?"

Danny blanched. "To the spa? *Twice* in one week?"

I crossed my arms. "You're my bodyguard, right?"

"I'm your security specialist," he corrected. "I don't have to shadow your every move to make sure you're safe.

Besides, unlike your hotel room, the spa is a public spot. You'll be okay. I have . . . something to do."

I quirked my mouth. "Is 'something' cute and blond?"

"Call me if you run into trouble." Danny didn't even pause to consider confiding his hot-date plans in me. "Or signal me."

Demonstrating, he scratched his head. *Slooowly.* "Remember?"

I swatted him. "I'm recently concussed, not stupid."

"Just making sure." He flashed me a grin. "For all I know, you might have forgotten our whole storied history together."

That would have explained why I'd been so bitchy to him earlier, when I'd snarkily offered to pay him to leave me alone. But that wasn't it. We both knew it. "I'll *never* forget that."

Looking alarmed, Danny held up his palms. "*Don't* start reminiscing. Now is not the time. We've got a spa to visit—"

"A hot date to keep." I waggled my eyebrows teasingly.

"—and a murderer to find," he went on. "Or maybe two."

I gulped. That was daunting. "Do you really think so?"

Danny shook his head. "I think we'll know more soon."

Then, with that cryptic comment, my track-pants-wearing buddy rotated his burly shoulders, gave me a grin, and left.

I took a minute to savor the fact that Danny was really alive. (What can I say? I'm a secret softy at heart.) Then I took my shorts-wearing self to the spa to meet Isabel Lemaître.

Forty-five minutes after being undressed, showered, steamed, slathered with a chocolate-fondue mixture that smelled like my sweetest dreams, rolled up in a gigantic heated foil electrified wrap, and left alone on a spa table to bake like a huge cocoa-buttered burrito (or a person-size hot *bûche de Noël,* minus the merengue mushrooms and fondant icing—take your pick), I finally realized I was being stood up. Isabel wasn't coming.

Honestly, I was relieved. And let down. Simultaneously.

I still liked Isabel, despite everything. After all, if I suspected the worst of everyone who'd ever argued with Rex . . . well, that long list would include *me.* I admired Isabel's free-spirited attitude and her cosmopolitan outlook. I envied her bodacious figure and her talent for effortlessly accessorizing. I even appreciated her ability to pour multiple cocktails down her gullet without so much as a boozy stumble (unlike *me* last year in Mykonos, when the local taverna's Greek ouzo did me in).

But I *didn't* like wondering if my glamorous newfound friend might have pushed Rex Rader to his death in a fit of pique. That was seriously scary. So was the idea that Isabel could have had at least one good reason to overdose Adrienne: Bernie. Now that Rex was dead, Isabel was rapidly moving up in the suspect ranks.

Isabel's opportune no-show gave me lots of time to consider those suspects, too. I thought about Bernard. About Christian. About Rex and Adrienne. About my own place in this whole mess.

I didn't belong poking my nose into things—at least not things that weren't 65 percent bittersweet, caramelized, and/or ganache-filled. Travis knew it. Deep down, so did I. Most likely, Danny did, too. But as Adrienne's friend, I had a unique perspective on her final hours. I'd been close to her. I'd helped her. Heck, I'd sipped the same killer green drink she had! For all I knew, I remembered with a shiver that made a macabre joke of my body wrap's decadent warmth, *I'd* been the killer's original target.

I still couldn't rule out that frightening possibility.

That meant I still had things to do. Maybe. If Rex *had* been the killer (and he'd been unreasonably driven to murder me by my initial refusal to consult for him at Melt—or to murder Adrienne and score her chocolate secrets for free), then the problem was solved . . . although that meant there was *another* murderer loose. If someone else had overdosed Adrienne *and* killed Rex, then . . .

. . . then *Isabel* could have done it! Gobsmacked by the obvious, I groaned aloud. I couldn't do much else, honestly. The spa technician (not Britney this time, but Portia) had wrapped my arms inside my heated foil wrap. I'd been wrapped like a mummy head to toe and left to bake, soaking up moisturizers and chocolate aromas while I waited for Isabel to join me. But Isabel wasn't coming.

Maybe because she'd killed Rex and then skipped town.

It was conceivable. But so were several other theories— such as the idea that poor, confused Bernard had learned about his wife's liaison with his onetime protégé and had pushed Rex off the ridge-side trail in irrational fury. Danny and I might not have been the only ones lurking in the shadows last night. I didn't think Bernard would have killed Adrienne, but . . .

Don't even think about telling him! Rex had warned Isabel last night. She'd warned Rex, too. They'd had to mean *Bernard.*

But I just couldn't believe Bernard was a murderer. Not even after he'd grabbed me, warned me, gotten frosty with me, and gotten confused with everyone else. But Isabel . . . well, just then, she seemed to be the likeliest suspect in Rex's death—and Adrienne's, too. Isabel had had plenty of reasons to kill her husband's mistress. *Of course,* I decided. *It* has *to be Isabel.*

Burning to tell someone, I wiggled. "Portia? Hello?"

No one answered. I could hear other retreat attendees in

other treatment rooms, enjoying the spa services. I could hear the spa's melodic New Age music. I could smell . . . *burnt chocolate*.

"Portia?" I called louder. "Britney? Is anyone there?"

I wasn't just burning to share my murder theories, I realized with unease. I was just plain *burning*. I hadn't noticed because of all my homicide-related conjecturing, but my wrap was overheating. I'd been sweating before; I dripped now. *Gross*.

But I didn't care about aesthetic issues just then. Not when I was *burning*. The acrid fragrance of burnt chocolate reached me. So did a prickling sensation on my legs. It hurt.

Confused, I craned my neck to stare at the wrap's controls. Its electronic panel flashed red. That was bad. When it came to mechanical things, exposed skin, and lipstick on my complexion, *red* was *bad*. My headache returned with a throbbing vengeance. My heart pounded, working overtime to push blood to my overheated extremities. Feeling even hotter, I swung my foot toward the control panel, trying to unplug my malfunctioning foil wrap.

No dice. Grunting with effort, I rocked atop my spa table. I moved a few inches. "Britney?" I yelled. "Portia? Anyone?"

At this rate, I'd turn into a human Ho Ho (no jokes *not* involving the famous creme-filled chocolate-rolled snack cake, please) before my spa treatment was over. I didn't want that, I told myself crazily. Everyone knew Zingers were better.

Sweat dripped into my eyes. Feeling woozy, I rocked harder. I managed to get to my feet, still burrito-wrapped in space-age foil. I swayed with the effort, my equilibrium as shaky as my ability to regulate my own temperature while fully insulated.

This must be what it was like to be baked at 350 degrees,

the most common temperature in today's kitchens. I'd be damned if I was going to die covered in chocolate fondue, though. Mustering a surge of effort, trailing power cords and dollops of spa goo, I hopped toward the control panel. *Almost there . . .*

The treatment room door opened. Cool air rushed in, almost making me pass out with partial relief. Nothing had ever felt that good—except the sight of a baffled, momentarily motionless Portia. She stared at me, obviously wondering if I'd drunk both my share of the complimentary choco-mosas *and* Isabel Lemaître's.

"It's malfunctioning!" I gasped, flailing at the control panel with my foil-wrapped hip. I felt like an overcooked baked potato. I probably looked like one, too. "I can't turn it off."

Wearing a look of enlightenment, Portia strode to the control panel. She peered at it. "Yeah. I think it's broken."

"Unplug it!" Feebly, I tried to wave at the outlet.

"Oh. Right." Portia giggled. "That would work, huh?"

I gritted my teeth as she used her handy *non*wrapped hand to yank out the electronic wrap's plug. My temperature plummeted.

I sagged with relief. Portia studied me blankly.

"Are you ready for your soothing *après-chocolat* soak?"

I shook my head. The only thing I was ready for was finding out who kept targeting me. This incident couldn't have been an accident. "Does this wrap equipment malfunction often?" I asked.

As far as I knew, no one had been in the treatment room with me. But someone could have tampered with it beforehand.

Portia's eyes widened. "You'd have to speak with my boss about that. We're not supposed to discuss the equipment."

I just *bet* they weren't. Disgruntled and scared, I wiggled my shoulders. "Fine. Can you just get me out of here, please?"

Fifteen minutes later, I was done with my first (and last) chocolate body wrap, and on my way to track down a killer.

The first person I intended to talk to was Christian. After all, he was (nominally) in charge at Maison Lemaître. He needed to know that his renowned chocolate-themed spa services were *this close* to involuntarily brûlée-ing his retreat attendees.

Fed up, I got dressed in my shorts and Marais-district sweatshirt, then wound up my hair in a slapdash ponytail. In the spa's gilded mirror, my face looked back at me, screamingly pink. It was truly disturbing. I looked sunburnt. All over.

Hoping the effects of my "inadvertent" chocolate bake were temporary, I pocketed my room keycard and stormed out of the changing area. The chime-filled New Age music didn't comfort me. Neither did the fragrances of chocolate and ginger or the sight of multiple retreat attendees *not* being heatstroked to death.

I didn't know if a heated body wrap could really kill someone, but it seemed likely. After all, restaurant foods cooked *sous-vide* style don't get very hot (only around 135 degrees), but given twelve hours or so, even the gnarliest cuts of beef are transformed into succulently cooked morsels. Home slow cookers only heat their contents to a slightly higher temperature, but they manage to morph tough pork into saucy, tender barbecue with no trouble at all. I didn't know if the spa employees needed more supervision or if I'd made a mistake in not forcing Danny to get burrito-wrapped with me. Either way, I was shaking with indignation when I reached the spa's central area. Its subdued colors and slate-and-bamboo wall of trickling water were all very Zen. At that moment, I certainly wasn't.

I stormed over to the main desk. "Would you please page Mr. Lemaître for me? I have something urgent to discuss with him."

I didn't plan to wander all over the resort's extensive grounds trying to locate him myself. All that effort would only dissolve my current ire-filled momentum. Given my sometimes short attention span, I needed to act on things immediately.

The attendant blinked up at me. "There's a courtesy phone in the café," she said in a pleasant tone, "if you'd like to—"

"I'd like," I said firmly, "for you to page him. *Please.*"

At my tone, she looked alarmed. "All right." With vague snippiness, she reached for her phone. Then she hesitated. "You know, I don't think Mr. Lemaître is available right now."

"I think Christian will speak to me," I said. *He'd better.*

"Oh! I'm sorry. I thought you meant *Bernard.*" The attendant gave an uneasy laugh. "He's on all of our minds today, because of what happened with Mrs. Lemaître." She traded a glance with her coworker. "We all feel really bad for him. He's *so* nice."

The other attendant nodded emphatically. "He brings us boxes of chocolate—the old-fashioned kind they sell at the Lemaître Chocolates shop down near Pier 39. It's *so* good!"

I would have given them ten pounds of milk chocolate creams and dark-chocolate mints if they'd simply quit dithering.

"Yes, it's unfortunate what happened at the banquet," I agreed, thinking that word had spread about Bernard's emotional breakdown while accepting his award, "but I really do need—"

"Oh, we don't mean the banquet!" They exchanged quizzical glances. "We mean Mrs. Lemaître turning up missing today."

Isabel was *missing*? That was . . . damning information. That explained why Isabel had been a no-show with me. I couldn't help concluding that she'd fled after killing Rex Rader last night.

Poor Bernard. Still, that didn't explain that malfunctioning equipment. "Could you please page Christian?"

Already, I could feel my ire starting to cool . . . unlike my seared skin. My arms looked like well-moisturized lobsters.

With a shrug, the second attendant announced the page.

Nothing happened at first. Disgruntledly, I imagined Christian hearing that page, deliberately blowing me off, and laughing about it. *There. That* got my outrage fired up again.

Moments later, I finally heard . . . "Hayden? Is that you?"

I turned, surprised to hear a feminine voice. "Nina?"

She marched toward me, business suited and all clipboarded up, wearing a pleasant but befuddled smile. She was such a professional that she didn't even blink at my flamingo-colored complexion. Maybe it wasn't as bad as I thought it was.

No, it was *worse,* I assured myself, trying to stay mad.

"I was in one of the spa's 'unify' theme rooms, making sure everything would keep until tomorrow for the canceled workshop session, when I heard the page for Christian." Nina kept her gaze (conspicuously) locked on my eyes instead of my beet-red torso. "I thought I'd come see if I could help. Can I?"

"Thanks, but no. I don't think so." I tossed a thank-you

glance to the spa attendants, then moved away from the desk to talk with Nina. "I've got a bone to pick with Christian."

Nina laughed. "Join the club! *He* was the one who was so keen on the workshop I canceled. A week ago, Christian couldn't *wait* to explore new ways to employ chocolate essences in spa-based fragrance utilization, but now he can't even be bothered to deal with all the fallout from canceling today's sessions."

"Well . . ." Uncomfortably, I looked away. "That *was* because of Rex's accident," I pointed out. "It's only decent to cancel."

"Oh, I know that." Nina gave an embarrassed-looking wave. "I agree. Of course, I do! Poor Rex." She lapsed into a moment of respectful silence. Then, "It's just . . . well, *you* know what I mean, right? Christian is *so* mercurial. Sometimes it's hard to deal with him. But tragedy or not, work must go on, I'm afraid."

My work hadn't been "going on" at all. I'd tried to change that, though. Last night, for instance, I'd had every intention of working on my Lemaître consulting report. Truly, I had. But then I'd spotted Rex's Melt portfolio and gotten drawn in.

"Are you *sure* there's nothing I can do for you?" Nina pressed, seeming concerned. She touched my arm. "It would be a welcome relief from thinking about chocolate! Almost everyone here is a whiz at it, but I'm afraid it's all Greek to me. I know how to make it sound good, but that's as far as I go."

"No, thanks. I appreciate it, though." I dropped my gaze to Nina's hand as she withdrew it. Today, her fingernails were expertly shaped, I noticed, and polished a perfect Ballet Pink.

Double-checking on a workshop, huh? More likely, I realized, Nina had skipped over to the spa for a spur-of-the-moment manicure. I'd probably been too obvious about gawking at her chipped, chewed-up nails earlier. I hadn't meant to make her feel self-conscious. Since I felt bad (and didn't want to make the same gaffe twice), I decided to temporarily postpone going on the warpath with Christian and bolster Nina's excuse instead.

"You said the workshop is about using chocolate fragrances?" I asked, trying to show an interest. "You should encourage Christian to sit in on that one when it resumes. The Maison Lemaître toiletries need some fundamental refining."

Nina laughed and wrinkled her nose. "Chocolate and orange? Yuck! That's not my favorite, either. But Christian likes it."

I thought I could change his mind about that. *After* I read him the riot act for allowing unsafe equipment in his spa, of course. I'd already noted several fragrance alternatives that might be used (and *yes,* I might have been postponing working on my consulting report at the time).

"Well, to each his own, I guess." *There.* I'd duly upheld Nina's flimsy "workshop" excuse to cover her pampering. Maybe she'd thought I'd be offended because she'd found time for a manicure but not for a couples' massage with Calvin. With effort, I swerved away my gaze from Nina's manicure. "I'd better run. My tirade for Christian is at risk of burning out."

Burning out. Nope, no it wasn't. That did it.

"Don't be too hard on Christian when you find him." Nina gave me an admiring gaze. "You can be pretty intimidating."

That was the second time someone had said something similar to me today. Not that I believed it. I knew I was a marshmallow on the inside. Except when chasing down chocolate issues.

"Although . . ." For a second, Nina looked troubled. She glanced around the spa's main area, then pulled me into an alcove near the trickling wall of water. I felt its mist fall faintly over us, smelling of minerals. "You're not invulnerable, Hayden."

I laughed. "If you're worried about Christian—"

"No, I'm worried about—" Nina broke off. She clutched her clipboard harder, then frowned at me. "Your friend Danny."

"Danny? Why? I thought you two"—*wanted to get cozy and extramarital sometime soon*—"hit it off the other day."

"We did. That's why I Googled him. You know, to get some background on him. And maybe find a . . . picture or two?"

At that admission, Nina went almost as pink as I was.

Now it was my turn to frown. "You *researched* Danny?"

"Did you know he's a *criminal*?" Nina asked urgently. Her gaze searched mine. "He's been involved in some shady stuff."

I wished I could have denied it. I couldn't.

"I really don't think that's any of your business."

My icy tone didn't deter her. "I understand the whole 'bad boy' thing is appealing," Nina admitted. "I do! But have you really thought about this?" She paused to examine me, probably trying to gauge if she was getting through. "I know you were hurt yesterday. I get reports from the staff physician so I can identify any trouble areas that might need . . . *finessing*. You know, in a PR sense. Or anything else. I know about your concussion."

Oh. "You don't have to worry about me, Nina."

Especially if she was insinuating that *Danny* was responsible for my head injury. I couldn't believe *two* people had now warned me against him. Who did they think they were?

Nobody else knew Danny Jamieson the way I knew him.

"Fine. I hear you." Nina held up her palm in a peace-keeping gesture. "You're not ready to talk about it. But just know"—her gaze softened with compassion—"I'm here whenever you are."

Exasperated, I folded my arms. "I won't need that. Thanks."

"I mean it, Hayden. Sometimes it's hard to ask for help."

At Nina's still-grave tone, it occurred to me that maybe she was trying to tell me something. Maybe *she* had personal experience with being battered or beaten. Maybe by Calvin.

That would explain her deferring a cozy couples' massage.

Nina didn't *seem* vulnerable. But even strong, smart women got caught up in abuse. If Nina was cautioning me because she had an insider's perspective . . . well, she deserved my sympathy and help, not my defensive attitude. Nina *had* spent a lot of time with Adrienne, who was notoriously softhearted. For all I knew, my late chocolatier friend had once given Nina this same advice.

I was touched to think she might be passing it on to me.

"I really appreciate that, Nina," I told her in a kinder tone. "If I'm ever alarmed by anything, I'll call for help."

Proving it, the very next thing I did after saying goodbye to the PR rep was make a mental note to myself as I headed off to continue my search for Christian Lemaître. I didn't have my phone with me—since I'd thought I was going jogging that morning and hadn't been back to my room since—but as soon as I did, it was time for me to tap Travis's network again . . . and find out if Calvin Wheeler had "shady stuff" of his own to worry about.

Chapter 12

By now, you might not be surprised to learn that my fiery ire didn't even last the whole length of the walk back to Maison Lemaître's main building, where I expected to find Christian. On the way there, amid the flowers and fountains and bay views and acres of green grass, I spied one of those billowy white tents—the kind they'd used for the chocolate-themed scavenger hunt on the first day of the retreat—and slowed my steps in curiosity.

Judging by the crowd gathered around that tent, something major was going on. Judging by the sugary, caramelized scent of freshly baked waffle cones and hot fudge drifting on the breeze, it did not involve murder (for once). All of my expert senses suggested there was *chocolate* over there—chocolate *ice cream*.

Reasoning that a nice, frosty treat might cool the lingering scorched-skin sensation I'd been left with after my chocolate-fondue body wrap mishap, I beelined in that direction. Like I said before, my monkey mind sometimes takes over. Today, it was urging me to have ice cream. Since I hadn't even eaten breakfast yet, I figured a couple of scoops of frozen freckled-chocolate ganache or mocha sorbet would tide me over as capably as brioche toast with Nutella and an espresso would have.

Ten minutes later, I held a plastic tulip-shaped bowl full of both of those flavors, plus some chocolate chunk mint-infusion gelato for a chaser. I'd opted to have the waffle cone broken into a makeshift topping (the better to pre-serve its crunch), and to forego the optional caramel and/or hot-fudge sauce (which would have turned the whole delec-table concoction into soup within forty-five seconds) and whipped cream (no need to dilute all the chocolaty good-ness with superfluous dairy). I am, after all, a professional at making these sorts of decisions.

My first bite made me moan. My second bite made my eyes roll back in my head. *How* had they made this ice cream *so* good? I didn't know if my rage attack had worked up a monster appetite or what, but I *did* know that I wasn't devouring that ice cream quickly. It deserved to be savored. Cradling it, I retreated to a bench not far from a riotously pink-flowering bauhinia tree, then curled up to indulge my outer chocoholic. *Yum, yum.*

"Hayden!" It was Eden, the reporter. "Mind if I join you?"

I looked up from my blissful cacao haze to see the *Chocolat Monthly* headline chaser pointing her cell phone at me. I winced.

"Sure." Warily, I eyed her phone. "Off the record."

She hesitated, then shrugged and closed whatever app she'd (probably) been using to record everyone surrepti-tiously.

Satisfied, I pointed my spoon. "Have a seat."

Eden joined me on the bench. She glanced at my ice-cream extravaganza with undisguised disdain. "Is it good?" she asked.

"It's *nirvana.*" I scooped up another bite. With relish.

"I don't like ice cream. Especially chocolate."

Okay. That was it. I officially didn't trust her. I decided to get to the point. "You want to ask me about Rex, right?"

"Well, his death *is* a big story." Eden's eyes gleamed. "What can you tell me about Rex Rader's final hours?"

They were spent getting frisky with another man's wife.

Nope, I wasn't throwing anyone under the bus like that. Not even Rex. Now that he was gone, I felt sorry for him. "Nothing," I told her. "What can you tell me about Isabel Lemaître?"

"Isabel?" Eden blinked as though she'd never heard the name before. "Isabel Lemaître? Bernard Lemaître's wife?"

"I assume you've been covering her disappearance, too?"

Eden gave me a suspicious look. I blithely licked my ice cream, waiting her out. She needed me more than I needed her.

More quickly than I expected, she caved. "All I know is that Bernard reported Isabel missing this morning around six. Her clothes and things were gone. No one's seen her since last night." Eden glanced toward the parking lot. "Her Mercedes is gone, but the valet didn't remember retrieving it for her."

Every sign pointed to Isabel hotfooting it out of Maison Lemaître, that was for sure. I'd be willing to bet Isabel paid that valet to "forget" her. "Are the police investigating?"

"Investigating a runaway wife? Doubtful. Isabel seems to have packed all her things and left." A pause. "So. About Rex—"

"Oh, I'm sorry. I'm afraid I'm late for an appointment." *With Christian.* I still intended to give him a piece of my mind about the spa equipment—although now that I wasn't currently being roasted in chocolate, my mission did feel less critical.

I was up and headed away from the bench when Eden

said, "Is it true that you've been consulting with Christian Lemaître?"

I skidded to a stop. "Who told you that?"

If word had gotten out about my consulting gig with Lemaître Chocolates . . . that would explain why Christian had come to my room yesterday. He probably thought *I'd* bragged about it.

I couldn't let such an unprofessional idea stand.

"Bernard told me," Eden informed me. "I assumed he'd know?"

Whew. This was manageable. "Bernard is no longer in charge of Lemaître," I said, thankful for that obfuscating truth. "You really can't trust what he says about the business these days."

"Not even," Eden persisted, "when he says Lemaître Chocolates was supposed to have merged with Melt?"

That was a scenario I hadn't anticipated. Rather than bringing Rex to Lemaître, maybe Bernard had been planning to bring Lemaître to Melt? Maybe *Bernard* had been selling company secrets to Rex, not Adrienne. I wanted to believe it was true.

Except for the part where it vilified an adored chocolate patriarch, of course. I didn't like that part at all.

"You know the chocolate industry," I told Eden with a wave. "Rumors are rampant. You can't trust hearsay. Good luck with your story." *You're going to need it.* "Try the ice cream!"

Then I headed toward the hotel, ready to call Travis.

My day *needed* a dose of husky sexiness . . . and so did I.

By the time I'd called Travis to ask him to check on Nina's (potentially abusive) husband, gone online to look at news reports about Rex's death, texted Danny to arrange a meet-up later, and arrived downstairs at Christian's office, my outrage was a shadow of its former self. You could even say it had mostly disappeared altogether. Because as many ways as Danny and I were alike, we could be mind-bogglingly different in others, too.

Unlike him, *I,* for example, do not hold a grudge *or* get revenge. I don't even know how to do that. Most of the time, I'm moving on before any one person could get on my nerves.

I'm a live-and-let-live type . . . *unless* someone is trying to bake me like a potato in a chocolate-fondue body wrap, I reminded myself. Then I had no problem taking the necessary actions to deal with things.

Maybe I *was* formidable. And intimidating. I certainly felt that way as I burst into Christian Lemaître's office and asked to see him immediately. Unfortunately, Christian's bombshell of an admin didn't pick up on my *don't mess with me* mojo.

"Do you have an appointment?" she asked, blond and bored.

"He'll see me," I told her. "Hayden Mundy Moore."

"I'm afraid Mr. Lemaître is not in right now." Obviously unconvinced of my importance, she glanced up from her apathetic perusal of my shorts-plus-sweatshirt ensemble. "Sorry."

I listened. "I can hear sounds coming from his office."

She rolled her eyes. "Fine. He's in, but he's having his afternoon workout. He's not to be disturbed. For anything."

This was taking *way* too long. "I'm disturbing him."

Where the admin's ennui didn't help my ego, it *did* help my plan of action. I strode across the office and stepped inside.

Christian's inner sanctum was dimly lit. It smelled (not surprisingly) almost overwhelmingly of chocolate. The noise I'd heard was a deluxe treadmill, raising a commotion in one corner.

"You can't be in there!" the admin yelled, much too late.

I locked the door to prove that I could, then looked around. I identified Christian right away—mostly by the trail of candy bar wrappers that littered the floor. I followed them . . .

. . . all the way to Christian's desk, where the man himself sat in the spacious semidarkness, hands and face smeared unevenly with chocolate. In the background, the treadmill thumped away.

Another glance confirmed the setup he'd rigged. A hexagonal dumbbell had been tied to the treadmill's rigging with a length of stretchy exercise tubing. It was currently *thumping* along to simulate (I assumed) Christian's footsteps as he "worked out."

I nodded at it. "That's going to void your warranty."

He dropped his chocolate and gawked at me. "Get out!"

"Nope." I moved to his desk. "That's not Lemaître chocolate." Evidently, Christian had a hankering for cheap drugstore chocolate—the kind kids bought at the corner bodega.

"It's been a difficult day." With a defiant expression, he stared at me. "The police, the questions, *another* person dying—" Christian broke off, his voice warbling. "I'm scared for my life! Aren't you? For God's sake, this place is a death trap!"

Completely unexpectedly, I felt sorry for him.

Christian Lemaître, one of the premier bullies of my industry, was *petrified.* With good reason, I had to admit. He'd holed up in here—probably after finishing talking with the police—to binge on comfort food.

Yes, I know. You're thinking I'm too soft, right?

Well, that's too bad. I didn't get to be famous for my

insight with chocolate without having some of those intuitive skills transfer to the real world of people. That's how I am.

"As soon as word gets out, I'm *ruined*!" Christian went on. "The press will crucify me. The public will turn their backs on me. I'll be a laughingstock in the chocolate industry."

All right. Forget what I said earlier. Christian didn't deserve *that* much sympathy. He was still 100 percent *me, me, ME*.

"I can do something about that," I told him, helping myself to a seat in one of his luxurious leather-bound executive chairs. (*Mm, cushy.*) "But you have to do something for me, too."

"Nobody can do anything!" Christian wailed before I could exact my part of the bargain—a check-and-repair mission of the spa's malfunctioning wrap equipment. "My retreat is supposed to be my triumphal moment! Now it's ruined." He pouted. "First Adrienne offed herself, making *me* look like a bad boss in the process—and *then* she took my new product launch with her!"

The Lemaître nutraceutical chocolates line, I surmised. I'd told Travis to keep the truffles. My report would (eventually) make clear my objections to them . . . and offer some alternatives.

"Then my uncle gave everyone an earful when he went all nuclear winter on my banquet last night," Christian went on, continuing his insensitive diatribe, "and now *Rex* is dead!"

"Yeah. You must be really broken up about that."

"I am! Everything is falling apart!" Looking distraught, Christian wiped his chocolaty fingers on his shirt.

That absentminded gesture of his niggled at me. Christian had also smeared chocolate on his shirt on the night that Adrienne had died, I remembered. Danny and I had both noticed that detail. But why had Christian been stressed on the night of the welcome reception? He'd been the boy wonder of the show.

"Not *everything* is falling apart," I told him. "As soon as my report is finished, you'll see that you have options to—"

He held up his chocolate-smudged hand. "Don't even worry about your report. I've got bigger fish to fry."

I was offended. "My report is *not* inconsequential."

I might have postponed writing it, but that was . . . temporary.

"That's not what I mean." Christian gave an impatient wave. "I've been trying to catch up with you for days." Suddenly, he seemed much more astute. Maybe the sugar buzz was wearing off?

"I heard," I said dryly. "Dunning me won't work."

I don't respond well to pressure. Funnily enough, it makes me . . . procrastinate. Badgering *me* about delays is a zero-sum game.

Christian shook his head. "I want to offer you a job."

I couldn't help perking up at that. At the same time . . .

Did I *really* want to do more work for this soap opera of a chocolate company? Lemaître had *not* been the idyll I'd expected.

"I don't know, Christian," I demurred, wanting to be professional. "You remember that stipulation in our agreement that limits my consultation to three months? That's because—"

My uncle Ross's will demands that I keep moving, I was going to say, *or go broke*. But I never had a chance.

"I *need* you, Hayden," Christian begged. "Please do it!"

I'll admit it. Blatant pleading gets to me every time. I'm a sucker for anyone who really, *really* wants my expertise.

"Well, I might be able to wrangle a consultation for your troubled toiletries line," I compromised. "It's a new area for me—being nonedible, that is—but I know I can do better than—"

Tang-flavored Tootsie Roll soap, I meant to say, but . . .

"What? There's nothing wrong with our house toiletries! They're fantastic!" Christian frowned. "I *mean,*" he said with the elaborate (and insulting) patience of someone conversing with a child, "that I want to offer you a job. A *real* job." He paused. "I want you to take over Adrienne's job. Immediately."

It took at least thirty seconds for that offer to sink in. Once it did, I reeled. It hadn't even occurred to me that Christian might be proposing a full-time post. "I'm flattered, but"—*at the moment, "San Francisco chocolatier" looks like a literal dead-end job*—"I'm not looking for anything permanent."

"Don't tell me your answer right now," Christian urged.

"I just did. My answer's *no.*"

But even as I said it, my mind started drifting toward my potential alternative future as Lemaître Chocolates' head chocolatier. I could move into one of those cute Victorian houses in the Lower Haight, plant petunias in my Painted Lady's window boxes, take the Muni to work (on a cable car, natch), get myself a little cocker spaniel or a French bulldog for company. . . .

I was halfway to signing imaginary mortgage papers before I came to my senses, prompted by Christian's agitated expression.

"Take some time to think about it," he insisted. "Really."

I didn't plan to do any such thing. But while I was there . . .

"I'll confess, I thought Rex was a shoo-in for the job," I remarked, blatantly fishing for more information from him. "With Adrienne gone, I figured Lemaître would need another expert—"

"*Rex?*" Christian gave a moue of disgust, then ripped into another candy bar. Perfunctorily, he offered me half. I shook my head, rescuing my taste buds from an assault of cheap tropical oils, dubious chocolate, and stale peanuts. "Rex was my uncle's protégé, not mine. The last thing I wanted was for Rex's arty-farty 'cacao essences' and 'artisanal aroma pods' to infect Lemaître. You'd think the guy invented chocolate-based molecular gastronomy, the way the city press wet themselves over him."

Maybe that had been true a year or two ago. I'd seen the media clippings myself in Rex's portfolio. But I couldn't help thinking about Eden's (almost guaranteed) unflattering profile.

However brightly Rex's star had shined, it had dimmed by the time I'd met him. Melt had definitely been on the skids.

"But there's a reason I ousted Bernard," Christian went on after swallowing a huge bite of cheap candy, "and there's a reason those rumors about Lemaître and Melt merging are bogus."

Then they weren't *true? That was interesting.* Eden had seemed pretty sure she was onto something with that approach.

Maybe I wasn't the only one with a penchant for angling.

"I guess if those rumors had been true," I observed, "they would be history, now that Rex is out of the picture."

"Yep. Can't merge with a dead man," Christian pointed out prosaically. He took another bite, mindlessly chomping.

He didn't exactly seem racked with grief about Rex. Which only made me wonder . . . *how* dead set against the idea of a merger between Lemaître and Melt had

Christian been? Enough to have taken desperate measures to make sure it would never happen?

Maybe Christian was stressed because he'd followed his uncle's hated protégé to the ridge and pushed him to his death. Even homicidal maniacs probably got ulcers and acid reflux.

I wished I didn't have to consider it. But given the several murderous looks I'd seen on Christian's face during our acquaintance, he absolutely seemed capable of impulsive violence. Plus, he'd just confirmed Bernard's status as Rex's mentor. Until now, only Isabel had mentioned that—and she (along with being currently on the lam) was notoriously unreliable.

Things were gradually starting to come together, though. Bit by bit, I was compiling a more complete picture of the Lemaître empire . . . and all its scheming, double-crossing denizens.

"It must have been hard for you, having your uncle mentor Rex instead of you," I said. It was odd that Bernard—the king of traditional chocolates—would have taken a shine to someone with avant-garde tastes like Rex. "How did you cope with that?"

Eden would have been proud of my leading question. All I lacked was a recording device and a bloodthirsty demeanor.

"By being *better.*" Christian wadded up a candy bar wrapper, unbothered by the persistent racket coming from his treadmill. "And by keeping an eye on Rex, just like I do everyone else."

I nodded. "Keep your friends close, and your enemies—"

"Right under your nose. Exactly." Christian eyed the wreckage of his chocolate binge, then shook his head. "Nobody else has the balls to invite their competitors to a retreat. Just me. It happens here, on my turf, where *I* control it."

I pointed out the obvious. "You can't control *everything.*"

"I can come damn close to it." For a heartbeat, Christian's expression filled with malice. Then, resignation. "At least I used to be able to. These days . . ." He sighed. "The excitement is all in the chase. You know what I mean? When I was taking over Lemaître, I *loved* coming to work. People used to run scared from me. They did *everything* I asked, right down to abandoning their offices and moving into dinky little cubicles. It was so—"

"Tyrannical?" No wonder Nina was frazzled. Under Christian's regime, Gandhi would have developed a few tics.

"—*gratifying.*" He shook his head, looking me over with new and appreciative eyes. "You're sassy. I like that about you."

He thought I was kidding. I hadn't been. Christian wasn't doing much to sell me on his *non*murderous side. Any man who relished putting people out of work and inspiring fear might be a man who was capable of murder, too. Especially of his rival.

But of Adrienne? *Yes,* I decided, remembering the way he'd bullied her—the way he'd accused her of sabotaging him. The Christian I now sat across from would have unquestionably taken personally her selling secrets. He might have wanted revenge.

Struck by the thought, I shivered. Hey, at least I wasn't choco-roasted anymore. Maybe I wasn't quite so pink, either.

There was a bright side to everything—even confronting another human being's fundamentally avaricious nature. Right?

"I was wrong about you, Hayden." Christian beamed

at me. I felt as if I'd passed a creepy secret admission exam. "It wasn't until you had the sense to withhold Adrienne's notebook and use it for leverage that I realized we were on the same page."

Ugh. Viscerally, I wanted to *turn* the page. Christian and I weren't at all the same. I hadn't "withheld" Adrienne's notebook as a bargaining chip. I'd done it—was still doing it, with the help of Danny's street smarts—out of loyalty to my departed friend. I couldn't see that changing anytime soon, either.

"I'll expect to have you *and* that notebook when you accept my offer, of course," Christian went on blithely. "But the way you schooled me at 'Name That Chocolate!' was the cherry on top. That's when you really sold me. Anybody else would have had the sense to let me win. You saw how everyone else buckled, right?"

They'd "buckled," I knew, because they'd been beaten— not because they'd thrown the charity contest on purpose. But since Christian was willing to gab, I was willing to listen. For now.

"But *you* didn't." He smiled at me again. "I can't say I wasn't pissed you won. I was. I was going to fire your ass."

I gulped, belatedly realizing I'd almost "expertised" my way out of a lucrative consulting job. If my pride had cost me another gig (don't ask), Danny would have been appalled.

"Firing me would have been a mistake," I told Christian evenly, "given everything I know about your company."

His eyes narrowed. "Is that a threat?"

I almost laughed. I'm about as menacing as a sleepy kitten. But I guess people tend to see themselves everywhere, don't they? "I don't know," I said coolly, revising my opinion of Christian's intelligence downward. "What do you think?"

"I think maybe I underestimated you *twice.*" Christian

leaned back, steepling his hands over his taut abdomen. How did he stay so buff while munching cut-rate candy? "I think maybe you were a little pissed yourself. You couldn't troubleshoot my nutraceutical chocolate line, so you erased the evidence of it."

His smug expression baffled me. "Your nutraceutical line was doomed from the start," I told him. "No one has ever devised a truly successful 'healthy' chocolate. We both know that."

There'd been numerous attempts to commercialize the cacao bean's inherent heart-healthy properties. But no matter how tasty those "good-for-you" chocolates may (or may not) have been, the fact remained: Nobody wanted their indulgences to be endorsed by a buzzkill board of white-coated doctors. Chocolate was *supposed* to feel decadent, luscious, and oh-so-bad for you.

"But I bet you thought *you* could do it, didn't you?" Christian pressed. "Hayden Mundy Moore: the famous 'chocolate whisperer.' If anybody could achieve the impossible, it was *you,* right?" He paused. "Except in the end, you couldn't do it."

I wasn't sure what he was driving at. I'd thought I might be able to work miracles, given recent advances in culinary-based nanotechnology. I hadn't, but I'd learned a few things in the attempt. In my book, that was progress. "My report is full of critical information that you didn't have when you began, as well as solid procedures for moving Lemaître forward, so—"

"Lemaître Chocolates was your only failed consultation, wasn't it?" Christian interrupted. "Adrienne just . . . stymied you."

Okay. Now I was getting annoyed. Remember how I told you I'm not easily ruffled? I guessed I'd spent too much time with Christian, because suddenly my live-and-let-live policy felt deeply shortsighted. "Exactly what are you suggesting?"

He shrugged. "You tell me. How ruthless are you, Hayden?"

I looked at Christian sitting there, ostensibly waiting for me to (I'm spitballing here) fess up to *overdosing Adrienne* to hide my "failed consultation" at Lemaître. My blood boiled.

At least I knew now how ruthless *he* was. That he could even contemplate such a cold-blooded scheme spoke volumes about him.

At the very best, he had a *really* morbid sense of humor.

With effort, I kept my cool. "Look, Christian. I'm in demand. I intend to deliver my report—on our agreed-upon due date—and then go on to my next consultation. In the meantime, you should really have a look at your abysmal house amenities. Trust me, they need work. The fact that *you* aren't aware of their defects only shows exactly how much you need someone like me." Not that it was going to *be* me. Not after this. "Consider that info a parting gift," I added, just in case my intentions weren't clear. "Oh, and by the way—your killer spa equipment needs some serious refurbishment, too. See to it."

I'd already left the pertinent details with Portia and Britney. I got up, intending to leave Christian sitting there, looking chocolaty and stunned. He obliged me— for a few seconds.

Then he applauded. "Bravo! Now I want you more than ever!"

Well . . . "You're just going to have to go on pining, then."

There was no way I was taking another job with Christian. Not now. Not in this crazy place. I didn't even break my stride.

I'd almost made it to the office door by the time he reacted. "Hayden, wait!" His chair creaked loudly behind me. Candy bar wrappers rustled as Christian trod over them. Amid the thudding of his treadmill, he followed me. He grabbed my arm.

I froze, fighting an urge to unleash some choice self-defense moves on him. It was Barcelona all over again.

I clenched my jaw. "Don't touch me, Christian."

He let go, then spread his arms wide. "You're mad? Hey, no. Don't be mad about *that*." Hastily, Christian circled around to face me, partially blocking the door. He nodded toward his desk. "That, back there, between us? That was just a technique I learned in B-school. Pressure-cooker interviewing. You passed!"

"I'm thrilled," I deadpanned, then opened the door.

At least I tried. It thudded into Christian's shoulder.

"Whoa!" He chuckled, rubbing his arm with a fake whimper. He shook his head. "Easy there with the killer instincts!"

I frowned, then hesitated. As long as we were being all chummy, I realized, I might as well push a little harder.

"Speaking of killer instincts," I said, crossing my arms as I faced him again, "where were *you* when Adrienne died?"

Christian balked. Then seeming enlightenment crossed his face. He pointed at me. "Hey—clever! You double-bluffed me."

I'd done no such thing. I arched my eyebrow, waiting.

At least he didn't *really* think I was a murderer. It just went to show you—sometimes conjecture could get out of hand.

"I was with my uncle," Christian told me, semi-huffily. *Hmm. Bernard told me he was with Isabel,* I remembered. "And Isabel?" I pushed. Maybe they'd made a threesome. No, not *that* kind of threesome.

Christian made a face. Plainly, there was no love lost between him and his uncle's younger wife. "Who knows? Plastered someplace would be my guess. Probably topless, if I know her."

I guess I wasn't the only one who'd noticed Isabel's proclivity for nudity. Could she and Christian have . . . *Nah.* No way.

"Well?" Impatiently, Christian eyed me. "What's your decision?" He hesitated. Then, "Don't think I didn't recognize that tactic you just ran on me, either. I'm savvy to that. Sun Tzu could have taken notes from *me* on *The Art of War.*"

I didn't know what kind of "B-school" gibberish he was rattling on about. All I wanted to know was if Christian had an alibi for the night of Adrienne's murder. Now I did.

I didn't believe it, but I did. Either Christian or Bernard was lying about his whereabouts. But until I saw Bernard . . .

"No, I don't want Adrienne's job," I told Christian in no uncertain terms. "No one can fill her shoes. Not even me."

Then I gave him a pointed look, waited for him to back up, and sailed through the doorway, past the obviously eavesdropping (and now far less ennui-filled) admin. Somewhere, I figured, Eden's girl-reporter instincts had to be clanging like crazy.

She'd obviously scrounged up a few informants during the chocolate retreat. If she wasn't there within half an hour to interview Ms. Bored Blonde for *Chocolat Monthly,* I'd eat one of Christian's economy candy bars . . . with a waxy Magic Shell coating poured on top and a discount diet soda to wash it all down with.

If I was going to terminate my taste buds, I decided in a burst of recklessness, I might as well go *all* the way.

Chapter 13

I wanted to have a steadying recap with Danny next (not to mention try to find something more substantial than ice cream for at least *one* meal that day), but fate wasn't on my side.

First, I couldn't find Danny in his adjoining room (which may have been a good thing—for him—given that he'd kinda/sorta been going on a date with the blond server earlier). Next, I was too late for lunch and too early for Maison Lemaître's all-chocolate happy-hour spread (which was definitely a good thing for my waistline, but left me too hungry to think straight). Room service was a possibility, but I don't like holing up in my room with a tablecloth-covered cart. (It makes me feel like a luxurious prisoner enjoying a gourmet-catered lavish last meal—pampered, yes, but ultimately destined to come to a bad end.)

Nobody traveled as much as I did and survived on room service chow. Driven by my rumbling stomach out onto the resort's posh grounds, I shaded my eyes, looking for another source of sustenance. Yesterday there'd been a chocolatier selling chocolate-chip *gaufres de Liège*—the scrumptious, buttery waffles that Belgians made, with crackly caramelized sugar bits inside. One bite would transport me straight to Ghent—and at least keep me from keeling over from low blood sugar. But today that tent was shuttered, probably out of respect to Rex.

At least a few people—besides me and Nina—were sorry Rex was dead. The city's newspapers had done a 180 on Melt's CEO in their coverage, deeming him everything from "respected" to "innovative." Several of Rex's tearful exes had been interviewed, too, blinking rapidly to safeguard their mascara and letting their artfully lip-glossed lips wobble just so. Their numbers had posthumously confirmed Rex's reputation as a ladies' man *and* made for a day's worth of salacious local news. I couldn't help feeling that Rex would have been *thrilled* by all the attention.

A breeze lifted the ends of my ponytail and pulled me back from contemplating Rex's premature demise. Forcing my attention on the mission at hand (find a nosh, stat!), I looked around.

Nearby, the valets ran to and fro while parking cars. I watched them for a minute, wondering which one of them might have covered for Isabel's getaway. Maybe the hunky surfer dude?

The whole setup didn't look super secure. Testing it, I sailed past the valet stand, glanced at Mr. Hang Ten, then beelined toward the remote lot designated as valet parking.

As I expected, he followed me. "Uh, miss? Yo, wait up!"

I kept going, wondering if I could brazen it out.

Nope. "Hey! You're, like, not supposed to be here!"

I stopped while eyeing all the parked cars, arrayed neatly beside some trees. Isabel's Mercedes would have been parked in this lot, right alongside all the BMWs, sporty MINI Coopers, Jaguars, Lexuses (Lexi?), and hybrids. (Hey, it *was* California.) But so far, it looked as though Isabel probably couldn't have sneaked in and retrieved her car herself—not without catching the attention of one of the Dudley Do-Rights of valeting.

"Oh, hey!" I turned, trying to look apologetic. "I, um, I'm, like, totally sorry to bug you?" I said in my best So-Cal patois, giving him the old baby blues. "But I think I must have, like, left my purse in my car, or something? You know?"

He nodded. "Yeah, that's a bummer, dude."

"I know, right?" I played with my ponytail, then went pigeon-toed like a socialite on the red carpet. "So, like, I was just hoping to, you know, look in my car? I didn't want to bug you? But I *really* need my purse? You know, girly stuff and all?"

All my uptalk was giving me a headache. But I had girlfriends who *lived* the full Valley Girl lifestyle, complete with beaches and malls. Sometimes their lingo came in handy.

This was one of those times. "Sorry," Surfer Guy said, giving me a goofily elaborate frown while checking out my bare legs in my shorts. He shook his shaggy blond locks. "Guests aren't supposed to be over here. It's, like, a liability issue?"

Great. Now we were both doing it. "Really? For reals?"

"I'm afraid so." He glanced back at the valet stand.

As he did, I caught sight of a uniformed resort employee striding toward the farthest row, jangling keys in her hand.

"But it's my first day!" I improvised, getting in deeper. I bit my lip. "And, like, my name badge is still in my purse?"

"Oh." Comprehension dawned. He smiled. "You want employee parking. It's on the far end." He gestured to the last row.

"Oh! Thanks!" I followed his pointing finger, then pouted a little. "Should I, like, go a different way next time? I mean, this has been fun and all?" I gave him another dose of goo-goo eyes. "But the next guy who busts me might not be so cute?"

Surfer Guy broadened his grin. He puffed out his chest a little, too. "Yeah. You want the path over there." Helpfully, he put his arm around my shoulders. He turned me to face it. "See?"

I did. "Oh! Thanks!" I enthused. I gave him a flirty wave. "Well, see you next time? Okay? Thanks, like, a million!"

I scampered off with a little extra wiggle, knowing he was watching, then veered toward the farthest row of parked cars, feeling a little disgusted with myself for my ditzy subterfuge.

If Danny could have seen me, he would have broken a rib laughing. But as I've told you before, I can be a chameleon when it comes to fitting in. Sometimes that's a pretty useful skill.

At least now I knew, I told myself as I fell into step behind two more (uniformed) employees, then gave Surfer Dude a twee over-the-shoulder wave, how Isabel could have sneaked out her Mercedes and left Maison Lemaître unnoticed last night. All Isabel would have had to do was wait for a little shielding darkness, head for the designated (unmonitored) end of the valet parking lot, then make a play for her car when the valets were busy elsewhere. It would have been easy—except for one thing, I reflected as I caught sight of one of the resort's typically understated signs. FOR PROTECTION OF VEHICLES AND GUESTS, the sign informed me, THIS AREA IS MONITORED WITH SECURITY CAMERAS. PLEASE BE ADVISED.

That was a new wrinkle in my breakdown of Isabel's getaway. It was a potential big lead, too. How many *other* security cameras might be in use on the Maison Lemaître property?

I had to find out. I knew just the guy to help me.

* * *

If I told you I collapsed cold, faint from hunger, right about now, you shouldn't be surprised. Ice cream (however delicious) is not an all-day meal. My stomach growled in protest as I ducked away from the parking lot while Surfer Guy's back was turned, then hurriedly doubled back toward Maison Lemaître.

Right about then, Danny's sad leftover banana sounded pretty good. I felt light-headed with hunger and wobbly from my still-healing knee injury . . . which might have explained why I weaved on my way to meet up with Danny. Deciding it was better to be safe than double concussed, I sat on a nearby bench beneath a ginkgo tree. Its leaves rustled in the bay breeze, lending a sense of serenity to the resort's lush surroundings.

As I looked out over the acres of grass and landscaped shrubs, the rows of flowers and the distant bay, I could almost forget that two people had died at Maison Lemaître this week. In the distance, the Golden Gate Bridge arched over the sparkling water, freed of the blanket of fog that had cloaked it earlier.

I could really learn to love it here, I knew. I liked the Noe Valley, the Mission, SoMa . . . all of it. I liked San Francisco's temperamental weather and its attitude of rebel nonchalance. I even liked climbing its hilly streets, which rivaled the steep, labyrinthine *rues* of any number of seaside Côte d'Azur villages.

I didn't want to think about Christian's preposterous offer to take over Adrienne's job. My mind was made up. Still, I couldn't help mulling over everything it would mean. A place to unpack my duffel for good. A home base for family and friends. A routine that *didn't* involve airports and customs checks and jet lag, but *did* include normality, coziness . . . a cuddly dog of my own.

Sometimes, when striding through a piazza on my way to a job or dodging commuters headed for the Yamanote Line in Tokyo, I spotted a street vendor or a boutique selling pet supplies. Sometimes I stopped to examine the food bowls and leashes, whimsical collars and tiny outfits made for four-footed friends.

Sometimes I even imagined I saw a dog coming right toward me. I blinked. *Nope.* That was a *real* dog. It was Isabel's dog.

What was Poopsie doing here on her own? Isabel had seemed to *cherish* her little Yorkie. I couldn't believe Isabel would have left—of her own volition—without her travel companion.

Cautiously, I held out my hand. "Poopsie! Here, girl!"

The dog perked up. She glanced at me, tongue lolling.

"Come on!" I slapped my thighs, hoping I hadn't gone off the deep end and hallucinated Poopsie altogether. "Come here!"

Obediently, the Yorkie did. Her collar tags rattled.

When she was within reach, I cooed. I caught her—not that Poopsie put up a struggle. She all but collapsed in my grasp as I hauled her onto my lap. She slobbered on my bare arm while I examined her. She must have been outside awhile, I realized. Her formerly pristine fur was dirty and studded with burrs.

"Where have *you* been?" I baby-talked, petting Poopsie. For one crazy moment, it occurred to me that the Yorkie was technically a stray. She'd been abandoned. I could keep her!

I was already making wild plans to ditch my wheelie bag and invest in a small pet carrier when I remembered: *Bernard.*

He'd given Poopsie to Isabel. The Yorkie belonged to him.

Resigned to doing the right thing, I got up.

Then I sat again, the dog still cradled in my arms. Her little face turned to me quizzically. Her tongue lolled. *Aw.*

A few minutes wouldn't hurt, I told myself. With a fast glance around to make sure no one was watching, I gave Poopsie a pat on the head, then gave in to baby talk all over again.

Hey, it was my only chance. I was taking it. For now.

By the time I made it to Bernard's (and Isabel's) deluxe cottage on the outskirts of Maison Lemaître's main buildings, I was in love. Poopsie had the most adorable quirks, the most brilliant melty brown eyes, the most lovable canine demeanor *ever.* When I'd sat down with her, she'd collapsed trustingly against me like a real, live teddy bear and then gazed up at me adoringly. And okay, so there'd been a *tiny* bit of that gooey, boogery stuff at the corner of her eyes, and she *had* dribbled dog slobber all down my couture sweatshirt, but I didn't care.

Poopsie and I were *forever.* Or for the next ten minutes.

Still intending to do the right thing, I ascended the steps of Isabel and Bernard's cottage, then stood on the tidy door mat and looked around interestedly. In the daytime, the place was a Pacific beach cottage in miniature, with a covered front porch, Craftsman-inspired construction and trim, and a crisp pastel paint job that coordinated with the main resort's subdued tones.

The cottage was, in a word, well-appointed. (Or is that two words? Do hyphens count?) Either way, every similar cottage on the resort's grounds offered two primary benefits: privacy and spaciousness. Here, unlike in my room, a retreat attendee could play the bongos, indulge in scream therapy, or blast Beyoncé at full volume without disturbing anyone. It was the perfect place to cheat on your husband.

Sabotage your nephew. Or simply disappear from in the dead of night, abruptly and mysteriously.

Before I could knock, the door opened with a *whoosh*. Bernard stood there, white-faced and considerably less twinkly-eyed than usual, staring at me with a mixture of hope and fear.

As I watched, his face crumpled. "I heard footsteps." He swallowed hard, trying to compose himself. "You're not Isabel."

I wasn't the police, either, come to give him bad news about his wife. I could see that dawn on him as I waited.

Bernard's gaze dropped to Poopsie. "You found her!"

I didn't want to let her go, either. "She was wandering around the grounds. I recognized her and brought her home."

"Thank you, Hayden." Bernard's face softened. He looked at me, his expression less muddled than before but no less forlorn. "Please, come inside. I'll get you some iced tea."

Chivalrously, he stepped back. He nodded invitingly at me.

I cast a guarded glance over my shoulder. Given all the scary things that had been going on at Maison Lemaître, it probably wasn't wise to sequester myself with anyone who wasn't Danny. But I figured I could always outrun elderly Bernard.

Besides, I was still starving. From my vantage point, I glimpsed an extravagant spread of fresh fruit, crusty baguettes, nuts, and a variety of artisanal cheeses, all neatly laid out on the cottage's homey, white-painted sideboard, just steps from its flowery upholstered sofa. I decided I *had* to come in.

Somebody had to help Bernard eat all that food, right?

He caught me eyeballing his lunch and smiled. "The staff are very kind to me. They brought those things here a

little while ago, but I'm afraid I haven't made a dent."
Bernard took a step back, then gestured for me to give him
Poopsie. I did, then watched as he cuddled the small filthy
Yorkie. "You need a bath, don't you?" he cooed lovingly to
the dog. "Yes, I think you do!"

His gaze flicked to the open door. I took the hint and
hastily shut it behind me. Neither one of us wanted to
chase Poopsie all over the grounds if she escaped again.
I doubted Bernard had the stamina. I would probably col-
lapse if I ran.

*Hmm. Maybe my plan to outpace danger wasn't entirely
well-thought-out.* I wasn't too concerned, though. I wasn't
exactly a CrossFit competitor, but I could still outmaneu-
ver a golf-shirted retiree. Unless, I mused as I examined
the cottage's tasteful furnishings and spotted at least two
heavy-duty lamps, that retiree came armed with a weapon.
Then I might have trouble.

"I've been here all day," Bernard told me, puttering with
a water-beaded pitcher of tea. Ice cubes clanked into a tall
glass as he filled it. "Waiting for Isabel to come back. I've
been afraid to leave, afraid to move . . . afraid to look for
Poopsie."

The little Yorkie scampered underfoot, sniffing everything. Bernard smiled at the dog, his eyes growing misty.
Poor Bernard.

He actually thought Isabel might be coming back.

"I'm sorry." I added a murmured thank-you for the tea
he gave me. He also nodded toward the impromptu buffet,
inviting me to sample the goods. So I did. "Have you heard
anything?"

"From Isabel? No." He shook his head. "That's not
unusual, though. She . . . sometimes goes away, you see.
Quite by surprise." He looked wistful. "I think she does it
to keep me on my toes."

If you asked me, that was a pretty terrible thing to do

just for kicks. But then I wasn't a sought-after lingerie model. Chances were good that Isabel got away with things I didn't.

"Then you think she'll come back?" I asked, scarfing more.

Wow. The fresh bread and cheese were *scrumptious.* Clearly, Bernard's nosh was culled from a different source than whatever the kitchen used to feed plebeian attendees. Feeling enlivened, I munched down a few almonds. Then a grape.

Too late, I realized Bernard was staring at me.

I almost choked on a mouthful of crusty sourdough baguette spread with moist, tangy Bucheret chèvre and chutney. It was a nice break from nonstop chocolate, but I didn't want to be rude.

"I was hoping *you* could tell me that," Bernard said.

The oddly expectant tone of his voice put me on edge. Everything I'd just consumed settled in an unmoving lump in my belly. Cautiously, I put down my unfinished bread and cheese.

"Why would I know whether Isabel is coming back?"

"The two of you spent a lot of time together."

Hmm. I'd hardly call one (injury-plagued) shared soak in a hot-cocoa mud bath and one (broken, nearly lethal) chocolate-fondue body wrap date "a lot of time together." But I didn't want to agitate Bernard. He seemed pretty upset already.

"I liked Isabel," I assured him. "I thought she was fun."

"'Liked'?" Bernard advanced on me. In the corner, Poopsie napped off her outdoor adventures. "You 'thought she was fun'?"

Oops. "I still do!" I assured him, realizing too late that I'd used the past tense. "Honestly, Mr. Lemaître, I do. I didn't mean to imply that Isabel was gone *forever* or anything."

Have I mentioned I can sometimes put my foot in my mouth?

He frowned. "What do you know that I don't know?"

"Nothing!" I put up my palms, frozen in place. "Nothing."

"You must have talked about things while you were spending all that time at the spa," Bernard persisted. "What did Isabel tell you?" His voice quavered. "Did you know she was leaving?"

Belatedly, the truth smacked me upside the head. Isabel must have used *me* as her excuse while she was enjoying lusty "personal training" sessions with Hank. No one could believably claim a need to "work out" multiple times every day without arousing suspicion. Not even an underwear model like Isabel.

"I promise you, I didn't know Isabel was leaving."

I really didn't want to be part of all this. It was painful enough to know that this nice man's marriage was unraveling.

"You must have told her!" Bernard yelled.

I jumped. Even as an older man, he was still imposing. I couldn't help being reminded that *he* used to be the head honcho at Lemaître. Like Christian, Bernard had probably done his share of intimidating underlings and menacing competitors.

"I . . ." I swallowed hard, willing myself not to bolt. Not yet. I took a deep breath, then smiled. "What would I have told her?"

"*You know.*" Bernard's low, rough tone didn't sound any less threatening to me. "*You're* the one who has Adrienne's journal."

I blinked, startled. "Adrienne's journal?"

"I saw her give it to you during the scavenger hunt." He examined me with distaste. "She was probably going to get on Isabel's team and show it to her herself." That was an interesting conjecture. "I know you must have read it."

I didn't understand how a notebook full of chocolate percentages, recipes, and formulas could have concerned Isabel. Or Bernard, at this point. But I *had* read it. Most of it.

Maybe, it dawned on me, I'd overlooked something crucial.

"*I'm* the one who should have that journal." Bernard looked away, out the cottage's window, where people *weren't* trapped with an angry sexagenarian. "*I'm* the one who loved her!"

I gawked at him. Did he mean . . . "You loved Adrienne?"

That would explain his entreaty to me at the awards banquet. *Don't forget Adrienne. Remember her the way she was.*

It also explained his breakdown while giving his speech.

I'll never forget you! he'd cried while holding up his award. *Never! No one will ever know what you meant to me.*

At the time, I'd thought Bernard had been referring to his absentee wife, not his older, less-attractive mistress.

It just went to show, youth and beauty weren't everything.

His red-rimmed eyes met mine. "Don't be coy. I know you know. I know you couldn't resist. You *had* to give Isabel all the dirty details, didn't you? Everything you read in Adrienne's journal, everything you knew, everything she ever told you!"

"Mr. Lemaître, I promise I did no such thing."

"I want it," Bernard said stubbornly. He closed his eyes. "To remember her by. Giving it to me is the least you can do."

"I don't have it," I said honestly. Danny did.

Why was Adrienne's journal so in demand, anyway?

"Give it to me!" Bernard bellowed, shaking with rage.

I shrank, then retreated a step. Poopsie woke up. The Yorkie skittered around on the wood floors, wagging nervously.

"That 'journal' is a chocolatier's notebook," I told him, shaking my head. "It's not a diary. It's not what you think."

He was completely unconvinced. I must have seemed like a capable liar to him. If so, that would have been a first for me.

"If it's so innocent, why did Adrienne give it to *you* to protect?" Bernard asked reasonably. "Why did she hide it?"

I couldn't answer that. I couldn't tell him that Christian had accused Adrienne of selling Lemaître Chocolates' secrets. But thinking about the scavenger hunt reminded me of Adrienne's eagerness to be on Team Yellow: Rex's team. *Not* Isabel's team—which Adrienne had drawn before I showed up. Had Adrienne been planning to sell her notebook to Rex—in plain sight of Christian and all the rest of the industry bigwigs—but then chickened out?

It would have been fittingly egomaniacal of Rex to stage an underhanded exchange that way. He would have appreciated an ostentatious *screw you* to his competitors . . . and to Christian.

"I don't know why Adrienne wanted to hide her notebook," I told Bernard. Warily, I tried to change the subject. "Are you *sure* Isabel left because she was upset about Adrienne?"

Bernard frowned deeply. "Why else would she leave?"

The words *überhot personal trainer* came to mind.

But so did Rex. "Did Isabel ever . . . step out with anyone?"

For a minute, Bernard looked befuddled. He blinked, then put his hands on his hips. He gazed out the window again.

He gazed some more. I hoped he wasn't going into

another dementia haze. That would have been colossally bad timing.

Just when I finally felt I was getting somewhere.

"You know," I went on awkwardly, keeping my voice gentle, "in retaliation for your relationship with Adrienne?"

"Well," Bernard finally said in a geezerish tone, "Rex always had a thing for Isabel. But *he's* gone now, so . . ."

So I gawked at him, wondering if Bernard was hinting he knew about their hookup. I was reminded of my earlier suspicions that Bernard might have killed both Rex *and* Adrienne—especially if he'd found out about his wife's fling with the Melt CEO.

"Rex?" I prodded. Wow, I was getting pretty pushy.

Bernard went dewy-eyed again. "I'm going to miss Rex."

Maybe this was all a dead end, I decided. Maybe Lemaître's revered founder was just as doddering as I'd suspected before.

On the other hand, recent events would have unsettled anyone, no matter how quick-witted they usually were.

"Yes, it's a shame about Rex," I said. "Poor Rex."

"His death wasn't an accident, you know." Bernard's voice became sharper. More venal. "I think Christian pushed him off that trail. Everyone knew how steep it was. My nephew always was jealous of Rex's work with me. He resented our closeness."

I doubted Christian resented anything except sharing the spotlight or being caught low on discount chocolates. But for the sake of information gathering, I went along with Bernard.

"Surely Christian wouldn't kill anyone!" I laughed.

Nervously (and unconvincingly), of course. But I managed it. Somehow. By now, I really, *really* wanted to know more.

"Why not?" Bernard's eagle-eyed gaze met mine. How

did he keep veering back and forth between lucidity and
senility? "I'm pretty sure he's the one who put something
in Adrienne's drink. He never got over her wanting to
'defect' to Melt when Rex offered her a job. The funny
thing is, Rex did that for me."

"For you?"

Bernard nodded. "I asked Rex to rescue Adrienne.
From Christian. After my nephew forced me out and took
over Lemaître completely, things were dreadful at the company. Everyone was worried. Resentful. Unhappy." A brief,
sardonic grin passed over Bernard's face. "Everyone
except Christian, of course."

Of course. That meshed with what I'd heard.

"Which means, I suppose, that if not for *me*—" Bernard
broke off, his voice cracking. "Adrienne might still be
alive."

Was Bernard pointing the finger at Christian . . . or
himself?

If I'd heard the Lemaître Chocolates' founder making
that statement an hour ago, I would have thought he was
confessing to killing Adrienne. I would have thought his
mistress had pushed him too far—maybe by demanding
that Bernard divorce Isabel once and for all, and be with
her instead. I would have thought that he'd had enough,
and—as autocratic and seemingly bulletproof as any CEO
of his stature—had decided to put an end to things with
Adrienne . . . either premeditatedly or impulsively. After
all, Bernard and Isabel *had* seemed dedicated to making
their marriage work while canoodling at the scavenger
hunt. Their behavior could have pushed Adrienne into
issuing an ultimatum—one she would pay for with her life.
It was all perfectly credible.

But now, given Bernard's desolate eyes and vaguely
shaky hands, none of that mattered. I still couldn't think of

the grandfather of San Francisco chocolate-making as a murderer.

Besides, all the evidence (except for Poopsie, at least) pointed to Isabel having left Bernard on her own. What else *could* have happened? Was I really supposed to believe that Bernard had overdosed Adrienne, pushed Rex to his death, and then—with nothing more to lose—had killed Isabel, too?

I imagined him bashing her unconscious with a heavy lamp, like the one that had concussed me. Packing up all her things. Piling those things (and Isabel's body) into her Mercedes under cover of darkness, and then . . . what? Driving her car off the steep curves of the Pacific Coast Highway and into the ocean below?

And what about Poopsie? Well, I deduced, the Yorkie had obviously run away during all the turmoil. Until I'd found her.

I had to admit, that sounded pretty far-fetched. Things (technically) could have gone down that way . . . you know, on TV.

Or maybe, I mused, Bernard was more invested in Lemaître Chocolates' future than I knew. Maybe he *wasn't* senile. Maybe he *didn't* want Adrienne's "journal" for sentimental reasons. Maybe he wanted her notebook to keep her chocolate-making acumen for himself—or to find proof of her selling secrets to a competitor.

Maybe vengefulness grew wild on the Lemaître family tree.

With effort, I pulled myself out of that morass of secrets, lies, double crosses, and prime-time-worthy shenanigans.

"I'm sure you did all you could for Adrienne," I told Bernard in a soothing voice. "After all, Christian isn't the only 'brilliant and accomplished man' in the Lemaître family."

"What?" Bernard snapped. "What do you mean by that?" He didn't seem comforted by Christian's "power phrase." But then, I hadn't expected him to be. I was angling again. Snooping around, I'd learned lately, was becoming kind of habit forming.

It wasn't so different from troubleshooting chocolates, actually. Both involved identifying problems, testing theories, and finding solutions. Except now I wasn't looking for the ideal chocolate-raspberry truffle or the ultimate malted milk shake.

I was looking for the not-so-perfect murderer.

Innocuously, I shrugged. "Only that you would have tried to save Adrienne if you could have." I watched him carefully. "You were there at the welcome reception, weren't you?"

"When Adrienne died, I was with Rex." Bernard looked haunted by that—far too haunted to be lying to me, I thought. "Trying to work out a partnership deal. I'll always regret that."

Well. So much for his earlier alibi, when he'd claimed to have been with Isabel. I guessed now, with her gone, Bernard no longer felt any loyalty toward his wife—or any obligation to protect her . . . if that's what he'd initially been trying to do.

Interestingly, he'd just scuppered Christian's alibi, too.

"Partnership deal? Were Lemaître and Melt merging?"

"Rex needed money. I had money—money I had no impetus to invest in Lemaître anymore." Bernard looked at his tasseled loafers. "I wanted to make Melt bigger than Lemaître. I wanted to make it succeed in a way that Christian never could." He cast me a prideful glance. "There's more to chocolate than minding the bottom line. But my nephew will never understand that."

"You were angry with him for pushing you out."

"Angry?" Bernard startled me by chuckling. "Maybe at first. But ultimately? No. What I said at the awards banquet was true."

I didn't think he remembered any of that gibberish. Wisely, I refrained from saying so. There were still those lamps nearby.

"I *am* grateful for Christian forcing me out," Bernard went on, echoing his awards speech. "It made me rethink my legacy."

He seemed so utterly enlivened by that idea, I couldn't help buying in. "What will your legacy be now?" I asked.

Bernard's irascible gaze swerved to mine. "Making sure that whoever hurt Adrienne pays for what they did." He gave me a cockeyed smile. "And making more yummy chocolates, too!"

His mood swings were creeping me out—and giving me antsy feet, too. Because if Bernard had thought that Rex had hurt Adrienne (and subsequently killed him for it) or that Isabel had hurt Adrienne (and . . . ditto), then maybe his wild-eyed vendetta could touch just about anyone at Maison Lemaître. *Including me.*

Or Christian, I had to admit. It wasn't *all* about me.

"Hey, I hear you there!" I said jovially, making a move toward the door. "Well, now that Poopsie's home safely and I've thoroughly raided your lunch, I guess I'd better be on my way."

I turned away and walked. I was almost home free when . . .

"Not so fast," Bernard said. His voice was low. Ominous.

I stopped, not looking at him. Instead, I gazed yearningly outside the window, where life went on as usual: threat free.

For one spine-tingling moment, I *believed* Bernard could have killed Adrienne. Rex. Isabel. Even *me.* What was I doing?

If a killer was threatening you, politeness wasn't called for. But social parameters were hardwired. I couldn't just *run.*

I've heard that the impulse to be polite—even in the face of obvious danger—sometimes got people killed. Now I understood.

I still couldn't quite force my feet to move.

"You forgot your dessert!" Bernard followed me. He pushed a napkin-wrapped bundle into my numb hand. "It's cookies. *Not* chocolate this time." He paused. "You want to know a secret?"

Not really. I gulped. My common sense vanished. I nodded.

"Some days, I don't eat *any* chocolate," Bernard confessed.

Then he gave me a chortle and herded me toward the door.

I practically sagged onto the floorboards on my way there, casting one lingering glance at my doggy buddy, Poopsie. Had I *truly* just gotten freaked out by a grandfatherly chocolatier?

Being around all this murder and mayhem was affecting me. Not in a positive, puppies-and-rainbows way, either.

"I don't, either," I squeaked, opting to play along.

Ahead of me, Bernard considerately opened the cottage door. Outside I smelled chocolate and life, fresh air and *freedom.*

He lingered. Maybe he was experiencing the same things?

Nope. Agreeably, he turned. "If you're the one who was selling us out," he said, "I'll find out. And you'll be sorry. Because you're right—I *am* a 'brilliant and accomplished man.'"

Then, as I gawked at him, Bernard shooed me out.

I didn't need to be told twice. I scrammed, his words still ringing in my ears as I sneakered my way down the cottage steps.

You'll be sorry. You'll be sorry. You'll be sorry.

I already was sorry. Sorry I'd come there at all.

Maybe I *had* been the target all along. I'd known as much about Lemaître's chocolate-making methods as anyone. I could just as easily have sold that knowledge to the highest bidder.

Not that I would have, of course. I have integrity. I have—

"P'tain!" Bernard yelped in my wake.

—enough knowledge of *le français* to recognize a colloquial French slur when I heard one. Either the beloved patriarch of Lemaître Chocolates was calling me something *very* rude or . . . A streak of fast-moving furriness flashed by me. *Poopsie.*

"*Putain!*" Bernard shouted more clearly, raising a ruckus as he hustled down the cottage steps right behind her.

He'd absentmindedly let out the dog while watching me leave. I knew I ought to catch Isabel's Yorkie, but hearing that expletive gave me a seriously sobering sense of déjà vu. Could *that* have been what I'd heard right before being clobbered?

Merde would have been more common . . . and less vulgar. I was reminded that Lemaître *was* a French surname. Maybe *everyone* in the family spoke unrefined *français*? If so—and that *was* what I dimly remembered hearing before hitting the floor—that wouldn't narrow down my list of potential lamp-wielding attackers much.

Poopsie scampered around my feet, wagging her tail. She ignored Bernard in her wake. *Aw.* She wanted to come with me.

I would have, too. Her owner might be a lunatic.

All the same, I scooped up the dog, then petted her.

Bernard huffed up. Wild-haired, he held out his arms.

I considered my options. They were few. A head-scratch signal to Danny wouldn't save me this time.

Sensing my reluctance, Bernard gestured for his dog again.

"Maybe you should just quit while you're ahead, Hayden," he urged pleasantly. "That might be better for everyone."

As menacing as that suggestion sounded, I *know* I should have agreed. Of course I should have.

"It wouldn't be better for Adrienne," I said, then I handed him his Yorkie and got out of there before things got hairy.

Chapter 14

I slammed into room 334 with my knees knocking, out of breath from the breakneck pace I'd used to escape Bernard.

Inside, things were peaceful and luxurious, freshly cleaned and faintly perfumed. The furniture gleamed. The myriad pillows on my king-size bed were plumped and perfect. The lamps and crystal chandelier (yes, I'm serious—this is a chichi resort, remember?) sparkled in the late-afternoon sunlight.

I exhaled. Maison Lemaître was *not* the kind of place where threats and conspiracies should have abounded. Maybe that's why I couldn't ditch the feeling I was over-reacting to all this.

Adrienne had died. Probably accidentally. Caffeine *was* toxic in high doses; we'd both learned that while working on the nutraceutical line. Rex had died. Probably accidentally. Falls were a major cause of in-home deaths, weren't they? If an ordinary Joe wasn't safe in his own castle, *of course* we were all taking our chances by living, breathing, and scarfing down chocolate on a jagged Northern California promontory in springtime.

It was so obvious it was laughable. Right?

Still feeling jittery, I decided to call Travis. By now, he might have the information I wanted about Calvin Wheeler. If Nina's husband posed a threat to her, I wanted to know about it.

But the idea of learning that Calvin was an abuser (and not merely spa shy) made a crushing weight of despair temporarily squash my attempt to cheer myself up. Because if a woman wasn't safe from the man she'd married, who was safe? Anyone? Ever?

Pacing and shaking my head, I went to the window. Below me, I glimpsed the valets scurrying around. Surfer Guy hopped out of a Bentley, then handed over the keys. He pocketed a big tip.

I envied him his happy-go-lucky job. Nobody was trying to kill *him*. There wasn't a lot of duplicity in valet parking.

What I needed was a dose of normalcy, I told myself. A nice, sexy chat with Travis would haul me back from the brink. I got this way sometimes, I knew as I searched for my phone. Away from family and friends and familiarity, my mind ran wild.

My phone was nowhere to be found. *Another break-in?*

Frantically, I hurried to the closet. My duffel bag looked undisturbed. So did my suitcase. I was about to open them when . . .

Danny burst through our rooms' connecting door, shirtless and barefoot. His dark hair was mussed, his expression dour.

"Looking for *this*?" He brandished my cell phone.

I didn't understand his bad attitude. "Yes, I am."

I made a play for it. He held it out of reach. Having obviously heard me come into my room, he'd planned this showdown and clearly now didn't intend to be denied his satisfaction.

Or maybe he'd already been denied some satisfaction. I

couldn't help noticing his jeans weren't buttoned correctly. He must have gotten dressed in a hurry. Wondering stupidly if Travis ever did the same thing (probably not— my financial advisor was *way* too methodical for that), I arched my brow at Danny. Knowingly.

"I guess things went well with the blond server?"

Danny didn't play along. "How were you planning to call me if you ran into trouble," he demanded, "without this?"

Again, he waggled my phone. He was being unreasonable.

I crossed my arms. "I didn't see *you* chasing me down to give it to me. If you were that bugged by my forgetfulness—"

"I'm not bugged by your 'forgetfulness,' you moron." Danny's tone softened. "I'm worried about your safety. Before going to meet Isabel at the spa, you were supposed to come back here, change clothes, get your phone—" He broke off, gazing at my bare legs. Or my shorts. They were considerably worse for wear after my cuddle with Poopsie. My sometime bodyguard frowned. *Danny Jamieson, fashion critic.* "What happened to you?"

No, not Poopsie. Too late, I remembered the rosy-looking aftereffects of my chocolate-fondue body wrap/baked-potato roast adventure. To Danny, I probably looked parboiled. I shrugged.

"I'm pretty sure someone else tried to kill me," I told him. "By tampering with the spa equipment. Can I have my phone?"

My supposed security man only gazed inscrutably at me. When we were both irked (and convinced we were in the right), things between us tended to go south quickly. But now, Danny seemed . . . fine with it all. He shrugged too, then crossed his arms. Sadly, his gesture spoiled my view of his muscular naked chest.

He narrowed his eyes at me. "Nope."

"Where were *you,* anyway?" I asked, feeling provoked. I considered inserting one of those handy French obscenities, then didn't. "*You're* the one who suggested I go to the spa alone."

Maybe, I thought obstinately, Nina and Travis had a point about Danny. Maybe he *did* just want my money . . . not my safety.

As though reading my mind, Danny scowled more deeply.

"If you're going to quit on me again," I said as the silence stretched uncomfortably between us, "just do it."

"If you're not going to be honest with me," he shot back with another obvious look at my scalded legs, "I might as well."

"Wow. Remind me to never interrupt you mid nookie again."

"I wasn't on a *date* with that server," Danny informed me. "If you think I'd take off in the middle of helping you—"

I stared at his bare chest and incriminatingly (erotic) misbuttoned fly. His jeans rode so low, I wasn't sure how he managed to keep them on. "It sure looks like that's exactly what you did."

He frowned at that, then threw my phone within reach onto the bed. It bounced on the comforter merrily, contradicting the peevishness between us. Maybe, I considered again, teaming up on a semiofficial basis was going to be hard on our friendship.

"Go ahead. Call Travis. Get your fix," Danny said with a dismissive gesture. "Snooping obviously makes you cranky."

"Ignoring my safety obviously makes *you* horny."

"I can't work in a vacuum. Next time, take your phone." With that edict, Danny stomped away. The connecting door slammed behind him, sealing me alone with my irritable thoughts.

I wished I'd never glimpsed my ultra-buff bodyguard's fine, tight butt as he stormed away from me, though. I didn't have time to deal with being threatened, being confused, being scared and concussed and almost baked to death, *and* being interested (however briefly and stirringly) in the way Danny's jeans fit.

Opting for moderation over burliness, I picked up my phone.

I dialed. When my call connected and Travis's deep, self-assured voice came over the line, I *did* feel a rush. I can't deny it. "Hey, hot stuff," I told him. "Do you ever wear jeans?"

As you might have expected, chatting with Travis calmed me right down. You know, if you could call feeling vaguely hot and bothered by an unseen man's bedroom voice *calmed down.* Maybe you can't. Because I *did* feel sort of breathless afterward. Let's just compromise and say that as I disconnected our call, then checked my phone's email for the attachment Travis had promised to send me (not there yet; was Travis slipping?), I was seeing things with new eyes . . . including my next-door-neighbor.

The sound of the TV blaring through the wall from next door told me Danny was still there. It also told me he was upset.

My buff pal only ever zoned out to an *Antiques Road-show* marathon when he was really, *really* wired about something.

Feeling similarly distraught, I put down my phone. Instead of checking and double-checking for Travis's tardy email about Calvin Wheeler, I paced across my room's sophisticated beige carpet. The whole color scheme was designed to be soothing, restful, and reminiscent of Lemaître's fine chocolates, I knew . . . but I still felt restless. It was obvious that being suspicious of Danny (even against my will) was making me crabby.

I was used to believing, without question, that Danny had my back—that he would always stand by me. Thinking otherwise was completely unsettling. Danny had known me for a long time—since before my inheritance. We'd met during my (just as footloose) backpacking-with-ramen days. We'd bonded immediately.

Funnily enough, I recalled, when the two us met, we were—

Nope. No nostalgia. How it all began didn't matter now. Not if we couldn't get past our current deadlock. I knew Danny wouldn't budge—not before a few more episodes of heirloom teapots and vintage whatnots aired, at least. It was up to me to make the first move. Sure, the odds against Danny were two to one. Casting suspicion on him was currently more popular than joining his bad-boy fan club. But Danny had always been misunderstood.

Most of the time, though, *not* by me.

Needing to make a decision, I quit fidgeting. I looked at the connecting door between our adjoining rooms. What I needed now was a leap of faith—and enough confidence in my own judgment to take it. Because the thing about trusting someone is . . .

. . . sometimes you just have to *do* it. *That's* the "trust" part.

Twenty minutes later, I'd changed into a black tank and my most destroyed (aka perfect) pair of jeans, blown out my hair, and slapped on some lip gloss. Carrying my clutch, I strode to Danny's door. I took a deep breath. If the door was locked . . .

It wasn't. Of course. That's how I knew my leap of faith was going to pay off. I breezed into the adjoining room.

"We're getting out of here." I picked up Danny's jacket and tossed it toward his lounging (now T-shirted) form on the bed. Without a word, he caught it, almost upsetting the laptop balanced on his thighs. "Put that on," I said, "and let's go."

His scowl deepened. "Do I get to dress *you,* too?"

"Nope. I'm not up for a bikini top and cutoffs tonight."

He grinned. We both knew I understood his kinks. The closer a woman looked to having just sexily soaped up a muscle car in a music video, the more Danny liked her. He was a simple guy.

Weren't most men, really?

"Where are we going?" he asked.

"That's for me to know and you to find out."

"Real mature." He turned off the TV but didn't budge.

I was getting closer. I took myself over to the bed. I looked down at him. I measured my options. Time was wasting.

I grabbed his jacket. "Fine. *I'll* wear it."

I slung it on. Danny's eyes gleamed. His *other* kink was any woman wearing a man's gear—oversize button-up shirt, suit coat, you name it. Preferably (he'd confided once) in her underwear.

I was partway there. I was playing with fire, sure. But making up with him meant more to me than anything else.

Besides, I'm not averse to a little risk now and then.

"You can go like that." I nodded at his T-shirt and low-riding jeans. "A big, burly guy like you won't feel the cold."

He grinned. That's right. Flattery got me everywhere.

My ability to make friends isn't confined to strangers.

"If I do," Danny told me as he levered off the mattress, then stood, "I know how to find somebody to warm up with."

As a peace offering, I let his macho boast go unremarked

upon. Danny was capable of making friends easily himself. It was just that he didn't bother most of the time.

"Tonight you're mine," I said, then led us out the door.

The dive bar Danny and I wound up in was (predictably) dark, gritty, and crowded. It smelled of spilled beer, stale tobacco, and pool cue chalk—all underlaid with a faint whiff of BO—just to let you know you were in the Tenderloin now, and not in Union Square with all the tourists and financiers. There was music, but it was live, sporadic, and relatively sullen. There were drinks, but they were beer, cheap beer, and cheaper beer.

Also, whiskey. Jim Beam, to be exact. A shot of that amber stuff whirled between Danny's restive fingertips as we sat at a corner table and got down to setting things straight between us.

"Her," I said, flicking my gaze subtly to a bodacious redhead standing at the bar. "Long weekend. *Easter* weekend."

Dubiously, Danny raised his eyebrow. "Why Easter?"

"She looks Catholic. You like corrupting people. It's a match made in heaven—especially on an official church holy day."

He laughed, then studied the crowded bar. When he'd made his decision, he aimed his chin at a business-suited man at the door. "Captain Spreadsheet. Two years. Starting tonight."

"*'Two years'?*" I guffawed. "No way. Drink up, pal."

Danny refused with a head shake. "I'm right. You know I am. You're jonesing for the whole picket-fence routine lately."

He was almost right. Did a dog count? Nah. I shook my head.

"That'll be the day." I pounded the table. "Drink. Drink!"

Relenting, Danny knocked back his whiskey. He pulled over another shot from the row he'd assembled for our reconciliation.

If you're wondering whether we were going to talk things over . . . you've obviously never met Danny. Or me. There's a time for getting sentimental, sure. But between us, it *wasn't* when pride and hurt feelings were involved. This game we played? It was it.

The idea was to pick out a fantasy partner for the other player, then estimate how long the resulting liaison would last. Whoever guessed wrong had to drink. Also, whoever was forced into admitting a correct pairing had to drink.

Basically, our game was all about drinking. And showing off our knowledge of one another. It wasn't complex.

It let me know things were okay between us, though. It took us away from the turmoil at Maison Lemaître for a night, too.

I hadn't realized how much I'd needed an escape hatch until we'd stepped out of the taxi (not Jimmy's this time), taken a look around, and unanimously decided on the diviest bar on the street. Danny wasn't afraid of any place. I wanted to unwind.

Together . . . we were . . . "Nerd alert. Jukebox. One month."

At Danny's assertion, I took a look. The "partner" he'd spied for me was tall, bespectacled, and cute. He looked brainy.

I'm a sucker for a smarty-pants. I quaffed my beer.

Danny looked smug. That was the lone pitfall of our game. We knew each other so well that eventually the self-satisfaction we felt at guessing correctly got to be overkill. Also, we usually got tipsy pretty quickly. That wasn't my goal tonight.

Besides, I was on my third watery beer. We'd already been there awhile. I wanted to get down to business before

I lost the ability to remember whatever brilliant insights we assembled.

Soberly, I zeroed in on Danny. "So, about Adrienne—"

"About Rex," he said at the same time, utterly in sync.

I know, it's pretty weird. But that's us. That's why I felt all right about blowing off all the warnings I'd had about him.

"You go first." Danny gave me a chivalrous gesture. It was pretty funny coming from a beard-stubbled bruiser like him.

Or maybe I was already tipsy. It was possible.

"I think we should break things down," I told Danny, thumbing the condensation from my beer bottle. That done, I started unpeeling the paper label. "After what happened today—"

Danny's hand covered mine, stopping me. Our gazes met.

"Stop abusing that label and get on with it," he said.

It was his way of showing concern, I knew. Danny wasn't the mushy type. So I nudged off his hand and then told him about the killer chocolate-fondue body wrap. About my meet-up with Eden. About my confrontation with Christian and my (occasionally bizarre) encounter with Bernard. I omitted (for now) my fleeting love affair with Poopsie and my spa-time girl talk with Nina.

The former made it look as though Danny was right about me and all that sappy picket-fence stuff. The latter only made me remember that Nina (wrongly) thought Danny had concussed me.

I wasn't sure how to finesse *that* misguided tidbit.

"Okay. We've got a few suspects lined up." No longer fiddling with his whiskey, Danny gave me a serious look. "What we need here are motives. That should clarify things for us."

"Motives are easy," I told him. "This one's love. People

kill for love—or love gone wrong, I guess—all the time. Right?"

Danny didn't disagree. But he made a hilarious face. "If I'm ever *that* far gone over someone, *you* should kill *me*."

As if I could. "It's a deal."

"Not that you'll have to." Then, "As a motive, love is . . ." Danny's gesture dismissed it. "It's got to be money."

"Money is the motive for someone to kill Adrienne? And Rex?" *And maybe Isabel?* I added silently. "Love is stronger."

"I think Travis would side with me on this one."

"Oh. Then I give up. You know what a pushover I am."

He wasn't intoxicated enough to forget how well he knew me. His head shake belied all the whiskey he'd drunk. "Obviously."

"I hate to say it," I told him, ignoring his teasing, "but I think Isabel did it. She wanted Adrienne out of the way so she could have Bernie all to herself to travel the world with her the way she'd dreamed of—especially now that Bernard is retired. She wanted Rex out of the way because he threatened to tell Bernard . . . *something*." I didn't know what yet. "Maybe Rex was going to tell Bernard about their fling? And Isabel wanted *me* out of the way because I was on the verge of catching her."

"Whoa. Good going, Sherlock," Danny cracked. He arched his brow at me, then swirled his finger absently around the rim of his half-full shot glass. He shook his head. "It wasn't Isabel."

It could have been. "Why not?"

"You're only pointing the finger at her because she's not here."

"What's that supposed to mean?"

Danny gave me a long look. "Isabel is your safest

suspect. She demands the least from you. That's what it means."

What? I took his whiskey. "You're cut off."

He relented. I hoped he was about to make sense.

"You hate thinking the worst of people, Hayden," Danny finally said. He looked at me. "It's one of your biggest flaws."

I frowned. "In what universe is being nice a flaw?"

"Mine."

"You're crazy."

"Mine, where people are trying to kill you," he persisted. "I'd be willing to bet that you've considered—and dismissed—Adrienne's real killer a dozen times already. You're *too* nice."

"I don't even know what you're talking about." Guiltily, I remembered thinking the worst of *him*. He was wrong about me.

Obviously, I could be doubtful with the best of them.

"But if it's Isabel," Danny told me, hooking his whiskey and taking another drink, "you can doubt her all you want. Risk free. Because she's already gone. If it's someone else—"

"Fine. Let's say Rex is the one who overdosed Adrienne."

"*Also* conveniently gone," Danny reminded me.

I was proving his point. Annoyingly. "I wouldn't call being dead 'convenient.' Rex *could* have killed Adrienne. *For money,*" I argued, pushing to sell my theory. "Maybe he wanted to get her notebook—and her chocolate expertise—at a heavy discount."

"Maybe," Danny agreed. We discussed Adrienne's supposed corporate espionage, Rex's financial woes at Melt, and his difficulties partnering with Bernard. "Then who killed Rex?"

We were back at square one. "Bernard?" I guessed. "He was there in the shadows, just like us, and saw Isabel and

Rex together last night. He lost his mind, followed Rex, and pushed him off the ridge. I know Bernard is strong enough to do that."

I reminded Danny of the way the Lemaître founder had grabbed me when I'd almost fallen from the ridge trail at the scavenger hunt—and of Bernard's eerie on-again, off-again warnings. He'd frightened me today. Then again, that was getting easier to do as the secrets, lies, and concussions mounted.

"Bernard could have killed Isabel, too," I went on, recounting some of my earlier theories, "then made it *look* as though she'd left the resort on her own." I remembered the Maison Lemaître security cameras I'd seen in the parking lot. "What we need is security footage of the nights in question."

Danny gave a shrewd smile. He knew what was coming next.

I didn't want to give it to him. But this was an emergency.

Casually, I looked around the bar. "Do you think you could, I dunno, maybe find a way to get ahold of some of that footage?"

Nothing but silence came from my buddy's side of the table. I knew what Danny was thinking, though. I was always on his case about cleaning up his act, going legit, *being on time* . . . even the merest transgressions sometimes warranted a lecture from me, Ms. Goody Two-shoes. He couldn't double-park without me hassling him about the risks he was taking. He wasn't on parole anymore, but—

"Are you asking me to *break the rules*?" Danny asked mildly.

I closed my eyes amid the din of the band tuning up for another round. Guitars assaulted my senses. My conscience had a good poke at me, too. I knew it was wrong, but . . .

"Only a little."

He laughed. "Already done." His sparkling eyes irked me. Why did Danny only ever look *truly* happy when he was putting one over on me? "What do you think I was watching on my laptop?"

"On your laptop?" I blinked, trying to remember. Maybe he'd had his computer with him on the bed. I couldn't be sure now.

I might have been too busy being badass to notice.

The only thing left to do was go on the offensive. So I did. "You were watching *Antiques Roadshow,* and you know it."

"Keep your voice down." He frowned, then looked around the packed-tight bar. "I don't want to break any heads tonight."

I stared at him. "You already *have* the security footage?"

"Did you forget who you're dealing with?"

I felt one step behind. It hadn't even occurred to me that such footage might exist until today. Whereas Danny had obviously thought of it *and* gotten it. "How did you get it?"

"The blond waitress. Her boyfriend works in security."

Aha. "But what about your pants?" I blurted.

He gave me a puzzled look. "What about them?"

I got busy chugging more beer. I shrugged. Extravagantly.

Time to change the subject. "Did you see anything?"

"On the footage?" At my nod, Danny elaborated. "It's pretty limited. Grounds, lobby, ballroom, meeting rooms . . . plus kitchens and other staff areas. That's it. The resort's security system sucks." He frowned, then had another drink of whiskey. "Whoever designed it had a clear focus on loss prevention, not safety."

Befuddled, I gave him a quizzical look. "'Loss prevention'?"

"Preventing employee theft," Danny translated with a hard look at me. "That means service elevators, but no guest room hallways—"

"So no evidence of who clobbered me," I surmised.

"—and no sign of Adrienne outside the kitchen or ballroom, where *we* saw her all night, until she stumbles into frame on the patio outside the welcome reception, with Nina helping her."

At that reminder of my friend's tragic death, I shivered.

"There's footage of Christian in the ballroom kitchen, where Adrienne was working," Danny told me, moving on quickly, "so he had access to the caffeine powder." We'd both agreed that was what Adrienne had probably accidentally "overdosed" on, now that Travis's analysis had ruled out the nutraceutical truffles. "He had access to Adrienne's green drink, too, while she was doling out chocolate to the big shots during the reception. But it's not clear on the footage if Christian tampered with anything." Danny leaned back, thinking about it. "Although since he's in charge around here, he would have known how to avoid being caught on camera. All I can say for sure is that Christian nearly put back his own body weight in chocolate that night."

That fit with what I'd seen in his office today. "If he was bingeing on chocolate again," I said, "that would explain why Christian looked so guilty when we ran into him that night."

"Yeah. He didn't want to be caught breaking his diet," Danny deadpanned. He rolled his eyes. "*Or* he murdered Adrienne."

We didn't seem to be getting any closer to a resolution.

"Bernard thinks Christian pushed Rex off the ridge," I told Danny. "He also thinks Christian killed Adrienne in retaliation for her wanting to 'defect' to Melt when Rex offered her a job."

"'Defect' is a pretty strong word."

"It says a lot about Christian's despotic mind-set, right?"

"But Adrienne didn't take that job," Danny argued—making me wonder, for the first time, why she hadn't. I knew she hadn't enjoyed working for Christian at the "new" Lemaître. "Is Christian *that* petty? He'd kill her for *thinking* of leaving?"

We didn't even need a nanosecond to nod in agreement.

"If she'd *think* it the first time," I speculated, trying to put myself in Christian's domineering, mistrustful, alligator-skin designer shoes, "then maybe she'd *do* it the second time."

"Christian wanted to make an example of her."

I nodded. But where did that leave us?

Still confused, actually.

"That sounds plausible," Danny mused. He gave a muttered expletive. "Bernard . . . wow. He really told you that? You've got to admire the old coot's willingness to backstab his nephew, straight up. Back in the day, I hear Bernie was a real—"

"Danny!"

"What?"

"Show a little respect, will you?" I shook my head, feeling my whole body start to vibrate in cadence with the band's bass guitar player's rhythms. It got louder. "Bernard Lemaître is the man who all but invented artisanal chocolate. Without him—"

"You might not have been concussed and left for dead?"

That shut me up. Temporarily.

"Pussycat," Danny yelled into the clamor of the band. "I hear Bernard was a real pussycat, back in the day. That's all I was going to say." His sarcastic grin was less than convincing.

"Yeah. Right." I shook my head, not persuaded. "I'm telling you, Christian is a *lot* meaner than Bernard is. He's *venal.*"

"And you know that . . . how?" Danny eyed my beer, probably wondering if I was going to finish it. He liked mixing it up sometimes. It was a good thing we were leaving via taxi.

I pushed my leftover beer across the table. Danny lifted it in a mischievous toast, then took a swallow. When he finished, he put down his glass, straightened a make-believe deerstalker hat atop his head (à la Sherlock Holmes), then gave me a grin.

"You know," I mused, "I think you're enjoying this."

"Nah." He wiped his mouth, then nodded at a woman who passed by while giving him a flirtatious look. "I like being *out,* away from all the stuffed shirts. On our own again."

I liked that, too. "I'm glad you're here with me."

"Hey. Settle down, sloppy. One of your *other* biggest flaws is getting mushy when you're drinking. Try to rein it in, okay?"

I saluted. "You know," I said, getting more somber, "it's possible that Bernard really *is* as nice as he seems to be— that he truly *is* grieving over Adrienne, sorry to have lost Isabel—"

"What was I saying about you not wanting to think the worst of people?" Danny shook his head. "Come on."

"I mean it! I *like* Bernard. When he's not scaring me."

"You need therapy."

Reminded of the info Travis was sending me about Nina's husband, I considered checking my phone for his email. Travis had gone above and beyond on that request. He'd let me know that he hadn't wanted to "skirt the law," but he'd done it. For me.

"Since you won't *leave* to be safe," Travis had told me on the phone, rumbly and hot, "you didn't give me much choice."

"Remind me to steal all your pants sometime," I'd joked, imagining *him* without "much choice" except to gallivant around in his tighty-whities, shirtless and—more importantly—available.

But my superserious keeper hadn't gotten in on the fun.

"This information came from one of my friends in the Fed," Travis had told me. "It's for your eyes only. *Not* Danny's."

Privately, I suspected Travis simply didn't want his nemesis to know that *he'd* done something borderline sketchy by calling in a few favors with his highbrow government buddies.

But I'd agreed to stay mum. Now I made keeping that vow to Travis even easier by not looking for his email.

"If Bernard is innocent," I told Danny, "then we have to consider what he said. He pointed the finger at Christian. Point-blank! No equivocating." Not beyond window gazing, at least.

"Maybe Bernard was redirecting you on purpose." Danny's keen gaze locked on mine. "There's no better way to dodge trouble than by throwing suspicion on someone else."

I scoffed. He held firm. I reconsidered. "You think so?"

He looked away. Tightly, Danny said, "I know so."

Well. That was all I wanted to know about *that.* I tended to overlook the nitty-gritty details of Danny's former life whenever I possibly could. It was better for us both that way.

Perkily, I moved on. "So, what do we do next?" I looked

around the busy bar, absorbing its energy and grittiness and music. "The retreat is winding down, which means *I'm* running out of time." I reminded Danny that it was still possible *I'd* been the original target, not Adrienne . . . and Rex was just a wobbly, unlucky ridge-trail runner. "If someone is after me, I want to know whodunit *before* I leave San Francisco all unaware."

And vulnerable, I couldn't help thinking. *Yikes.*

Danny nodded. "We have to flush out the killer."

I swallowed hard. "Make them tip their hand?"

"Otherwise, we won't have any proof. I have an . . . acquaintance who works with the SFPD," Danny told me, nodding at another frisky woman. She brightened. "I can bring help if we need it."

"But you don't think we need it."

He shrugged. "I think we need to set your mind at ease."

"You think I'm making this up?" I was offended.

"I think *you* weren't the target. But that doesn't mean there's not a killer on the loose. Who else have you talked to?"

We discussed all the other attendees I'd chatted with over the past few days. None of them had seemed even remotely suspicious to me—or had had any reason to want me (or Adrienne) dead. I sighed. "That leaves us with Isabel—"

"No good unless we can give the police proof."

"Rex—"

"If he killed Adrienne, he's already got what's coming to him."

"—Christian," I went on. I made a face. "And Bernard."

"Christian is the one to start with," Danny told me decisively. I was still hung up on Danny thinking I was being paranoid about this. I'd been *clobbered* and *baked*! "He's a bully, but I don't think he has the stones to kill anybody. We can eliminate him first, then cast a wider net if we need to."

"Okay," I agreed, "but how do we flush him out?"

Maybe it was the discount beer talking, but I liked the idea of settling this mess, once and for all. I wanted it *done*. I didn't want to spend the next decade looking over my shoulder.

"Greed," Danny said. "That's how. You'll have to make the first move. Christian would be suspicious if I approached him." His gaze squared up with mine. "I'll have your back, though."

With a shiver of trepidation, I nodded. We huddled up and made our plan together. We were drunk, we were amateurs at catching a killer, and we were probably out of our depth. But I didn't want to wait for another near disaster to take action. It had to be now.

Well, *tomorrow*. That's when everything would go down, we decided. Just then, it was too late for anyone but bar crawlers, club kids, and two world-traveling miscreants like us.

"This would be a very bad time," I warned Danny as we raised a toast to our plan, "for you to be late again."

He scoffed, then drank. "You can trust me," my pal said. He flashed me another grin. "Your first EFT hasn't even cleared."

Then, with that unsettling jokey rejoinder, Danny hustled me out of the bar and into the clear, dark night. I only hoped it wouldn't be my last lungful of Pacific breeze as I grabbed us a cab and sent us speeding across the bridge to Maison Lemaître.

Chapter 15

Predictably, by the time I woke up the next day, last night's bravado felt a million miles (and several beers) away.

What had seemed to be a stellar idea to me (trapping a killer) in the middle of a dive bar past midnight now seemed like a smoky dream. Or a movie. Who was *I* to augment my (already questionable) snooping activities with an honest-to-God *trap*?

I didn't have it in me, I decided as I showered and then got dressed. I wasn't anything close to a formidable killer-catcher. But I opted to look the part, anyway. Because what else would a cool, save-the-day type wear *except* for all black? All I needed to pull it off were my close-fitting black pants, a chic black top, my fast-getaway flats, and (in deference to the changeable weather near the Marin Headlands) Danny's jacket.

I'd kept it last night, after we'd parted at the door.

From the ankles to the waist, I was Audrey Hepburn. From the waist to the neck, I was James Dean. From there upward . . . I was stumped. My loose, shoulder-length hair and face (from the Slightly Hungover collection) stymied classification, until I remembered tomboyish '70s and '80s style icon Jane Birkin. That just about nailed it.

But I couldn't putter around getting my procrastination on all morning. Despite the rampant murder and confusion, I still had a consulting report to finish—and just hours to do it in before the plan Danny and I had brainstormed went into motion. I intended to finish writing my analysis of Lemaître Chocolates, *for sure,* today. I'd been working on my report in bits and pieces until now. All that remained was tying things together and formalizing my recommendations. All the necessary details were clear in my mind. Nothing was going to stop me. It couldn't.

Well, except for breakfast, I reasoned, swapping out my clutch for my reliable crossbody bag. No reasonable person would have denied me *breakfast.* I needed brainpower, didn't I? And I needed both hands free to navigate all the mouthwatering things on offer at the resort's everpopular all-chocolate buffet.

Ordinarily, the buffet was a weekends-only thing at Maison Lemaître, designed to entice resort-goers and coax local city dwellers into making the trip across the bay. Today, though, I'd learned that the chocolate-chip brioche French toast, chocolate waffles, pancakes with cacao nibs and fudge sauce, almond mocha scones, white chocolate cherry muffins, and everything else were going to be available in honor of the retreat's penultimate day.

It was a decision I applauded as I slipped out of my room, then eyed the door to Danny's room in indecision. Deciding in the end to leave him to his beauty sleep, I headed for the nearest stairs. The fire door clanged behind me with just as much hollow creepiness as usual, sealing me inside the typically uninhabited service stairwell. Shrugging into Danny's jacket, I descended the stairs at double speed, jostling my headache.

At least it wasn't a concussion headache, I figured as I

emerged onto the Maison Lemaître grounds and followed the sweet scents of chocolate and freshly brewed coffee toward the patio. What I was suffering from was a good old-fashioned overdose of lukewarm cut-rate beer (not to mention the ill-advised burritos we'd later stopped the taxi in the Mission to chase it down with).

In the buffet area, the lavishly dressed tables were full of retreat attendees. The sound of chocolate-business chatter rose to greet me; so did a few people I'd become friends with.

Getting to the end of the buffet spread took me a lot longer this time. Now that it wasn't dawn (or the early days of the retreat), my chocolatier cohorts were clearly feeling chatty. I entertained a couple of offers of consulting work (delivered on the QT, naturally), a few more offers of between-the-sheets "consulting" (Rex wasn't the only smarmy entrepreneur in my biz), and made a lot of promises to keep in touch with various suppliers, restaurateurs, and shop owners.

By the time I left the chocolate buffet, I had no memory of what I'd haphazardly dished onto my plate. Waving to the last friend I'd chatted with (the vivacious Torrance Chocolates rep), I veered toward an available table, then sat and took a look.

An overflowing plate looked back at me, chockablock with pastries, chocolate-chunk breakfast foods, a big smear of Nutella, whipped cream, and a mini ramekin of hot-fudge sauce. It was hardly balanced or complete, but that wasn't the point.

In my line of work, I see (and taste) a lot of chocolate. But I don't ordinarily get to do so off the clock, for my own pleasure. Eagerly anticipating doing exactly that, I unfurled my fancy napkin, fished out my heavy silver cutlery, then got down to business. With a never-ending supply of coffee coming from the attentive servers, a refreshing breeze blowing in across the grass and ruffling the nearby flowers, and no workshops, I was—

—unsurprisingly interrupted before I'd taken a single bite.

"Hayden!" Nina hustled over, smiling at me. Her gaze dipped to my overflowing plate. Her smile dimmed. "Are you okay?"

"I'm about to be, as soon as I tuck into all this."

"No, I mean . . ." After casting a hasty look around, Nina hugged her clipboards. She took a seat next to me, then leaned in. "Are you okay after *Rex*? How are you handling things?" Her concerned gaze searched mine, then wandered to my breakfast. "I mean, you and Rex seemed pretty close. You wouldn't be the first person to try to drown her heartache in chocolate sauce."

I burst out laughing. I couldn't help it. "*Me?* And *Rex*?"

She seemed taken aback. So did the people who glanced toward us at the sound of my chortle. Smiling, I waved them off.

"I'm not drowning my sorrows, Nina. I promise."

"If you say so." Her gaze skittered back to my face. "I *did* see the two of you cuddled up together fairly often, though."

That was because he'd been putting the moves on me. *Ugh.*

"I swear I'm not heartbroken over Rex. What happened to him is a tragedy, of course, but . . ." I put down my fork. It was apparent I wasn't going to be able to properly savor my praline *pain au chocolat.* "He wanted to consult with me. That's all."

Nina's next glance at my cacao smorgasbord disagreed. She evidently couldn't fathom eating all that food unless racked with grief. Which made no sense to me. I lose my appetite when stressed. Who wants to eat when everything tastes like sawdust?

"I don't know why Rex would need to consult with anyone!" Nina brushed back her hair—as if a single strand would dare to be out of place. As usual, her appearance was immaculate—whereas (thanks to my very late night last night) *I* looked like something Poopsie had dragged in . . . then chewed on, then slobbered on, then dragged back outside. "Melt is one of the premier chocolatiers in the city!" Nina said. "Rex was *very* successful."

Skeptically, I shook my head. "Nobody else says that."

"Well, if you've heard otherwise, you've heard wrong!"

Too late, I remembered that *Nina* was the one who'd been close to Rex. *They'd* been the ones who'd cuddled up together. Right near this buffet, in fact. Maybe elsewhere, too, I realized belatedly. After all, Nina hadn't seemed 100 percent opposed to getting extramarital with Danny (at least not until she'd learned about his wrong-side-of-the-tracks past). Maybe she'd been more serious about Rex than I'd realized?

Either way, I was being insensitive. Rex's death had been a shocking surprise. Nina was probably still reeling from it.

"Those business rumors don't matter now," I assured her in a gentle voice, patting her suit-covered forearm. "Rex *was* very well thought of in the end." Maybe she'd seen the TV news reports, too. "I'm sure he'll be missed by many people."

Including you? I wanted to ask, but didn't.

Mostly because Nina was getting worked up again.

"Who told you Rex was struggling?" she wanted to know. "Was it that *Chocolat Monthly* reporter? Eden had it in for Rex, you know. You can't take anything she says at face value."

"Nina . . ." I had to come clean. I could trust her with the truth. "I've seen Melt's business portfolio. Rex *really was* in financial trouble. I'm sorry if you didn't know that."

She fidgeted, then flung out her arm. "Well, that doesn't matter to *me*." She laughed, turning almost as pink as I'd been after my wrap adventure yesterday. "I just didn't want you to come away with the wrong idea, that's all. If *you* liked Rex, I wanted you to leave here with good impressions of him."

Oh? "That's sweet of you, Nina. But not necessary."

A breeze sent a whiff of chocolate wafting upward from my plate. I felt keenly aware of my rapidly cooling brioche waffle. Also, I remembered too late that I'd forgotten (in my postdive haze) to look at Travis's email about Nina's husband.

Probably, when I did, I'd learn that Calvin Wheeler had done something heinous like mix recyclables with trash. It was hard to say what kinds of things an organized, straight-arrow type like Travis would find outrageous. For all I knew, my late-night barhop with Danny had put me on Travis's naughty list.

"You know," I mused, unable to resist nibbling a muffin for strength, "I heard that Rex offered Adrienne a job at Melt. But she turned him down. Or was that just gossip, too? Do you know?"

It wasn't the most smooth or subtle segue, I'll admit. The link between Rex and Adrienne was tenuous. But Nina had known Adrienne even longer than I had. Maybe she could shed some light on one of the few things that still niggled at me about her.

Nina bit her lip. Her complexion had gone from embarrassed pink to mottled pink and white. I was glad I wasn't a redhead. For fair-skinned types like Nina, being out in the sun (the way we were on the serene and chocolate-scented patio) was brutal.

She gave the other breakfasters a cautious look. "No, that one is true," Nina finally confided in a low tone. "Rex offered to pay Adrienne a lot of money to take over as head chocolatier at Melt. He was too busy pressing the flesh to do it himself."

"That sounds like a dream opportunity," I said. Even idiosyncratic, often nomadic restaurant workers enjoyed a big payday. "Do you know why Adrienne turned him down?"

Nina's gaze swiveled to mine. She sighed. "Because of me."

I was surprised. "Because of *you*? What do you mean?"

She squeezed her clipboards, clearly reluctant to talk.

"I won't tell anyone, Nina," I promised. "Especially not Christian, if that's what you're worried about. I swear."

She gave me a ghost of a smile. "I heard he's trying to get his hooks into you next," Nina ventured. "Are you going to—"

I didn't want to talk about my nonexistent future with Lemaître Chocolates. I'd already made my peace with *not* having that Victorian house, those window box flowers, that cable car ride, or that adorable four-legged friend of my own. Besides, I wasn't sure how to explain my reluctance to work for Christian without inadvertently slamming Nina's ongoing employment with him. Nina was sensitive. I didn't want to spark a new tic.

"You can't sidetrack me," I interrupted with a smile, calling her out on her (probably automatic) PR gamesmanship. "How could Adrienne have turned down a job because of you?"

"It wasn't long after Christian took over," Nina admitted. "We were all under the gun, worried about how things would turn out. With Bernard at the helm, I'd been at the top—choice corner office, big salary, all the perks and privileges . . . you know." Her wave suggested those things were par for the course in our industry. Sometimes they were. Not always. "But all new execs like to make their mark. They like to put their stamp on things. Christian was no different. I thought he might bring in his own people. Adrienne did, too. We were both scared for our jobs."

That made sense. "Bernard recruited you *and* Adrienne, after all. Right? You were both part of the old guard."

"That's right." Nina nodded, warming up to what were clearly difficult memories. Absently, she scratched her neck. "But Christian didn't want to make those kinds of changes, after all. He's a devotee of new management tactics—strategies designed to bring in new blood and fresh thinking. We all got foosball tables, big-screen TVs, junk food in the break room—"

"Like one of those tech companies," I said, thinking of Google, Amazon, Twitter . . . any number of Silicon Valley start-ups.

"Exactly. We *also* got 'exciting' new cubicles instead of offices. They were supposed to foster teamwork and creativity."

I nodded. "You lost your nice corner office, didn't you?"

Nina nodded. "It wasn't that bad. Because I still had Adrienne! We were already friends. The new layout only brought us closer. After that, the kitchens weren't miles away from the PR zone anymore. We used to have coffee together every day."

That sounded nice. I was never in one place long enough to forge workplace routines with anyone. "With all the turmoil going on, Adrienne didn't want to leave you alone," I guessed, putting *two* and *two* together. I remembered how considerate my chocolatier friend had been. "That's why she turned down Rex's job offer. So you wouldn't have to deal with Christian alone."

Nina looked away. She fussed with her cuticles, then thoughtlessly nibbled on her fingernail. Then, "I'm afraid so."

I understood. "It *does* make it easier, you know," I told her, seeing how distressed she seemed. "If I didn't have *you* to talk to about Christian, I'd think I was going crazy for sure!"

At that, Nina laughed. She made a fist with her hands, seeming to realize belatedly that she'd started gnawing again.

"See? Now *I'm* going crazy!" she joked. "Thanks, Hayden. You always know just the right thing to say. I've been feeling so bad about all of this lately. I mean, if not for *me,* Adrienne—"

"Would have had a much less happy work life, I'm sure," I butted in. I didn't want to hear another person (after Bernard) beat themselves up for a past decision that *might* (or might not) have wound up affecting Adrienne's well-being. "Believe me, I know how special Adrienne was. I do." I had very fond memories of our time together. "That's why"—*I'm determined to track down her killer*—"I'll be so sad to leave Maison Lemaître tomorrow."

Nina gave a perceptive head shake. "You hesitated there, Hayden. I saw it!" She leaned in. "What's your plan, anyway?"

Lure Christian out in the open, make him confess what he did, then let Danny's police "associate" take it from there.

Nope. That sounded preposterous. It honestly did.

But whether she knew it or not, Nina could help make that happen. She had the direct line to Christian that I lacked. If my request to meet with him came through *her* . . . maybe that would be better than the approach Danny and I had dreamed up last night.

"I can't say," I told her, indulging in my best cloak-and-dagger routine to coordinate with my ninja outfit. "But it all starts with Christian." Handily, Nina would think I was talking about his job offer with Lemaître Chocolates. She clearly knew about it. So she wouldn't be suspicious when

I said, "Do you think you can pass along a message to him for me, though?"

She stared at me fixedly, clearly sensing my covert vibe. *"Absolutely,"* Nina promised. "What should I tell Christian?"

"Tell him . . ." I paused, relishing the drama of the moment. This might be the only time I ever actively participated in bringing down a killer. Even if Danny thought Christian was just the first guy to knock off our suspect list, I knew better. Christian was the one! Besides, let's be real: It *was* going to be the *only* time I ever helped to catch a murderer. "Tell him I have something *very* important to give him," I said. "Tell him he's *definitely* going to want this information. Tell him it's *more* than what he's been waiting for—*more* than I promised."

Okay, sure. I was overselling it a tad. But I was a newbie.

"Right." Gravely, Nina nodded. "Got it. I'll tell him."

"Tell him . . ." I stopped, realizing that maybe it would be smart to go even *more* off plan. Just a little. After all, Danny and I had been fairly tipsy last night when we'd conceived of this whole thing. I frowned. "Where's a good place to stage a clandestine meeting?" I asked Nina. "To exchange something?"

She wouldn't know that I meant Adrienne's chocolate notebook. That's what Danny and I had decided to use as bait to lure each of our suspects into the open. They all wanted it.

"The spa," Nina told me confidently. "It's deserted after hours. Even the staff members don't linger. You can meet there."

"Good idea." We broke down the specifics. "Thanks, Nina."

"Any time." She drummed her fingers on her clipboard. One of her omnipresent cell phones rang. At its tone, Nina jumped. Apologizing, she pulled it out. "I've really got to run."

"I know. I'm sorry to keep you so long." I felt bad for her. It was evident her stressful time hadn't ended yet. "I bet you'll be glad when the chocolate retreat is over with, right?"

Nina's newly flustered gaze met mine while she juggled her other ringing phone. For a heartbeat, she paused to look at me. "I'll be *so* glad when it's all over with," she said in a heartfelt tone. "It's been so stressful. You have no idea."

Then she scurried away, leaving me and my all-chocolate breakfast in peace. I looked down at it, considered having it reheated, then decided speed was utmost in this instance.

By now, Danny would be up. I'd need my strength to tell him that I'd gone (infinitesimally) off plan. Plus, there was always the risk he'd pester me to *jog* again. With a groan, I dug in.

Chapter 16

You know that feeling you get when you're trying to clear customs or waiting in line at the DMV or standing behind that one person at the supermarket who *still* keeps a checkbook? It's as though glaciers are melting while you watch. As though roses are blooming and dying in slo-mo time lapse all around you. As though time is absolutely *crawling* by, with no beginning or end. See, that's how I typically feel while thinking about working on any individual consulting report. I just. Don't. Want. To do it.

Actually, *writing* my report is fine. Always. Detailing all my analysis, explaining my recommendations, describing potential solutions for clients . . . I *like* those things. But every time I'm faced with breaking out my laptop and getting down to brass tacks, I feel the same old inertia trying to suck me down again.

In this frame of mind, going outside sounds awesome, for instance. So does taste-testing chocolates (to be double-triple-quadruple certain my initial impressions were accurate). Even reorganizing my duffel bag seems like a stellar idea. While trying to get psyched up to finish my report for Lemaître Chocolates, I'm not proud to say that I wound up engaging in all those time-tested pro-procrastination activities. And then some!

Maybe you've been there, so you know exactly what I'm talking about. Maybe you haven't. . . . In which case, you must be from Mars or something (sorry). In my universe, procrastination follows responsibility as night follows day. The only way out, I knew, was to channel Nike and "just do it." Because waiting to feel "inspired" to work was about as futile as waiting to feel four inches taller. It just wasn't going to happen.

As a professional, I knew that. That's why I did what I always do and went through the motions anyway. I got out my Moleskine notebook. I assembled my research materials. I spread my market analysis spreadsheets on the bed. I put my laptop in the middle (with Rex's Melt portfolio acting as a makeshift lap desk), grabbed Adrienne's notebook (for safekeeping), then climbed into the unholy nest I'd created. There, amid everything I needed, there could be no excuses. I was there to work.

Since it was crunch time, that's what I did. I squinted and recollected and typed. I reviewed and evaluated and typed some more. I proofread and edited, double-checked and expounded. By the time I was done, I had fifty pages of charts and graphs, recipes and recommendations, percentages and paragraphs. It was, as usual, a pretty kick-ass piece of consultancy work. I wasn't too shy to say so. In my business, modesty gets you *not* hired.

I sighed and looked up, bleary-eyed but pleased with the results I'd achieved. You might not believe me, but as loony as it seems, this is all part of my "chocolate whisperer" process.

Part of my work is methodical. Part is analytical. But a *big* part of it is intuitive; the rest is creative. I need time for all those parts to gel into a cohesive whole. Technically, I'm delaying doing the typing. I'll admit that. But while that's going on, the chocolate-expertise centers in my brain are doing their own things behind the scenes, collating information, making connections, and spitting out useful ideas for me.

It's not a system that would work for everyone, sure. But it works for me. I get no complaints from my clients, and I have all the work I can handle, besides. So it's all good.

Tense from sitting still, parched from my marathon stint, I glanced out the window. *Uh-oh.* It was getting dark outside.

That meant it was almost time for my rendezvous with Christian. Or maybe it was past time. I'd zoned out *too* hard.

With a glimmer of panic, I picked up my phone. If I'd left for my spa-set meeting with Christian ten minutes ago, I'd only have been five minutes late. *Argh.* If chronic latecomer Danny could have seen me now, the irony would have killed him.

Shoving aside that thought, I scrambled to collect my things. Danny and I had gone over our plan in detail after breakfast. He'd promised to alert his friend at the SFPD, then wait in the shadows while I made the exchange with Christian; I'd promised to sub one of my unused notebooks for Adrienne's. That way, we wouldn't be forced to surrender the real thing. Under the circumstances, a decoy would be sufficient, we'd decided.

Besides, I was supposed to play it cool and not *show* the notebook until Christian had thoroughly implicated himself in Adrienne's murder. Easy-peasy, right? I actually thought it might be. Given how much Christian liked to hear the sound of his own voice, it was possible he'd *love* blabbing about his misdeeds. Not that I especially wanted to *hear* them, but . . .

That was part of the deal, I knew as I shoved everything

I needed into my crossbody bag, slung it over my shoulder, then bolted out the door and down the (creepily deserted) service stairs. I'd be lying if I said I wasn't nervous; I was. But just as with writing my report, the only way to have any peace of mind was to have this thing *done with,* once and for all. I needed to know who'd killed Adrienne (and maybe Rex). I couldn't rest easy otherwise. I couldn't exactly ramble around the world with my usual joie de vivre unless I knew I was safe, could I?

Breathless, I exited onto the freshly watered, twilit grounds with a sense of purpose, then followed the path toward the spa. In the distance, I heard laughter and conversation, music and the clatter of kitchen workers. I wished I was among those line cooks and sous chefs tonight, instead of heading toward a furtive meeting. I wasn't completely sure I could get Christian to come clean. But I figured I had as good a shot as anyone.

Ahead of me, the luxurious spa building looked peaceful and dark. Only its security lighting was illuminated. Far away behind me, the Maison Lemaître cottages and outbuildings dotted the lawn, barely visible squares of darkness against the ever-deepening sky. I would have thought the need for stress relief and pampering offered by the spa would have been a 24/7 thing, but apparently (I'd learned) it wasn't. Once happy hour rolled around, Portia and Britney had told me earlier, demand for spa services starting dipping; before dinnertime, it nose-dived.

I guessed once people were able to start knocking back cocktails, they started feeling pretty stress free anyway.

Wishing I'd thought to grab a tequila shot for courage (a handy tactic I'd picked up in Mexico City), I approached the spa's imposing entrance. As predicted, everything was quiet.

I glanced around, looking for Danny. Predictably, he and his SFPD friend were nowhere in sight. But they were the experts, right? They shouldn't have been visible. Unlike me.

I hauled in a breath, reminded myself of Danny's promise to have my back, then knocked on the spa door. Thrice.

That was supposed to be the signal I'd arranged. Using it felt ridiculously clandestine. Also, just plain ridiculous. I wished I'd arranged this liaison inside Christian's office.

Three (long) minutes later, I *really* wished I'd arranged to meet the younger Lemaître indoors. I hadn't thought to grab Danny's purloined jacket. It was getting chilly now that the sun had completely set. Shivering, I paced in the spa's entryway.

Was Christian standing me up? It looked that way, but I just couldn't believe it. He *really* wanted Adrienne's notebook, and I'd done a masterful job of (over)selling it. Frowning, I gazed across the darkened grounds, looking for him. Nada.

Unsure whether to stay or go, I pulled out my phone to check for messages. There was a confirmation text from Danny, letting me know he was at the Maison Lemaître bar with his law enforcement pal, a reminder to myself to read Travis's email, and a notification about my upcoming departing flight from SFO, but nothing from Christian. Grumbling with uncertainty, I decided to kill a few more minutes reading Travis's email.

It wasn't easy to view the whole thing on my phone's tiny screen, but I got the gist readily enough. Calvin Wheeler wasn't a thoughtless nonrecycler *or* an abusive husband, as it turned out—but he *was* unemployed. Travis's contact had turned up details of Calvin's arrest for "harassing" his former employer and making threats after having been dismissed from the firm.

The arrest was four months old, though. Calvin's accounting firm hadn't pressed charges. The whole matter had been dropped.

Its timing did make me wonder, though. . . .

Suddenly, the spa's door silently *whooshed* open.

Nina stood in the entryway, unsurprised to see me.

"Nina!" I blurted, *quite* surprised to see *her.* "Where's Christian?" Surely she'd understood that she'd been supposed to arrange the meeting, not be present for it. Then I thought of another possible explanation for her being there. "Was tonight our spa date with Calvin and Danny? I should let him know."

She waved. "You don't have to do that."

But I whipped off a quick text to Danny anyway, just in case. A girl couldn't be too safe. "It's okay. Already done."

With my plan engaged, I stepped inside the low-lit spa's reception area, eager to get this over with. It was probably going to be a no-go if Nina was there, though, I realized. Christian would be unlikely to spill the beans in her presence.

I wouldn't have wanted to confess to murder in front of her, either. Nina's enviable grooming, impeccable posture, and nonstop organizational skills were fairly intimidating. Heck, I wouldn't have wanted to confess to a hangnail in her hearing. Although, I noticed as I looked at her now, today Nina's manicure was history. She seemed to have finished what she'd started at breakfast this morning by gnawing all her newly polished nails to the quick. The end result looked . . . painful.

That wasn't all, either. Nina's blotchy complexion was back as she turned to me, then dropped her gaze to my bulging bag.

"Did you bring it?" she asked.

Her tone suggested we were swapping spreadsheets or finalizing marketing campaign plans, not (potentially) trading corporate secrets. But then, Nina didn't know all the details.

I doubted Christian would have enlightened her.

"I brought something for Christian," I specified, putting my hand protectively over the spot where I'd stashed the decoy notebook. I looked around. "Is he here? Or is he running late?"

I hoped he was running late. That would disguise my own tardiness. I had a professional image to uphold, after all.

"Why don't you come this way?" Nina gestured toward the treatment rooms. A few feet away, the Zen fountain sparkled.

"Okay." I was thrown by her being there, but I shrugged and followed in her wake, anyway. "I guess Christian just won't stage a meeting without turning it into a big production, huh?"

He obviously wanted Nina, his right-hand gal, to be there—probably for appearances. I didn't know if Christian imagined himself as some sort of cartoon supervillain or what, but he did like to seem important. His hubris didn't surprise me.

Maybe I'd inadvertently caused this snafu by going off script. Danny had warned me that I shouldn't have improvised.

Speaking of him . . . I peeked at my phone as we traversed the spa's silent and serene lounge area, then headed for the treatment rooms. "Christian had better not be planning on sharing chocolate-fondue body wraps with me!" I joked, glancing into that room as we passed it. "I'm off those for life."

Nina said nothing. Probably, she was as irked to be taking part in this sneaky scenario as I was to be instigating it. I would have preferred that Adrienne was still alive, creating wonderful chocolates, and Rex was still kicking, smarming it up.

Nina was nothing if not forbearing, though. There was no trace of irritation in her expression as she showed me into the same room where I'd shared the hot-cocoa mud bath with Isabel.

Automatically, I glanced overhead, looking for security cameras. Earlier (while I'd been procrastinating), Danny had explained how they worked at Maison Lemaître. I wasn't surprised that there weren't any cameras in the treatment room. That would have been a serious violation of guest privacy. Also, what were the spa workers going to steal in here? Towels and pricey mud?

I didn't see Christian. "He *is* late. That figures."

Nina turned. Her expression looked . . . pretty *weird,* frankly. The mottled pinkness I'd noticed earlier seemed to have spread from her face to her neck and lower, making her look blotchy all over. Her hands trembled. So did her voice, when she spoke.

"Christian isn't coming," she said. "No one is coming."

I didn't understand. "Didn't you give him my message?"

"He wants you to give *me* Adrienne's notebook."

"Adrienne's—" I broke off, confused. I studied her more closely. "I never said I was bringing Adrienne's notebook."

"But that's what it *had* to be, wasn't it?" Nina's voice echoed in the luxuriously tiled room. Nearby us, the hot-cocoa mud bath burbled away, making it feel vaguely steamy. I guessed the staff didn't turn down the heat all the way—probably, it was too expensive to crank it completely up and down every day.

"Either that," Nina went on, clenching her fists, "or your consulting report." She narrowed her eyes. "You found out *lots* of interesting things while working on *that,* didn't you?"

Her demeanor baffled me. The PR exec seemed more on edge than ever, but there weren't any official events going on here.

"I *knew* you had," she told me before I could interrupt,

pacing near the mud bath. Her businesslike pumps clicked on the sleek tiled floor. "You couldn't resist taunting me about it, could you? Christian said you were the best. He was right."

Ordinarily, I liked hearing praise. Who didn't?

But Nina's odd behavior bothered me. She was obviously upset about something. Her belligerent attitude seemed out of place, especially in such a tranquil setting—even for someone forced to act as Christian's (unwilling) one-woman entourage.

"He was more right than he knew about you," Nina told me. "I guess when he gets his 'report,' he'll get more than he counted on. Unless *you* never give it to him, that is."

Was that a dig at my procrastination habit? Confusedly, I shook my head. "Christian will get a pretty typical report from me," I assured her. "I just finished writing it today."

"I heard you two talking about it at the scavenger hunt," Nina said. "You and Christian." She said his name as though it disgusted her. "The two of you were so *gleeful,* discussing your 'fascinating' assignment and the 'problems' at Lemaître."

Loosely, I remembered the exchange I'd had with Christian. He'd seemed determined to pester me about my overdue report. I remembered Nina leaving abruptly during our conversation.

At the time, I'd thought she was annoyed, like I was, by Christian's overbearing ways and heavy-handed tactics. But now, I couldn't help wondering . . .

"You knew we were talking about Lemaître? You guessed I'd been consulting for Christian?"

So much for my super-stealth undercover MO.

"I knew you were talking about *me*!" Nina corrected.

Her eyes looked a little . . . wild to me. What was going on?

"I knew, at that moment, that you'd figured out what was going on."

"I wish I could say the same thing," I cracked, wanting to go back to the easy camaraderie I'd had with her. I shook my head, then softened my voice. "You seem upset, Nina."

I knew it wasn't because of Calvin. Maybe Rex?

"Of course I'm upset! You've been rubbing it in my face all this time. You think you're so clever, Hayden, with your world-traveler ways and your expertise about chocolate. But you don't know anything about *me*. You don't know how hard I worked."

"I do," I tried to soothe her. "You told me, remember?"

"I didn't tell you half of it," Nina all but sneered. "Did you find out, anyway? Did you go back to your shady friend afterward and find out? Did the two of you laugh about it?"

Danny. I remembered him . . . and kind of wished I'd sent him an SOS text instead of an innocuous "I'm in!" message.

I may have been being a little overconfident at the time. I'd thought I'd been about to come face-to-face with Christian.

"Of course we didn't laugh about you," I assured Nina, wishing I hadn't jumped *quite* so eagerly on the idea of a deserted location for this meeting. I'd thought an out-of-the-way locale would encourage Christian to confess. He wasn't likely to do that amid all the chocolate-retreat attendees. "I wouldn't do that. I haven't been rubbing anything in your face, either. I don't—"

I don't understand what you're talking about, I wanted to say. But Nina's abrupt, humorless laugh cut me short. "You haven't? What do you call 'Christian is a brilliant and accomplished man'? Huh? You stood there with me and *threw it* in my face!"

I frowned. "I asked, sure. But I just wanted to know—"

"If I'd crack? Close to it!" Nina paced. Absently but furiously, she scratched her arm. "That 'sympathetic listener' routine you pulled on me at breakfast today was the last straw, though. I liked you, you know. In spite of everything, I did." Her pleading, fast-blinking gaze met mine. "I thought maybe if I explained my situation, you would understand. I thought maybe you would leave me alone. Because you knew what it was like to be browbeaten by Christian. You knew how difficult it was!"

"Your situation . . . doesn't seem that bad," I tried.

Another harsh laugh. "Oh no? Getting demoted, losing my office, losing part of my salary, having my stock options cut. . . . None of those things sound 'that bad' to you?" Nina put her hands on her hips, then whirled to face me. The enmity in her expression startled me. "How about having all those things happen and *then* having your husband lose *his* job? How about that, huh? How about having *everything* fall on your shoulders?"

Aha. Now I knew where Calvin's unemployment came in.

"That sounds . . . I'm sorry, Nina. That sounds awful." I still didn't understand what she was driving at. "If you just want to vent until Christian shows up, I guess I get that, but—"

"You 'get that'? How very generous of you." Again, Nina sounded almost beside herself with hostility. "You're not as smart as everyone thinks you are. I already told you—Christian's not coming."

"He's not?" I wasn't sure what to think. "Why not?"

Maybe he wanted Nina to handle all the dirty work? But Nina couldn't possibly know about Christian killing Adrienne.

"Because he still doesn't know what I did, and I intend to keep it that way." She inhaled, then held out her hand. "Give it to me."

"Adrienne's notebook? But why? You don't know anything about chocolate." She'd told me so before. "Why do you want—"

Christian is a brilliant and accomplished man. The phrase I'd supposedly taunted Nina with. Belatedly, I remembered her referring to that phrase days ago. I remembered Bernard mentioning it. I remembered seeing it in Rex's Melt portfolio.

That was a *watchword,* I realized—a phrase that let all the players know who was in on selling chocolate secrets.

"Adrienne's notebook has Lemaître's recipes in it, doesn't it?" I asked as the truth dawned. "All those formulas, all those techniques . . . they weren't the result of years' worth of Adrienne's personal chocolatier experience. They were all of the trade secrets that Lemaître uses to dominate the market—all handily written down for a competitor to use." *For Melt to use.*

"You can't stall me by stating the obvious," Nina said.

But it hadn't been obvious. Not to me. So far, I'd only heard two people say that phrase aloud: Nina and Bernard. A third person had written it down: Rex. But only two of those people had been using it to coordinate corporate espionage.

Because only Bernard had *also* co-opted that phrase to threaten me with yesterday. Only *he* had been oblivious to its hidden meaning . . . just as I'd been. How had I missed that?

Probably the same way I'd missed something else: the significance of Bernard purposely "redirecting suspicion." The important part of Danny's informative tip *didn't* have to do with Bernard's suspicions of Christian at all, I realized too late. It had to do with someone *else* who'd "redirected suspicion."

Nina. She'd pointed the finger at Danny—probably as a means of making sure I wouldn't suspect *her* of anything untoward . . . such as searching my room for Adrienne's notebook, then walloping me on the head with a lamp when I'd disturbed her by surprise.

Alarmed, I backed up. I'm pretty sure my eyes went comically wide, too. How often are *you* faced with somebody's obvious duplicitousness in real life? It's terrifying stuff.

"Don't act as if you don't know what's in Adrienne's notebook—what *I've* been up to with it," Nina scoffed. "It's too late for that. I know you were planning to tell Christian all about it. That's why you set up this little meeting with him."

She'd never given my message to Christian. I held up my palms, hoping to placate her. "I wasn't going to tell Christian anything about you," I swore—honestly, as it turned out. "I mean, I have to admire your ingenuity, right? What a way to put one over on Christian. After this, he'll be ruined for sure."

I tried to chuckle knowingly. I'm pretty sure I bombed.

"That's the idea." Nina gave me a skeptical look. She scratched her arm again, then her neck. Her speckled complexion was getting worse. So was the twitch in her foot. "At least it was until *you* came along," she said as she paced. "It was until Adrienne died! I had such a good setup going until then. Adrienne to write everything down . . . and *me* to benefit."

I got it. I thought. I wanted to be sure. "Christian suspected someone of selling Lemaître's secrets." I remembered him telling me so. "He thought it was Adrienne, but it was you."

"Of course it was me! Don't think I don't know *that's* what you're here to uncover. I needed the money after Christian took over and Calvin got downsized out of a job. Adrienne was too dumb to realize what a gold mine she was sitting on. But *I* wasn't."

Reeling, I stared at Nina. No wonder she was riddled with nervous tics and a burgeoning rash. She'd been keeping a whole host of secrets. *And* she thought I'd been at Lemaître to uncover her espionage, not to consult on the nutraceutical line. That's what I got, I guessed, for having clients who demanded "the utmost discretion." That left my presence open to rampant (wrongheaded) speculation. I still needed to know more, though.

"No wonder you and Rex were so cozy," I mused. Leadingly.

But Nina sneered. "Rex. He was just like you—"

"Hey!" I couldn't help protesting. I didn't want to be a member of any club that included smarmy Rex. God rest him.

"—always pestering me, threatening me, *hounding* me."

Too late, comprehension dawned. At the buffet that day . . .

"He wasn't comforting you over Adrienne's death," I said.

Nina snorted. "He was demanding I give back the money he'd already given me—an advance payment for Adrienne's notebook." That partly explained Melt's dire financials. Rex must have overextended himself when prepaying for Adrienne's notebook—which Nina hadn't possessed to deliver. "But I couldn't do that."

I glanced at the treatment room door. It was open, but there was still nobody around. I doubted I could just laugh off Nina's (partly) incoherent confession and sashay out of there.

I needed to keep her talking. "You'd lost your partner."

"Adrienne wasn't my partner! She was my golden goose." Nina shook her head. "There was no one else like Adrienne."

"*I* could be." Tensely, I nodded. "I know chocolate. I know Lemaître. Christian already offered me the head chocolatier job. Things can go on the same way they always have for you."

"*You'll* help me sell Lemaître's secrets?"

I hedged. "You don't think Danny is the only one who's open to 'unconventional' business opportunities, do you?"

Nina eyed me skeptically. She was right to look at me that way. I would be about as adept at corporate espionage as I would be at hockey.

I tried to appear shady. "I already told you about Danny's forgery skills," I improvised. "We're the complete package."

For a minute, Nina almost seemed to waver.

Then she shook her head. "No. I'm retiring after this. I just want it all to be over with finally!" She sighed, then scratched her neck again. "Just when I'd dealt with Rex—"

I froze, horror-struck by what Nina undoubtedly meant. I could picture her following Rex to the steep ridge trail, confronting him, pushing him off. Or maybe just pushing him.

Most likely, Nina didn't feel such a rapport with all her victims, I mused with a sickening feeling. Just me. I was special. Appalled and scared, I wanted to bolt. But I didn't.

Because if I didn't make it out of this alive, no one would ever know what Nina had done to Rex. To Lemaître. To Adrienne?

"—*you* had to come along and mess things up again!" Nina said. "I thought you'd eventually give in and give Adrienne's notebook to Christian. God knows, I reminded him about it often enough." *Aha.* That explained his constant badgering.

But maybe I'd misunderstood. "You 'dealt' with Rex?"

"I wanted out," Nina explained. "I was willing to take what he'd already given me and forgo the rest. But Rex refused."

"So you . . . ?" I held my breath, not wanting to hear the worst.

Nina shrugged. "It's a pretty slippery ridge up there," she mused aloud. "What happened to Rex could have happened to anyone." She pawed at her blotchy neck, then frowned. "It wasn't really *murder,* if that's what you're thinking. Not since it *could* have happened accidentally without me even being there."

"But it didn't," I couldn't help pointing out, aghast.

Nina gave me a merciless grin. "If people could see you now, struggling to figure out something so simple . . ." She looked away, then shook her head. "*Mierda.* You'd never get hired."

Mierda. That expletive gave me chills. It hadn't been rude French I'd heard when surprising my lamp-wielding room-ransacker, after all. It had been rude Spanish. It had been *Nina.*

"It was considerate of you to set up this nice deserted meeting place," Nina went on next, looking around. The tiled walls had beaded with condensation. So had the floor. "That made things much easier for me. Easier than the chocolate-fondue body wrap equipment thing. It's so hard to arrange an accident when a bunch of chocolate-retreat attendees are hanging around."

"That was *you*?" Then Nina hadn't been at the spa to have a manicure at all. She'd come there to get *me.* "But why?"

"Because I didn't succeed the first time, of course." Nina's tone was eerily matter-of-fact. "It's all your fault that it's come to this. It was supposed to have been a simple overdose—"

I felt my heart stutter, then kick into overdrive.

Oh no. Oh no. Oh no. It had *all* been Nina, all along.

"—but somehow the glasses got switched," Nina went

on jumpily. "You got Adrienne's green juice, and *she* got yours."

This was all getting a little too real for me. I backed up again, scanning the treatment room for a weapon. I noticed that the hot-cocoa mud bath still burbled innocently away, as though Nina and I might patch things up and then become spa buddies.

"It was supposed to have been *you* dead, all along. Not Adrienne. *Now* it's going to be." Erratically, Nina beamed at me. She hugged herself, free (for the first time I could remember) of her clipboards and phones. "I've tried to kill you *three times* now, Hayden, but you just keep on getting away!"

"'Three times'?" I stalled. My throat was so dry, I could barely force out the words. The hypercaffeinated green energy drink, the killer chocolate-fondue body wrap machine, and . . . ?

"I thought I had you with that lamp," Nina explained conversationally, "but your friend Danny interrupted me." She frowned. "That's how I thought of blaming him for it."

Aha. "If it's any consolation, I had a monster headache."

"It's not." Nina rummaged in her handbag. She pulled out something cylindrical, black, and compact. A collapsible umbrella? "Honestly, it's kind of a relief to have it out in the open," she told me. "I've been *really* stressed about this."

"No kidding?" I eyed her multiple nervous tics. Then I started panicking. I breathed in, forcing myself to regroup.

"Well, you'd better get undressed." With whatever she'd withdrawn, Nina gestured to the side. She'd (helpfully?) placed a Maison Lemaître spa robe on the closest hook. "Your accident isn't going to be believable if you're fully dressed." She pointed at my crossbody bag. "Just leave me your purse."

I clutched it. Silently, I shook my head. I knew enough

to try to delay her—to try to humanize us both. "It doesn't have to be this way, Nina. We can both leave here safely! I can make sure everyone understands that Adrienne's death really *was* an accident." I wasn't sure how I was supposed to gloss over the fact that *I'd* been the intended target. Details. "Let's talk about this! I can see that you're feeling pretty overwhelmed."

I backed up, all knowledge of my "brilliant" plan to flush out the killer falling out of my brain. I wondered if Danny and his friend had arrived—if they were somewhere near. If so, they were the most lackadaisical save-the-day cavalry ever. It looked as though I was on my own. Just in case, I scratched my head.

Danny did *not* burst in to save me. I almost sobbed.

"You won't find what you want in my bag," I warned Nina as I pulled it off my shoulder. "All I put in here is a decoy."

Everything felt surreal. I wanted this nightmare to end.

Apparently, so did Nina. She reached into the hot-cocoa mud bath, withdrew a hefty handful of mud, then tossed it on the floor. Then another handful. She smiled at her handiwork.

"There," she announced. "That ought to just about do it."

With a sinking sensation, I understood. I was supposed to "slip" on that mud and fall—probably to my death. A well-placed blow to the head would do it, sending my noggin squarely against the tile. This time, I'd have much worse than a concussion.

"I'm not just going to let you murder me," I warned.

Nina looked exasperated. "It's not *murder,* remember? It's an accident. You're going to have a terrible, tragic accident."

I swallowed hard. "I'm tougher than I look." I thought it was only fair to say so. "I have backup right behind me, too."

"Your macho buddy?" Nina laughed. "I think he's late."

I did, too. Unfortunately. Goose bumps rose on my arms.

"Besides," Nina added, "I brought backup, too."

With a brutal gesture, she jerked the thing she'd brought. It telescoped outward with a horrifying sound. It was, I saw too late, an expanding baton—the kind police forces used worldwide.

With as much franticness as Nina had, I scratched my head. But my "help!" gesture did not summon my burly bodyguard, Danny.

"Come on," Nina coaxed irritably, stepping nearer— probably to grab my bag. "There's no point delaying the inevitable."

"I'm a master procrastinator," I cracked, my voice warbling. "It's *always* possible to delay the inevitable."

Nina didn't appreciate my attempt at humor. But she did come close enough for me to take a swing at her. Because one thing I'd learned in Barcelona was to never take *yourself* closer to an attacker. Only defend yourself in ways that let you keep your distance.

So as Nina came closer, her gaze fixed on my bag . . . I swung that thing as hard as I could. I caught Nina right in the face with my crossbody bag's full weight. She staggered.

I followed up with a sturdy kick, aimed right at the side of her kneecap. You couldn't aim for the front—that hurt, but it didn't throw an attacker (or streetwise mugger) off balance. As I'd prayed it would, my kick made Nina crumple. She went down.

So did her baton—and my trusty bag. Her weapon skittered across the floor; my favorite bag flew into the tub full of hot-cocoa mud bath muck. But I couldn't think about that just then. I was too busy mentally planning my next self-defense move.

Swearing a blue streak of Spanish profanities, Nina

tried to get up. She slid on the mud, which she'd dropped on the floor a minute ago. Breathing hard, full of wild adrenaline, I adopted a ready pose.

Nose strike or eye gouge, I repeated to myself, arranging my arms and hands. *Nose strike or eye gouge. Nose strike—*

"That's enough," Danny said calmly from beside me.

I whirled. He knew enough not to touch me. Not then.

He nodded at Nina on the floor. "Barcelona strikes again?"

Shakily, I shrugged. But we both knew that's what it was: the same fail-safe maneuver that had dropped that would-be mugger in Barcelona. Hey, I told you it was *effective,* right? I never said it was *complicated.* Sometimes it's better if it's not.

Tardily, I noticed Danny's uniformed friend dealing with Nina. It was a relief to have a police presence there—even if I couldn't help noticing that said police presence was curvaceous, brunette, and dishy . . . in an authoritative, capable way, of course.

"I thought you didn't like the police," I said to Danny.

"Sometimes I do." His gaze touched me, full of concern. "When it comes to you." He traded a decisive nod with his attractive friend. "It was touch and go when I heard Nina's baton go into action, but I'm pretty sure we got it all."

"Got all what?" Had they been outside the treatment room listening? "You couldn't have gotten anything." Suddenly, I felt overrun with fear and frustration. "You were *late*! Again!"

Unable to hold back, I gave him a good smack to the arm.

"I wasn't late," Danny argued, eyes widening from my blow. He held up his hands. "I was hanging back. Getting Nina's confession. You were handling things okay." He eyed my head. "You'd better watch that itch, though. Might be dandruff."

I couldn't believe he was laughing about this.

"We need a new SOS signal," I told him sternly. Danny's police officer friend's radio burst to life. Raising my voice above the comforting sound of the SFPD deciding what to do with Nina, I added, "I think the old one is too complicated for you."

"I think you're waiting too long to deploy it."

"'Too long'? I was scratching my head like crazy!"

"Like I said, you had it covered." Danny slung his arm around my still-trembling shoulders. "Congrats, Hayden. You just caught a killer," he said cheerfully. "How does it feel?"

"It feels . . ." I paused. "Like I *never* want to do it again."

Then, at the officer's instructive nod, we headed outside together to give our statements (I assumed) and formalize my first (and last) covert catch-a-killer operation.

Chapter 17

As you might have expected, word spread quickly about Nina's arrest at Maison Lemaître. It might have helped that police cars came screaming up the resort's long, luxurious driveway just moments after my encounter with Nina in the spa. Even as Danny and I stepped outside, more officers were there waiting to meet us. We spent quite a while talking with them.

"This is serious stuff. And here I thought you were just making time with your hot detective friend," I told Danny during a lull in the action. We watched as Nina was put into a patrol car. She looked dazed, defiant, and (obviously) irrefutably guilty. "You didn't tell me your 'associate' was so cute."

"There's a reason I was willing to hang out in the bar with her while you worked your way through our suspects." Danny grinned at that reference to his role in our catch-a-killer plan, then nodded at his friend. "It wouldn't have been so bad if the effort had taken two or three or four nights."

"It couldn't have taken that long," I protested. "I would have had to leave San Francisco without knowing who was after me." I shivered, remembering that I *had been* the target, after all. "I guess I'm not as 100 percent well-liked as I thought."

"Nah. You're very well-liked with me."

"Well, then. That's all that counts, right?"

"Damn straight," Danny agreed.

I was pretty sure he was being extra nice to me. I had, after all, just been through a traumatic experience. I'd been really brave about it all, too—even if I had to say so myself.

"What I still don't understand," I mused, standing in the darkness with the police lights flashing over us and all the officers hurrying around, "is *you*. You *liked* Nina. You stuck up for her. You made me have breakfast with her while you jogged!"

"All part of my cunning plan."

"Ha. As if." I poked him. "You had a crush on a killer."

"I didn't have 'a crush' on Nina. I was watching her!"

"Mmm-hmm." I folded my arms against the cold. "Remind me to be skeptical of your people skills in the future. Whereas *I*—"

"Was totally fooled about Nina's intentions all along."

Whoops. He had me there. "I can't be expected to be *good* at sniffing out a killer. I've never done it before!"

I hoped never to do it again, either. I hadn't been kidding. This was not something I wanted to make a habit of.

"Especially not when *this* is the result." I lifted my still-soggy crossbody bag, which I'd fished from the hot-cocoa mud bath. It felt heavy with mud residue. "It'll never be the same."

Danny shrugged. "It could have been worse. At least your overdue report wasn't in there."

"My report *isn't* overdue!" At least it wasn't, as long as I delivered it to Christian tonight. "Plus . . ." Woefully, I eyed my bag. We'd made a lot of memories together. Vietnam, Wales, Denmark—I'd lost track of the countries

I'd traveled through while wearing that bag. "You're clearly not a woman, if you can dismiss the loss of a favorite bag that easily."

Danny looked down at himself. "You're just figuring that out now?" He grinned. "I think you need glasses."

We both knew I didn't. But there was no point going there.

"What's more important is that Adrienne's notebook wasn't in there," I informed him, grateful that I'd stowed it elsewhere before leaving for my rendezvous. "It's safe and sound. Although I still don't understand why Adrienne brought it to the chocolate-themed scavenger hunt in the first place. Even if Nina was right—and Adrienne didn't realize how valuable it was—that doesn't explain why she was carrying it around with her."

"Maybe she needed it to work on her chocolates?"

"Maybe." But if that had been the case, I knew, Adrienne would have needed it to finish the gilded caffeinated truffles we'd worked on together at the last minute for the reception.

"Well, what matters is that her killer's been brought to justice," Danny said in a voice that meant he was ready to move on. He gazed toward the Golden Gate Bridge. "Now what's next?"

"The same thing that's always what's next," I told him, joining his unsentimental gaze toward the bay. "Moving on."

But first, I had a few people to square things with.

First up was Christian. I felt bad for suspecting him of murder (wouldn't you?), but more pressingly, I had a report to deliver to him. So I went back to room 334, pulled myself together, and grabbed my masterwork before I ran out of juice.

This time, Ms. Bored Blonde (Christian's admin) wasn't

stationed outside his office. So I hefted my report and took myself inside. At his desk, Christian scowled at me.

"I have to go speak to the police," he complained. "*Again.*"

Leave it to him to make Nina's arrest all about *him*.

"I won't keep you long." I plunked my report on his desk. "There. Job done. Follow my recommendations, and Lemaître will flourish. If you have any questions, you know how to reach me."

Via Travis, of course. All my official business was channeled through him. Travis said it was because I was too softhearted—because I would take every hard-luck chocolatier job that came around. I didn't think Travis was right. . . . However, looking at Christian's woeful face, I began to have my suspicions about me.

Trying to ignore my (supposedly) inherent softhearted-ness, I turned and headed for the door. Christian's voice stopped me.

"Hey, Hayden?"

"Yes?" I waited for him to try to make amends. After all, there *were* good reasons I'd suspected him of cold-blooded murder.

"When you talk to Eden from *Chocolat Monthly* about me, try to make me sound good, okay? I'd really appreci-ate it. Thanks."

I laughed. "I won't be talking to Eden."

"But if you *do,* just remember to talk me up. Thanks."

"I won't." I raised my hand. "Good luck, Christian."

I made it a few more feet before . . . "Uh, Hayden?"

I sighed—then smiled liked the professional I was. "Yes?"

"Are you sure," Christian prodded, "you won't recon-sider that head chocolatier job?"

"I'm *absolutely* sure." I wanted out of this cabal of liars, thieves, and backstabbers. Because even though Christian had turned out to be innocent of murder, he wasn't *innocent*.

Besides, now that I'd glimpsed that upcoming SFO flight reminder on my phone, I was feeling pretty keen to get going.

Once a globe-trotter, always a globe-trotter, I guessed.

"I'm, uh . . ." Christian cleared his throat. He frowned, then gave me an honest look. "I'm sorry I was such a jerk about your report. Nina was really riding me about it. Every time you dodged me and I came away empty-handed, I felt like a loser."

Did he want me to comfort him? "Forget about it. It's fine." That was the closest I could bring myself to reassurance.

But Christian wasn't done. "So much so," he went on—speaking rapidly, as though he didn't want to lose his nerve—"that I'm quitting Lemaître. I'm giving the company back to Bernard and going to work for someone else, doing what I really love."

"Contract dictator work? Belittling people full-time?"

"Very funny." He rolled his eyes. "Corporate raiding."

That sounded about right to me. "Good luck," I said.

God help the companies he tried to take over. I could only hope that none of them were good chocolatiers, like Torrance.

Then I took myself out of there before Christian could headhunt me into abandoning chocolate to rule the world instead.

The funny thing about packing, I've learned over the years, is that it's *clarifying*. While trying to fit all your worldly possessions (in my case, I *do* mean *all* of them) into a 22-by-18-by-10-inch bag weighing not more than fifty-one pounds, it's necessary to figure out what you *really* need and when.

Will this scarf double as a poolside sarong and a

mosquito net? you ask yourself. *Can I get by with only one pair of shoes, even on cobblestone streets in a European village? How much duct tape is really necessary for a flight to New Zealand with one layover?*

The answers to those questions can be more illuminating than you might think. For me, packing up my things to leave the Maison Lemaître chocolate retreat behind me was . . . bittersweet.

Once I was gone, I knew, Adrienne would fade from my memory. Just a little. So would Bernard and Poopsie, Isabel and Rex, Christian and the murderous chocolate-fondue body wrap machine. Thankfully, so would Nina. I felt much *less* melancholy about that eventuality. I was still shaken by her breakdown.

I guessed desperation made people do desperate things. That was true even when those people had regular access to cocoa oil massages, cacao-bean-and-espresso-nib pedicure scrubs, and molten chocolate cakes (an oldie, but a goodie) with ice cream.

In the bright light of another springtime California morning, Nina's desperation felt much farther away from me than it had last night. I knew it would fade even more in time. I was glad that I'd caught her and relieved that I'd escaped. I didn't want my obituary to be printed for a *long* time yet. I definitely didn't want it to read "death by chocolate" as the cause of my demise. The irony of that would be too preposterous.

As clarifying as my packing ritual was—and as satisfying as crossing off Lemaître Chocolates from my to-do list was—it didn't take long. Within moments of hearing Danny's shouted (now routine) "Going for a run!" through the connecting door, I was up and in action. I was headed for breakfast.

This time, on the very last day of the chocolate retreat, I was getting some of those chocolate goodies—and I was getting them *hot*. But first, I had one more thing to do. So I grabbed Adrienne's notebook, skated downstairs, and caromed onto the grounds. As usual, they were stunning. So was the view. But I was content (for now) to keep moving. Anything else was a dream.

Seeing my little Yorkie buddy scamper up to me as I approached Bernard's cottage made me falter a *tiny* bit. But only that. Because as lovable as Poopsie was, I wasn't in the market for anything that would make me settle down. A dog. Travis. Or—

Isabel Lemaître ran in her dog's wake. "Poopsie! Come here, *ma petite*!" Laughing, she scooped up the Yorkie. "*Ma belle!*"

On the porch behind her, Bernard watched inscrutably.

On the walkway leading to the resort's private cottages, a *very* well-built man stood wearing track pants, sneaks, and a muscle shirt. Hank, I presumed. Everything fell into place.

Isabel had run off with Hank, the personal trainer.

She glanced up, spotted me, and smiled. "Hayden! *Mon amie!*"

Just as though it were perfectly normal to do such a thing while her lover and (I'm assuming) soon-to-be ex-husband looked on, Isabel rushed over to give me *les bises*—kisses on the cheek.

Have I mentioned that lingerie models can get away with things that ordinary mortals (like me) simply can't?

For a long, awkward (for me) moment, Isabel held my hand. She smiled at me. "Hank and I are in love! *So* in love that I simply forgot to bring my precious petite Poopsie!" She nuzzled the dog, still holding her Yorkie in her other hand. "I had to come back to get her, of course. And to explain to Bernie."

Isabel gave her husband a jovial nod. He nodded back.

It seemed there were no hard feelings between them.

"But I simply cannot linger! Good luck, Hayden!"

Then, as unexpectedly as she'd appeared, Isabel hugged Poopsie closer, released me, and rushed across the grass to Hank. He caught her in his arms, gave Bernard a wave, then left.

Left alone on the porch, Bernard lowered his arm. Standing there all white-haired and abandoned, he no longer looked scary. He only looked . . . well, "relieved" was the best description. Probably because he didn't have to worry about what had happened to the missing Isabel. Bernard really *had* only been grieving, I guessed, not losing his mental sharpness to rapid-onset dementia.

My supposition was confirmed when I reached him. The founder of Lemaître Chocolates greeted me with a hearty handshake. "Hayden! I'm so glad you're here." He lowered his voice, then gave me the full twinkly-eye treatment. "I got the impression last time that I scared you, and I'm sorry."

He'd petrified me. Now I laughed it off. "No worries."

"I didn't mean to," Bernard explained. "I've been a little up and down lately. Ever since losing Adrienne, you see. The resort physician gave me some medication to help, but I think it was making things worse. I felt so foggy all the time. So moody." Dolefully, Bernard shook his head. "It's not like me."

"I never thought it was." *Only for a few seconds. Over and over again.* Gladly, I patted his arm. "You heard about Nina?"

He nodded. "It's better to know. Just as with Isabel." He scanned the resort's grounds. In the distance, his (soon-to-be) ex-wife walked arm in arm toward the valet stand with buff Hank. "Isabel knew that my heart really belonged with Adrienne. That only became clearer to us both after Adrienne died so suddenly."

I understood. "That brings me to the reason I'm here."

As Bernard watched interestedly, I pulled out Adrienne's notebook. With a heartfelt sense of rightness, I handed it to him. "It's not a diary, like you wanted, but I think you should have this."

"Thank you." Seeming moved, he ran his wrinkled fingers over the notebook. When he lifted his gaze to mine, Bernard seemed contemplative. "Despite what I told you before, I don't think there ever was a diary," he confessed. "Adrienne said she was bringing it to the scavenger hunt, full of details about our affair, to show Isabel—to try to force me into making a decision. She wanted me to get divorced, but I was too worried about hurting Isabel." He gave a sheepish smile. "I guess I shouldn't have been. I'm an old softy like that sometimes."

I believed him. Plus, now I knew why Adrienne had brought her chocolate notebook with her. Like the one I'd brought to my ill-fated meeting last night, it had been a decoy. A bluff.

Adrienne must have changed her mind about confronting Isabel, I realized. She'd tried, but she had been too kindhearted to go through with it. That explained why she'd seemed so torn about having drawn a Team Yellow T-shirt when I'd first run into her that day. It explained why she'd given *me* her notebook, too.

She'd realized, with Christian bearing down on us both, that exchanging her notebook would make it seem as though she'd needed to consult with me about something work related. That action would have ostensibly explained her presence there (against Christian's rules). It turned out that I'd been Adrienne's cover story for attending the scavenger hunt. Nothing more. I'd been drawn into all the intrigue just by being there.

Way to go, Hayden, I thought ruefully. *Come for the chocolate—stay for the murder!*

With the last piece of the puzzle in place, I smiled at

Bernard. "I hear you're back on top at Lemaître Chocolates."

Bernard nodded. Now that he was unmedicated, he seemed much sharper than before. "I am. Christian and I still have a few details to work out, but I'm ready to get back to work."

"You look it." He did. With his gingham shirtsleeves rolled up and his khaki pants freshly creased, Bernard looked ready to resume his role as San Francisco's grandfather of chocolate. "I'm happy for you, Bernard. I really am. I'm sorry we didn't meet under happier circumstances, but I'm glad to know you."

"And I, you." He gave a faint, chivalrous bow. "Good luck, Hayden. May the chocolate always temper correctly for you."

I grinned at his use of our industry lingo. As a substitute for part of that old Irish proverb, it seemed apt to me.

"You too, Mr. Lemaître." I shook his hand, then left.

I still had one more thing to do . . . and it was a doozy.

At our shared breakfast table at the final Maison Lemaître all-chocolate brunch of the retreat, Danny gave in first.

"Ugh. That's it!" He dropped his napkin on his chocolate-smudged plate with a groan. "I can't take any more."

I looked. "You haven't even finished your French toast."

"It's got chocolate chips in it. It's dessert."

"Or your almond croissant with caramel and chocolate."

"Why is it called a croissant when it's rectangular? In French, croissant means crescent. You know that as well as I do."

"Or your white-chocolate whiskey bread pudding with cherry sauce and candied almonds. The drizzle of ganache on top is—"

"Too much! Plus, it's alcoholic. Even I don't want whiskey at breakfast—at least I don't if I haven't been up all night. Maybe not even then." Danny switched his gaze to my plate, which I was currently struggling not to lick clean. He gave me an incredulous look. "Where did you put all yours, anyway?"

"Right in here." Contentedly, I patted my belly. "Every last bite was *delicious,* too. The chocolate was sweet but complex, melty when it was supposed to be and smooth when it wasn't. The pastries were delectable, the ganache *incredible,* and that chocolate-swirled speculoos butter . . . out of this world!"

"You're an animal," Danny told me.

"You're broken somehow. You really don't like chocolate?"

"I like it." He looked away, mulling it over. "I guess."

Sacrilege. "You need some serious rehabilitation, mister."

He gave me a fond look. "I guess you're just the expert I need for the job, then. I don't think you can do it, though."

"Those sound like fighting words." I was up for the challenge. When *wasn't* I? "Where are you off to next?"

"Wait, what?" Danny gave me a faux astonished look. "We're not going every place together from now on?" He shook his head. "I thought I was your bodyguard. I thought you needed me."

"You're my *on-call* bodyguard. I told Travis to put you on retainer," I explained blithely. "If I need you, I'll call."

"You'll need me," he assured me. He'd never lacked confidence. Only the gene that involved chocolate tasting.

Danny couldn't possibly be tasting it correctly, I knew, and still wind up so utterly apathetic about chocolate's ambrosial qualities, could he? No. He couldn't.

"So . . ." I arched my eyebrow, then exercised all my

willpower to allow the server to clear away my plate. "Where to next?"

"No place." He shrugged his burly shoulders. "I'm staying here for a few days." His gaze arrowed to mine, full of sudden, inexplicable exasperation. "Your dumbass financial manager—"

"You can call him Travis." It sounded as though they were having another one of their feuds. That was my cue to vamoose.

"—only booked me a one-way ticket, that cheapskate. So I thought I'd spend a little time exploring San Francisco."

Ah, I got it. "Exploring, huh? With your detective friend?"

"Maybe." Mischievously, Danny looked up. "You?"

I shrugged, reluctant to say good-bye.

"You're already booked," Danny prodded, "to . . . ?"

Anguilla. That's what it was supposed to have been. Except . . .

"I changed my flight," I told him with a nonchalance I didn't begin to feel. I wasn't ready to embark on a new job. I didn't have a home to speak of. But I *did* have an intriguing offer, I remembered. "The Caribbean can be so crowded. After this, I feel like going someplace a little moodier. Rainier."

"London," Danny surmised. He knew how I loved it there.

I stayed mum while I signed for our breakfast. My treat.

I stood, grabbing my (temporary) clutch. *RIP, crossbody bag.*

"Not London." With feeling, I grabbed Danny, then gave him a hug. With him staying in California, we wouldn't see each other again for a while. "Not this time. Soon, though."

If I'd hoped to distract him from his original question about my destination, I'd forgotten who I was dealing with.

Danny leaned back. He frowned. "Where are you going?"

I gave an offhanded wave. "Seattle. You know, just for a few days." I gave Danny a grateful smile. "Thanks for all your help with . . . *everything*. You know you're the best, Danny."

He crossed his arms. "You can't sidetrack me. Seattle?"

We both knew what that meant. I didn't want to admit it.

But with a successful consultation behind me, a first-time murder resolution to my credit, and a belly full of scrumptious chocolate, I guess I didn't have the where-withal to hold out.

"I thought I might pop in on Travis," I admitted. Stupidly, my heart rate picked up just from saying it. "You know . . . see what he's like in person. I think it's about time we met, don't you?"

"Nope," Danny grumped. "I don't."

"Well, then, it's a good thing you're not the boss of me, because I'm doing it," I said lightly. Then I dared myself to lean in, give Danny one of Isabel's Parisian *bises,* and squeeze his shoulder. "Hey, catch you next time, Jamieson."

"You'd better believe it," Danny told me. "I wouldn't miss it."

"Me either," I said. Then I left the patio, left Maison Lemaître, left its cacao-scented breezes, and embarked on my next adventure—footloose, chocolatified, and ready for whatever came my way.

YOU-WON'T-BELIEVE-IT CHOCOLATE MOUSSE

Serves four to six

10 ounces good quality bittersweet chocolate,
 chopped
1 cup water
2 tablespoons granulated sugar
1 teaspoon vanilla extract

GET READY: Fill a large bowl about halfway with ice and water. Have ready a slightly smaller metal bowl that fits inside it. Set aside. (You'll use this to rapidly chill the mousse while whipping it.)

Place the chopped chocolate, water, and sugar in a microwave-safe glass bowl (Pyrex is good). Microwave until chocolate is melted. Add vanilla extract.

Pour melted chocolate mixture into prepared small metal bowl. Place the metal bowl in the prepared ice bath. (Make sure not to let any stray ice water get into the bowl!) Whisk chocolate mixture by hand until mousse reaches desired thickness, about two minutes.

Spoon into serving dishes and enjoy!

Notes from Hayden

The success of this mousse is all about the quality of the chocolate you use, so choose a good one! Any brand that's around 70% cocoa solids should be delicious.

This recipe might seem complicated, but it's really not! It's basically whipping melted chocolate while swiftly cooling it, which makes it fluffy and delicious. The mousse reaches the desired consistency as if by magic, with only a little whisking.

It seems counterintuitive in a world filled with creamy desserts, but dairy products actually dull the flavor of chocolate. Without milk fat getting in the way, this mousse is super chocolaty. Try it!

SPA-STYLE CACAO NIB AND ESPRESSO BEAN PEDICURE SCRUB

¼ cup cacao nibs, ground
¼ cup ground espresso beans
2 tablespoons granulated sugar
2 tablespoons olive oil
a few drops of vanilla extract

In a small bowl, stir together ground cacao nibs, ground espresso beans, and sugar. Add the olive oil and vanilla extract; stir thoroughly until combined.

TO USE: Wash feet; leave damp. Apply a small scoop of pedicure scrub to each foot. Massage well.

Leave on for 3-5 minutes while you relax and enjoy the delicious mocha scent. Rinse off and pat feet dry. This scrub is exfoliating and soothing!

Notes from Hayden

This mixture is best while fresh—don't try to save it for later! There's enough here for one good scrubbing. If you don't like olive oil, you can substitute any neutral oil—

almond oil is especially nice. Don't use canola oil, corn oil, soybean oil, or peanut oil! They make the scrub too greasy (and don't smell nice).

You don't have to use espresso beans for this scrub—any coffee bean will do—and they don't have to be dry (aka un-brewed). If you're feeling thrifty and/or "green," just recycle your coffee grounds from this morning's java. Also, a mini coffee-bean grinder or spice grinder works well for crunching up the cacao nibs. If you leave them as is, they're too rough.

HAYDEN'S ANYTIME CHOCOLATE CHIP COOKIES

½ cup granulated sugar
⅓ cup brown sugar
⅓ cup milk
1 teaspoon vanilla extract
⅓ cup olive oil
1 cup all-purpose flour
½ teaspoon baking soda
½ teaspoon salt
1 cup chocolate chips

GET READY: Preheat oven to 375°.

In a medium mixing bowl, combine the sugars, milk, and vanilla extract. Mix well. Add olive oil; beat with a spoon until thoroughly combined. Add the flour, baking soda, and salt; stir just until no streaks of flour remain. Mix in chocolate chips.

Scoop rounded spoonfuls of dough onto greased or parchment-lined baking sheets, spacing each about two inches apart. (A #20 portion scoop—which holds 3 tablespoons—is handy here.) Flatten cookies slightly. Bake for 10-13 minutes, until golden brown. Enjoy!

Notes from Hayden

Your cupboard's almost bare, but you're craving some delicious chocolate chip cookies? This recipe is for you! It's my almost-instant, no-mixer-required, small-batch special recipe. You can make it from pantry staples you probably have on hand every day.

It might seem unusual to use olive oil in cookies, but give it a try! Italian bakers use olive oil in sweets all the time. Or, if you're not feeling adventurous, you can substitute any neutral-flavored oil—grapeseed oil, canola oil, and coconut oil are all good.

CHOCOLATE BUTTER

¼ cup refined coconut oil
¼ cup pure maple syrup
¼ teaspoon vanilla extract
½ cup unsweetened cocoa powder
tiny pinch of salt

Melt the coconut oil in a microwave or on the stovetop over low heat. Stir in the maple syrup and vanilla extract. Add the cocoa powder and pinch of salt; stir until chocolate butter is smooth. Enjoy!

Notes from Hayden

The keys to this recipe are the coconut oil and the pinch of salt. The coconut oil gives the chocolate butter just the right luscious consistency. The salt (flaky sea salt is good, if you've got it!) adds complexity.

Natural cocoa powder and Dutch-processed cocoa powder both work well in this recipe. Honey can be substituted for maple syrup, if you prefer.

Chocolate butter is delicious spread on toast, fresh fruit, graham crackers . . . whatever you've got!